Even in the dark, he was hot.

I sat on the side of his bed and he jerked awake, sitting up, his hand flashing out and curling, hard and tight, around the back of my neck as I gasped.

He came fully awake. His hand didn't leave me but it relaxed and he growled sleepily, "Jesus, you scared the shit outta me."

And I would. I hadn't thought about it but the last time someone snuck into his room while he was sleeping, they'd been wielding an ax.

"God, Ham, I'm sorry. I didn't think," I whispered, lifting a hand and putting it on his chest, feeling the crisp hair there, wanting to slide my fingers through so badly, my mouth watered with the need.

"You okay?" he asked.

"No," I answered.

"You sick?" he asked.

"No," I answered.

"What's up, baby?"

Before I lost my courage, I blew on the dice and let fly. In other words, I leaned into him, aiming fortunately accurately, and my mouth hit his.

His body stilled.

I touched my tongue to his lips.

His mouth opened.

My tongue slid inside.

Acclaim for Kristen Ashley and Her Novels

"A unique, not-to-be-missed voice in romance. Kristen Ashley is a star in the making!"

—Carly Phillips, *New York Times* bestselling author

"I adore Kristen Ashley's books. She writes engaging, romantic stories with intriguing, colorful, and larger-than-life characters. Her stories grab you by the throat from page one and don't let go until well after the last page. They continue to dwell in your mind days after you finish the story, and you'll find yourself anxiously awaiting the next. Ashley is an addicting read no matter which of her stories you find yourself picking up."

—Maya Banks, *New York Times* bestselling author

"There is something about them [Ashley's books] that I find crackalicious."   —Kati Brown, DearAuthor.com

"Run, don't walk…to get [the Dream Man] series. I love [Kristen Ashley's] rough, tough, hard-loving men. And I love the cosmo-girl club!"   —NocturneReads.com

"Punctuated by blistering-hot sex scenes and fascinating glimpses into the tough world of motorcycle clubs, this romance also delivers true heart and emotion, and a story that will stay with the reader long after the final page is turned."

—*Publishers Weekly* (starred review) on *Fire Inside*

"[*Law Man* is an] excellent addition to a phenomenal series!"

—ReadingBetweentheWinesBookClub.blogspot.com

Jagged

KRISTEN ASHLEY

FOREVER

NEW YORK   BOSTON

Copyright © 2013 by Kristen Ashley
Excerpt from *Kaleidoscope* copyright © 2014 by Kristen Ashley
All rights reserved. In accordance with the U.S. Copyright Act of 1976, the scanning, uploading, and electronic sharing of any part of this book without the permission of the publisher is unlawful piracy and theft of the author's intellectual property. If you would like to use material from the book (other than for review purposes), prior written permission must be obtained by contacting the publisher at permissions@hbgusa.com. Thank you for your support of the author's rights.

Forever
Hachette Book Group
237 Park Avenue, New York, NY 10017

hachettebookgroup.com
twitter.com/foreverromance

Printed in the United States of America

OPM

Originally published as an ebook

First mass market edition: September 2014
10 9 8 7 6 5 4 3 2 1

Forever is an imprint of Grand Central Publishing.
The Forever name and logo are trademarks of Hachette Book Group, Inc.

The publisher is not responsible for websites (or their content) that are not owned by the publisher.

The Hachette Speakers Bureau provides a wide range of authors for speaking events. To find out more, go to www.hachettespeakersbureau.com or call (866) 376-6591.

Maryse Courturier Black
You know why.
And it's not just because we both love shoes.
I figured you'd like a Colorado Mountain
Man dedicated to you.
So here you go, beautiful.

Acknowledgments

At the risk of repeating myself, gratitude to Chasity Jenkins-Patrick and Erika Wynne for keeping me sane and making me look like I know what I'm doing when usually I don't.

To Emily Sylvan Kim, my agent, who has a lot more patience than me (or anyone I know) and who has my back. Always.

To Amy Pierpont, Lauren Plude, and Madeleine Colavita, for listening to me wax on about my "vision" without getting annoyed and sending me really good bottles of champagne whenever we do good. Here's to hoping there's lots more champagne in the future, my lovelies!

And to Gib Moutaw for always being excited when good things happen to me, for giving the best advice ever and for not being pissy when I don't take it (but I've learned, I promise!).

Jagged

PROLOGUE

No Promises. No Expectations.

MY EYES OPENED and I saw dark.

I was wide awake and I knew it was early.

This was weird. It might take some time for me to get to sleep but once I found it, I didn't wake up until morning. I usually woke up groggy, though, more willing to turn around, curl up, and fall back to sleep than get up and face the day.

But I was awake in a way that I could easily get up, make coffee, do laundry, and clean my apartment. In a way that I knew I'd never get back to sleep.

Which was totally weird.

On that thought, my phone rang.

I blinked at the clock on my nightstand and saw it was almost four in the morning. Warmth rushed through me and, following close on its heels, dread.

Only one person called at this time. The calls didn't come frequently enough for me, but they came.

Ham.

Shit.

I knew this would happen one day. I'd hoped for a different ending but deep in my heart I always knew this would be how we'd end.

I wanted to delay, let the phone go to voice mail, do what I had to do another time, but I knew I shouldn't. He'd worry.

I always picked up. The only time I didn't was when I'd

fallen off the ladder in the stockroom at my shop. I broke my wrist, conked my head real good, and they'd kept me in the hospital overnight for observation. When Ham got ahold of me after that and found out what happened, he drove right to Gnaw Bone and stayed for a week to take care of me. It was just a broken wrist and I was banged up a bit, but for that week I didn't cook, clean, or do anything but work at my shop.

Ham did all the rest for me.

One of the many reasons why I wished this would end differently.

I also couldn't delay because this needed to be done. No time would be a good time, not for me. I didn't know how Ham would feel about my ending things, which was a problem, and explained why I knew deep in my heart this would be our ending.

So I might as well get it over with.

I grabbed my phone and put it to my ear.

"Hey, darlin'," I greeted, my voice quiet and slightly sleepy.

"Hey, babe," he replied and that warmth washed through me again.

Graham Reece, Ham to me, didn't have an unusual voice. Though, it was attractive. Deep and masculine. But there were times it could go jagged. For instance, when I did something Ham thought was cute or sexy. Or when we were in bed and I was taking him there.

I loved it when his voice went jagged. So much so that even hearing his voice when it was normal reminded me of those times.

Good times.

The best.

I forced my mind from those times.

"You off shift?" I asked.

"Yep, just got home," Ham answered.

Graham Reece worked in bars and, as often as the life he led meant he was looking for a new gig, he never had a problem landing a job. He had a reputation that extended from Bonners Ferry, Idaho, to Tucson, Arizona; Galveston, Texas, to Rapid City, South Dakota.

This was mostly because although he might move around a lot, when you had him, he was as steady as a rock. Not to mention, he poured a mean drink and was so sharp he could take and fill three drink orders at the same time as well as make change in a blink of an eye. Further, he had so much experience he could spot trouble the instant it walked through the door and he had no aversion to handling it. He knew how to do that with little muss and fuss if the threat became real. And, last, he had a certain manner that I knew all bar owners would want in their bar.

This was because there was an edge of mean to his look. If you knew him, you knew that menace was saved only for times it was needed. But if you didn't know him, one look at his forbidding but handsome face, the bulk of his frame, the breadth of his shoulders, his rough, calloused hands, his shrewd eyes, you'd think twice about acting like an asshole.

For men, I would guess this would be off-putting and I knew from experience it stopped many of them from being assholes before they might even start. Though, some men found it a challenge, poked the sleeping bear, and ended up mauled. I knew this from experience, too, seeing as I'd witnessed it more than once.

For women, the look and feel of Graham Reece had one of two results. They were either scared shitless of him, but still thought he was smokin' hot, or they just thought he was downright smokin' hot.

I was the latter.

But I had to quit thinking about this stuff. Thinking

about this stuff made it harder. Thinking about this stuff made me want to rethink ending things.

More, it made me think I should consider why I was rethinking ending things.

I had to suck it up, get this done, even though I didn't want to.

Therefore, I hesitated.

It was a mistake.

"Listen, darlin'," he went on, "tonight's my last night. Got a gig to get to in Flag."

This wasn't a surprise. Ham was in Billings. He'd been there awhile. It was time to move on. New horizons. New pastures. Trading Montana for Arizona. From beautiful to a different kind of beautiful.

Ham's way.

Ham started his life out in Nebraska, but from what he told me, through his adulthood, he was a travelin' man. As far as I knew, the longest he stayed in one place was a year. Usually it was six to eight months.

Ham was not a man who laid down roots. He moved from place to place, rented furnished apartments, and everything he owned could fit easily in the back of his truck.

"Takin' a coupla days to pack and load up," he continued. "Thought I'd swing your way, drag my shit in your place, unload the bike, and we could take off for a few days."

The dread moved through me again as I tossed off the covers and threw my legs over the side of the bed.

"Ham—"

He cut me off. "You can't close the shop. I'll find somethin' to do during the day and we'll go out, do night rides."

Night rides.

The best.

Oh God, I wanted to do that.

But I couldn't do that.

"Darlin'—" I started.

"Or, you can swing it, I'll hang with you for a few days, then you close up and take a vacation, ride with me down to Flag, hang with me for a while."

He was talking time and lots of it.

And he wanted me to be with him for that time.

And, man, oh *freaking* man, I wanted to be with him for that while.

Not to mention, I'd heard Flagstaff was amazing. I lived in the mountains of Colorado so I knew amazing but that didn't mean I didn't want to check out Flag.

I pushed to my feet, moved through the dark to the window, and did this while talking.

"Honey, I have something to tell you."

"Yeah?" he prompted when I said no more.

I pulled my curtains aside and looked at my not-so-spectacular view of the parking lot. They broke ground on my new house in one of Gnaw Bone's land magnate, Curtis Dodd's, developments only four days ago. In the meantime I was living in an apartment facing away from the mountains, with a view of nothing but cars, asphalt, and storage units.

In my new three-bedroom, two-and-half-bath house, I would have panoramas of the Colorado Rockies all around in a development that the HOA decreed would be appropriately, and attractively, xeriscaped.

I couldn't wait.

Though I *could* wait for having a mortgage payment, but everyone had to grow up sometime.

This was my time.

"Zara, you there, babe?" Ham asked when I still didn't speak.

"I'm seein' someone."

It came out in a rush and was met with nothing.

I held my breath and got more nothing.

"Ham?" I called when he didn't speak.

"It exclusive?" he asked and I nearly smiled at the same time I nearly cried.

Again, pure Ham. No promises. No expectations. He called when he called. I called when I called. We hooked up if it worked and we enjoyed ourselves tremendously when we did. If it didn't work, both of us were disappointed (me probably more, but I never let on) but we kept on keeping on, waiting for the next call. The next hookup. The next two days or two weeks when we'd hang out, have fun, laugh, eat, drink, and make love.

Ham understood the concept of exclusive; he just didn't utilize it. He'd respect it, if necessary. But, if he could, he'd also find ways to work around it.

So Ham had no hold on me like I had no hold on him. He had other women, I knew. He didn't hide it nor did he shove it in my face.

He asked no questions about other men.

He wanted it that way.

I did not, but I never said a word because I suspected, if I did, I'd lose him.

Now, he'd lost me.

I just wondered how he'd feel about that.

"We've been seein' each other for almost four months. We haven't had that discussion but exclusive is implied," I answered quietly.

"You into him?" Ham asked.

There was a smile in my voice when I reminded him, "We've been seein' each other for almost four months, darlin'."

But the smile hid my uncertainty.

My boyfriend, Greg, was a great guy. He was steady. He was sweet. He was quiet and there was no drama. He was

better than average looking. And there was no doubt he was
into me and also no doubt that I liked knowing that.

There *was* doubt, though. All on my side and all of it had
to do with if I was into him.

But I wasn't getting any younger. I wanted kids. I wanted
to build a family. I wanted to do it in a way that it would take,
no fighting, cheating, drama, heartbreak, all this ending in
divorce. I wanted to be settled. I wanted to come home at
night knowing what my evening would bring. I wanted to
wake up the next morning next to someone, knowing what
my day would bring. I wanted to give my kids, when I had
them, stability and safety.

I also wanted that for myself. I'd never had it, not in my
life.

And I wanted it.

And, after being friends with benefits with Graham
Reece for five years, I knew that was not going to happen
with him. No matter how much I wanted it to.

"So you're into him," I heard him mutter.

"Yeah," I replied and tried to make that one word sound
firm.

"Right, then, will he have a problem, I swing by and take
you to lunch?" Ham asked.

No, Greg wouldn't have a problem with that. Greg didn't
get riled up about much and I knew he wouldn't even get
riled up about an ex-lover swinging by to take me to lunch.

Thus me having doubts. Part of me felt I should be cool
with a man who trusted me not to fuck him over. Part of me
wanted a man who detested the idea of his woman spending
time with an ex-lover. Possessiveness was hot. A man who
staked his claim, marked his territory.

It wasn't about lack of trust. It was about belonging to
someone. It was about them having pride in that and wanting
everyone to know it, especially you.

Ham *looked* like a man who would be that way. Knowing I wasn't the only friend he enjoyed benefits with and his ask-no-questions, tell-no-lies approach to relationships proved he just wasn't.

"No, Greg'll be cool with that," I told him and I shouldn't have. With nothing holding him back, that meant Ham would go out of his way to hit Gnaw Bone, take me to lunch. I'd have to see him, want him, and, as ever, not have him. But this time, it would be worse. I wouldn't have him *at all,* including in some of the really good ways I liked to have him.

"Okay, babe, I'll call when I'm close," he said.

"Right," I murmured.

"Now you get to bed, go back to sleep," he ordered.

That was not going to happen.

"Okay, Ham."

"See you soon, darlin'."

"Look forward to it, honey."

"'Night, darlin'."

"'Night, Ham."

He disconnected and I stared out at the parking lot.

That was it. He wanted lunch. He wanted to continue the connection even if the connection had changed.

That was good.

But he wasn't devastated or even slightly miffed that I was moving on, changing our connection.

That was very bad.

I bent my neck until my head hit the cool glass of the window and I stared at the cars in the lot without seeing them.

I did this for a long time.

Then I pulled myself together, moved from the window, made coffee, did laundry, and cleaned my apartment.

*   *   *

Five days later...

I sat in a booth at the side of The Mark, a restaurant in town. I had a ginger ale bubbling on the table in front of me. I was in the side of the booth where I could see the front windows and door.

I knew Ham was about to show because, ten minutes ago, I saw his big, silver Ford F-350 with the trailer hitched to the back holding his vintage Harley slide by. With that massive truck and the addition of a trailer, it would take him a while to find a good parking spot.

But he could walk in any second now.

I was nervous. I was excited.

I was sad.

And I knew I should never have agreed to this.

More sunlight poured through the restaurant and I looked from my ginger ale to the door to see it was open and Ham was moving through. I watched as he smiled at Trudy, a waitress at The Mark who was standing at the hostess station. He gave a head jerk my way. Trudy turned to look at me, smiled, and turned back to Ham, nodding.

Then I watched Ham walk to me.

Ham Reece was not graceful. He was too big to be graceful. He didn't walk. He trudged.

But he was built. He was a bear of a man, tall and big. His mass of thick, dark hair was always a mess. He constantly looked like he'd either just gotten off the back of a bike he'd been riding wild and fast for hours or like he'd just gotten out of bed after he'd been riding a woman wild and fast for hours.

Now was no different, even though he'd just spent hours in the cab of his truck.

It looked good on him.

It always did.

Although big, he was fit and he worked at it. It was not lost on him with the years he'd put in in bars that he needed to be on the top of his game so, although not quick, he was in shape. He ran a lot. He also lifted. Every time I'd been with him, he'd found time to do what he needed to do, even if he was doing crunches on the floor of a hotel with his arms wrapped around something heavy held to his chest.

This meant he had great abs. Great lats. Great thighs. A great ass.

Just great all around.

Yes, I should never have agreed to this.

He got close. His eyes that started out a tawny brown at the irises and radiated out to a richer, darker brown at the edge of his pupils were lit with his smile as his lips grinned at me while he approached.

I slid out of the booth.

Two seconds later, Ham slid his arms around me.

"Hey, cookie," he greeted, his voice jagged. My lungs deflated. He was happy to see me.

"Hey, darlin'." I gave him a squeeze.

He returned the squeeze and let me go but didn't step away.

His eyes caught mine and he stated, "Pretty as ever."

"Hot as could be," I returned, and his grin got bigger as he lifted a hand toward my face.

I braced, waiting for it. No, anticipating it with sheer delight.

But I didn't get it. His grin faded, his hand dropped away, and then he took a half step back and gestured to the booth.

That was when I felt it, all I'd lost with Ham. One could say it wasn't much but when you had him for the brief periods you had him, *you had him*. His attention, his affection, his easy, sweet touches, his deep voice that could go jagged with tenderness or desire. I knew that others might look at what we had and think I hadn't lost much, but they would be wrong. And I knew in that instant exactly how much I was losing.

It hurt like hell.

"Slide your ass in, darlin'," he ordered but didn't wait until I did. He moved to the other side.

I slid in, Ham slid in across from me, and Trudy arrived at our table.

"Drink?" she asked.

"Beer," Ham answered.

"Got a preference?" Trudy went on.

"Cold," Ham told her.

She smiled at him then at me and took herself off.

Ham didn't touch the menu sitting in front of him. He'd been to The Mark more than once. Anyone who had knew what they wanted.

His eyes came to me.

"How much time you got?" he asked.

"Couldn't find anyone to look after the shop so I had to close it down," I said by way of answer.

"In other words, not long," he surmised and he was right.

I owned a shop in Gnaw Bone called Karma. Ham had been there. Ham knew how much work it was. Ham also knew all about my dream of having my own place, being my own boss, answering to no one, and surrounding myself with cool stuff made by cool people. He also knew it was hard work and that I put in that hard work. There were things we didn't discuss but that didn't mean we didn't talk and do it deep. Not only when we were together but when one or the other of us got the itch to call. We could talk on the phone for hours and we did.

So I knew Ham, too.

I nodded. "I did try to find someone but—"

"Don't worry about it, darlin'," he muttered.

"Are you stayin' in town?" I asked. "Maybe, tomorrow—"

"Headed out after this, babe."

I nodded again, trying not to feel as devastated as I felt, an effort that was doomed to fail so it did.

"Thought you'd look different," Ham noted and I focused on his handsome face, taking in the exquisite shape of his full lips, his dark-stubbled strong jaw, the tanned, tight skin stretching across his cheekbones, the heavy brow over those intelligent eyes that was the source of him looking not-so-vaguely threatening.

"What?" I asked.

"Got a man, you're into him, you two got some time in, thought you'd look different."

I forced a smile. "And how would I look different, babe?"

"Happy."

My smile died.

Ham didn't miss it.

His intelligent eyes grew sharp on my face. "This a good guy?"

"Yeah," I answered. It was quick, firm, and honest.

Ham noted that, too, but that didn't change the look in his eyes. "Gotta find a guy who makes you happy," he told me.

I did. You, I thought.

"Greg's sweet. He's mellow, Ham, which I like. He's really nice. He also really likes me and lets it show, and I like that, too. Things are going great," I assured him.

Ham's reply was gentle but honest, as Ham always was.

"Things might be goin' good, Zara, but I can see it on your face, babe, they're not goin' great."

"He's a good guy," I stressed.

"I believe you," Ham returned. "And he's givin' you somethin' you want. I'm all for that, darlin'. But you can't settle for what you want. You gotta find what you need."

I did. You, I thought again and found this conversation was making me slightly pissed and not-so-slightly uncomfortable.

I knew this man. I'd tasted nearly every inch of him. He'd returned the favor. I had five years with him in my life. Four months of that solid and, for me *and* Ham, exclusive back in the day when I was waitressing at The Dog and Ham was bartending. Four months solid of me waking up in his bed every morning from our first date to the day he left town.

Now he was advising me on what kind of man I should settle for.

I didn't like this.

"Maybe we shouldn't talk about Greg," I suggested.

"Might be a good idea," Ham replied, his attention shifting to Trudy, who set his beer on the table.

"You two ready to order?" she asked.

"Turkey and Swiss melt and chips," I ordered.

"Buffalo burger, jack cheese, rings," Ham said after me.

"Gotcha," Trudy replied, snatching up the menus and then she was again off, which meant I again had Ham's attention.

"Last thing I wanna do is piss you off, cookie," he told me quietly.

"You didn't piss me off," I assured him.

"Good, 'cause, your man can handle it, I wanna find a way where I don't lose you."

The instant he was done speaking, I felt my throat tingle.

Oh God, we were already here. I suspected our lunch would lead us here, just not this soon.

We were at the place where I had to make a decision.

Greg wouldn't care if Ham and I worked out a way to stay in each other's lives. Maybe somewhere deep inside Greg would mind that I kept an ongoing friendship with an ex-lover but I'd be surprised if he'd let that show. Even so, I wouldn't want to do something like that to him.

So that was a consideration.

But also, I had to decide if I could live with even less from Ham than I had before.

No decision, really.

I couldn't. I knew it. I'd known it for ages because I couldn't even live with the little bits of him that he already gave me. I just told myself I could so I wouldn't lose even those little bits.

And, knowing this, finally admitting it, killed me.

"I don't think I could do that to Greg, darlin'," I told him carefully and watched his eyes flare.

"So this is it," he stated.

That was all he gave me. An eye flare and confirmation that he got that this was it. I swallowed past the lump in my throat.

"This is it," I confirmed.

"Do me a favor," he said, then kept talking before I could get a word in. "Don't lose my number."

That knife pushed deeper.

"Ham—" I started.

He shook his head. "You change yours, you call me. I change mine, I'll call you. We don't gotta talk. But don't break that connection, cookie."

"I don't think—"

"Five years, babe, through that shit your parents pulled on you. You breakin' your wrist. Your girl gettin' cancer. We've seen a lot. Don't break that connection."

We had seen a lot. He might not always have been there in person but he was always just a phone call away, even if he was hundreds of miles away.

I closed my eyes and looked down at the table.

"Zara, baby, look at me," he urged and I opened my eyes and turned to him. "Don't break our connection."

"It was always you," I found myself whispering, needing to get it out, give it to him so I could let it go.

I watched his chin jerk back, his face go soft, and then he closed his eyes.

He wasn't expecting that, which also killed. He had to know. I'd given him more than one indication over five freaking years.

Maybe he was in denial. Maybe he didn't care. Maybe he just didn't want that responsibility.

Now, it didn't matter.

"Ham, baby, look at me," I urged. He opened his eyes and there was sadness there. "I won't break our connection," I promised.

The last thing I had to give, I'd give it.

For Graham Reece, I'd give anything.

Unfortunately, he didn't want it.

"Not that man," he said gently.

"I know," I told him.

"Not just you, cookie, know that. I'm just not that man."

"I know, honey."

"Also not the man who wants to walk away from this table not knowin' his girl is gonna be happy."

He needed to stop.

"I'll be happy," I replied.

"You're not being very convincing," Ham returned.

"Broke ground on my house last week, Ham. It's sweet," I told him and watched surprise move over his features. "Great views," I went on. "Roomy. Got a good guy who thinks the world of me." I leaned toward him. "I need to move on, honey." I swallowed again and felt my eyes sting before I finished. "I need to be free to find my happy."

After I was done delivering that, Ham studied me with intense eyes for long moments that made my splintering heart start to fall apart.

Finally, he stated, "I could never give that to you, baby."

You're wrong. For four months, you gave me everything. Then you left and took it away, I thought.

"I know," I said.

"Want with everything for you to find it," he told me.

"I will, Ham."

"Don't settle, cookie."

"I won't."

I saw his jaw clench but his eyes didn't let mine go.

"I'm sorry," I said. "I should have said this over the phone. I wasn't ready then. I hadn't… well…" I lifted my hands, flipped them out, and then rested them on the table. "Whatever. I shouldn't have made you come out of your way—"

Ham interrupted me. "You gave me the brush-off without me seein' your pretty face, that would piss me off, Zara. I'd come out of my way for you any time you needed it. You know that."

I did. It always confused me but I knew it.

"Yeah, I know that, Ham."

"Him in your life, he fucks you over, it goes bad, it doesn't and you still need me, you'll have my number and that always holds true."

Really, he had to stop.

"Okay, Ham."

"It'll suck, walkin' away from you."

I looked at the table.

"But, one thing I always wanted is for you to be happy," he continued.

I looked at him.

"You mean the world to me, cookie," he finished.

So why? my thoughts screamed.

"You, too, darlin'," I replied.

He reached a hand across the table and wrapped it around mine.

We held on tight as we held each other's eyes.

Then we let go when Trudy came with a refill of my drink.

* * *

Half an hour later...

"Go," Ham ordered.

We were standing on the boardwalk outside The Mark. My shop was a ways down the boardwalk, same side.

Now was the time.

This was truly it.

And I didn't want to go.

Tears flooded my eyes.

"Ham, I—"

"Zara, go," he demanded.

I pressed my lips together.

Suddenly, his hand shot up and curled around the side of my neck. His head came down and his lips were crushing mine.

I opened them.

His tongue darted inside.

I lifted a hand to curl it around his wrist at my neck, arched into him, and melted into his kiss, committing the smell, feel, and taste of him to memory.

And Ham let me, kissing me hard, wet, and long. A great kiss. A sad kiss. A kiss not filled with promise of good things to come, a kiss filled with the bitter knowledge of good-bye.

We took from each other until we both tasted my tears.

Just as suddenly, his hand and mouth were gone and he'd taken half a step away.

It felt like miles.

"Go." His voice was jagged.

He didn't want to lose me.

Why? my thoughts screamed.

"Bye, Ham," I whispered.

He jerked up his chin.

I turned away, concentrating on walking down the boardwalk to my shop, ignoring anyone who might be around, and trying to ignore the feel of Ham's eyes burning holes into my back.

I didn't get relief until I turned to my shop, unlocked the door, and pushed inside.

No. The truth was, I didn't get relief at all, not that day, that week, that year, or ever.

Because I'd walked away from the love of my life.

And he let me.

CHAPTER ONE

Ax Murderer

Three years later...

I SAT CROSS-LEGGED on my couch, pressed the tiny arrow on the screen of my phone, and put it to my ear.

Again.

"Zara? I, uh...signed the papers. Took them to George. It's, uh...done. I, well, uh...just wanted you to know. Okay? I just..." Long pause, then, quieter, "Wanted you to know. I'll, uh...I guess I'll, um...see you around."

I closed my eyes when I got silence.

Greg.

He'd signed the divorce papers.

It was done.

Shit, we were over.

The end.

I'd done what I never wanted to do. Never thought I would do. Hell, never thought I had it in me to do.

I'd broken a man.

I sucked in a breath through my nose, brought the phone down, and forced myself to lean forward, grab my remote, and turn on the TV rather than listen to the voice mail.

Again.

The news flashed on and I made myself pay attention to it.

Now, tonight's top story, the newsman said. *Dennis*

*Lowe, the man who has been on a multistate killing spree,
his chosen weapon an ax, was shot dead in the home of one
of his victims by law enforcement officers today. After a
short standoff with the FBI and local police, officers entered
the house where Lowe was holding three women hostage.
One hostage, Susan Shepherd, is in stable condition in a
hospital in Indianapolis.*

"Holy crap," I mumbled. "An ax?"

A picture of a relatively good-looking—strangely, considering his chosen weapon was a freaking *ax*—mild-
mannered-appearing man flashed on the screen behind the
newscaster.

*Lowe's body count right now is unknown, although four
murders are confirmed as being attributed to him. However,
there's a possibility that his victims number at least seven,
with murders in Colorado and Oklahoma, and another
man today in Indiana, suspected of being Lowe's gruesome
handiwork. In addition to Ms. Shepherd, a police officer and
a bartender in Brownsburg, Indiana, were severely injured
during the kidnapping of one of Lowe's hostages, February Owens. Ms. Owens was allegedly the object of Lowe's
obsession and the reason behind his grisly spree. In Texas,
Graham Reece, until today the only survivor of Lowe's
attacks, was released from police protective custody.*

My breath became painfully stuck as I stared at Ham
on the screen, looking hugely pissed and wearing a sling
holding his left arm tight to his chest, prowling to his silver F-350. Reporters were crowding him, bright lights in his
angry, hard face. You could see the reporters' mouths moving but Ham's was tight.

The news anchor droned on as I dropped the remote to
my lap, fumbled with my phone, and flipped through my
contacts.

As promised, I'd kept Ham's phone number. I had not

changed mine so, luckily, this meant I had not had to contact him.

He had also never contacted me.

For three years.

He was listed as *Z Graham Reece* because that would make him the only *Z* I had in my phone and it would, therefore, make it so I wouldn't ever have to see his name accidentally as I scrolled through my contacts.

But right then, I went directly to the *Z*s, hit his name, hit his number, and put the phone to my ear.

It rang four times while I breathed so heavily I was panting, at the same time despairing that Ham might not pick up.

Then I heard, "Zara?"

As promised, he kept my number, too.

I thought this at the same time a lot of other thoughts clashed violently in my head.

Therefore, the only response to his greeting I was capable of was to chant, "Oh God. Oh fuck. Oh shit. God, God, God."

"Cookie," he whispered.

At that, I burst into tears.

"I take it you've seen the news," he remarked.

I made a loud hiccoughing noise, which was the only ability I had at that moment to answer his question in the affirmative.

Ham understood me.

"Honey, I'm okay," he assured me gently.

I pulled in a breath that broke around five times and then I forced out a wobbly, "Ax murderer."

"Yeah, sick fuck," Ham told me.

That was all he had to say?

Sick fuck?

So at that, I shrieked, *"Ham, you were attacked by an ax murderer! That shit doesn't happen. Ever!"*

"Zara, baby, I'm okay," he stated firmly.

"Oh God. Oh shit. Fuck, fuck, *fuck*," I chanted.

Ham said nothing.

With effort, I pulled myself together and asked, "You're okay?"

"Said that twice, babe," he replied quietly.

"You sure?" I pushed.

"Zara, darlin', no fun havin' some guy come at you with an ax but he's very dead and I am not so, yeah. I'm sure."

I gave that a second to move through and slightly calm me before I muttered, "Okay."

Ham again said nothing.

Suddenly, I was rethinking this call, the first time I'd spoken with him in three years.

A lot had happened to me. Nothing as big as being attacked by an ax murderer but it did include marriage, divorce, and a lot of other not-so-fun stuff.

I no longer knew Ham. He no longer knew me.

Sure, any girl who'd been in love with a man who was attacked by an ax murderer would want to call to make sure he was okay.

Then, that girl should think again and maybe not make that call the day her now ex-husband signed their divorce papers, a day that was just one day in months of super-shitty days, each one leading toward the likely outcome that her life was going straight down the toilet.

Or, perhaps, she shouldn't make that call *ever.*

Finally, Ham spoke.

"Are *you* okay?"

"Ham, darlin', no fun havin' a guy you care about show up on the TV while they're reporting on the multistate killing spree of a freaking *ax murderer* but he's very dead and you're not so, yeah. I guess I'm okay."

"Okay," he replied and I could hear the smile in his voice.

God, I missed him.

Shit, *I missed him.*

This was a bad idea.

"Talked to Jake," he stated unexpectedly and I knew right then for certain this was a bad idea.

Jake worked at The Dog. Jake had worked at The Dog for ages. Jake was installed behind the bar at The Dog in a way that everyone knew he wasn't going to leave.

It wasn't just about longevity in the job. It was about the fact that The Dog could get crowded and rowdy, which meant he got good tips. I suspected it was also mostly because it got crowded and rowdy, half that rowdy crowd was female and drunk, so Jake also got a lot of action.

Jake was a Gnaw Bone native, like me. And, in his position of working at the bar in town where the locals frequented, Jake knew more of what was going down in Gnaw Bone than the police did.

So that meant, if Jake talked to Ham, Ham knew about me and Greg.

"Ham—"

"Says you split up with your man."

Okay, totally certain this was a bad idea.

And totally certain that, when I could next afford to buy a drink at The Dog, I was going to drink it and then throw my glass at big-mouth Jake.

"Yeah," I confirmed.

"First stop," he declared.

"What?" I asked.

"Comin' to see you. First stop."

Oh God.

Not only was calling Ham a bad idea, it was a catastrophic one.

"Ham—"

"Babe, you shot of him?"

"Yes, Ham. Though I wouldn't refer to it as 'shot of him,' but—"

"First stop."

I wanted that. I so very much wanted that.

But not now. Not after what I did to Greg. Not with all that was going on.

And probably not ever.

Because seeing Ham might destroy me.

I'd walked away from him once and that was hard enough.

I didn't think I could endure watching him walk away from me.

"Darlin', I think—" I began.

"Care about you, cookie, you know I do. Been years, sucked, not knowin' what's up with you but, babe, I just got an ax embedded in my shoulder. You think shit through when that kind of thing happens, trust me. And, Zara, you matter. I can give respect to you and him. You're together, hitched, you both deserve that. You shot of him, this disconnect we got goin' ends."

"I—"

"First stop. I'll be there tomorrow."

I lost my cool and exclaimed, "Ham!"

He didn't care that I lost my cool.

"Tomorrow, babe," he replied.

Then I had dead air.

I stared at my phone for several beats before I told it, "Yep, that was not a good idea."

The phone just sat in my hand.

The news anchor droned from the TV.

I got up and headed to the kitchen.

I came back with a glass of ice, a two-liter of ginger ale, and a bottle of vodka. The last of my vodka that I'd been saving for the right time, seeing as I couldn't afford to replace it and I couldn't see on the horizon a day soon when I would.

This was definitely that time.

Ham's voice slid through my head.

Tomorrow, babe.

I decided not to bother with the ginger ale.

Or the glass.

CHAPTER TWO

Tatters

I HEARD THE growl of a big truck's engine.

My eyes shot open.

That growl was coming from my driveway.

Then it stopped.

That was when my body flew into motion. I threw the covers back and jumped out of bed.

It was dark. I didn't care. I rushed through my bedroom into the hall and straight to the front door.

I unlocked it, yanked it open, and Ham was standing there, one arm in a sling, the other hand lifted toward the doorbell.

I threw myself at him, wrapping my arms around him.

He grunted, part in surprise but mostly in pain.

I jumped back.

"God, sorry!" I cried.

He stared at me through the shadows. The only illumination we had was dim and coming from the muted streetlamps of my development. I felt his eyes move over my face as I drank him in.

Then his hand shot out, hooking me at the back of the head. He yanked me to him, planting my face in his chest.

Cautiously this time, I rounded him with my arms.

"Cookie," he whispered into the top of my hair.

Warmth washed through me and I closed my eyes.

"Ham," I whispered back.

"Missed you, baby," he said softly.

I closed my eyes harder and pressed my face into his chest.

He let me, and we stayed that way a long time.

Finally, he broke the moment by lifting his lips from my hair and saying, "Let's continue this reunion inside with a beer."

Shit, I didn't have beer.

And shit again, I forgot in the thrill of hearing his truck in my drive that I'd spent that entire day alternately freaking out about the state of my life and freaking out about the fact that Ham was coming back and what I was going to do when he did, with Ham winning most of my freak-out time. Though, even with all the time I gave it, obviously, I didn't come up with a plan, nor did I steel myself against the thrill of hearing his truck in my drive.

And shit a-freaking-gain. In the thrill of hearing his truck in my drive, I forgot to throw on at least a robe so I was standing there in a clingy, sexy rose-pink, spaghetti-strapped nightgown that showed cleavage, exposed some skin through strategically placed lace, and had been purchased in a time when life was a whole lot better.

I tilted my head back, leaving my arms where they were, and he curled his hand around the back of my neck.

"I don't have beer," I informed him and watched his brows shoot up.

"Did hell freeze over and I missed it?" he asked and I wanted to keep distant. I wanted to control this "reunion." I wanted to guard my heart and my time.

I just couldn't.

So I smiled.

"Don't have a line to the devil, Ham."

"Bullshit, babe. Somewhere along the line, you made a deal with him. No woman who gives head the way you do hasn't sold her soul for that ability."

I blinked at this quick, explicit reminder of our bygone intimacy.

Then again, Ham was an honest guy. He didn't hide anything, even when he kept things from you. I knew that didn't make sense. I couldn't explain it. But I knew he was good at it.

He also didn't pull any punches. If he liked something, he liked it and said he did. Same with the opposite. Same with anything. If he had something to say, he said it. That didn't mean he didn't have a filter. That just meant he was who he was, he did what he did, he said what he said, you liked it or you didn't, and he didn't give a fuck.

I, unfortunately, liked it.

Ham let me go, moved back so my arms were forced to drop away. He bent and carefully picked up a big black duffel that I hadn't noticed was sitting on the concrete beside him.

This, I didn't think was good. This meant Ham thought he was staying with me.

And Ham couldn't stay with me.

"Uh . . . Ham—"

"Move back, babe."

"But, your bag—"

"Babe, back."

I moved back.

Ham moved in.

I shut the door and hustled in behind him.

"Got lights?" he asked.

I held my breath and flipped a switch.

Ham's ability to notice pretty much everything all at once honed by years of working bars had not dulled and I knew this the instant he muttered, "Jesus. What the fuck?"

Of course, the state of my house was hard to miss.

On the whole, my house was awesome. The best of the five floor plans offered by far, even if it wasn't the biggest. I loved it. It was perfect. The development was perfect, pretty, friendly people in it, well taken care of.

After growing up in a home that was not all that great, and living a life that had its serious down times, this house was all I ever wanted.

The narrow, cool, covered walkway outside was flanked on one side by the garage and on the other by the recessed portion of the kitchen. The front door opened to a short entryway that led to an open-plan area, the living room straight ahead, dining area to the left back. The kitchen was also to the left, part of it recessed toward the front of the house with a wide, curved bar that fed into the overall space.

The living room was sunken two steps, which gave a vague sense of breaking up the space and a not-so-vague ratcheting up of the awesome factor.

The colors on the walls and ceiling were sand and cream, the carpeting a thick, cream wool, so the feel was warm but serene.

I'd gone with a variety of upgrades, something I was paying for now in a number of ways, all of them literal. I'd gone for premium cabinets, granite countertops, Whirlpool appliances, and a built-in unit in the living room, with glass doors and recessed lighting. It was the shit.

I'd also upgraded the doors, so instead of sliding glass,

there were French doors leading from the living room, dining room, and the master bedroom to my backyard.

Most of the wall space was taken up by windows covered with custom-built Roman shades that I'd splurged on back in the day when things in Gnaw Bone were golden.

When Greg lived here with me, we'd decided to get rid of my old stuff, which wasn't that great, and he'd bought furniture and decorations that made an awesome space spectacular.

That was all gone.

Now I had a couch, and beside it a standing lamp, and in front of it, a nicked, scratched, not-altogether-stable coffee table that I'd actually picked up on the side of the road. The coffee table was the worst of the lot, seeing as I purloined it from a Goodwill pickup. The lamp and couch were only slightly better and that slightly was by a small margin.

My friend Maybelline had donated the lamp and couch to the cause when Greg moved out. She hadn't been thrilled to do it, knowing it was crap that had been sitting in her garage waiting for her husband to get the lead out and sell it on Craigslist, but she also knew something was better than nothing.

Except for a huge box television that saw the launch of MTV (donated by another friend, Wanda), the rest of the large space was empty.

"Greg got the furniture in the divorce," I explained.

Ham dropped his duffel and slowly turned to me.

I pressed my lips together when I saw the look on his face.

"You're tellin' me your ex left you in a home that's in this state?" Ham asked, seeking further details about the situation.

During one of my many freak-outs that day, I really should have figured out a way to keep Ham away from my house. Unfortunately, I was only thinking about seeing Ham, not about my house. In fact, I thought distractedly, I didn't even know how he knew where I lived since he'd never been here.

I didn't question this.

I thought, considering the look on his face, it was more pertinent to share. "I told him to take the stuff, Ham. It was his anyway."

"You're tellin' me your ex left you in a home that's in this state?" Ham repeated.

I decided not to reiterate my answer.

His eyes moved toward the kitchen then back to me, and when I got them again, I braced.

"Why don't you have beer?" he asked.

Again, Ham noticed everything, and along with noticing everything, he was capable of making scary-accurate deductions about things he noticed. And Ham's deductive powers, which could rival Sherlock Holmes', made things very uncomfortable for me at that moment.

I should have called and told him I'd meet him the next day at The Mark.

I should not have answered the door.

And the idea of cutting and running from *everything* was getting more and more attractive by the second.

The problem was I didn't have money for gas.

I took two steps forward, peered around the wall into the kitchen, saw my microwave clock said it was twelve thirty, and I looked back at Ham.

"You've been drivin' awhile and doin' it in that sling. Why don't you crash and we'll talk tomorrow?"

"Why don't you have beer, Zara?" Ham asked again.

"You've got to want to relax, unwind, and get some shut-eye," I said.

"What I want is to know why a woman who I've known eight years, five of 'em she never was without beer, and even once she dragged my ass out of bed to drive her two towns over to hit an all-night liquor store when we ran out, doesn't have beer."

That had been a good night.

I didn't want an interrogation and I *really* didn't want a trip down memory lane.

"Okay, how's this?" I began. "I'm happy you're here. I'm happy to see you safe and sound. I didn't expect it but it's cool if you want to crash here. But I have to open the shop tomorrow so *I* need some shut-eye. We'll talk tomorrow night when I get home from the shop."

"I don't like you avoiding this conversation, babe, but I mostly don't like why that might be," Ham returned.

"And I don't care, Ham," I snapped, losing it and watching his eyes narrow. "In case you haven't gotten it, I'll say it straight. The answers to your questions are none of your fuckin' business."

I'd never spoken to him like that. In fact, we never fought. Ever. Not in all the time we were together, not in all the years we'd known each other.

Ham was mellow, funny, and fun to be around. He'd seen it all, done it all, and had an air about him that he knew that there were things worth getting riled up about, but not many, and life was precious enough not to spend it pissed and shouting at someone. I went with that flow. We had always been easy. I couldn't remember once, not even *once*, when things had even gotten mildly heated. Ham made it that way. He just didn't go there, kept you snug in his laid-back aura, and it felt so good you didn't want to go there either.

Ham being laid-back, taking me along with him for that ride, and hearing me snap for the first time since I knew him had to be why he whispered a surprised, irritated, "What the fuck?"

"Three years have passed, Ham. Shit has happened. And *none* of it is your business," I carried on.

"Zara—"

I shook my head and lifted a hand. "No. We're not having this conversation now. I fucked up, callin' you. But I care. I never stopped caring. You matter to me, too, Ham, and it isn't every day someone I know gets attacked by a serial ax murderer. I had to know you were okay. I wasn't sure I wanted it but I'm glad actually to get to see for my own eyes you're okay. But we're not doin' this now. I'm tired. You have to be tired. We need sleep. But I'll warn you, I might not do this tomorrow either. You made a decision three years ago and we're stickin' with that."

His eyes narrowed further and his face got hard. "*I* made a decision?"

"Yeah, you did," I confirmed.

"You found a man, babe. You walked away from me."

"You let me."

He flinched and his torso swung back an inch.

I watched him in shock.

His flinch was not minor. My words cut him. Deep. So deep, his torso moved through the laceration.

What was that?

"Ham?" I called.

He recovered, wiping his face blank, or I should say wiping the pain away so it was back to hard.

"I told you to find a good man, not settle," he stated.

"You told me that three years ago. That's over and done. Now is now. And I'm tellin' you *now* we're not talkin' about this shit."

"You didn't find a good man, babe. You settled."

God, when had he become so stubborn?

I was already angry but I was getting angrier.

"Ham, this is none of your business."

Ham ignored me. "I know this because no man who's a good man cleans out his wife like this fucked-up shit." He used an arm to indicate the space and turned back to me.

"We're not talkin' about this."

"I also told you, he fucks you over, he did you wrong, you call me. You did not call me, Zara."

What the hell?

"Are you serious?" I whispered.

"Fuck yeah, I'm serious," he shot back.

"Rethink that answer, Ham," I returned.

"No, babe, *you* think back to that shit your parents pulled, how that shit meant you landed in my bed and I kept you there and took your back through that nightmare."

Again, memory lane, but this time, not such good memories.

"That was more than eight years ago, Ham."

"Yeah, it was. And my point is, over eight years, I've always been there for you."

"Only when you weren't gone."

His face turned to stone. "Bullshit, Zara, and you know it."

I threw up my hands. "Jesus, Ham, I'm seeing you for the first time"—I leaned toward him and yelled—"*in three years!*"

He leaned right back. "And it was fuckin' *me*"—he jerked a thumb at his chest "who told you to keep that connection, babe, and you kept it. You dialed that line that connected us just last night."

"A fuckup I knew was a fuckup last night but has now been elevated in status to a *major* fucking fuckup," I fired back.

"Jesus Christ!" he exploded, shocking me. As I explained, we never fought so this meant I never saw him lose it like that. It was freaking scary but it also weirdly made me angrier, especially when he scowled and went on to inform me, "This is *precisely* why I don't do this shit."

"What shit?" I clipped.

"You find a woman you think is a good woman, you make the big fuckin' mistake of lettin' her in an inch, she tears her way through, leavin' you bloody in her wake," he answered.

"Oh my God!" I shouted, raking a hand through my hair. "Are you insane?"

"*You* walked away from *me*," he bit out, jerking a finger at me. "And I see that took a bite outta you, Zara. I can fuckin' *see* the hole it left behind right in your goddamned eyes."

"Don't flatter yourself," I scoffed on a snap.

That was when he threw my words of three years ago right in my face, using them to tear through me, leaving me bloody in their wake.

"It was always me."

Standing there in tatters, unable to take more, I whispered, "Get out."

"Gladly," he returned, bent, and snatched up the handles of his duffel.

He stalked past me and I followed.

He used the only hand he had, the one carrying the duffel, to yank open the door and I watched him move through.

I also followed him out, stopping on my welcome mat, something I bought and one of the few things I didn't encourage Greg to take, in order to give Ham my parting shot.

"I'll give you a call, darlin', let you know the state of hell, seein' as I'm checkin' in with Satan to sell my soul for the ability to shield myself from assholes like you."

At my words, he swung around and informed me, "Takes more than your soul, baby. He also takes his pound of flesh. I should know, seein' as I made that deal with him years ago in an effort to protect myself from pain-in-the-ass women like you. Though, you might have noticed, seein' as we're havin' this cheery conversation, sometimes his spell doesn't work."

"Then he can take two pounds of flesh so I can buy a stronger one that'll work," I retorted. "After this shit, I'm sure you're not surprised that I'm willin' to pay a high price."

"That number might be busy, darlin', but keep tryin' it. I 'spect, after you ran him through the ringer enough for him to be so pissed he cleaned you out, your ex is on the line right about now, makin' his deal."

Already in tatters, that struck so close to the bone, it was a wonder I didn't dissolve.

"You're a dick," I hissed.

"Yeah, and a grateful one, seein' as you led with this bullshit so I could get the lay of the land real fuckin' quick, cut my losses, and get the fuck outta here."

I felt my face start heating with fury. "I led with a hug, you asshole."

"It was not ten minutes ago, Zara. I remember. Then I got whiplash with your one-eighty. You sure you aren't already tight with the guy downstairs?" he asked with deep sarcasm. "Five more minutes, I reckon I'd have watched your head spin."

"God! Can you get worse?" I snapped.

"Yeah, there it is. All woman. Pure woman. You don't know what you want, except the part where you want what you can't have and, somehow, that's my fuckin' fault."

"If you have heretofore unshared issues with women, Graham, work them out with another unwitting female."

"Not a chance. Haven't done this shit in years. Gonna do my motherfucking best not to do it again, *ever*. I drink, I eat, I fuck, I *leave*."

"Well, you got that down to an art."

"Why the fuck am I still standing here?" he asked.

"Beats me," I answered.

I barely got out the second word before he turned to go. But I wasn't done.

"Now look who's walking away," I remarked and he turned right back.

"Yeah. And advice. Take a good look, baby, 'cause this is the last time you'll see my ass and you like my ass. You want it. I know 'cause I still got the scars from your teeth the last time you took a bite outta me."

Fury and remembered desire rushed through me. So much of both I was paralyzed. I could do nothing but stand immobile and stare.

Ham raked me with his eyes from head to toe and fired the final shot.

"Christ. All the proof I need standing right there. All that pretty. Shiny. Looks sweet. Tastes sweeter. So goddamned good, you fuck up, put your trust in that sweet, then she sinks her fangs in you and releases the venom. Only one woman I know not filled with poison, knew her own goddamned mind, her shit was fucked up but she didn't make it anyone's problem but her own, and I let her walk away from me, too. The difference with her and you, babe, is that I regret lettin' her do it. I drove here thinkin' the same about you. Glad to know right off, I was wrong."

After I took that bullet, he turned, prowled down the walk, and disappeared.

I stood there listening to the door of his truck slam.

I kept standing there as the powerful beast growled to life.

And I stayed standing there as I saw his headlights illuminate the drive and I watched him back out and drive away.

Only then did I move into my house, close and lock the door, and wander to my room.

I laid in the dark, stared at the ceiling, and let his words shift through my brain, over and over.

Then she sinks her fangs in you and releases the venom.

And as those words shifted through my brain, I thought, *Yep, that's me.*

CHAPTER THREE

Mendin' Fences

Five months later...

WITH FILLED GROCERY bags in my hands, my phone ringing in my purse, I struggled through the door to my studio apartment. Dashing to the counter of the kitchen, I dumped the groceries, shrugged my purse off my shoulder, snatched my phone out, and hurriedly took the call before it went to voice mail without looking at the display to see who it was from.

"Hello?"

"Cookie."

At the surprise of Ham's deep voice calling me his nickname, my body sagged into the side of the counter even as my heart turned over.

"Are you okay?" I asked immediately.

"Yeah, but you aren't."

Just as quickly, I jerked away from the counter and my back went ramrod straight.

"Talked with Jake," he went on.

God. Jake.

I hadn't heard from Ham since that horrible night.

Now, he'd again talked with Jake, who I was distractedly surprised he was tight with, seeing as they worked together for just over six months eight freaking years ago and obviously kept in touch, which I knew Ham could do but Jake doing it shocked the shit out of me, and he was calling because Jake had spilled all my secrets. Again.

Not that they were secrets. Everyone in town knew that I'd had to close down my shop and had my house taken away from me by the bank.

This would have been humiliating if this freaking recession didn't mean that not a small number of the residents of Gnaw Bone, most specifically the inhabitants of the now-dead, as in murdered, as in killed by a freaking hit man, Curtis Dodd's developments weren't in the same pickle.

"Baby, why didn't you tell me?" Ham asked.

His voice was jagged.

I closed my eyes.

His voice sounded beautiful.

And it killed.

Damn it, I was not going through this again.

We were done. He clearly had issues with women. I wasn't stupid. I sensed that during the five years we'd been friends with benefits, five years in which he wouldn't commit to me or anyone.

But he'd made it plain during our last conversation.

"I seem to recall that I told you it was none of your business," I reminded him.

"Serious financial problems that mean you lose your house and your shop, babe, are absolutely my business."

"I'm not having this conversation again," I declared.

He ignored that and asked, "And you're workin' at Deluxe Home Store? You? Zara. Jesus."

"I need to eat, Ham. When a woman needs to eat, she does what she has to do. Thus the continued prevalence of prostitution, strip clubs, and porn films."

"Fuck, Zara," he growled and I heard the sharp edge of alarm in his tone. "What the fuck are you talkin' about?"

"I'm not talkin' about anything, and by that I mean I'm

done with the conversation, as in, hanging up, Ham. Don't call again."

"Cookie, don't hang up on me."

"Good-bye, Ham, and I hope your shoulder healed all right."

"Za—" I heard before I hit the button to hang up.

I turned the ringer to mute.

Then I fought back tears as I put away groceries in my tiny kitchen in my tiny studio apartment, which was the only thing I could afford on the shit wage I made at fucking Deluxe fucking Home Store. A big chain store that my friend Maybelline helped me get a job at when my life took its last major nosedive. A store that I liked working at *only* because Maybelle worked there, as did our other friend, Wanda. A store that was all right but so far from the coolness that I'd created in Karma, it wasn't fucking funny.

*   *   *

Twenty minutes later...

I jumped when the doorbell rang and didn't stop ringing.

"What the hell?" I whispered, pulling myself out of the couch.

I had a new couch. Not *new* new but new to me. My friend Mindy gave it to me. She'd put all her living room furniture in storage when she moved in with her husband, Jeff. The instant Mindy saw the state of what Maybelline gave me, she tasked Jeff and his best friend, Pete, with going to the unit, pulling out the furniture, and delivering it to my very humble new abode. Mindy also tasked Jeff and Pete with carrying away the stuff Maybelline gave me and, as she phrased it, "putting it out of its misery."

Thus, I now had nice, but used, furniture that included an armchair. All of this was in one room, as studios tended to be, stuffed in with my queen-sized bed and Wanda's mammoth so-not-flat-screen-it-wasn't-funny-but-on-the-bright-side-it-had-a-remote TV.

It was good that I didn't have to worry about furniture but I did have to worry about giving Mindy and Jeff money for their castoffs after Mindy breezily said, "Keep it. I don't know why I did, except my obvious-but-to-this-point-unknown clairvoyance of knowin' you'd eventually need it. Not to mention, you saved me the bother of havin' to do something with it."

She refused to take a cent mostly because, at the time, I didn't have any. I still didn't. But I was going to give her one (or a lot more than one) as soon as I had a few of them to rub together.

After giving Mindy some dough, next up, a new freaking TV.

In getting my life back in order, I had priorities. Thinking these thoughts, I went to the door cautiously as the bell kept ringing. Even in Gnaw Bone, a small town that was mostly sleepy but could do more than a decent tourist trade, or did back in the days when people had disposable income, one couldn't be too careful.

And anyway, all sorts of freaky shit was happening in the county lately, starting with Curtis Dodd's murder, which happened within days of Ham letting me walk away from him three and a half years ago.

It made me feel lucky that Gnaw Bone only had Dodd's murder and all the resulting muss and fuss with his wife, a woman I'd always loved, Bitsy, and her friend, a guy I'd always liked, Harry, ordering the hit. Harry had even killed a few other people after losing his mind and not exactly going on a rampage, but any amount of bodies that dropped that added up to more than one seemed like a rampage to me. Holden Maxwell and his girlfriend, now wife, Nina, got involved in that mess, Nina by getting kidnapped and nearly shot on the side of a mountain.

This made me feel lucky because Gnaw Bone only had that.

Carnal, the town one over, had much bigger messes and that was plural.

In other words, next up, it was discovered that Carnal had a serial killer, thus making Ham the victim of one freaking me out even more, seeing as a lot of people lived their whole life not having a serial killer in it, not one town over and definitely not some whack job planting a hatchet in your ex-lover's shoulder.

After that, again in Carnal, the fact their chief of police was a racist dickface became clear when it was discovered he framed a local—but seriously hot if the pictures in the paper were anything to go by—black guy for murder in freaking LA of all places. Not long after this dastardly deed was exposed, the dude lost his mind, that dude being the ex-chief of police. He kidnapped the black guy's pregnant wife and, luckily, she shot him dead on the side of another mountain. This was "luckily" because that outcome was what it was, rather than it being the other way around.

Then *another* whack job in Carnal had been at work. This one was a fanatically religious woman who killed some lady up in Wyoming and kidnapped her kids, holding them captive for ages in her house before one was discovered by a local cop and his girlfriend, taken care of, and then that whole thing exploded in a mess that somehow got his girlfriend buried alive. Though I didn't get that. Then again, I didn't really want to. I quit listening at "buried alive." That was enough for me.

Suffice it to say that, even though it was probably Mindy, Maybelline, Wanda, one of my other friends Becca, Jenna, Nina, or possibly Arlene, Cotton, or anyone else in Gnaw Bone seeing as I lived there all my life (everyone in town knew what had happened to me so everyone was watching over me), I still kept the chain on when I opened the door because my shitty apartment didn't have a peephole.

When I saw who was outside, my mouth dropped open.

Luckily, the doorbell buzzing stopped.

Unluckily, the last person on earth I wanted to see was standing outside my door.

"Jesus, you don't have a peephole?" Ham growled, looking incensed and Graham Reece looking, or worse, *being* incensed was a very bad thing. I'd learned that five months ago.

I didn't have it in me to concern myself with Ham being incensed. I was more concerned with him being there *at all*.

To express this, I asked, "What the hell?"

"Open the fuckin' door, Zara."

I stared a beat, then pulled myself together.

This was not happening.

We were done.

I pushed the door closed.

The problem with this was it didn't work, seeing as the toe of Ham's boot was wedged between it and the jamb.

"Open the door, Zara," he repeated.

"We're done," I told him through the gap in the door. "Move your foot."

"Open the door."

"We're done, Ham," I snapped.

"Right, then move back."

"What?"

He didn't repeat his order. He moved his foot but only so he could rear back and plant his shoulder in the door.

The chain popped right open, as did the door, and I went flying.

I righted myself as Ham, now in my apartment, slammed the door.

"You're payin' for that!" I yelled.

His eyes were beyond me, examining my new space as his mouth moved.

"Not a problem. I'll reimburse what they take out of your security deposit when we move you out of this dump."

I didn't know what he meant and I also didn't care.

I switched subjects.

"How did you get here so fast?" I asked, and his eyes finally came to me.

"I hope to Christ you didn't miss local gossip because you're spendin' your days at Deluxe Home Store and your nights at some titty bar."

"I'm not working at a titty bar, Ham, so you can stop concerning yourself with me and move on"—I paused—"*again.*" I bit off the last word then what he said penetrated and I asked, "What gossip?"

"Managing The Dog, Zara, have been for a week. I live in Gnaw Bone."

I felt my eyes get huge as my stomach clenched.

"You're managing The Dog?" I whispered, aghast.

"Yeah. And you just got a new job. You start after you work out your notice at Deluxe," he returned.

"What?" This also came out quiet and horrified.

"You're waitressin' for me. Shit hours but, if I remember correctly and since the view hasn't changed except to get better, with your face, tits, and ass, great tips. In the meantime, we're movin' you out of this shithole and, you don't got a girl who can take you on, you're bunkin' with me."

Bunking with him?

Was he high?

"I am *not* moving in with you," I declared.

"You aren't livin' in this place either."

"It's fine," I snapped.

"It doesn't have a fuckin' peephole, and, babe, reminder, I just popped that fuckin' chain not two fuckin' minutes ago."

"Well, seeing as my other callers won't force themselves into my place, that shouldn't be a problem," I retorted.

"Zara, got a scar on my shoulder that proves fucked up can hunt you down just 'cause you're breathin' and you've lived in this county through some serious, crazy, sick-fuck shit. You need a goddamned peephole and a decent lock. And, you can get it, a man at your back and that man's gonna be me."

"You're either high or you've lost your mind, Graham Reece, because there is no way in *hell* I'm moving in with you."

"I don't want your body, Zara. I want your safety," he shot back.

Ouch. That stung.

With no other choice, I powered through the sting. "Either way, neither are yours to have or give anymore, Ham. We're done."

"Don't let pride or bein' pissed stand in the way of reason, babe."

It was then, I'd had enough. More than enough. Of Ham. Of life. Of *everything*.

And, seeing as I'd had enough, I totally lost it.

"You're not *listening to me!*" I leaned in and shrieked the last three words so shrill Ham's head jerked. "We. Are. *Done.* I don't want to see you again. I don't want to talk to you again. I do not want you in my…*fucking*…life. Now get out, get gone, and please, God, *stay* gone."

Shockingly and infuriatingly, this tirade did not make him move toward the door. Instead, it made him take a step toward me, lift a hand my way, and say in a soothing voice, "Cookie, take a breath and calm down so we can talk."

"I'll calm down when you're out of my fuckin' house."

"Babe—"

I took a step back, turned, didn't know why the hell I

was turning since, in that tiny pad, I had nowhere to go, so I faced Ham again, and said quietly, "I lost my home. I lost my dream when I lost my shop. I nearly lost my stupid car and I had to sell a bunch of shit like my stereo so I wouldn't. I lost my husband and with him went my furniture. I'm working at a place I hate, making practically nothing. I have no idea what my future will bring. I have nothing to look forward to. I live day to day doin' nothin' but gettin' through the day. I do not need this shit. Not now. Not from you. Not from anyone. If you care about me even a little bit anymore, Ham, you'll get gone and *stay gone*."

"I've always cared about you, Zara."

God! Killing me!

"Then get gone."

"You gotta listen to me—"

"You're not getting gone," I snapped and he leaned in.

"Shoe's on the other foot, babe, you knew I needed you, would *you* leave *me*? No matter how much I said I wanted it, you knew my shit was fucked, would you walk away from me?"

Seriously, it was exasperating that he had a point.

I decided not to speak.

Ham saw his advantage and took it while taking another step toward me.

"You saw me on TV, babe, and I know, the way you were freaked, you picked up the phone within seconds. We were disconnected for fuckin' years, you saw the shit that went down with me, you reached out. So I know you wouldn't turn your back on me."

Definitely exasperating.

Ham kept going.

"I got a two-bedroom condo, good views, balconies off both bedrooms and the livin' room, and you'll have your own bathroom."

"You can't think I'd even consider movin' in with you," I replied.

"And I got a decent fuckin' TV."

Damn.

I wished he hadn't mentioned the TV.

I stared at him and Ham held my stare.

I found this nerve-racking so I tried something new.

"I have a year lease that I signed one month ago."

"And I have a way with talkin' folks around to my way of thinking."

I knew that. In fact, I was experiencing it at that very moment.

I tried something else.

"I have furniture and I don't have the money to put it in storage."

"That's good," he returned instantly. "Since I got a place that's not furnished and I haven't got 'round to buying anything."

"I thought you said you had a decent TV?"

"Darlin', I'm a guy. We can't breathe without a decent TV. I don't have furniture in the living room but I bought a bed and TV my first day in Gnaw Bone."

And again. Exasperating.

"Do you have an answer for everything?" I clipped.

"When it comes to gettin' you safe. Yes. I do. Absolutely."

And *again*. Killing me.

"Okay, then tell me this, Answer Man," I demanded. "I lose my mind and move in with you, who do I get? The Ham I thought I knew or Dickhead Ham who came to my house months ago and broke into my place just now."

"Never had a roommate, babe, except those four months you lived with me, and we did all right back then."

My stomach muscles contracted with the force of that blow.

He'd never had a roommate?

Except for me?

I decided not to go there.

"Right, to speed this along, I'd appreciate it if you'd leave so I can consider your gracious offer."

"Not leavin' without an answer."

"Ham—"

"Strike that. Not leavin' without the answer I wanna hear."

I glared at him before something hit me.

"What are you doin' here?"

His brows shot together. "Babe, I'm here offerin' to help you deal with your shit."

"Not here." I pointed to the floor. *"Here."* I swung my arm out wide. "Gnaw Bone. Why did you take the job at The Dog?"

"'Cause I got a hatchet to the shoulder, made me slow down, think about shit, and reconsider. Don't mind tendin' bar. Prefer doin' it paid a manager's salary. Been a lot of places and got treated kind. When I thought on it, this one stuck out. Don't know why. Don't care. It did. Just happened as I was thinkin' that shit through, The Dog needed a manager. Jake didn't want the promotion, he gave me a call. I told 'em I was interested. I'm here."

That was unsurprisingly forthcoming yet surprisingly thorough.

"And what about me?" I asked. "The town isn't all that big, Ham, and I doubt I have to remind you that the last time we shared breathing space, we didn't leave things all that great."

"Mendin' fences with you was on my list of things to do."

I had no idea if he wanted to do this so we could exist in the same town where we would undoubtedly run into each other or because he didn't like the way things ended the last time he'd seen me.

I told myself it didn't matter. What mattered was moving on.

To do that, I took in a deep breath, drawing in rational thought as I did so and, on the exhale, I shook my head and said, "Ham, our fight was extreme. I think we need to learn from that situation that we can wound each other, be smart, and steer clear. Gnaw Bone isn't that big but if you promise to act like a decent person should you see me, I'll do the same."

"Zara, our fight was extreme 'cause I just got hunted by an ax murderer. He was a sick fuck, obsessed with Feb, and did something about it to a woman I care about, and I got caught up in that mess. And I walked in on you while you were dealin' with some serious shit you were not in a place to process with me. We took that shit out on each other. It got outta hand and we wounded each other. Now, I got a life plan and you gotta find a place where you're safe while you make one. That place is with me. No strings. No bullshit. You work for me and make decent money. You live in my second bedroom. You sort your shit out. You make a plan. You move on. And in the meantime, we find the way to the new whatever-it-is we're gonna build with each other. No pressure. Nothin'. Just you safe, me not havin' to worry about you, and us not up in each other's shit."

Why did this suddenly sound completely reasonable?

"Honestly, Ham, I need some alone time to think about this," I told him.

"You can't have it. You don't move in with me, I'm sleepin' on your couch 'cause if police chiefs can kidnap pregnant women one town over, anything goes. So with your chain popped, no fuckin' way I'm leavin'."

I closed my eyes and dropped my head.

"Cookie, you've had it shit for a while," he continued. I opened my eyes and lifted my head to look at him. "Everyone's worried about you. Way I hear it, they're doin' all they think you'll let 'em do to help you out. Told you, you matter to me. For fuck's sake, babe, let me help you out."

"Livin' together is not a good idea, Ham."

"Worked for us before."

"We were lovers before," I whispered and Ham's jaw got tight.

Then he stated, "Right. I get your point. So, ground rules. You hook up, you do it at his place. I return the favor. Agreed?"

Me sleeping in Ham's second bedroom knowing he was out all night, hooking up.

That would be devastating.

I wasn't going to let on that I felt that.

I was also not going to share that I was never hooking up. Not ever again. For the rest of my life.

"That's a good rule," I said instead. "Another one, you replace any of my beer you drink."

His mouth twitched and he agreed. "You got it."

"And you're weirdly tidy," I informed him. "If I leave my shoes out or something, you can't light into me."

"Babe, I'm not weirdly tidy. I'm just not a slob like you are."

"I'm not a slob," I returned.

"I've known three times where you had to take emergency trips to the mall to buy underwear. This somethin' you actually did instead of laundry."

"That was before I had a washer and dryer in my house. I didn't have an aversion to laundry. I had an aversion to that weird guy who's always sleeping in the Laundromat."

At that, Ham grinned. "Lucky for you, I got a stackable in the hall."

"Yippee," I muttered.

Ham's grin got bigger.

It faded and he said quietly, "We'll work it out."

"Ham—"

"Cookie, we'll work it out."

I pressed my lips together.

"Tell me what I wanna hear," he prompted.

"Uh...just sayin', even if I do, my lock's still broken, seein' as you charged in here like a lunatic. Does this mean you're sleepin' on the couch until I move in?"

"No, you tell me what I wanna hear, it means we're loadin' your bed in my truck right now, movin' your ass in, and you're sleepin' in your new room tonight. We'll get the rest of your stuff later."

Something new to learn about Ham. He wanted something, he didn't mess around.

I made a mental note of this (and underlined it, repeatedly) as I studied him.

Ham let me.

Finally, I remarked, "You do know this is totally insane and will end in disaster."

"Last time I had you under my roof, it led to five years of good with a number of times in those years that weren't good. They were fuckin' great. So, babe, no. I don't know that at all."

At that point, I decided I needed to stop talking mostly so *he* would stop talking.

So I did and I considered his offer.

What I knew was I couldn't do this. I also knew I shouldn't.

"You gonna strip your bed or you wanna air the sheets on the way?" Ham asked.

Damn.

I was going to do this.

Because he was right.

Dennis Lowe, who attacked Ham, hadn't discriminated.

He'd attacked men and women, including killing his wife. The dude in Carnal *had* discriminated. He'd only killed women. And Lexie Walker, the pregnant lady who got kidnapped by the ex-chief of police, had obviously been a woman. Not to mention, Faye Goodknight, who got buried alive but fortunately rescued before she became buried dead, had also obviously been a woman. A wife. A pregnant lady. And Faye Goodknight was a freaking librarian.

No one was safe.

And I didn't even have a peephole.

"Strip it," I answered.

Ham smiled.

I sighed.

He wasn't insane. I was.

But, I told myself, at least I could be insane and safe at the same time.

Ham moved to the bed.

I stood there, hoping like hell I'd survive this.

Then I followed him.

CHAPTER FOUR

Easy

Two days later...

"LET ME GET this straight," Maybelline, my friend, my boss, a plump, attractive black lady in her forties, sitting across from me in the break room of Deluxe Home Store, started.

"You and this boy were together years ago. He took off. You both carried on an on-and-off fling for years. Mostly off. You let him go to explore things with Greg. He got axed by a psycho, you gave him a call, he shows, you rip into each other, now he's livin' in Gnaw Bone, and, yesterday, you moved in with him?"

Her brows were up and her face was a study in incredulity.

I understood her reaction. Breaking it down like that didn't sound so good.

I'd known Maybelline a long time even though she lived in Chantelle. We became friends after she became a regular at my shop. She liked the candles a local candlemaker made. She also had a habit of giving the unique-looking and stunningly melodious wind chimes another local artist made as gifts to friends out of state. When I lost the shop, seeing as she was the staff supervisor who did all the hiring, she worked it so I got a position at Deluxe.

And I'd just handed in my notice.

"You did me a solid, honey, but you also know things are serious tough for me right now and I make just above minimum wage," I reminded her. "Waitresses wages are crap but everyone goes to The Dog. It's packed nearly every night. I worked there before and tips were unbelievable. I'll at least double, if not triple, what I'm makin' here and I need it."

"Okay, I get that. I don't like it, but I get it," Maybelline replied. "You're good here. Good with customers. Show up on time, and you work instead of sneakin' into the stockroom or hiding out in the shelves to take calls from your boyfriend or to set up meets with your pot dealer. Most folk suck. Spend half my time dealin' with them. Only ones on staff don't have my head about ready to explode are you and Wanda. So I don't wanna lose you. But I get it. What I don't get is you're suddenly livin' with this guy who, sorry, baby, does not sound like a well-adjusted man who's got it goin' on."

"Ham's adjusted," I protested.

"He's a drifter," Maybelline shot back. "That's not adjusted. And then he shows at your house after midnight and lays into you?" She shook her head. "No."

"We fought because he'd just got axed by an ax murderer," I told her, thinking, of all reasons for emotions to run high, that was a doozy.

"I get he'd have issues after that, honey, but it isn't like I haven't learned anything, havin' three sisters and three daughters, not to mention bein' a woman myself. I see your face, Zara. You're strung out *more* than you're normally strung out and I know it's because you spent the last two nights sleepin' under this man's roof and wakin' up makin' coffee for him."

"I don't make coffee for him, Maybelle. He doesn't get up until nearly noon. I've barely even seen him except to move in."

"You know what I mean," she said gently.

I knew what she meant.

I held her gaze.

Then I told her, "I do. But he's a good guy and he's looking out for me. He talked to my landlord and got me out of my lease without any penalties or any hassle and it took him, like, fifteen minutes. He corralled Jake into coming around and they did all the heavy lifting with getting my stuff to his place. And his place is really nice. Clean. Newish. I have my own balcony. And there's not only a peephole but a security system."

"All that's good for your life right now, Zara, but none of it is good for your heart."

She was absolutely not wrong.

"I'm over him," I declared and she sat back but didn't let go of my eyes.

She didn't speak for several beats before she stated, "I'll remind you, you're talkin' to a woman with three daughters and three sisters, baby."

Okay, so I couldn't pull one over on Maybelline.

"Right, then, I'm not over him but I'm not doin' that shit again with *any* man. I'm determined about that. I'm determined to get my life back together. So even if I was open to having another man, having one would take attention away from getting my life together. And that's not going to happen so it's lucky I don't want one."

Before she could reply, I leaned toward her and grabbed her hand.

"I'm thirty-two years old, Maybelle, and I'm starting fresh and that *sucks*."

"I know, hon," she whispered.

I kept talking, telling her stuff she knew because she lived through it with me.

"The bank took my house and I got so deep with my creditors for the store, my credit rating is totally in the toilet. I have to sit for seven years to wait out the black mark of the foreclosure and to get my credit history back on track. I'm screwed with all that. I have my two-hundred-dollar security deposit in the bank and that's it. I don't know what rent's going to be at Ham's but I do know that if I don't have to drive all the way out here to go to work, I'm gonna save a whack on gas."

"Well, you got that right," she mumbled.

I figured that meant I was getting somewhere so I went on.

"Like I said, my pay is going to at least double. And one thing I know, even with our history, Ham will do right by me. I'm hanging on to that for today. Tomorrow, I'll build on that. And then build some more. Until this shit time is done and I finally, *finally* have something to look forward to again. I don't know what that is. I just know I have to find it, Maybelle. Because not havin' anything good, anything to look forward to, anything to work toward sucks. It can beat you. There were a bunch of times when I almost let it beat me. And I gotta do what I gotta do to keep that streak and not let it beat me."

When I was done talking, Maybelline was holding my hand tight.

"You been doin' real good, girl," she told me.

"I don't know how," I told her. "Honestly, Maybelle, the times I wanted to run away or felt humiliated because I had to sell plasma, fighting tears the whole time my blood dripped out of me, just so I could buy some cereal and put a bit of gas in my car, jumping at the shot to babysit Nina and Max's kids so I could make twenty bucks. It's a struggle, not letting it beat me. Ham's giving me a shot at pulling myself out. Bein' with him while having feelings for him, that'll also be a struggle. But it's the best shot I've had for a really fucking long time and I gotta take it."

Maybelline kept holding my hand tight as she held my eyes.

"You need me, I'm there," she declared.

I smiled, let her hand go, and leaned back. "You always are."

"Okay, no. What I meant to say, you need me or not, I'll be there," she amended.

My head tilted to the side in confusion. "What?"

"Me and Wanda, we're gonna be on the case," she announced.

I was still confused. "On what case?"

"Don't know this boy. Gonna get to know him *real* quick. Gonna keep our fingers on the pulse. Make sure he doesn't play games with our girl."

I didn't have a good feeling about this.

"Maybelle—"

She lifted a hand my way, palm out. "Love you, baby. You know it. Wanda thinks the world of you and you know that, too. But you're not out of that hot water yet. We're gonna make sure you don't drown in hot guy."

I leaned in again. "Maybelle, seriously, honestly, I'm not pulling wool. He's a good guy."

"He left you."

"Yes, but—"

"Left you but kept you, then let you walk away from him."

"This is true, but—"

"Boy's gonna have to prove to me he's a good guy."

I sat back again and let it go.

Maybelline and I graduated from shopper and shop owner to meeting for coffee to having a gab over drinks to talking on the phone for hours about her boy-crazy daughters and man-eating sisters to her having me over to dinner twice a week so she could ascertain I got a decent hot meal in me so she could strike at least that worry off in all her worries about me. In other words, I knew her. I could talk for days and she'd still do whatever-it-was she was going to do with Wanda to keep an eye on Ham.

"Just don't get me kicked out of my new pad. It's the shit," I said.

"You can move in with me and Latrell, that happens."

"Latrell would lose his mind if the female quotient of his house upped from four to five," I returned.

"This is true," she muttered. "But I'll give him regular foot rubs. He'll get over it."

Latrell, I knew, liked his foot rubs and Maybelline got away with a lot in utilizing them strategically.

Still, I thought it important to warn again, "Don't get me kicked out of my pad, Maybelle."

"We'll go easy on your supposed good-guy hot guy."

This was, most likely, a big fat lie.

Therefore, I repeated, "Don't get me kicked out of my pad, Maybelle."

That was when my phone on the table started ringing.

"It'll all be good," she assured me, getting up. "Now, I accept your resignation. Grudgingly. Get your phone. And you're on register three when you're done with your break."

She gave me a finger wave and took off.

I looked at my phone and took the call.

"Hey, Arlene," I greeted.

Arlene was the dispatcher at the local taxi company in Gnaw Bone. She also part-owned it. She'd inherited it when her husband, who had part-owned it with his brother, passed. Since Gnaw Bone wasn't a thriving metropolis and taxis were needed sometimes for tourists but most times about thirty minutes after last call, this meant she spent her days having plenty of time to get in everyone's business.

I could see it was now my turn.

"What's this I hear you movin' in again with that Reece guy?" she asked instead of saying hi.

"Arlene—" I tried.

"Didn't that boy leave you high and dry years ago?" she pushed.

"Well, not exactly high and dry. I knew he was a rolling stone and it was a matter of time. But that's not what this is. We're just roommates. The place I was stayin' at wasn't safe. His place is. He's just makin' me safe."

"Know that about that dump you lived in already, Zara. Told you you should never move in there. It doesn't even have a blasted peephole."

My eyes rolled to the ceiling.

"Anyway," she continued. "Whatever. We're meetin' for drinks tonight at The Dog. Seven thirty."

"Arlene, I've got boxes to unpack."

"So? Unpack 'em tomorrow night. Seven thirty. See you there."

Then she hung up.

I guessed I was going to The Dog that night.

Oh well, this wasn't a bad idea. Outside of moving me in, I hadn't seen much of Ham and we needed to iron some things out. Like rent and utilities.

I had two hundred dollars. I could afford a drink.

So The Dog it was.

I put my phone away in my locker and hightailed my ass to register three.

*   *   *

At a quarter after seven, I walked in to The Dog, saw Ham behind the bar, and caught my breath.

I hadn't seen that in eight and a half years.

And I missed it.

Both my sister, Xenia, and I wasted no time getting out from under our parents' roof the minute we could.

For me, this meant hostessing at The Mark from age eighteen to twenty-one when I could legally serve alcoholic beverages. It was then I moved to The Dog and went from existing on practically no dough and living with a girlfriend in an apartment that was a half step up from my studio to having loads of cash in my pocket every night and getting my own place that I kept until I moved into my house, even through the time when I'd all but moved in with Ham.

So I'd had three years at The Dog under my belt before Ham got a job there.

Looking back, I'd fallen for him on sight. But he capped it being not only hot but cool and fun to work with. I never expected anything to happen. He was eleven years older than me, and back then, that was a lot. Even now, it still seemed like a lot.

But it happened for us. It didn't take long. My parents never really got done screwing with me or Xenia. Not until they did it when Ham was around, he took my back, as he said, I landed in his bed, and he took care of that situation for me.

Not for Xenia, unfortunately. By then, Xenia was beyond anyone taking care of her, even professionals with years of training and experience.

I turned my thoughts from my sister like I always turned my thoughts from my sister but doing it meant I caught the sexy smile Ham threw at me when he caught sight of me.

Yes, this was going to be a struggle.

He moved down the bar when he saw I was moving in that direction.

I hefted my ass on a stool as he hit the bar in front of me.

"You didn't tell me you were comin' in," he said as a greeting.

"Command performance," I explained. "Arlene."

He smiled another sexy smile as he muttered a throaty, sexy, "Ah."

I ignored the sexy, throaty "ah" *and* smile as well as my mild surprise that Ham obviously remembered Arlene from back in the day (then again, Arlene was unforgettable), though there was the possibility she'd been in since he'd been back, and stayed on target.

"I got home, unpacked some stuff so your head wouldn't explode at the mess, and headed out or I would have called to let you know you needed to have a cold one waiting for me."

Without hesitation, he moved back two steps, bent, pulled a cold one out of the glass-fronted fridge under the back of the bar, twisted off the cap, and came back to put the bottle of beer on the bar in front of me.

I grabbed it and took a deep pull.

When I dropped it, I noted, "Just to say, I only got a few

boxes unpacked so don't let your head explode. I'll finish tomorrow."

"Tell me you unpacked the dishes," he ordered.

"Seein' as you got paper plates, a weirdly ample supply of chopsticks, and that's all, not even mugs, yes. I prioritized unpacking the dishes."

He grinned. "Then my head won't explode."

"Good," I mumbled and took another pull from my beer. When I dropped it, I asked, "You got a second to talk before Arlene gets here?"

"Jake's out back, so I do but I do only if no one needs a drink."

"This'll be fast."

His brows went up. "What's up?"

"We need to talk about rent, utilities, stuff like that."

"Why?"

I blinked and repeated a perplexed, "Why?"

"Well, seein' as you're not payin' either, nothin' to talk about."

I didn't blink then. I stared, wide-eyed and with lips parted.

I pulled it together to ask, "I'm not payin'?"

"Babe, told you, helpin' you get on your feet."

"But—"

"To get on your feet, you need cash."

"Yes, but—"

"Yo! Barman!" a man's voice called.

I looked to the right and saw a man holding up a ten spot.

"Be back," Ham muttered and moved to the man.

I took a pull of beer, thinking about our brief discussion and how I felt about it.

Then I decided how I felt about it.

Luckily, Ham was quick getting beers for the guy, making change, and getting back to me.

"We good?" he asked.

"No," I answered.

"Zara—"

I leaned in. "Please, listen to me."

Ham held my eyes. "I'm listenin'."

"I can't let you do that. Even if we were together, I couldn't let you do that. I've made my own way since I was eighteen."

"Darlin'—"

"Please. Listen," I urged.

Ham shut his mouth.

"We have to work something out. I know what it costs to rent there because I checked it out when I was moving. It was totally out of my range and I wasn't even looking at two bedrooms with three balconies. I suspect half of your rent is more than my rent on the studio so, it sucks, but I can't hack that. But I have to do something and you have to let me, Ham. I'm moving right back out if you don't. Maybelline said I could stay with her and her husband if—"

He cut me off. "Half utilities, a hundred dollars the first month, a hundred fifty the second, two hundred the third, we stick with that for the next three and see where you're at."

I took a deep breath and felt the tension ease from my shoulders.

"Thank you," I said quietly.

"So we got a deal?" he asked.

I nodded.

His intelligent eyes moved over my face.

"Easy," he murmured.

"What?" I asked.

He shook his head. "Nothin'."

"No, Ham, what?"

He again studied me and then he bent into his forearms in the bar and my stomach muscles contracted at the blow delivered from that memory.

Before we were together, and especially when we were, I couldn't count the times when I stood outside the bar, Ham stood behind it, leaned into his forearms, leaned into *me,* while we flirted, chatted, talked deep, teased, joked, whatever.

I missed that, too.

Huge.

And my working there, Ham leaning into me now, I was getting it back.

Just not the way I wanted it.

Oh yes, this was going to be a struggle.

"Hesitate to say this, darlin' "—Ham took my mind from my thoughts—"but we had what we had and the deep part of that where we shared, I want us to get back to, so here it is. I think you got in that shit I spewed at you that, for the most part, I'm not a big fan of women. I'm a man, so basic needs, I've had my share, didn't hide that from you but only two of those women I had were easy. Until that night we had our thing, one of 'em was you. You were goin' through shit so I get it. But I want you to know, I'm glad you're back to easy. It's how I always thought of you and, when I didn't have you, it was what I remembered of you." He grinned. "That and your smile, how soft your hair was, and how good you were with your mouth."

I hid the shiver his words caused and warned, "I'm not out of the woods, Ham. You're helpin' a lot but I have a loose hold on easy."

"We'll get you there," he promised.

"Thank you for being cool," I replied and smiled. "That's what I remembered of you. You bein' hot and cool."

His hand came up and reached out. I braced, hoped, but feared that it would drop away.

It didn't.

Ham did what he used to do. He tucked my hair behind

my ear, his fingertips running the full length of the shell to the lobe, then dropped to my neck. He ran them down the skin there and they fell away.

Depending where we were back in the day, his fingers didn't stop at my neck.

But I'd take that. As desperate and wrong as it was, it felt good. It made my scalp tingle, my eyelids feel heavy, my skin heat, and I missed that from Ham, too.

And when I could lift my eyelids again and focus on Ham, the look on his face, his eyes aimed at the spot where his fingers last touched, made my breath catch because he looked like he missed it, too.

"Just makin' you safe? Yeah, right," Arlene broke the moment by grumbling as she hefted her ass up on the stool beside me. "Coors, now, player," she ordered, her eyes sharp on Ham.

"Player?" he asked, his eyes on Arlene, and then they moved to me.

Arlene turned to me. "Isn't that what they call a Lothario these days?"

"Ham's not a player or a Lothario, Arlene," I told her firmly.

Arlene ignored me and looked at a displeased-looking Ham. She also ignored that Ham looked displeased.

"Know her, don't know you 'cept what I knew of you years ago when you were right where you are now. Like her and have for years. Don't know if I like you yet. Also want her to get on her feet, and she don't need no man playin' with her heart while she's doin' it. So, just sayin', this thing you two got goin' "—she put her fist toward her face, extended her index and middle fingers, pointed to her eyes then to Ham then back again—"I'm watchin' you."

Terrific. Now Maybelle, Wanda, and Arlene were all going to be up in Ham's face.

Instead of getting pissed, the Ham I'd always known came out and his lips twitched.

"You wanna watch me get you a beer?" he asked.

"Yeah. And incidentally, that'll go a long way to making me like you," Arlene answered.

"So it doesn't take much," Ham noted.

"I don't have a beer," Arlene prompted.

Ham smiled flat-out, turned it to me, then got Arlene a Coors, putting it in front of her, murmuring, "Girl time."

"Damn straight," Arlene replied.

Ham gave her another smile, shot it to me, reached out and touched my fingers that were curled around the beer, and wandered down the bar.

"Yeesh, didn't know a bear matin' with a human could create somethin' that divine but there it is. Proof," Arlene remarked and I looked at her to see her checking out Ham.

So I looked back at Ham, who was now down the bar, grabbing the empty glass from in front of a woman he was also grinning at.

She was giving him come-hither eyes.

I looked away.

"Yeah, he's hot," I agreed.

"Hot or not, you be careful," Arlene warned.

My gaze went to her.

Arlene was ornery, nosy, and in your business, but still lovable mostly because she was only nosy and in your business because she cared. She also had short hair permed in tight curls dyed a weird peachy color. Last, she was petite and very round but had tiny, graceful hands and feet. I'd always found that strange, but at the same time beautiful.

"We're just roommates," I stated firmly.

"Mm-hmm," she mumbled disbelievingly.

"Seriously," I told her.

"Take twenty years and fifty pounds off me, I was under

that man's roof, I'd do my damnedest to be just his room-mate for about five seconds."

"Been there, done that. We've moved on," I told her firmly.

Arlene speared me with her eyes. "Got some life tucked under my belt along with this belly, girl. Remember him. Remember you. Know you. Now he's back and I got a good look at him, his behind, *and* his smile. A girl doesn't move on from that."

"Okay," I gave in. "So let's just say I have approximately five thousand seven hundred and twenty other things on my mind that *don't* involve Ham's behind or smile that are priorities."

"Stay focused," she ordered and I smiled.

"I will, Arlene."

"I will, too, Zara."

Right. Confirmation. Arlene was going to be in Ham's face *and* mine.

I looked away, took a pull off my beer, swallowed, and muttered, "Do what you gotta do."

"Always do," she muttered back after her own pull.

"But don't get me evicted from my new pad by being nosy and in your face with Ham," I demanded.

Her brows shot up. "Girl, I got finesse."

"The finesse of a rhinoceros," I returned.

She looked away, put her beer to her lips, but didn't drink.

Instead, she said, "I'm gonna pretend I didn't hear that." Then she drank.

I put my beer to my lips but didn't drink, either.

Instead, I smiled against it and replied, "Whatever works for you." Then I drank, too.

"Suck that back. I'll get us another one. Then another. And I'm payin'. I'm also not takin' any lip about payin'. You can catch me on the flipside," Arlene ordered.

"I drove here, Arlene," I informed her.

"And I own a taxi company, Zara," she shot back. "Bottom's up. Girls' night, on me. Live it up."

That was an order, too.

Arlene, incidentally, was like Maybelline.

You just didn't fight it.

So I bottomed up, caught Ham's eyes, lifted my empty, and got another smile as he moved our way.

Yes, absolutely.

This was going to be a struggle.

Luckily, beer helped.

And so did knowing Arlene and Maybelline cared so much about me.

I just might make it through after all.

CHAPTER FIVE

Fair

Three weeks later…

I FELT RATHER than saw Ham round the corner into the kitchen as I was wiping the counters.

"I'll be ready in a few. Just gotta get this done and get my boots on," I told him.

I'd been back at The Dog for three weeks now.

I'd also been wrong. Waitressing at The Dog didn't double or triple my pay.

It quadrupled it.

It had been a long time I'd been away. I guess I didn't remember how good it could be.

And it was good.

In fact, it was all good. Living with Ham. Working with Ham. Having cash in my pocket. Not freaking because my gas tank was edging toward empty. Having beer in the fridge.

And Ham and I were back. Not, of course, the good stuff like my having his fingers, his tongue, and other parts of his anatomy but the *other* good stuff, like Ham making me laugh, Ham being mellow and tucking me snug in that mode, Ham being cool about everything.

I couldn't say that occasionally things didn't hit me and sting. Like when I saw him flirt with a customer. Or when I'd let my guard down while looking at his hands or his lips and remember those used to be mine for a time, I was free to touch them, put them on me, put mine on him.

But I found my way to beat that back and move on. These ways mostly had to do with my having cash in my pocket, a job I actually enjoyed, and Ham in my life on a daily basis, even if it wasn't how I would want him.

"We gotta talk," he told me.

"We can talk in the truck," I replied as I tossed the sponge into the sink. "I'm on shift in twenty."

Incidentally, there was another reason I had cash and didn't freak that my gas gauge was heading to empty. Nearly every night, Ham drove me to work.

"I know you're on in twenty, babe. I wrote the schedule. Remember? We gotta talk now."

At his tone, my eyes went from my hands, which I was drying with a towel, to him.

His tone wasn't angry but it was unyielding and, therefore, surprising.

I looked to him even as I folded the towel and said, "Okay."

"You did my laundry," he stated.

"Yeah," I agreed.

"You did it last week and the week before, too."

"So?"

"You cleaned my bathroom yesterday," he said, sharing something I knew since I was the one washing his whiskers down the sink.

I felt my eyebrows draw together. "And?"

"Darlin', we're roommates."

I was no less confused at this short explanation. "I know."

It was then he moved into me. Not only moved into me, he lifted one of his big, calloused hands, curled it around the side of my neck, and pulled me to him so I had to tip my head way back and he had to dip his chin deep so we could hold each other's eyes.

Ham had to be six-four, maybe even six-five. I was five-six. Even in heels, he towered over me.

I'd always loved that.

I especially loved it in times precisely like that one, where we were close, he was in boots, I was in socks, and his big bearness seemed to engulf my frame, surrounding me, protecting me, dominating me.

I held my breath.

Ham spoke and he did it jagged and sweet.

"I get you're grateful, baby. I get it because you told me. You don't have to show me."

I was too overwhelmed by his nearness, the roughness of his hand on the sensitive skin of my neck, to understand what on earth he was talking about.

So I asked, "What?"

"I can do my own laundry. I can clean my bathroom. I come to the kitchen meanin' to turn on the dishwasher, I find it's been turned on and the dishes put away. I get up in the mornin' ready to make coffee, you not only got the coffee made, babe, you've pulled down a mug and put sugar in it for me. Again, Zara, you're my roommate not my maid."

"I'm just tryin' to keep things tidy," I told him. "You like things tidy."

"You're attemptin' payback," he contradicted. "You live here. You pay rent. It's your place, too. You aren't an indentured servant. This is your pad. Just live and stop knockin' yourself out to show gratitude to me. I don't need that. I'm good knowin' you're safe and gettin' on your feet."

All right, it must be said, I was knocking myself out to keep things ordered and do bits here and there to make it easier on Ham because he was being so cool with me.

I just didn't think he'd notice.

I should have known better.

"How about, until I'm in a place to go halfsies, I do a little bit extra," I tried.

"How about you don't worry about halfsies and just keep your shit sorted. I'll worry about mine and the common space we take care of as it gets taken care of. Not you runnin' yourself ragged to take care of it before I got a shot to take care of it in an effort at payback I don't want. Deal?"

My eyes fell to his throat as my chest warmed but my throat tingled. "That's not very fair."

"Babe."

That was all he said but it made me look back up into his eyes.

When I caught his gaze, his face got closer and I was back to holding my breath.

"Said it before, more than once, you matter. You beddin' down in a bedroom I don't use is no skin off my nose. Stop worryin' about shit you don't need to worry about and just breathe easy for a while."

For me, it was him.

It had always been him.

And this was one of the myriad reasons why.

To be certain I didn't let on to that fact, I said, "Okay, you're all fired up to unload the dishwasher, have at it. I'll go back to my slob ways. Just don't bitch when I do."

He grinned and unfortunately moved back.

But he didn't move his hand from my neck. He gave it a squeeze before his calloused thumb glided out and stroked across my throat.

Then he let me go and moved away, ordering, "Get your boots. You're gonna be late and the boss doesn't like that shit."

I smiled at the folded towel in my hand before I tucked it into the handle of the oven and started out of the kitchen to get my boots.

I stopped dead when I heard Ham call, "We're enjoyin' this weather but it'll get cold later so dress for the bike."

It was nearing on September, unpredictable in the Colorado Mountains. It could mean we'd be up to our knees in snow tomorrow and stay that way until April. It could mean we could go out in swimsuits tomorrow and get sunburned.

But every man who had a bike who lived in unpredictable weather took it out as often as he could before that unpredictable weather hit.

We'd been in the truck since I started at The Dog.

I hadn't been on the back of Ham's bike in years.

I loved being on the back of Ham's bike, wrapped around Ham.

This was one of those times that stung.

I sucked it up, ignored the sting, and went to get my boots.

*   *   *

It was a Thursday night and The Dog was crowded but it wasn't packed.

This was good, seeing as Bonnie, one of the other waitresses, had called off sick. This meant I'd be busy, get a slew of tips, and the night would go fast. I'd be exhausted when it was over but it would be worth it.

I turned the corner from the back where the pool tables were and my eyes automatically went to Ham behind the bar.

His eyes were already on me but he jerked his chin in front of him, silent indication I knew meant a customer had come in I hadn't seen.

I nodded, looked to the mess of high tables with their tall stools that were scattered all over the bar, and stopped dead.

I did have a new customer.

A lone man, wavy dark hair, slightly sloped shoulders, jeans jacket. His legs were spread wide with his feet on the rung of the stool. His thighs were thick, a leftover from playing football in high school.

Greg. My ex-husband.

Greg never came to The Dog. He wasn't a Gnaw Bone native. He worked at an environmental engineering firm based in Chantelle, moved from Kansas to take the job. He was quiet, liked to play board games, watch movies, concoct meals in the kitchen out of ingredients that it was always a shock tasted good together, and would have a beer with me on occasion at home but he wasn't a nightlife kind of person.

There was only one reason he'd be at The Dog.

He knew I was there.

I hadn't seen him in months. This wasn't a surprise, seeing as he moved to Chantelle after we split up to be closer to work and was a homebody.

We'd promised, though, to keep in touch. See each other. Go out and get a bite to eat. When I'd asked for the divorce, I'd told him I didn't want to lose him from my life. I just didn't want to be married to him anymore.

Greg, being Greg, went for that.

He'd do anything for me.

Even let me go.

Something the men in my life always seemed able to do.

Then again, I also seemed perfectly capable of asking them to.

But I hadn't kept my promise. I had reason. My life was swirling down the toilet. We'd talked a couple of times and Greg knew this so he didn't pressure me. Then again, he wouldn't pressure me anyway. That wasn't his style.

On leaden feet, I moved to his table and rounded him, carefully arranging my face so he saw I was welcoming, not wary. He caught sight of my movement and his clear, bluish-gray eyes came to me.

"Hey," I greeted.

"Heard you were working here," he replied.

I leaned into the table and tucked my tray under my arm. "Yeah. Better money."

He nodded. He'd offered to help me out financially, repeatedly. I'd declined. Repeatedly.

"It's good to see you," I told him.

"Yeah, you too," he told me.

I forced my lips into a grin. "Breakin' the seal on The Dog," I noted on a careful tease.

"Like I said, heard you were working here and haven't seen you in a while. Thought I'd take a chance."

"Glad you did," I lied. It was a lie not because I didn't want to see him, just that I didn't like being surprised by his showing up at my work.

It was then Greg forced a smile.

"Can I get you a beer or somethin'?" I asked. "I... well, our other girl is out sick so it's only me on tonight. I probably can't hang at your table but I'll get you a beer and do my best."

"That'd be good, Zara."

I nodded and asked, "Newcastle?"

"Yeah."

I forced a smile, turned away, and moved toward the bar.

Ham moved toward me, his eyes sharp on my face.

"Newcastle," I said the minute I hit the bar.

"Who's that guy?" Ham asked a nanosecond after the final syllable left my mouth.

And again, Ham never missed anything.

I held his gaze. "My ex-husband."

Ham's jaw got tight and his eyes went to Greg

"Ham," I called and his eyes came to me. "It's cool. We're cool. It wasn't ugly."

"Way I see it, babe, your house cleaned out, him leavin' you stuck with a mortgage you couldn't afford, that's plain not true," Ham returned.

I leaned into him. "I'll explain later but, honestly, Ham. It's cool. Seriously."

"Right, you want me to believe that then you best stop lookin' like takin' a Newcastle to him is like walkin' to the electric chair."

Luckily, Greg didn't have superhuman perceptive and deductive powers like Ham did so I was relatively certain I'd pulled the wool over his eyes.

I'd never been able to do that with Ham.

"I hurt him," I said quietly.

"Shit happens. People deal. They don't show where you work and make you look like you look right now, cookie."

I couldn't do this now so I asked, "Please, can you just get me his beer?"

Ham studied my face before he got me Greg's Newcastle.

I took it to Greg and slid it in front of him. "There you go."

"Should I open a tab or pay for this now?" Greg asked and that was so Greg. He didn't know how to pay for a beer in a bar.

I tipped my head to the side and forced another smile. "You plannin' on gettin' hammered?"

Greg's eyes moved over my hair before they came to mine and he answered, "No."

"Then feel free to pay as they come, honey, but that one's on me."

He shook his head and straightened his back. "No, Zara. I'll—"

I put my hand on his bicep. "Let me buy you a beer."

I watched him pull in a breath and then he nodded.

"I'm gonna do a walk-through. Soon as I have everyone sorted, I'll come back. Okay?"

"Sure, Zara."

"Okay," I said softly, then did as I said I would.

This took a while because I had a lot of customers. This was also not easy, knowing Greg was there and feeling Ham's acute attention on me and my ex-husband the entire time.

When I was free for a few minutes, I took Greg a fresh Newcastle and put it in front of him, whisking away the empty.

"This one, I'm paying for," Greg announced.

Again, I forced a smile. "I'll allow that."

"You got two seconds?" he asked.

Damn. Greg didn't get out and about much so I had a feeling he was there for a reason and not just to see me. And I really didn't have it in me with all that had been going on to deal with this if his need for two seconds was going to hit deep. He'd been really cool with me all along but I always worried one day, something would trip, he'd realize I did him wrong, and he'd stop being cool.

I worried these two seconds would show he was done with being cool.

I could give him that. He deserved it.

But not with no warning, at work, and with Ham watching.

"Yes," I answered.

He looked to the beer, the wall, then twisted on his barstool so as better to face me.

"It's public record but I didn't find out that way. Guy at work's wife works for a judge and she talks. She mentioned you. He knew about you and me, so he mentioned you so I know you changed your name back to Cinders."

Of all the things I thought he might say, and truth be told, I had no idea what he was there to say, I just guessed he was there to say something, that wasn't it.

"Yeah, I petitioned the judge a while ago. Why?"

"You took their name back."

I pressed my lips together.

He knew about my parents. Then again, everyone in town did but Greg knew more than most because I told him.

He hated them. He didn't hate anyone. He was a kind soul and didn't have a judgmental bone in his body. But he hated my parents and he'd never even met them.

"You said you'd never take their name back," he went on.

"Greg—"

"You asked for us to be over, Zara, and I didn't like that but I left and the only thing I could think of to make me feel better, not having you, was that I gave you that. I took away their name and gave you mine. I thought you'd keep it."

"Honey, we aren't married anymore. It's not mine to have."

"That's the only good thing I gave you."

Oh God, now *this* was stinging.

"That's not the only good thing you gave me, Greg," I told him gently.

"It's the only thing you let me leave with you. Made me clear everything of mine away. I thought you'd keep *something*."

"I asked you to take your stuff because it's *your* stuff.

That's fair. I wasn't making you clear everything of yours away," I corrected.

"Well, it felt like that," he returned.

Man, oh man, that wasn't what I intended. I was trying to do right.

"I didn't mean it that way," I replied carefully.

"You've got nothing of me. You even gave back the rings."

"You bought those, too," I reminded him. "That's also fair, honey."

Again, his back went straight but this time with a snap.

"You know, stuff like this, Zara, it isn't about fair. That has nothing to do with it. It's about a lot of other stuff but not about being fair. I didn't want to leave you but you wanted that so I let you go. Then you made me leave you like I left you and I hated that but you wanted it so I did it. But what *I* wanted was some indication that maybe a day or an hour or a second of what we had meant something to you. Enough you'd want to keep it. And I could live with all that, thinking that the best thing I gave you, the most important thing I had to give outside my love, was my name. I thought at least you'd keep that. But you got rid of that, too."

"Greg—"

He stood, pulled out his wallet, and threw a twenty down on the table.

"Don't make change. I know that tip is above fair but at least let me give you that," he said before he turned and walked away.

Yep. He was done being cool.

I stared at his back long after the door closed behind him.

Long enough for Ham to get to me, come close, for me to feel his warmth behind me, his bigness surrounding me, but nothing was going to take away this sting.

"You're on break," Ham growled above my head.

"I gotta do a sweep of the tables."

"You go back to the office, sit down, pull your shit together, or I carry you back there and lock you in until your shit is together."

I turned and looked up at him.

He was wearing his scary look.

"My shit is together," I lied.

"Bullshit. Motherfucker gutted you. I watched," Ham returned. "Go. Now. Break."

I held his eyes.

Then I went back to the office, took a break, and got my shit together.

Or, more truthfully, I got myself to a place where I could pretend that it was.

*   *   *

I was right.

When the night was done and Ham took us home on his bike, I was so exhausted from work and dealing with Greg, I couldn't even enjoy the ride.

But I'd made a shitload of tips.

I was in my bedroom, sitting on the side of my bed yanking off my boots, so ready to go to sleep it wasn't funny.

Because sleep would erase the sting of Greg, at least for a while.

My bedroom door opened, and I turned to watch Ham, in socks, his usual faded jeans, his navy shirt unbuttoned all the way down, a bottle of vodka in one hand, two shot glasses in the other.

"What the hell?" I asked.

"Get comfortable, cookie, story time," Ham answered, and without delay, *he* got comfortable.

That was to say, he sat on my bed, stretched his legs out, poured two shots of vodka, put the bottle on my nightstand, lounged back against my headboard, and held a glass out to me.

"Ham, I'm exhausted. I need sleep."

"You need sleep, stretch out, throw this back, and give it to me fast."

"Give what to you fast?"

"The explanation you said you'd give me later. Just sayin', darlin', it's later."

I had the feeling Ham was in the mood to be stubborn and unyielding because he was lounged on my bed like he used to lounge when we were together-together and we'd relax in front of the TV. That was to say, stretched out, shirt open, boots off. And when we'd relax in front of the TV, Ham did it like he intended to do it forever. Which was the way he looked now.

So I decided to give in so I could get it over with and get some shut-eye.

I avoided looking at his broad, muscled chest and defined abs as I crawled into bed and took the shot glass from him.

Ham had a hairy chest. It wasn't profuse. It wasn't a dusting either. I'd never been one to like men with hairy chests but his was just so...*Ham*. If the first time we made love and he took off his shirt (or, if memory serves, as it actually happened, I yanked it off), and I found a smooth chest, I would have been disappointed.

Even though on another guy I did not like this, with Ham, I loved it. In the times he was mine, I slid my fingers through it. I trailed my nails down it.

And after a night like that night, I would have liked nothing better than to cuddle up next to him, put my cheek to his shoulder, sift my fingers through his chest hair, rest my hand against the warm hardness of him, and let his mellowness melt my physically and emotionally exhausting night away.

Alas, this was not an option open to me.

To get my thoughts off his chest hair and stop myself from even beginning to think about his abs, which would not bring on thoughts of relaxation and stress relief, but instead orgasms, which would be a better kind of stress relief, I threw back the shot.

Ham leaned forward, took the glass from me, his was empty, too, and he twisted for a refill, demanding, "Stretch out, babe."

I stretched out, my head to the foot of the bed, on my side, up on an elbow, head in hand, eyes on him.

He reached out an arm with the filled glass toward me. I leaned to take it and settled back in.

"Talk to me," he invited.

I didn't sugarcoat it.

"I fucked him over," I declared.

"You cheat on him?" Ham shot back.

"No."

"Steal from him?"

"No."

"Lie to him?"

"No."

"Then what?"

"I loved him."

Ham's brows shot together, giving me his scary look. Or, I should say, *scarier* look and he asked, "What?"

I rolled to my back, rested the shot glass on my belly, and told the ceiling, "I loved him. When we got married, I was happy. I was thinking house, babies, settled, safe." My eyes slid to Ham. "I really did love him, darlin'."

"Okay. So . . . what?" Ham asked slowly.

"I didn't love him enough," I whispered.

His face lost the scary look, went soft, and his voice was jagged when he said, "Cookie."

He got me.

He always did.

I turned to my side, got up on my forearm, and explained. "Six weeks in, Ham, six weeks into our marriage, I knew I didn't do right. I had second thoughts, too late. He was a homebody. I knew that. I still married him even though I was not a homebody. I'm social. I don't like stayin' at home all the time. That's all he liked. He likes foreign movies—you know, the ones with subtitles. He watches them a lot. I don't like them. Reading and watching"—I shook my head—"did my head in. And half of them are just plain weird. After we tied the knot, he didn't spring that on me as a surprise, tying me to a chair, and making me watch Polish movies. Before we were married, I knew that about him, too."

"So you fucked up," he said in his jagged voice.

"Yeah," I replied. "Huge. Time went on. He'd talk babies. I'd delay because I knew. I knew I wanted out and I didn't want a baby caught in that mess. I wanted something he couldn't give me. I didn't try to change him. Make him into what I wanted. In the beginning, I just thought I could deal with who he was if I had all the rest."

"All the rest of what, darlin'?"

"Babies. Home. Safety."

"But you couldn't deal."

"In the end, it was a life changer," I told him. "He tried to go out with me but I knew he wasn't havin' a good time, so much so he was even miserable, so we quit goin' out. He tried to watch the shoot-'em-ups with me but he didn't get into them so I quit suggesting we watch them. I just stopped doin' more and more of what I liked doin', what made me who I was, until I started feelin' like I was losin' me. Then the recession hit, the tourist trade dwindled, the shop started to get in trouble, and I got deeper in that bad place. I couldn't control what was happening with the shop but I could control what was happening in our marriage. Or, that is to say, I could end a marriage that wasn't makin' me happy. In fact, it was like I was losin' hold on all that was me, fading away, and weirdly lonely even though I had someone to come home to. So I did. I ended the marriage."

"And he's pissed," Ham surmised and I shook my head.

"No. I hurt him. I..." I pulled in a breath and admitted, "I broke him, Ham. He was happy. He enjoyed our life, our marriage. He hated losing me. He liked me just the way I was."

"Doesn't seem like it to me, him not lettin' you go out. Be you."

"He never tried to stop me. I just stopped goin' because he preferred to stay in and that's what I thought I was supposed to do."

"Darlin', a man can put pressure on a woman to change without sayin' a word," Ham contradicted and that rocked me.

I hadn't thought of it like that.

"All right," Ham kept going. "So what was tonight about?"

"He heard I changed my name back to Cinders."

"So?" Ham asked.

"So, the house was mine, we just never got 'round to puttin' his name on it, so it was him that left because it really was always mine. He wanted to give me some money to tide me over but I wouldn't let him. I didn't think with what I was doin' to him that was fair, takin' his money after I broke his heart and essentially kicked him out. And I made him take his stuff. I told you that already. And I did do that. I made him. I was firm about it. He didn't want to but I made him take everything he bought because I thought it was fair. I gave him back his rings. I didn't know me doing that was sayin' to him that I didn't want any memory of him but he told me tonight that he took it like that."

"Not your problem," Ham stated.

"It is. I don't want to hurt him…" I paused. *"More."*

"This divorce final?" Ham asked.

"Yes," I answered.

"Then you don't worry about that either. He's no longer your man. That's also not your problem."

"Ham, you're making it sound like it's okay I got involved with a man I shouldn't. I hurt him and ended a *marriage*. You don't just end *marriages*. This wasn't a little fuckup. It was huge."

"No, you're right. You don't just end marriages. You get in 'em knowin' as best you can you're in for the long haul," Ham replied. "But you went into it like that, bein' in love, thinkin' you were gettin' and givin' what you wanted. It just didn't turn out that way and, babe, you start losin' you to anything, a guy, a job, to any-fuckin'-thing, you get out. If he loved you the way you think he loved you, he knew who he was marryin', too. And he wouldn't want you at home watchin' fuckin' Polish movies. He'd *want* you to be you."

I hadn't thought of it like that, either.

Ham wasn't done.

"You're also right it was a big fuckup. But that kind of fuckup doesn't end in capital punishment, cookie. People do it. You tried. It failed. You hurt him. That sucks. Your punishment is what you feel right now, the hurt, the guilt, him able to come in and cut clean through you with a few words. That'll heal. What you gotta do is learn from your mistakes, cut your losses, and move on. Includin' changing your name back if you want."

"But he hates my parents. He thought giving me his name was a gift."

"It is. Absolutely," Ham stated with an inflexibility that was surprising. "Means everything. Means a woman's got him, his protection, his money, his love. That's everything. Best thing he's got to give because it symbolizes all that. But you two are done, babe. His name is yours to keep or give up as you please."

"He took that, too, as me not wanting any memory of him."

"I see that. But I don't see him walkin' into a place where you work, you're busy, you're on your feet, you gotta be on your game, and layin' that garbage on you."

"He's really a nice guy, Ham. He's never been to The Dog. He wouldn't know it was an imposition. He didn't even know how to pay for his beer tonight. He probably thought it was the only way to connect with me, to share what he had to share so he pulled up the courage and did it."

"Well he did it wrong."

"Ham—"

Again with the inflexibility. "He did, Zara. You worked in an office or as a pilot on a plane or a lawyer in a courtroom, your ex doesn't walk in while you're doin' your gig and lay shit on you."

I hadn't thought of it like that, either.

"He's got the wrong end of the stick about what you were doin'," Ham continued. "You feel like it and wanna sort that, you call him. Have a drink with him. But tell him The Dog is off-limits. Your boss wants your head on your work, not on your ex. He comes in again, he comes in for a drink and to make you laugh or he doesn't come in at all."

"Okay, Ham," I muttered, put the shot glass to my lips, and threw it back.

"Zara," he called when I was done and I looked at him. "That is not me bein' an asshole boss. That's me takin' care of my cookie. He doesn't come in because I'm worried about you droppin' drinks. He doesn't come in because I didn't like watchin' him gut you, but more, I didn't like knowin' you felt him sink in that blade."

I'd known for a long time why it wasn't Greg for me.

Because, for me, it was Ham.

It had always been Ham.

And this was another of the myriad reasons why. Why I should never have married Greg. Why it would always be Ham.

"Thanks, darlin'," I whispered and watched Ham's face get soft again.

"Take him out for a drink. Unburden his mind about that shit. He's feelin' crap about that, you set him straight," Ham advised. "But take care of you while you do it, baby. And if you gotta use me as an excuse to take care of you, do it."

I needed to stop him from being so *freaking* cool.

Therefore, I shared, "I'm feeling the need to do another load of your laundry."

At that, Ham threw his head back against my wall and laughed, the rich, booming sound filling my room and warming my soul.

I watched, smiling.

CHAPTER SIX

Moving On

One week, two days later…

"OH MY GOD."

"Baby."

"Ham."

"Oh yeah. *Fuck.* Love that, baby. Love *you*, Zara."

I opened my eyes and saw sun peeking through the blinds.

I was hot, bothered, my nipples hard and aching, perspiration was dampening my chest and between my breasts, and my girl parts were throbbing.

I'd had another dream.

Since Ham talked me through the Greg thing, I'd had three.

This one made four.

All of them hot, so freaking *hot*.

All of them ended with Ham telling me he loved me.

This was not good.

I rolled to my back and turned to see my clock.

It was twelve fifteen. I often went to bed late, and slept in late, but today I'd slept in later.

I listened and heard no noises.

Back in the day, Ham had a routine and it hadn't changed. Even if he went to bed at four in the morning, he woke up between eleven thirty and twelve, slugged back a mug of coffee, and went for a run with coffee as his only sustenance.

I not only didn't know how he could run (at all); I didn't know how he could run with only a cup of coffee fueling his endeavors.

I figured it was a macho guy thing. A test of endurance. If he could lug that big body of his five miles in what was considered his morning on just a cup of coffee that was the same as cage fighting a bruiser by the name of Butch Razor and coming out the unqualified victor.

Ham's "morning" run meant I had time to do what I needed to do. And I hadn't done it since I moved in with Ham.

So I was going to do it.

I reached into my nightstand and grabbed my toy. Pulling up my nightgown and sliding it in my panties, I turned it on.

Then I replayed the dream. I also made up more bits of the dream. They were really good additions, seeing as, when it came to Ham, I had an excellent imagination.

It had been a while so I came relatively quickly but it still snuck up on me. It was long. It was good. I gave a soft cry when it hit me and I moaned through it, whimpering at the end.

When I was done, I returned my toy to the nightstand, stretched, snuggled into my pillow, lounged, and when my body's call for coffee could no longer be ignored I threw the covers back, put my feet to the floor, and headed to the kitchen.

I hit the door to the kitchen and stopped because a sweaty, track-pants wearing, tight-shirt-wet-and-plastered-to-him Ham was standing at the counter in the kitchen with his head turned, glowering at me.

"New rule. You don't do that shit when I'm in the house," he growled and I blinked.

"What shit?"

"You use your toy to get off when I'm not fuckin' here."

Oh my God. He heard me.

How humiliating was this?

"Ham—"

"Heard the toy. Heard you. Don't do that again."

"I—"

"Hear it again, make no mistake, babe, I'll join you."

Oh my God. Did he say what it sounded like he just said?

I didn't have time to ask him to confirm, not that I could speak at that moment anyway. He came my way and I had to jump to the side to avoid him bowling me over.

He disappeared down the hall to the master bedroom.

"What the hell?" I whispered.

Okay, so that was humiliating.

Why Ham would be pissed about it, seriously pissed, pissed enough to bring it up, which he shouldn't have—he should have never said a word—and lay down the law about it, was beyond me.

He told me straight up he didn't want my body. We were roommates. We had been for over a month and he gave no indication whatsoever he wanted anything more or was even nostalgic for what we once had.

Until just then with what he said but it was said in anger so he probably said it just to be a dick.

I stared down the hall as my thoughts came into order.

He couldn't tell me when I could or could not touch myself.

That was insane.

And why was he mad about it? He wasn't a prude. Far from it. He'd helped me do what I just did to spectacular results more than once. And I'd participated and watched as he'd done the same to himself.

"What the hell?" I hissed.

Suddenly, I wasn't mortified.

I was mad.

I stomped to my room and decided his penalty for being an asshole was my getting into the shower at the same time as he got into his. I was quick in the shower but he could stay in there a year. I didn't know what he did in there but he took the longest showers of any man I knew.

And our hot water heater wasn't that big.

"So there, dickhead," I muttered to the shower spray.

Then I got ready and took my time. Blowing out my blonde hair with a roller brush, I used blasts of heat on my hair with the roller tight so it had big soft curls and flippy waves. Giving my makeup that tad bit of extra attention. Dressing for work, which was where I was going after I somehow whittled away the day, because once I left the condo, I wasn't coming back until I'd calmed down. All of this was done in what I considered was an heroic attempt at not committing murder.

I was dressed, jacket on, purse on my shoulder, and ready to go but I made one stop.

Back at the kitchen where Ham was.

He was at the counter again, and he again had his head turned to me, face wearing a scowl.

"I'm in the shower after a run, babe, do me a fuckin' favor and don't jump in yours," he growled.

"Kiss my ass," I retorted.

His eyes narrowed dangerously.

I ignored that and kept going.

"FYI, bruiser, you can't tell me when to touch myself. I may not be able to go halfsies but you told me yourself this is my pad, my home, and I'll touch myself whenever I want in *my* pad that's *my* home and if you walk in on me, I'll throw my vibrator at you."

On that somewhat pathetic parting shot that still managed to make me feel better, I turned on my boot and stomped out of the condo.

* * *

"Oh my God, that's crazy," Becca breathed.

I had chosen to whittle away my Saturday with my girls Becca, Mindy, and Nina.

Becca was a pretty brunette who used to work at The Dog but moved to waitressing at The Drake because her live-in boyfriend, Josh, was a musician who did acoustic nights there and she liked to be there when he played.

Mindy was tall, very pretty, with curly strawberry-blonde hair. She'd also worked at The Dog once upon a time but now she worked as a counselor at a rape crisis center while going to school to be a social worker. She was almost done. She was graduating next year.

Nina was a bit older than all of us, blonde, exceptionally pretty, and she dressed like a model. She was an attorney and married to Holden "Max" Maxwell. I'd met her yonks ago when she first came to Gnaw Bone for a vacation and visited my shop to buy some earrings made by my other girl-friend Jenna. We didn't become friends until after she was kidnapped, nearly shot on the side of a mountain, went back to England to sort stuff there, and officially came home to Gnaw Bone to start her life with Max.

Looking at them as we sat at a table outside at the riverside café in town drinking coffees, I thought they looked like Charlie's Angels, except without jobs as private detectives with a mysterious boss and the Pinto.

I'd just told them what happened with Ham earlier.

"That's scary," Mindy added.

"It's not scary. It's *crazy*," Becca replied.

"It's scary crazy *and* crazy scary," Mindy stated.

Neither of them was wrong but Mindy was more right.

Becca's horrified eyes suddenly lit and she sent a grin my way. "Though, it's pretty funny, the part where you told him you were going to throw your vibrator at him."

I was glad she thought that was funny since I thought it was lame.

It hit me Nina wasn't saying anything so I looked to her to see her studying me closely.

"What?" I asked.

"You need to flirt," she answered.

"What?" I asked again, but it was higher pitched this time.

Nina put her mug down on the table and sat back, still studying me.

Then she said, "Honey, I get your thing of swearing off men, focusing on getting stuff sorted because you need to do that. You need to take care of you, and you're right, a man in that mix right now would probably not be a good thing."

She'd said "probably."

And, incidentally, Nina was half English and she had the kick-ass accent to prove it. So even if she said scary stuff, it came out cool.

"Okay," I replied cautiously.

"But that doesn't mean you should cut yourself off from having fun, forget you're a girl and the good parts that come with that. So you should have fun and flirt," she stated.

"I'm not flirting with Ham," I returned.

"I'm not talking about him," she said. "You work at The Dog. With your pretty face, fabulous hair, and fantastic figure, I bet there are tons of guys who would love to flirt with you."

"Tips'll get better, I know that as fact," Becca put in.

I heard Becca but I was too busy trying to figure out what Nina was saying that she wasn't exactly saying.

"I'm not sure how that will help me deal with what happened with Ham today, Neens," I pointed out.

"You're focused on getting your life in order, so determined you're forgetting to have fun, and further, you're mired down in the history you have with your roommate," she replied and leaned toward me. "Things are better, Zara. You've landed on your feet. You have a good job. You're making decent money. It's time to let your hair down, have fun, remember you're pretty and you can turn a man's eye. Enjoy that. You're young and you should. You shouldn't miss a moment of feeling that feeling if you can. And if you do, if you remember to enjoy life a little bit and stop thinking all the time about how bad it's been, your mind might clear of some of the things bogging it down and you can move on. Including move on from being hung up on a man you can't have."

This, as Nina was prone to do, made sense.

Still, I wasn't certain I was ready for that, the flirting part that was.

Nina kept talking.

"You're now at a place where you can find ways to move on from *all* the bad things that have happened to you, honey. You also need to move on from this guy. He's being very nice, helping you out. And I'm not sure what was in his head this morning. What I *am* certain of is that you shouldn't worry about it. That bothers him, that's his problem." She grinned. "Be quieter next time or, since you're roommates and you doing that bugs him, do as he asks and do it when he's out so you can avoid the drama. But you need to fill your life and mind with good things, fun times, happy times, and push out the bad things, what happened with Greg, your house, your shop, this guy coming back into your life. It's time. And when you do, something like what happened this morning won't mess with your head so much."

I wasn't certain this would work. I'd tried to "move on" from Ham for years and, in the process, I broke a good man.

But I was certain she was right about the rest.

I was in a good place, not back where I started but not living in an unsafe studio apartment and barely existing on close-to-minimum wage.

I had to stop obsessing about all that happened and rejoice in the fact that, with help from friends, I was making it through. I needed to have fun like I used to. I needed to begin to enjoy life again. I'd divorced Greg, hurting him, to be free to be me, to do all that, and I wasn't doing it.

And maybe, if I did, if I got back to me a little bit, those stings I experienced being with Ham without getting to be with Ham wouldn't bite so deep.

"You're the shit, Neens," I told her quietly.

She grinned.

"I say that to her all the time," Mindy put in.

I grinned at Nina then I grinned at Mindy, lifting my latte and taking a drink.

Girl talk shifted but, fifteen minutes later, I caught Nina staring at the river, a small smile on her face. Becca and Mindy were in a deep discussion about when they were going to schedule their next facials, so I leaned toward Nina.

"Thinking about Max?" I asked on a smile.

She turned her eyes to me. "No. About you."

My brows went up. "Me?"

She reached out a hand and squeezed my knee. "You."

"Why?"

"Things are looking up for you, I feel it."

"Uh...yeah, I know. And I know because I can afford a latte."

She smiled but shook her head and sat back. "No, in ways you don't know yet but I'm thinking I do."

"And what are those?"

"Be more fun if you find out yourself."

I was confused. "What?"

She leaned in again but, this time, took my hand.

"Life has certain things planned. I find, for some people, it takes you places you don't want to go but the path leads to where you need to be. That happened to me. You just have to learn to trust it. And, for you, have fun while it's happening. And last, honey, go with your gut. Take risks. Roll the dice. You've been beaten down but you kept getting right back up. Still, when that happens it can make you hesitant to roll the dice. Don't be. You might find the payoff is beyond anything you could even dream."

"Now I'm more confused and maybe a little freaked out," I shared.

She squeezed my hand, smiled again, let me go, and sat back. "Like I said, it's going to be fun as you find out for yourself." Her eyes grew sharp on mine. "But only if you're strong enough to roll the dice."

"No less freaked out, Nina," I informed her.

To that, she freaked me out more by smiling bigger and replying, "This is going to be fun."

"I'm not sure I agree and I don't even know what you're talking about," I returned.

She didn't respond to my words.

She just said, "I can't *wait*."

Nina was really smart and not just the kind of smart having a law degree made you. She was just smart.

And knowing that, I had a feeling that I could. I definitely could wait. What might be fun for her might not be such great fun for me.

But even so, because she was smart, when my time came, I was going to take her advice, blow on those dice, and let them roll.

* * *

That night at work proved positive that the reprieve I'd had spending time with the girls, after such a shaky start to the day, would not hold because it wasn't a shaky night.

It was a disastrous one.

I knew this right off when I walked into The Dog to start my shift and Ham was already there. My laidback Ham was history, and scary, pissed-off Ham was still in his place because he scowled at me, didn't say hi, didn't even give me a chin lift. In fact, he didn't say anything to me. He just glowered, then moved down the bar to get a customer a drink.

I decided to give him a wide berth and, since it was Saturday and things were hopping, thought I could lose myself in work.

Things looked up when Nina and Max came in and sat at one of my tables.

Max, by the way, was nearly as hot as Ham but what made him hotter was how into his wife he was. They'd been through hell together, but his love and affection for her and their two babies had not dulled and he wasn't afraid to let it show. I thought that was the hallmark of a true man, being in love and not giving a shit if people saw how deep he'd sunk into that emotion.

I'd always liked Max. He was a seriously good guy. But I liked Max with Nina even better.

Things took a turn for the worse when Arlene showed up with Cotton.

Jimmy Cotton was a world-famous photographer. Cotton also had some reclusive tendencies, in so far as he didn't stray much from the environs of Gnaw Bone and when he did, it was to travel the width and breadth of the Rockies to take his photos. Other than that, Cotton stuck with what and who he knew. He was old, crotchety, and, contradictory to the latter, entirely lovable. He liked me, always had and always showed it in his crotchety Cotton way.

So I gave that back but without the crotchety part. The jury was out on if I gave it back without a healthy dose of sass.

Now, he'd walked into The Dog, a place he'd come to but not often, and headed straight to the bar with Arlene. Not a table where a waitress could serve him. No, to the bar, where Ham would.

Once settled in, they made it very clear they were checking out the lay of the land with Ham and me. They did this by openly watching us nearly constantly, only taking breaks to huddle and confer, more than likely about Ham and me.

Things nosedived when Maybelline and Wanda wandered in and *they* took places at the bar, opposite Cotton and Arlene, but for exactly the same purpose, a purpose they didn't try to hide either. I had hoped, since time had slid by after Maybelle threatened to wade in, that she'd forgotten she intended to get up in my business.

Alas, this hope that night was dashed.

Making matters worse, I saw them talking to Ham for not a short period of time during which his unhappy eyes cut to me twice and Maybelline's hands gestured, *a lot*.

I continued with my strategy of giving Ham and the bar a wide berth, taking my drink orders exclusively to Jake and getting the hell away from the bar as quick as I could once they were filled. I added ignoring all that was happening because it was all scary and I was pretending it was occurring in an alternate universe. I decided to live in my own universe.

In other words, I found a guy who I didn't know but who had been in a couple of times since I started there and I tested out the flirting business.

Matters degenerated significantly when, after a few jokes, smiles, and a bit of tension building of the good kind, I turned away from the guy to take his drink order to the bar and saw Ham leaned into his forearms in front of a very pretty blonde woman who was baring not a small amount of cleavage. He was grinning his flirtatious grin, one I knew was just that because it had been aimed at me enough times that I had it memorized.

That stung, the bite deep, the pain radiating, but I ignored it and went straight to Jake.

My friends saw what Ham was up to, and they didn't like it any more than I did. Arlene was crinkling her nose Ham's way. Cotton was scowling at him. Wanda and Maybelle were glaring. Max was studying him, looking weirdly displeased.

But Nina...

Nina was smiling at the table.

And it was her reaction that freaked me out the most.

I ignored all that, too. I flirted with my guy. I even gave him my number.

We had a packed house but Ham, like me, found his times to drift back to the blonde, lean into his forearms, and give her some attention.

This carried on for ages, nearly to closing. And even though Cotton and Arlene took off and Wanda and Maybelline had a brief visit with me before they took off and Nina and Max went back to relieve their babysitter, Ham kept flirting and so did I. This carried on to the point where I was finding it difficult to keep hold on my alternate world and not let the pain of what Ham was doing overwhelm me.

Finally, the situation ended but the ending wasn't a relief.

The ending was me nearly bumping into Ham on my way to the bar. I had my head bent to my tray, my mind filled with cashing out tabs, so I didn't see him until the last second.

I rocked to a halt, tipped my head back, and stared into his unhappy face.

"Call off your dogs," he ordered, his voice not unhappy but downright pissed. "I don't need you dealin' with your shit walkin' in this bar and I *really* don't need *me* havin' to deal with your shit walkin' in this fuckin' bar."

Maybelline and Wanda had not gone cautious and Arlene and Cotton had showed zero finesse so I knew what he was talking about to the point that I couldn't even lie to deny it.

He didn't give me a chance to lie.

He walked away.

It was nearly closing, last call come and gone, and it was unusual, as in unheard of since I'd been back at The Dog and even before when we'd worked there together, but when Ham walked away, he walked to his blonde. Once there, he put his hand on her elbow and she slid off her stool, head tipped back to him. She smiled a sultry smile and Ham guided her to the back.

He didn't come back out to help or even supervise clean up.

He wasn't in the back when I went to get my purse.

And, when I checked, his truck wasn't parked behind the bar where he always parked it.

And last, he didn't come home that night.

*   *   *

The next morning, or more accurately, half past noon, I was sitting on my balcony in track pants, a hoodie, and thick wool socks, feet to the middle rung of the railing, holding aloft a steaming mug of coffee, when my door slid open.

I turned to see Ham walk out wearing his clothes from last night.

That didn't sting. It burned.

But I battled the burn, telling myself I had to move on. We were roommates. He wanted nothing more. Even if he did, he couldn't give me what I wanted. He wasn't that man, not for me, not for anybody. He'd told me that himself. I had to find a way to unhook myself from a man who wanted nothing hanging on him. Not a house. Not furniture. Not a steady job. Not a woman. Not anything.

I had to find my way clear. Find a different happy that didn't include him at the same time it did.

"Hey," he greeted.

"Hey," I replied.

Ham moved to the railing and leaned a hip on it, crossing his arms on his chest, all this while I watched.

"I was a dick yesterday," he announced. "Was in a shit mood. Don't know why but took it out on you. That was uncool. It won't happen again. You're right. This is your place, do what you want. I shouldn't have said shit. It was a nasty thing to do, totally out of line, and you don't need that crap."

"You're right. It was a nasty thing to do but it's over. You're bein' cool about it now but I'd prefer it if we never discussed it again," I said.

"I can do that."

I nodded, put the coffee cup to my lips and my eyes to the mountains.

"Babe, just sayin', I was a dick about your friends last night, too," he stated and I looked back at him. "That said, cookie, be good you had a word with them and let them know what this is so they don't give me anymore shit. I get where they're comin' from. I dig that you got that. Good friends are hard to beat. But just like you don't need the crap I gave you yesterday, I don't need that crap."

"I can do that," I told him.

"Thanks, darlin'," he replied.

I looked back at the mountains.

"Zara," he called.

"What?" I answered, eyes still glued to the mountains.

He said nothing.

I looked to him.

"What?" I repeated.

His head turned to the mountains and he muttered, "Nothin', darlin'."

I looked back to the mountains and took a sip of joe.

"More of that?" Ham asked.

"Plenty," I answered.

"Need a refill?" he asked.

"I'm good," I lied, but not about the coffee.

"Right, baby," he murmured and I heard the door open and shut.

I kept my eyes to the mountains and pretended not to feel the wet gliding down my cheeks.

CHAPTER SEVEN

Roomies

Two weeks, three days later…

IT WAS MY day off and I was going to use it to do something I hadn't been able to do in a long time.

I was going shopping. I was going to blow money (or, at

least, a little bit of it) on whatever struck my fancy. Then I was going to a shoot-'em-up movie.

I was wandering down the hall toward the living room and my ultimate destination, the front door, as I was thinking distractedly that Ham also had the day off. I was also thinking that, in all the time Ham and I had been back to working together, we always but always had the same days off. And I was further thinking this was weird, seeing as this was his doing since he wrote the schedule.

And last, I was thinking not so distractedly that, since it was his day off, I should ask if he wanted to go with me.

I'd shopped with Ham in the past. He didn't mind it. I couldn't say he was overwhelmed with joy to do it, but he didn't bitch about it like other guys. That was, as long as you didn't drag him around from store to store for hours.

But he liked movies.

I knew I should ask him. Things had been weird since our blow up about my vibrator usage weeks ago.

We weren't the same.

This was mostly my doing. I was finding ways to live my life and have fun. I was reconnecting with friends, meeting for coffee, lunch, or dinner before I'd have to go to work. I went to the library in Carnal, met the famously-still-alive-after-being-buried-alive Faye Goodknight and got my library card so I could check out books and rediscover my passion for reading, something I did in my room a lot but more often did at the café with a latte. And it was near on harvest festival time and I was looking forward to going, with money, so I could eat the amazing food and maybe splurge on something cool from one of the vendors.

I was also kind of avoiding Ham.

If he noticed it, he didn't show it. He was back to mellow, grinning easy, quick to tease or joke in the minimal time I spent in the common areas of the condo and in the not minimal time we spent together at work.

Roomies. For Ham, easy.

Truth be told, Nina was right. It was cool to get back to doing things I liked to do and I was having fun. It felt good not to wallow in what was done and gone and wasn't much fun and find things to look forward to. I'd waited to have that back for a while and it was more than nice having it.

But the invisible chasm that separated me from my roomie was still there. I felt it even if he didn't and I didn't like it.

He was my friend who did me a solid. He was a guy with, as he put it, "basic needs" so he was going to see to those and I needed to get over it because it was none of my business. And he'd been a dick but he'd explained and kind of apologized, meeting the issue head on and guiding us around it.

I needed to sort my shit out.

At least I'd sorted out Maybelle, Wanda, Arlene, and Cotton (I hoped). I'd spent some time with each of them over the past few weeks and when we'd sat down, I'd told them in no uncertain terms to back off. I also told them my new lease on life and that I need them to accept the fact that I was finding my way off the dark path and into the light.

And last, I'd been brutally honest about the fact that I was working through being hung up on Ham, but it was mine to do, I was determined to do it, and I didn't need their help. I also shared that it was no help, them getting in the face of a guy I was tight with who had my back. If they didn't trust him, they should trust me so they needed to back off.

Wanda seemed contrite. Maybelle was noncommittal but I thought I got through to her. Arlene stated, "I'll do what I do," but she'd been a frequent visitor to The Dog and she hadn't been in Ham's or my business once since we had our chat.

Cotton said nothing except, "Find a day. I need an assistant. Feelin' the urge comin' on to take me some pictures. And you're luggin' my stuff."

I wasn't sure if that was Cotton's way of giving me what I wanted without telling me he was going to give me what I wanted or vice versa. I just knew he didn't come back to The Dog.

I was sure I was looking forward to "luggin' his stuff" while he worked. He'd never asked me to do that. He was famous, his photos more so because they were the freaking bomb, and there were likely not many people who had the privilege of working with him.

So all that was good...I hoped.

I stopped nearly to the mouth of the hall that led into the living room when I heard Ham's voice talking quiet.

And jagged.

I sucked in a silent breath.

"Yeah, darlin', dyin' down. That's good, Feb."

Feb.

February Owens. The woman he cared about who was the obsession of an ax murderer.

After the finale to that grisly debacle, it was impossible to miss the aftermath news reports about it, but even so, I didn't try.

I was curious. Curious about February Owens.

Eventually, my curiosity was assuaged. They showed pictures of her and her boyfriend, and she was gorgeous. Older than me, probably closer to Ham's age. But she looked a little like me. Blonde hair. Brown eyes. Her man, who apparently had been her man way back in the day and they'd hooked up again, was phenomenal. Definitely on par in hotness to Ham, if leaner and not quite as tall.

"No, probably won't go away. But it will come further between," Ham went on and I suspected he was talking about the situation with Dennis Lowe, the resulting media onslaught and continued morbid fascination of the public when stuff like that happened.

"No, nothin' this way. I'm a footnote, babe. And way good with that," Ham told her.

I started to slink back when he continued.

"You good? Happy?"

At that, I stopped. Mostly because he sounded like he wanted that for her even if her being that way meant she was that way with another guy.

Which was, apparently, Ham's way.

"Good, beautiful," he whispered.

He wasn't saying something was beautiful.

He was calling February Owens "beautiful."

And that hurt. A lot.

Why did that hurt so much?

She was "beautiful." February Owens, who had to be one of the women he had when he also had me, was "beautiful."

I was "cookie."

She was closer to his age and she was inarguably beautiful. I wasn't jailbait but I was a lot younger than him so I got "cookie."

That had to be why it hurt so much.

What hurt more was I'd always loved him calling me cookie. No one had ever given me a nickname. Not even my sister, Xenia. We were tight and she messed around with me all the time, definitely the kind of person to give me a nickname. And I thought "cookie" was cute, it was sweet and it was mine.

"Right, yeah, got the day off," Ham carried on. "No clue. Relax, do nothin' ..."

His voice trailed off as I finally moved back to my

room. Once there, I stayed there, gave it time, and as I did, I blanked my mind.

I knew about the other women, and anyway, that was then. This was now. She had a man and Ham was just my roommate.

And roommates didn't get in their roomies' business about past lovers.

Also, roommates did shit together. Like go to movies.

When I thought it would be safe, I again left my room and went down the hall.

I hit the living room to see Ham stretched out on Mindy's couch, his superior quality flat-screen TV on and his eyes to it.

When I came in, they came to me.

"Hey, I'm goin' shopping and to a movie. Wanna come?" I asked, pleased as all hell my voice sounded normal, friendly, inviting.

His eyes moved over my face before he replied, "I'm gonna sit back, relax, do nothin' but eat and watch TV. Wanna join me?"

I shook my head. "I'm in the mood to spend money on nothing I need and something I want for the first time in what seems like decades. Then I'm going to go see Holly-wood movie stars drill fake holes in each other and crash cars. Your day sounds fun but mine sounds more fun."

"Limit the shopping and that's agreed," Ham returned.

I tipped my head to the side. "Changing your mind?"

"You gonna limit the shopping?"

"I can do that."

"Then, yeah."

I smiled at him. "Get your boots, bruiser."

He gave me a full-on grin when he passed me to go get his boots.

I waited, wondering if this was a good idea.

But he was just my friend, my roomie, and anything was more fun with company.

So I told myself it was a good idea.

Even though I knew it was a lie.

*   *   *

"Venice," I stated and Ham's brows went up.

"No shit?" he asked.

I grinned and nodded.

We'd gone shopping and I'd bought nothing I needed but two killer tops that I loved. Then we'd gone to a movie and watched movie stars crashing cars. After the movie we'd had dinner together, chatted, and laughed. After *that* we moved to a bar and had drinks but left before we got tipsy.

So now, we were continuing drinking, chatting, and laughing, just doing it in the safety of our living room.

Ham had just asked me where I would go if I could go anywhere.

I was on my back on the couch, my legs thrown over the back, my head to the armrest. Ham was at the opposite end, his body twisted so his feet were crossed at the ankles on the coffee table.

I had a bottle of beer in my hand resting on my belly. He had one resting on his thigh.

"Italy?" he asked.

"Not Italy, so much as Venice. I've seen pictures. It looks beautiful. And I like water and boats." I lifted my beer, took a drag, and replaced it on my belly. "What about you? Where would you go?"

"Anywhere with a beach."

I grinned again as I noted, "You don't strike me as a sand man."

"Babe, was on St. John once, walked out in the water up to my neck, looked down, could see my feet clear as if I was standin' on land. Water warm but cool, fuckin' sweet. Sun hot and bright. Beauty all around me. Those clear blue waters, tranquil. Nothin' like it."

"So, not a beach but St. John," I suggested.

"Yeah. Go back there in a second."

I felt my grin fade and my face get soft. "Hope you get back there, Ham."

It was then I watched his face get soft. "I will, darlin'."

He took another drag so I took one and when I was done, I queried, "Can I ask you something?"

"Anything, cookie."

"Didn't think about it at the time, except later…" I paused. "How did you know where I lived? Both times?"

"What?" he asked.

"When you came to my house and again to the studio apartment. You didn't ask me and I didn't tell you, so how did you know?"

"Asked Jake."

Right. He asked Jake. No surprise.

"Okay, this brings me to question two," I went on. "When did you and Jake get so tight?"

"When my girl told me she was movin' on and didn't want to adjust what we had so I could stay in her life as she did that. Jake and I got tight so I could keep my finger on her pulse, make sure she was all right."

He stopped talking but I'd stopped breathing.

He took my nonresponse the wrong way. "Didn't require monthly reports, babe. I wasn't in your business. Just keepin' a finger on the pulse."

"It's not…that isn't…" I swallowed and my voice was soft when I said, "That was sweet of you to do, Ham."

I watched his body relax and I hadn't noticed it got tight.

"You matter," was all he said in reply.

"If I had a Jake, I would have kept tabs on you, too. Just

so you know," I informed him and gave him a teasing smile. "Though I would have required monthly reports."

Ham smiled back but his intelligent eyes were intense and didn't leave me and I didn't know what that meant. I just knew it felt nice.

The mood was right and it seemed we were back on track. Lastly, we'd always been honest.

So I kept to that and shared, "I missed you when you were gone, Ham."

"Right back at you, cookie," he replied, voice jagged.

To lighten the mood, I asked, "Are we going to get mushy? Because mushy requires vodka."

He lifted his feet off the coffee table and leaned toward me. "No mushy. Don't do mushy. But do need shut-eye, so even though this was a great day, babe, you and I got work tomorrow and I need to hit the sack."

"It was a great day, Ham," I agreed. "Thanks for comin' with me."

"Thanks for askin'," he replied, pushed to his feet, moved down the couch, and stopped at me.

He leaned down, touching his lips to the top of my hair before pulling back.

I tipped my head to catch his eyes and saw his were warm.

"Sleep tight, cookie."

"You too, darlin'."

He grinned and I steeled myself against the beauty of it when he tucked my hair behind my ear, traced it, drifted his fingers down my neck, then straightened and sauntered away.

I sat in the living room, alone and silent, sipping my beer until it was gone.

Then I went to bed.

*   *   *

"Ham."

"Fuck yeah. Love that, Zara. Love *you,* baby."

My eyes opened, my pulse spiked, my nipples ached, my sex throbbed, and my skin was damp.

I'd had another *freaking* dream.

"God, this sucks. This fucking *sucks,"* I whispered into the dark.

I turned, trying to beat it back, finding it difficult at night, the dream so fresh, so real, and Ham in bed down the freaking hall.

I tossed, considered getting out my toy and taking care of business but Ham was down the hall. He slept like me, hard and deep. I didn't know him to wake up in the middle of the night but, with my luck, I wasn't taking chances.

Nina suggested I be quiet while I took care of business but that was impossible because my toy was not quiet and, well, I wasn't either. I wasn't loud but I made noises. Who didn't?

I didn't know if I could squelch them and I was too afraid to try.

I turned then tossed and it didn't leave me.

Basic needs.

Ham's words hit me at the same time it hit me I had them, too.

Basic needs.

Oh yes. I had them, too.

"Damn," I whispered.

It was then Nina's words came to me.

Roll the dice.

"Oh God," I moaned.

Except for that disastrous night at The Dog, Ham had not once spent the night somewhere else.

And, if memory served (and I knew it did), he had a high libido. When we were together, we would go out and do stuff, chat, cuddle, goof around.

But we had a *lot* of sex.

Even knowing my mind forced by my desires, my *need,* was leading me through a ludicrous rationalization, I threw the covers back and got out of bed.

Then I sat back down on the bed.

"What am I doing?" I asked the dark.

Roll the dice, Nina urged.

I could roll the dice. Just that. Roll the dice.

Ham could say no. He could turn me away. That would be mortifying but I was already dealing with tough crap with regards to Ham on a day-to-day basis. I could live with that.

Or, if I rolled the dice, we both could understand we knew what this was and we could give each other something.

I pushed up from the bed and headed to the door.

"This is crazy, stupid, scary," I whispered.

I still opened the door and walked down the hall to Ham's room.

I stopped at his door.

Was I going to do this?

I opened his door.

I guessed I was.

I moved to his bed. He was on his side, facing me. He had the blinds open and a hand shoved under his pillow. The covers were to his waist and he had nothing on up top. Not unusual. If it was cold, Ham would put on pajama bottoms but mostly he slept nude.

Even in the dark, he was hot.

I sat on the side of his bed and he jerked awake, sitting up, his hand flashing out and curling, hard and tight, around the back of my neck as I gasped.

He came fully awake. His hand didn't leave me but it relaxed and he growled sleepily, "Jesus, fuck, you scared the fuckin' shit outta me."

And I would. I hadn't thought about it but the last time someone snuck into his room while he was sleeping, they'd been wielding an ax.

"God, Ham, I'm sorry. I didn't think," I whispered, lifting a hand and putting it on his chest, feeling the crisp hair there, wanting to slide my fingers through so badly, my mouth watered with the need.

His hand slid to the side of my neck.

"You okay?" he asked.

"No," I answered.

"You sick?" he asked.

"No," I answered.

"What's up, baby?"

Before I lost my courage, I blew on the dice and let fly.

In other words, I leaned into him, aiming fortunately accurately, and my mouth hit his.

His body stilled.

I touched my tongue to his lips.

His mouth opened.

My tongue slid inside.

Then I was on my back in his bed, his arms around me.

Way back when, we could get heated. Especially after a period of absence, the first time was fast and rough and wonderful.

This was different.

It was fast. It was rough.

And it was desperate.

Ham took over the kiss even as he yanked up my nightgown. I lifted my arms over my head. He broke the kiss and the nightgown was gone.

He came back, mouth to mine, kissing me, hungry. No, *greedy*. Devouring. Amazing. And I kissed him back the same way, my hands moving on him, roaming, pressing, nails scratching, just as greedy as our mouths.

Ham broke the kiss to shift down, lifting one of my breasts. His lips closed around my nipple and he pulled hard.

My back arched. My leg forced its way out from under his and curled around his thigh as I drove my hands into his hair.

He came back to my mouth,, drinking, consuming, his thumb now at my nipple, pressing deep and circling, rubbing, pulling. I moaned into his mouth, unwrapped my leg from his thigh, planted my foot in his bed, and rolled him.

Then I took from him. Everything. My mouth, tongue, and teeth at his neck, his chest, his nipples, down, down, he opened his legs, cocking his knees, and I saw his cock, hard and thick, resting on his stomach.

And I wanted that. Badly.

So I ran my tongue up the underside from base to tip.

He grunted, one hand plunging in my hair, fisting. I wrapped his cock in my hand, shifted, moved my hand away, and took him deep.

"Jesus," he growled, his hips thrusting up, his other hand coming to my face, palm to my cheek, thumb out and resting along my lower lip so he could feel it two ways as I worked his cock.

I was giving it to him, God, finally giving it to him and loving it.

Head was not my favorite thing to give. I'd do it, I liked it all right, but I'd pick other things to do above that.

With Ham, I couldn't get enough. I never could. I loved his reaction. I loved how I could make him lose control. I loved the taste of him. The feel of him in my mouth.

I loved everything about it.

As it would turn out, I loved it too much.

So much, I had to shove a hand between my legs and touch myself because just taking him there was making me hot. So hot, I was close to exploding.

But I had him so I should *have* him.

And I was going to take him.

I slid him out of my mouth, dropped to a hip, tugged off my panties, threw them to the side, and crawled over him.

"Zara—" he called, his deep voice guttural.

I didn't reply.

I wrapped my hand around his cock again, guided him to me, and, with a rough, desperate downward plunge, I impaled myself on him.

His groan shook the room, his hips thrust up, and his hands went to my hips. My hands went to me, one finger to my clit, one hand to my breast, fingers closing around my nipple as, head back, mindless, I rode him and I did it hard.

"Babe—" he called again but I didn't respond because I was there.

Crying out, moving with abandon, I came, the fire of it exploding between my legs and shooting through me, splitting me open, ripping me wide, and I loved every second.

Vaguely, I felt Ham's arms come around me and I was on my back, Ham driving rough and deep. With one of his arms under me, hand curled around the back of my neck to hold me stationary, I took his beautifully brutal thrusts as I came down and he took himself there.

I knew when he made it because his fingers at my neck drove into my hair, fisted, holding my head steady and he slammed his mouth down on mine as he thrust his cock to the root and groaned down my throat.

I held him tight, my arms around him, my legs bent, feet in the bed, thighs pressed to his hips, and I traced his lower lip with my tongue, thinking Nina was right.

Rolling the dice was a good thing to do.

I barely finished this thought when Ham unexpectedly pulled out and rolled off, settling on his back.

I blinked into the dark in surprised confusion.

Something about this was not right. Ham was affectionate, especially in bed. He never pulled out until he had no choice. He caressed, cuddled, nuzzled, nipped, licked, kissed, whispered.

He'd never pulled out and rolled away.

I shifted to my side, preparing to lift up on a forearm and reach out to him but I froze solid when he spoke.

"Got a taste for your fuck toy, babe, at least let me roll on a goddamned condom before you use me to find it."

Oh shit, part one. We didn't use protection.

This wasn't exactly bad. I was on The Pill but Ham always used protection.

And oh shit, part everything. He thought I'd used him as a fuck toy?

"Ham?" I called, beginning to reach out but he rolled off the bed and started through the shadows to the bathroom.

He did this speaking.

"That was fuckin' awesome. Mood strikes you, you know where I am." He stopped at the bathroom door and turned to me. "But I sleep alone, baby, and we're done tonight so do me a favor and find your bed."

After delivering that, the bathroom door closed behind him.

Evidence was suggesting that maybe I shouldn't have rolled the dice.

My body was hot everywhere and not in good ways. I was scared, worried, and I had no clue what to do. I had no clue why Ham reacted like that.

I just knew, when he got out of the bathroom, he didn't want me in his bed.

So I jumped out of it, snatched up my panties, found my nightgown, ran naked to my own room, and closed the door.

*   *   *

For the next two days I avoided Ham as best I could, seeing as we lived and worked together.

During the days, this was easy. I got the hell out of the condo and stayed out until I went to work.

At work, Ham helped. He seemed just as happy to avoid me as I did him and, luckily, Jake was working so Ham stayed distant any time I approached the bar and I used Jake.

Driving to The Dog myself and Ham being the manager and not picking up any blondes, he stayed later. When he was my ride, I usually hung out while he dealt with shit. Now, I used it as a way to get home and behind my bedroom door before he got home.

It was the second night, lying in bed, hearing him come home and close the door to his room, that I understood what had happened with Ham.

Greg and I, in the beginning, had a good sex life. It wasn't as good as Ham but then, unfortunately for Greg and bitchily for me, nothing about Greg was.

After we were married, when I was losing myself and the distance was forming between us, the sex went bad. We had it but we had it in a way where we had it only, it seemed, because we were supposed to.

Greg got off entirely, my guess, due to biology.

I never did.

So with that and with the fact I hadn't had a man in some time, I lost myself in what I was doing, what was happening, and the fact it was Ham.

And he would know I lost myself.

I'd never done that with him. I could lose myself in sex with him but it was always *with him*. I never rode him like that. Usually, when I was on top, I was bent to him, touching him, kissing him, nuzzling him. Or he was sitting up, doing all that to me.

The other night, I didn't use him to get off. I knew who I was riding.

But I could see how he didn't think the same.

I could also see how that could piss him off.

I'd walked to his room in the dead of night, scared him, came onto him, and rode him to climax without even discussing protection and stupidly not using it.

It was a shit thing to do.

I'd fucked up and I needed to do what he did when he was out of line.

I needed to apologize so we could get past it.

I also needed to do it soon. We lived together. We worked together. If there were different-sized elephants in rooms, ours was one of the biggest. If I didn't sort this out, we'd both be smushed.

"No time like the present," I muttered, throwing back the covers and, with determination, walking to his room.

He wouldn't be asleep. He'd just gotten home.

Though there was no light coming from under his door and no answer when I lightly knocked.

I sucked in a breath, opened the door to dark, and stuck my head in.

"Ham?"

"What?"

Damn. That wasn't inviting.

I considered backtracking, telling him we'd talk later or just saying, "Nothing," and getting the hell out of there.

I didn't do that.

I slowly walked in and went to the side of his bed where I could see the shadow of his body.

I stopped close and started to speak.

"I know it's late but we . . . *eeeek!*"

The "eek" came when Ham's hand darted out, latched onto my wrist, and yanked me off my feet so I fell on him then he rolled us both so he was on top and I was pinned under him.

Then he kissed me.

Not thinking, not for an instant, I kissed him back.

We didn't do this very long but we did it very well. So well I was completely lost in him when he broke the kiss and growled, "Tonight you get *my* mouth. Nightgown off, cookie."

If there was a world record for getting a nightgown off, I was sure I beat it as I yanked mine up and over my head.

While I did, Ham slid down me, hooked a finger in the side of my panties, and tore them down my legs. He barely got them clear and tossed away before his hands went to the backs of my knees. He lifted them, spread them wide, settled, and his mouth was on me.

"Oh my God," I breathed, my head pressing into the mattress, my legs tensing, my sex spasming against his mouth.

He could do this, Ham could. He got off on it like I got off on taking him in my mouth.

But this was different.

This was like our kiss the other night. His mouth was hungry, greedy, *desperate*. He sucked my clit. He fucked me with his tongue. He nipped the juncture of my thigh with his teeth, making me whimper, then he came back to me and gave me more. All the while his big, rough hands held my bent legs high and spread wide.

It was magnificent.

So much so, I came in his mouth, moaning, whimpering, my fingers fisted in his hair to hold him to me.

I was nowhere near done when he was gone, for too long, and before I could come down and figure it out, he was back, covering me, his cock slamming inside me.

"Yes," I breathed, wrapping my arms and legs around him, shoving my face in his neck.

He thrust hard and fast and grunted in mine.

"Yes, baby," I panted and one of his hands slid down my side, in, over my belly, and then his thumb was *right there*. "Ham!" I gasped, my entire body jolting as his touch seared through me.

"You're comin' with me," he grunted into my neck.

"Baby, that's … it's too …" I panted then a new climax rolled through me and I whispered, *"Ham."*

"Fuck yeah," he groaned, burying himself inside me, his hips deep and planted, the rest of his big, heavy body jerking as he came.

I descended from the high, my body melting into his bed, my arms softening around him.

Ham nuzzled my neck with his nose and lips.

I closed my eyes.

I held his weight. He held me, stayed planted inside me, his mouth moving on my neck for a long time before his hand slid up my body between us, up my neck. He swept my lips with his thumb and his lips came to my jaw where he kissed me.

Then he pulled out, rolled off, exited the bed, and sauntered to the bathroom.

I exited the bed, too, grabbed my stuff, and ran naked to my room.

I pulled on jeans, shirt, boots, grabbed my keys and purse and ran to the front door, through it, and straight to my car.

*   *   *

I spent the night in Carnal Hotel.

I woke up to three missed calls and a voice mail, all from Ham.

I'd turned my phone to mute.

I didn't listen to the voice mail.

I went into super-sleuth mode. That was to say, I staked

out our parking lot and dashed into the condo when I saw Ham head out for his run.

He did this later than usual.

I knew why because I had two more missed calls from him.

I dashed up to our place, took the fastest shower in history, tugged on new clothes, grabbed some stuff to get ready for work with, and drove back to Carnal Hotel where I'd paid for two nights and where I intended to hide out, and since the owners seemed like really nice people and they had a heated pool, I decided to do this maybe forever.

*   *   *

As I knew with the phone calls he wouldn't, Ham did not assist me in avoiding him that night when I got to work.

I had confirmation of that when his eyes came right to me when I hit the floor from the back where the staff parked their cars and stowed their stuff in the office.

I looked away immediately and grabbed a tray off the end of the bar, which was luckily opposite to where Ham was.

I needed to find out which section I'd be covering tonight. To do that, I moved toward Christie, my waitressing partner for the evening, and I had made it the length of three feet before an arm clamped around my ribs, I was hauled back into a hard frame, and a mouth was at my ear.

"Tonight, we talk."

Oh hell.

"Okay, Ham," I lied.

"Been worried sick about your ass all day," he stated.

I said nothing.

"You avoid me at the bar, I'll not be best pleased," he warned.

"Copy that," I replied, breathing heavily and not wanting to get my drink orders from him or even look at him until

I figured out what the fuck was happening in my head, not to mention make a wild stab at what might be happening in his.

He gave me a sturdy squeeze so my heavy breathing got heavier then he touched his lips to my neck and let me go.

The lip touch was interesting.

It was also terrifying.

Even so, it felt beautiful.

I didn't avoid him at the bar and I told myself that was my punishment. Although I didn't avoid him, Ham didn't push conversation. That didn't mean he wasn't watchful of me, his eyes moving over my face, studying me closely before filling my orders, making my anxiety increase tremendously.

At the beginning of the shift, things were not busy or even steady. So I got my drink orders from Ham but I did my best to stay busy and away from the bar. Away from Ham.

Luckily, it got busier and I didn't have to find work to keep me occupied.

Finally, it was closing time.

Ham was talking to Christie and I took that opportunity to go get my purse, get in my car, and get my ass to Carnal Hotel.

I accomplished one of these goals. I got my purse and I got *to* my car but I didn't get in it because, as I was standing beside it, digging through my purse, I couldn't find my keys.

"Reece wants to talk to you, honey," Christie told me as she made her way to her Hyundai.

Man, oh man.

"Okay," I called, forcing brightness in my tone and, as she got in and I moved to the back door, I saw Ham lounging in its frame holding up what appeared to be my keys.

"Lookin' for these?" he asked.

I stopped four feet away and didn't answer.

He palmed the keys and shoved them in his jeans pocket.

"I'm your ride home tonight, cookie," he informed me.

"My car is here," I informed him.

"It'll be safe."

"I'm not sure it will, Ham. We're not exactly in town."

And we weren't. There was good reason why The Dog was almost completely populated by locals—because they were the only ones who knew how to find it out here in the boonies.

"Got security cameras, babe, so even if your car is stolen, we'll catch on film who did it and you got insurance. So it's stayin' here and I'm your ride."

"I—" I started but Ham swiftly cut me off.

"You say another goddamned word, I'll kiss you quiet, drag your ass into the office, fuck you on the goddamned desk, and do it until you're so exhausted, you can't speak and *then* we'll talk seein' as I'm the one who's got somethin' to say."

I snapped my mouth shut.

Ham did not.

"Now either you open your mouth and get that or you keep it shut and ride home with me. Which is it gonna be?"

Although, in an alternate universe, I'd jump at option A, in this universe, I was definitely going with option B.

So I pressed my lips together and, just in case he couldn't see that from where he was lounging in the doorway, I slid them to the side to make sure I made my point.

"Good fuckin' choice," he stated. "Now get your ass in here while I finish shit."

He stepped to the side and I got my ass in there, squeezing by him, so I could wait it out while he finished shit.

Then, clearly, we were going home to talk.

And I was utterly terrified of what he had to say.

CHAPTER EIGHT

I Lied

WE MADE THE ride home in silence but I knew I couldn't avoid the talk just as I knew I shouldn't.

We had to get this out and move on.

And I knew how we were going to move on and that was me moving out and finding another job (again) because this was messed up.

I couldn't live like this.

I'd tried but I'd rolled the dice and fucked it up.

I was in love with Ham. I had been since I was twenty-four. I probably would be forever.

So as he "finished shit" at the bar, I blanked my mind, stayed quiet, and waited.

The ride home was silent and tense. And when we got home, I moved to the living room, shrugged off my purse and jacket, and threw them on the armchair before I turned to sit my ass on the couch in order to get this done and prepare to move on.

Before I could make it to the couch, my hand was seized, my arm tugged, and I found myself being dragged behind Ham toward the hall.

"Ham—"

"Shut it five seconds, baby," he told the hall, taking us on a direct trajectory to his room.

It took more than five seconds but I kept it shut the entire time, mostly because I was bemused, sad at the thought of losing Ham for good, and freaked way the hell out at the way Ham was acting. I was also wondering why I managed to always fuck up my life. I had no one else to blame but me about everything.

And especially this.

I knew better than to move in with him. I *way* knew better than to go to him that first night.

But I did.

Now we were broken, just like I broke Greg.

Ham was right, Greg knew me. He knew who he'd married, so I'd come to uneasy terms with that being not exactly all my fault.

This, I had no leg to stand on.

When we got to his room, Ham switched on a bedside lamp, used his hand in mine to maneuver me to the bed, and then let me go to put his hand in my belly. He gave me a little shove so I was sitting on his bed.

I looked up at him. "Ham—"

"Five more seconds, cookie," he muttered as he bent, lifted my leg, yanked off my boot then he did the same with the other.

After that, he straightened and shrugged off his jeans jacket, letting it drop to the floor. He then stooped to take off his own boots and only after that did he come to me, plant his hands under my arms, and haul me into the bed so I was on my back, head to the pillows.

I belatedly started breathing heavily when he put a knee to the bed, hiked his other leg over me, and settled his big body mostly on me, partly to my side.

He put his elbow in the pillow, head in hand, and locked eyes with me.

That was when he asked, "What the fuck was that?"

My mind was now blanked for a different reason, primarily freaking way the hell out that we were having this conversation in his bed, so I didn't know what he was asking.

Even if I wasn't freaking, I still would be confused.

Therefore, I asked, "What the fuck was what?"

"Last night," he answered. "I go to the bathroom to get rid of the condom, come out, you're gone. By the time I make it to the door, buck naked, mind, I see you dressed and runnin' down the hall. Seein' as I'm buck naked, I can't get to you before you disappear. You're gone all night, don't answer your phone, don't answer it all fuckin' day. I'm worried sick, you stroll into the bar, and then you're beyond weird at work."

I stared into his eyes, marveling how the light brown at his pupils spiked through the dark brown that edged his irises. I'd never seen anything like that and it was all kinds of fascinating because it was all kinds of gorgeous.

I did this memorizing it because, soon, I wouldn't see it again.

Then I focused not on the color of his eyes, but him.

"I need to move out," I whispered and his body seemed to grow heavier on mine as his eyebrows snapped together.

"What the fuck?"

"I need to move out," I repeated, louder this time. "And, um, give notice."

"What the fuck?" he said again, pissed this time, then he bit out, "For fuck's sake, why?"

"Why?" I asked.

He had to know.

"Yeah, babe, *why*?"

He didn't know.

"I can't do this," I told him. "I can't be like we are now. I can't be roomies."

"Yeah, your sweet, hot, middle-of-the-night visit clued me in to that. Or, I should say, your sweet, hot, long-fuckin'-overdue visit clued me in to that."

I felt my lips part as my eyes went from looking into his to staring.

"What?" I breathed.

"Zara, for nearly two months, I've been waitin' for you to come to me."

What did he just say?

I didn't get a chance to ask; he kept talking.

"I didn't handle it right that first night. Got the wrong end of the stick. You weren't you. Thought your head was fucked. You gave me plenty of time to think about it, though, and I get it. You *were* you, and Christ, never knew a woman who liked my cock in her mouth so much. You got lost in that, lost control and, my guess, it's been a long time so that made you totally lose control. It was fuckin' hot, don't get me wrong, but you got so lost it made me feel like available meat. But I shouldn't have been a dick. I should have talked to you about it. But I'd been waiting so goddamned long for you to come to me, and that was not how I wanted it to go when you did, that I got pissed and acted like an asshole. But *you* shouldn't have run away when we sorted that out last night in my bed before we could totally sort it out by havin' a goddamned chat."

I heard all that.

But I honed into one part of it.

"You've been waiting for me to come to you?"

"Babe, you're my Zara, my cookie, so fuck yeah, I've been bidin' my time, givin' you space to sort your head out, but waitin' to get you back, as in"—his hand slid up to cup my jaw and his face dipped closer—"*back*."

Was he serious? Two months...no *seven*, if you counted when he came back after hatchet man got to him, I'd been in misery and *he'd* been waiting to get me back?

I felt my eyes narrow.

"Last night, you rolled off me and didn't say a word about a chat before you went to the bathroom," I reminded him.

"Zara, what we shared, so good, so hot, so close, us bein' back to us, didn't feel I needed to say a word," he replied.

Was he for real? "Back to us" and he didn't feel he needed to say a word?

"Well, you did," I stated.

"I see that *now*," he returned.

Okay, then, time for a different subject.

"You said you didn't want my body," I accused.

"I lied, Zara. Fuck, when have I ever not wanted in there?" he asked, a question that had one answer, that being *never*. But he didn't give me the chance to give that answer, he kept talking. "I would have said anything to get you out of that shithole, get you safe, and get you *with me*."

"You lied?" I asked.

"I lied," Ham answered.

"Lied?" My voice was getting higher.

"Asked and answered, darlin'," he clipped.

"So you thought it was a good idea to lie," I noted unhappily.

"Babe, I came to you, we almost instantly got up in each other's shit. You had a lot you were dealin' with and one of those things didn't need to be me. You weren't lettin' anyone do anything for you. You needed time to deal. I wanted you with me. I did what I had to do to give you that and make that happen for me."

My head gave a jerk as what he said tardily hit me.

"You wanted me *with you*?"

He was beginning to look impatient.

"You've known me years. I ever go back?" he asked.

"Go back to what?"

"Go back *anywhere*."

"Ham—"

"I don't go back," he declared.

"I don't get—"

"Now I'm back in Gnaw Bone, back at The Dog, babe, why do you think that is?"

I didn't speak. I was back to staring.

Because I knew why I *wanted* that to be.

I just rarely got what I wanted.

Then Graham Reece finally gave me what I wanted.

"Because you're here."

"Holy shit," I whispered.

He stopped looking impatient, his eyes warmed, his face went soft, and his lips twitched.

But, "Yeah," was all he said.

This was too much. Too fast. Too good.

I didn't know if I ever had good.

Well, my shop, Karma, was good and the four months I had of Ham years ago were good. Not to mention the times in between with Ham. Those were good, too.

But I'd never had *good*.

"I don't know what to do with this," I told him quietly.

"First thing you're gonna do is, after we fuck, stay in my goddamned bed for more than five seconds. Next thing you're gonna do will happen tomorrow and that's you movin' your shit in here because here's where you're gonna be sleepin' from now on. And after that, I don't know." He shrugged and concluded, "We'll wing it."

We'd wing it?

Yes, this was too much and it was too fast.

There were things to be said.

"Ham, you . . . we . . . when you . . . that is when we—"

His lips twitched again before he urged, "Spit it out, darlin'."

"I can't go back."

There was no lip twitch then. His hand slid to my neck, palm at my throat, fingers digging in the side.

"Cookie," he whispered.

I shook my head. "I want that but I can't have it because it's not what I really want. We've always been honest so I have to lay it out so you know where I'm at." I took in a deep breath that was nevertheless shaky and laid it out. "I barely survived walking away from you. I couldn't handle you walking away from me."

Strangely his face got a mixture of hard and soft, his eyes warm and sharp before he stated, "Zara, you're not paying attention."

He was wrong. I so totally was. I was paying so much attention, if I paid more, my head would explode.

"I am, Ham. You said it yourself. You have issues with women. You're a rolling stone. You—"

I stopped speaking when he rolled into a seated position, back to headboard, taking me with him so I was straddling his lap, my torso pressed close.

He had one arm clamped tight around my waist and he had sifted the other hand into my hair and was cupping the back of my head.

"I'm here," he stated.

"I know you are, but—"

"Baby, please be quiet for a bit and listen to me," he requested gently.

I shut my mouth.

"I'm here, Zara, as in, I intend to stay here. I own a TV. A bed. Bought fuckin' nightstands, a dresser, and lamps. This is it. This is where I wanna be. It's where I wanna be because I like the people, I like the work, I like the bar where I work, all in God's country. But this is mostly where I wanna be because *you're* here."

Now that was not too fast.

That took a long fucking time.

"Oh my God," I breathed.

I wanted to believe that. I would have paid him to give me that. I would have sold my soul to the devil to have that.

But after wanting it for so long and never having it, I couldn't believe in it.

Fortune seemed finally to be shining on me because Ham wasn't done.

"Baby, a man lives his life runnin' from history, hopin' it doesn't catch up and repeat itself, goes to sleep one night, opens his eyes in the dark to a man wielding an ax, suddenly findin' himself facin' an end that's a fair bit worse than most, a footnote to a far uglier piece of history, I've told you before, he reflects. I also told you I did that. And you haven't paid attention but I'm not just a bartender anymore. I'm a manager. I got responsibilities and I gave promises of longevity. I can't put everything I own in my truck and move on." His fingers tensed against my scalp. "Darlin', I'm settling. What you didn't know, what I was keepin' back 'til the right time, that time bein' now, was, I'm doin' it with you."

Was he serious?

Please tell me he was serious.

To get Ham, the only one who could answer that question, to do that, I used one word, "Why?"

"'Cause you're my cookie, you're easy, you're funny, you're honest, you're fuckin' sexy, you love my dick, and you're not hard on the eyes."

That was all awesome.

But somehow it also was not.

It was...flat.

Luckily, he wasn't done.

"And I want kids. Hope I didn't wait too long but I want them. I want a family, always have. Lost my parents young, Mom when I was seventeen, Dad when I was twenty-one, didn't have any brothers or sisters but had it good with Mom and Dad. I want that back, want to give that to kids. You want them, too, and I know, what went down with your family, you've learned. So you'll be a great mom."

Okay. Again.

Please tell me he was serious.

Please, God, tell me this was happening to me.

I mean, I knew about his parents. His mom had always had really bad diabetes so even though Ham told me often she was a great mom that illness was always hanging over their heads.

His dad was a shock, heart attack at a young age. Then again, Ham said he drank, was overweight, and had a deep affinity for anything fried so during one of our heart-to-hearts when Ham and I first got together, he told me, even though his dad's dying was a shock, it wasn't a surprise.

But until then, I didn't know my travelin' man had always wanted a family.

Something I'd always wanted, too.

One that was better than the one I was born into, that was.

"Ham—"

"Plus, you're all kinds of pretty. We'll make beautiful babies, have fun doin' it, and have fun raisin' 'em. You'll get my history because you lived a lot of it with me. I'll share the rest. I'll get yours because I've been in your life to share it with you. We never fight unless your head's a mess because shit is fucked in your life and I've been recently attacked by an ax-wielding fuckwit. Or because I'm actin' like a dick because listenin' to you make yourself come after spendin' night after night in a bed a door down from you was doin' my motherfucking head in and I hadn't been in there for years drove me to act like a dick."

"So that's what that was about," I replied.

That got me another lip twitch and his arms pulled me closer. "Yeah, darlin', that was what that was about." His eyes dropped to my mouth and his voice dipped deeper. "Fuck, it sounded hot, good, went on so goddamned long. Torture."

My stomach pitched.

"Ham," I called and his eyes came to mine but his hand in my hair slid to my jaw.

"What, baby?"

He asked his question but I was lost in his eyes.

They were hooded and heated. Burning into mine.

Thus I knew his mind was not on what I was going to say. It was elsewhere.

My mind joined it.

His thumb slid over my lower lip.

I lost my mind and pressed my lips to his.

He opened his lips over mine, slid his tongue inside and his hand back up into my hair, and my arms slid around him.

He slanted his head. I tipped mine the other way and Ham took the kiss deeper.

Then I was on my back in his bed and Ham was on top of me.

Not long after, I was naked on my back in his bed and Ham was moving inside me, his lips to mine but not kissing.

Breathing.

Heavily.

"When we're done, you're comin' with me to the bathroom," he ordered, voice thick.

"I won't leave your bed, babe," I assured him through panting.

Ham's hips powered faster and I gasped against his mouth.

"You're comin' with," he stated, voice now gruff.

I was so very close but still managed to force out a breathily exasperated, "Ham, I won't leave your bed."

"Makin' sure and killin' two birds with one stone by fuckin' you in the shower while we're there."

Now, *that* I could do. Gladly.

I didn't say that.

I arched my neck, wound my limbs tight around him, tipped my hips into his thrusts, and came.

*　　*　　*

Dawn was just lighting the sky when we were done and lying together in Ham's bed. I'd gone to my room to get my nightgown, but I was back plastered against Ham's side, cheek to his shoulder, fingers lightly raking through the hair on his chest. Ham, on his back, his arm tucked under and wrapped around me, was drawing random patterns with his fingertips on my hip.

"There's more to say," I told his chest softly.

"We'll say it," he replied.

"I'm scared," I admitted.

"I get that. We got a shift to get through, baby, moving us to somethin' we've never had. You promise to hold on to me, I'll promise to hold on to you and we'll make it through."

God, I wanted that. I so, so wanted that.

But I had to be sure before I lost myself in the beauty of it.

"I need to know your issues with women," I told him.

"And I'll tell you, tomorrow night, when I take my girl out to a nice dinner. We'll lay our shit bare, baby, and then we'll move on."

I lifted my head and looked at his face. "You're going to give me that?"

His hand came up to cup my cheek and he whispered, "Cookie, pay attention. I'm gonna give you everything."

That was when Ham gave it to me. What I wanted. What I needed.

Proof I could lose myself in the beauty of it.

In him.

Oh my God, I was going to cry.

Man, oh man, I was crying.

I planted my face in his chest and let loose.

Ham wrapped his arms around me, pressed into me so we were both on our sides as he pulled me up, and tucked my face in his throat. Then he held me while I cried.

And while I cried, it happened.

It came to me.

All of it.

Ham was in Gnaw Bone only a week before he made the ludicrous sound reasonable and talked me into moving into his second bedroom.

Ham gave me a job at his bar when, with the reduced rent I was paying him, I could get on my feet working at Deluxe Home Store. Ham took me to work nearly every night when I wasn't pissed or freaking out.

Ham scheduled us both off on the same days so we had the opportunity to spend the maximum amount of time together that we could, definitely at work, but also at home.

And when I went to him that first night, Ham not hesitating but a half a second before I was on my back in his bed.

And, last, when I went to him again, he'd yanked me into his bed.

Something else hit me and, with all the rest, it didn't make sense.

"You fucked that blonde," I accused his neck, my breath hitching through it because I was still crying.

"What?" he asked.

"That blonde you were flirting with, you fucked her."

"What blonde?"

I stopped crying because I was shocked at his question and the fact that he sounded baffled. I was also, but more so, pissed.

How could he forget the blonde? He'd had her only a couple of weeks ago.

I yanked my face out of his throat and tipped my head back, watching his chin dip down, and I caught his eyes in the semi-dark.

"That blonde, Ham, that blonde you were flirting with the other night who you took down the back hall of the bar."

To this, he strangely replied, "She was hammered."

"What?"

"Blitzed, babe, totally out of it. I took her home. She lived in fuckin' Chantelle, so it took a while. I came back to the bar, you were gone. I finished the shit I needed to finish, and seein' as *you* were flirtin' with that fuckwit, I was pissed so I sat in on a poker game so I could get my mind off you and your shit." He paused, then finished with, "I won fifteen hundred dollars."

"She was hammered?" I asked.

"Passed out in the truck. Got her to come to in order to walk her to her house. She passed out on her living room couch before I took two steps back to her front door."

This was good news. Not only had Ham not fucked her, she'd been so blotto, she passed out, which meant her punishment for flirting with my guy was her having a hangover the next day.

It didn't make me a nice person, she had no idea he was my guy, *I* didn't even have any idea at the time he was my guy. But still, I liked this.

Onward.

"You won fifteen hundred dollars?" I asked.

I saw the white flash of his teeth and his arms gave me a squeeze.

"Yeah. Means we can go crazy at The Rooster tomorrow night."

We were going to The Rooster? I *loved* The Rooster.

I let The Rooster go and narrowed my eyes.

"Since when does the manager of The Dog take drunk women home?" I queried. "Jake calls a taxi"—I paused to drive my point home—"unless the woman is hot."

"They do that shit when they spend a night gettin' crap from their girl who doesn't know she's his girl's friends and watchin' her flirt with some jackass and give him her number. Had to get the fuck outta there so I didn't rip that jack-ass's head off."

That explained that.

My eyes un-narrowed and my body melted into his.

"That guy ever call you?" Ham asked.

"I didn't pick up."

"How many times did he call you?" he pushed.

I pressed my lips together and when his eyes narrowed, I answered, "Twelve...*ish.* I quit counting."

"Fuck," he muttered to the ceiling.

I decided to stay silent.

Ham looked back at me.

"You thought I fucked her?"

"You were flirting with her."

"I was pouring her drinks. My job is to sell booze, babe, and you and me both know tossin' a smile at a randy drunk is a good way to do that."

He wasn't wrong about that.

"You also left with her," I reminded him.

"Wouldn't ever do that shit to you."

"You said that the ground rules were, if I hooked up, I did it at his place and you'd return the favor."

"Baby, *I lied,*" Ham stated with firm emphasis that was made firmer by his arms going tight around me.

"Well, I didn't know that," I snapped.

"Is that why you were brooding on your balcony?" he asked.

"Yeah, Ham. I thought the love of my life, who I was living with and working with but I couldn't have, had spent the night with another woman, so that was why I was brooding on my balcony," I clipped.

Only when I was done speaking did I feel the air, the stillness of his body, and the fact that his arms were now very tight around me.

"Ham?"

"Fuck, now I gotta fuck you again," he muttered, rolling us so I was on my back.

"What? Why? What's going on?" I asked, rounding him with my arms.

His lips came to mine, where he whispered, "Love of your life."

I stilled.

Then I drew in a soft breath.

After that, I admitted, "It's always been you."

"Fuck, now I gotta fuck you again," he murmured, but his murmur was jagged.

I smiled against his mouth and slid my hands up his back.

Ham slanted his head, took my mouth with his, and proceeded to fuck me again.

CHAPTER NINE

Our Beginning

"HAM," I BREATHED.

"What 'cha need to take you there?" Ham growled.

"Oh God," I whimpered.

"Baby, hurry, I'm close," Ham grunted.

We were in the living room. My panties were dangling from my ankle. My back was to the wall. The bottom of my wraparound dress was gaping open because my legs were wrapped around Ham's hips, my arms around his shoulders, and he was powering deep.

Suffice it to say, when I wandered out of his bedroom in a clingy dress that showed cleavage, spiked, high-heeled sandals, hair out to there with soft curls and sweet flips, and sultry makeup, Ham liked what he saw.

Thus me against the wall getting it from my guy.

"Keep going," I begged.

"Fuck, should have dropped to my knees and ate you before I fucked you," he groaned.

That did it. My head flew back and hit wall, my hands slid up and clenched in his hair, my legs squeezed him hard, my sex squeezed him harder, and I cried out as I came hard.

"Thank fuck," he muttered, shoved his face in my neck, thrust his cock inside again, again, *again,* jolting me, prolonging my fantastic orgasm, making me moan then he finally buried himself deep and groaned into my neck.

I pressed my face into his, held on tight, and started sliding my lips on his skin and nuzzling his jaw and ear with my nose when his cock started gliding in and out of me.

He kept gliding as he whispered against the skin of my neck, "Just in case you hadn't noticed, glad to have you back, cookie."

I smiled against his skin when I replied, "Glad to be back, bruiser."

I felt his smile as he clarified on an inward glide, "All the way back, babe."

"All the way back, darlin'."

He slid in and stayed there but lifted his face out of my neck so I tipped mine to catch his eyes and saw his brows raised.

"Bruiser?"

"You run on nothing but coffee," I explained.

His raised brows lowered but drew together in confusion as he asked, "What?"

"Only a bruiser who could kick the ass of a cage fighter

named Butch Razor can run five miles on nothin' but a cup of coffee," I expanded my explanation.

Ham stared at me.

Then he threw back his handsome, dark head with messy hair I'd delightfully made messy and he burst out laughing.

I saw it, heard it, and felt it, the last in very, very good places.

And I loved every bit of it.

*   *   *

We both had the day off, as Ham always arranged, and we spent nearly all of it in bed, taking a long, happy trip down memory lane.

Seeing as we woke up after noon, we had to make up for lost time before dinner at The Rooster. Ham made us some eggs and toast. We had the annoying errand of taking a trip to Carnal Hotel to get my stuff (my fault). Ham helped me drag my stuff from my room into his and then we showered together before Ham left me to get ready.

The trip to The Rooster was long, an hour, but we didn't talk about anything important on the way there. I was too busy being happy that first, Ham held my hand while he drove; second, he always looked hot but in dark denims and a black untucked, straight-hemmed tailored shirt that he left open at the collar, he looked *hot*; and last, I was going to The Rooster at all.

I'd been there seven times, all of them with other guys, four of those times with Greg pre- and during marriage. It had fabulous décor, with Cotton prints hanging on the walls, so many windows you could see through it, it was high up on a mountainside, you didn't go there unless you dressed up, and its menu was pricey. Mostly steaks. Everything good.

It was the perfect place for the celebration of Ham and me being back, *all the way* back, so far back that we were at a place we'd never been, and for us to lay it bare so we could understand each other and move on with no surprises.

I was riding a happy wave the likes I'd never felt *in my life*.

Ham had bought a TV.

Ham had talked about settling.

Ham had talked about having a family.

Ham had come back to Gnaw Bone for me.

Thus I wandered into The Rooster in the curve of Ham's arm around my shoulders, mine around his waist, my head tipped to the side and resting on his shoulder, my face, I was sure, wearing a goofy but gleeful smile, thinking that nothing could pierce this happiness.

At the same time I marveled that, not a year ago, I had been at what I thought was my lowest, only to sink lower.

And now I was here.

Ham muttered, "Graham Reece," to the hostess. She murmured, "Right this way," back, I came out of my bubble of happiness, focused on the room, and my bubble burst.

I also tripped over my feet.

This was because, in the far back corner, sat Greg, his eyes on Ham, his face pale, his company clearly business associates.

And in the front corner was Kami Maxwell, Max's sister, a woman I'd known years who had always been slightly bitchy and constantly in a foul mood but had mellowed a bit when her brother's girlfriend had faced imminent death and bested it. Still, she was unpredictable, and right then, her eyes were sharp on me in a way I didn't like. In a way I worried Cotton or Arlene had got her ear. And if Kami Maxwell had something to say, whether you wanted to hear it or not, she said it.

And last, at the back wall sat my aunt, my father's sister, a woman I hadn't spoken to in nine years, a woman I detested, a woman I never wanted to see again in my life. Which was an impossible feat since we both lived in the same town. She was also sending a venomous stare my way.

"Cookie, you good?" Ham asked, his arm giving me a squeeze and I tipped my head to look at him.

"This is a disaster," I whispered.

His brows shot together and the hostess announced, "Here we are."

I looked at her, motioning to a booth and declared, "We have to go."

She blinked.

"What the fuck're you talkin' about?" Ham asked under his breath.

"Greg's here," I told him.

His head jerked, his eyes scanned, they narrowed when he caught sight of Greg, and he muttered, "Fuck."

"And Kami Maxwell," I went on.

He looked down at me and asked, "Who?"

I didn't answer. I continued.

"And my aunt. Dad's sister."

His arm tightened reflexively, curling me into his front, and his head shot up, his eyes scanning again. He'd seen her but never met her and I knew when he caught sight of her because his jaw got hard.

"Mr. Reece?" the hostess called.

A muscle jumped in his cheek and he looked back down at me.

"Fuck 'em, this is our night."

"Ham—"

His arm tightened further. "Fuck 'em, cookie, this is our night. I want this, a nice place, good food, you lookin' fuckin' amazing sittin' across from me, me sharin' important shit you gotta understand. They don't exist. The room is meltin' away. It's just you and me, good food, and me givin' you all of me. This is our night. You with me?"

Ham giving me all of him.

"Yes," I whispered.

"There she is," he whispered back. "Easy."

He dipped his head to touch his mouth to mine and I tried not to think of Greg, seeing that only seven months after our divorce was final and my aunt seeing it, since my father hated Ham nearly as much as Ham hated my father. Dad had thought Ham was too rough, too old, too coarse and he shared that with me, Ham, and, undoubtedly, my aunt.

Ham curled me away from his body, nodded to the hostess, guided me to one side of our booth, and, when I'd settled, slid into the other one.

The hostess waited until I'd stowed my purse and shrugged off my coat before she handed us menus and swept away.

A waitress wearing a white shirt, black trousers, long slim black tie, and a long white apron hit our table approximately half a second after our hostess left.

"Two Coors, draft," Ham ordered before she opened her mouth to speak.

"Certainly, would you like to hear the specials?" she asked.

"Later," he answered. "Beer first."

She nodded and floated away.

I only half heard this. Mostly, I was trying to make the room melt away and praying our waitress didn't dillydally with the beers.

"Babe," Ham called.

"Mm-hmm," I mumbled in answer, my focus on smoothing my napkin in my lap.

"Cookie, baby, come back to me," he urged gently.

My eyes went to him.

"This is our beginning. Don't let them fuck it up."

This was our beginning.

I reached a hand across the table to him.

Ham caught it.

"Okay," I replied.

He gave my hand a squeeze and let me go.

"Decide what you want. We'll get into the deep shit when we won't have interruptions."

I nodded, picked up my menu, and read.

The beers came. We both ordered steaks. And loaded baked potatoes, sautéed mushrooms, and appetizers.

Ham ended this session by tipping his head to his beer and stating, "These get low, don't ask. Bring more."

"Of course," she muttered and took off.

I stared at him with some unease.

"Am I going to need to be drunk?" I asked.

"No. How Rachel fucked me was a long time ago and it was me she fucked," he answered.

"I, uh...Rachel?" I prompted when he didn't continue.

"The bitch who aborted my babies."

My mouth went dry, my hand resting on the table twitched, and I stared.

Did he say *babies*? Plural?

"What?" I breathed.

"Woman's right to choose, I'm down with that. It wasn't that, seein' as we were married, planning a family, worked toward it, she got pregnant, I was fuckin' beside myself, and she hauled off and ended it without one word to me."

My throat was moving convulsively. It took effort to get it under control and when I did, I asked, "You were married?"

"Yeah. Got hitched when we were both twenty-one. Young, but I loved her, thought she loved me. It was all good."

"I, uh...thought you said you'd never had a roommate except, well...me," I reminded him and his head tipped to the side.

"A wife's not a roommate, babe. She's a partner."

This was true.

It was time for the tough stuff.

"Why did she...she...end the pregnancy?" I queried.

"Said she didn't know what she wanted," Ham answered immediately. "Said I pressured her into it. Said a baby was a big deal and she should be sure."

This was all true, except the part where he said they'd planned and worked toward it.

"I—" I began.

"Thing is," Ham spoke over me, "she shoulda said that *before* she got knocked up. And she sure as fuck shouldn't have aborted my kid without fuckin' talking to me."

Yes, she sure as fuck shouldn't have done that.

"I don't belicve this," I whispered.

"It was twenty years ago and, still, I don't believe it either."

I held his eyes. I knew mine were soft and I told him, "Ham, darlin', I don't know what to say."

"Nothin' to say," he replied. "That started years of serious sick shit, which I participated in, bein' stupid, young, in love, addicted to her pussy, and, again, fuckin' stupid," he went on. "I left. She coaxed me back, promises of together forever and family. We'd get down to talkin' about tryin' again. She'd be all for it and then I'd find her birth control pills."

This just got worse.

Ham wasn't done.

"I'd confront her. She'd twist shit, convince me that I was layin' it heavy on her. I'd back off, same shit would happen. I'd leave, she'd coax me back. Fuckin' stupid. Whacked. Now, for a long time, it's over."

"Man, oh man, I...Ham, I...I'm at a loss," I stammered.

"Yeah. Took a while for me to get old enough and smart enough to see things as they were. She was a self-ish, spoiled bitch who wanted what she wanted how and when she wanted it and would do anything to get it. But the problem was, she wasn't all-fired sure of what that was and she dragged me through that shit. Or it could be I didn't get old enough and smart enough, just angry enough after she aborted my second baby."

There it was. Babies. Plural.

I closed my eyes.

"Lost my fuckin' mind, left her, divorced her ass, found I had a type," Ham continued and I opened my eyes. "I didn't give up. I tried. Got tangled in other relationships. Got jacked around, not as bad, but not good, by the woman after her and the woman after her. The first one took money out of my wallet without askin', like I wouldn't miss it, and went shoppin' all the time, hidin' the shit she bought from me, like I wouldn't notice it when she eventually wore it. This was also somehow my fault because I didn't take her anywhere nice, but more, I didn't make enough money to do it and often."

Yes. This just got worse.

"Ham—" I started, only for him to talk over me again.

"Bitch three pulled much the same shit as my ex-wife, promises of together and babies, but she worked out half the time. I had to pry her away from her goddamned mirror, she admired the results so much, and by the time we got down to it, again, I found her birth control pills so I knew she was jacking me. This, too, was my fault because I didn't understand her issues with her body and how a baby would interfere with all her hard work, her body would never be the same, and she was uncertain she was prepared for that at her age. I knew she'd carried extra weight 'cause I was with her before she took it all off. And I knew she worked hard to get it off. I could understand that. Again, that's the way she is. I get it. What I don't get is her tellin' me one thing and doin' another. You don't want a baby, say it."

"They'd lose you if they did," I explained carefully.

"So jackin' me around is okay?" he asked disbelievingly.

"No," I answered hurriedly. "I'm not excusing them. I'm just trying to explain so you understand. Losing you—especially you—is a hard thing to do, Ham. You're a good guy."

"Right." He gave a curt nod. "I think I got that, babe. So exit good-guy Reece. From then on it was no promises, no expectations. Just good times and no bullshit. She starts feeding me bullshit, she doesn't get another call."

I pressed my lips together and Ham's eyes dropped to them before coming back to mine.

"You always got a call," he reminded me.

"I know."

"So what's with the look?" he asked.

"I'm just wondering how many women are out there, waiting for calls," I answered hesitantly.

"None, seein' as, when I made my decision it was you and Gnaw Bone, the only other one I had got a call explaining shit and how she wouldn't be gettin' future calls. She was in Taos. She was new, a good-time girl, and, babe, it might make me sound like a dick but she wasn't gonna make the cut anyway. Outside of her, there was only Feb and she'd already moved on."

All the air squeezed out of my lungs.

The good news was, there was only one.

The bad news was, he'd again mentioned February Owens and her "already moving on," which made me wonder what would have happened if she hadn't.

Would he be in Indiana with February?

"How fantastic is this? And you don't have food! Perfect timing for us to join you!"

Ham's eyes shot up, my head twisted around, but I already knew that English-accented voice.

Nina and Max were standing there.

Damn.

"Max, darling, isn't this great?" Nina asked when no one said a word.

Max didn't look like he thought it was great. His eyes were aimed Greg's way. Then they swung his sister's way. Then he looked down at his wife and lifted his brows.

She completely ignored him and shoved into the booth next to Ham.

"You're Graham Reece," she stated, pushing her hand his way.

Ham looked at her hand then at her face before he took her hand, muttering, "Reece."

"Delighted," she replied as he let her go and her eyes went to her husband. "Max, honey, sit down." Before Max could do as ordered, or not, she snapped her fingers at a passing waitress and said, "We're sitting here. Please, when you have a second, we need menus."

I scooted over when Max slid in beside me and I tipped my head back when his arm curled around my shoulders for a squeeze as his head came down and he kissed my cheek.

"Hey, Zara," he greeted.

"Hey, Max," I replied.

Max let me go and extended a hand to Ham. "Reece. Holden Maxwell. Max."

"Yeah, seen you at The Dog. Good to meet you," Ham murmured as they did a shake and let go.

Ham looked at me.

I widened my eyes to him.

He raised his brows to me.

I pressed my lips together.

"Can I get you drinks?" our waitress asked the newcomers while handing them menus.

"Beer and keep bringin' 'em," Max answered on a mutter.

"Martini for me. Vodka. Up. Olive," Nina added.

The waitress nodded and moved away.

"Duchess, I said beer and keep 'em comin'. You wanted to do this, I get to drink and you drive us home," Max told his wife.

I didn't know what "this" was that Nina wanted to do but I suspected it had something to do with them horning in on my special night with Ham.

And, by the way, Max's nickname for his wife was "duchess," this being because she had an English accent. He called her that all the time and I thought it was all kinds of cute.

"Just one," Nina told her husband. "By the time I'm finished with dinner, I'll be fine."

Max looked at Ham and there was a light in his eye and his lips were twitching before he informed him, "You heard it. Now watch as she gets fuckin' smashed and I stop at beer two."

I was beginning to feel a hysterical giggle forming inside me.

"I'm not going to get smashed," Nina snapped.

"We've been here fifteen times. Each time, except when you were pregnant, you had two martinis, half a bottle of wine, and an amaretto and passed out in the Cherokee on the way home," Max returned. She opened her mouth to speak but Max beat her to it, his lips now fully curved up. "And the passing-out part includes when you were pregnant and not smashed."

Definitely feeling a hysterical giggle forming.

Nina's eyes narrowed. "I'll remind you, Holden Maxwell, father of my children, love of my life, that we just met Reece and perhaps he doesn't wish to listen to us squabbling."

Max looked at Ham. "Kiss that good-bye. We'll be fightin' on and off through dinner. Prepare. She gets riled, we're all fucked."

The words sounded like Max was complaining but his tone sounded downright proud.

Nina swung her gaze to Ham. "Don't listen to him. Ask Zara. I'm very sweet."

"She's a goddamn hellion," Max muttered, now sounding proud and *amused*.

The hysterical giggle was choking me at exactly the same time Ham burst out laughing.

Still laughing, Ham cut his eyes to Max and asked, "You mind we switch sides? Since we got company, I'd like to sit by my woman."

"Not a problem. I'm closer to my wife, I have a better shot at controlling her," Max replied, sliding out of his side of the booth.

"Max!" Nina hissed as she slid out of hers.

"Not a good chance," Max told Ham as they switched sides, "but a better one."

Everyone settled. Max with his arm resting on the back of their side of the booth, Nina fuming, Max grinning at her. Ham with his arm on the back of our booth, fingers absently brushing my shoulder, both of us sipping beer and smiling.

When their drinks arrived, I took the chance to put my lips to Ham's ear.

"I'm sorry," I whispered there.

"I take it they're your friends," he whispered in mine.

"Yeah."

"Then don't be, baby. We'll finish later."

"Okay."

I pulled away but he caught me with his arm around my shoulders, pulled me back, and touched his mouth to mine.

When he let me go, we settled back and my eyes went to Nina.

She was sipping her martini.

When she placed the drink back on the table, her eyes were dancing on me and she said, "Told you."

It hit me then. She knew why Ham was pissed about the vibrator usage.

I smiled at her and replied, "You so totally did."

*　　*　　*

Nina was halfway through her martini and we were all the way through our bread basket when she leaned toward Ham and me.

"I know you think we're rude—" she started.

"That's because we *are* rude," Max murmured. Nina sent him a killing glance, to which Max grinned at her. She rolled her eyes and then looked back at us.

"But, I'm sure you know this, Greg is here," she finished.

"I noticed," I told her.

"And Kami," she told me.

"I know," I told her.

"When I saw that, we had to come over and interrupt. You needed reinforcements. Trust me, things can go bad at The Rooster," she stated gravely.

I found this intriguing, but before I could ask, Nina's eyes darted to the side and up and she inquired, "Can I help you?"

"No," my aunt snapped from where she stood beside our table.

I tensed. Ham went solid. I even sensed Nina and Max tensing.

"Walk away," Ham growled.

I looked to the side to see Ham's head tipped back to scowl at Dahlia Cinders, my maiden aunt, who had a black soul, a nasty mouth, a heart of stone, and a flair for drama.

She looked like she always looked, except older. Perfectly creased trousers. Flouncy blouse. Appropriate jewelry, all of it quality, none of it ostentatious. Now-fully-gray hair swept back in a not unattractive bun but, knowing her, nothing was attractive. Brown eyes that didn't hide she was mean as a snake.

She ignored his words but not him.

"Heard you were back in town. Heard you installed her back under your roof," she noted.

"Walk away," Ham repeated.

She again ignored him and went on. "Clearly she didn't learn the first time, good riddance to bad rubbish."

Nina gasped.

Max grunted.

My breath caught.

"Walk...the fuck...away," Ham snarled.

"Excuse me, I don't know you or why you're suddenly here, but we're trying to enjoy a nice night out," Nina butted in. "Please, make a choice and do it swiftly. You can do as Mr. Reece says or I'm calling the manager."

My aunt turned her venomous eyes to Nina. "I have a few words to say to my niece."

Nina didn't even blink but her back went straight.

She'd never met them but I'd told her. She knew all about my family.

"So write them down on nice notepaper and use our trusty postal service to deliver them," Nina retorted.

"Oh fuck," Max muttered, getting close and curling an arm around his wife's waist.

"Nice language," Aunt Dahlia snapped.

Max looked at her a moment, then, weirdly, grinned.

"Excuse me!" Nina hissed. "That's my husband you're talking to."

"He has a foul mouth," Aunt Dahlia returned.

"Better that than foul manners," Nina shot back.

This was semiamusing but mostly scary and it got scarier when Ham slid out of the booth, got close to Aunt Dahlia, looked down at her, his scary-scarier-scariest face unamused and entirely pissed-off, and he rumbled menacingly, "I said, walk...*the fuck*...away."

"Is there a problem here?"

Oh hell.

That was Greg.

"You," Aunt Dahlia sneered at my ex-husband. "I know who you are. Her one shot at respectability and you scrape her off? What, did she cheat on you?"

Greg ignored her, looked to me, and asked, "Are you all right?"

"This is my Aunt Dahlia," I stated as answer.

"I know. You pointed her out at the festival three years ago," Greg replied.

"So, obviously, no. I'm not all right, seeing as I'm choking on Cinders-infected air," I returned.

Greg looked at Aunt Dahlia. "You need to leave."

"I already told her that," Ham growled.

Greg ignored Ham like he didn't exist and said to Aunt Dahlia, "I'll ask the manager to have you removed."

"Since I dine here once a month, I doubt he'll choose removing me over removing the lot of you." She twirled her finger in the air to indicate us all.

"Do you think," Nina started and I looked at her to see her looking at Max, "that this is normal? I mean, does this kind of thing happen to other people in the world? I really want to know."

Max smiled at his wife.

I looked back at Aunt Dahlia to see, scarily, she was looking at me. "You need to phone your father."

"No, she doesn't."

This was said by Kami Maxwell.

I leaned forward and plonked my forehead on the table.

"Kami," Max said in a warning tone. "Stay out of it."

"The staff is excellent when they're serving food," Nina remarked irritably. "They disappear during drama. Where are they? I really want to know."

"Don't you call your father, Zara," Kami ordered.

I lifted my forehead off the table and aimed my eyes at Max's sister, a pleasantly plump, female rendition of her brother, which was to say she had great eyes, fantastic dark, wavy hair, and very attractive features.

"That's not a worry, honey. I've conditioned my body to spontaneously combust if I get six digits in," I told her.

"I don't find you amusing," Aunt Dahlia snapped.

"I don't give a shit," I shot back.

"Excuse me." Greg had hold of the arm of one of the waiters. "Can you please send the manager over here?"

"Of course," she muttered before she quickly scurried away.

"You're a mean old bitch," Kami said to my aunt, "and I've been bein' nice for a real long time."

Nina's eyes cut to me and got huge, eloquent indication that I agreed with that Kami's brand of "bein' nice" was not agreed on by all.

Kami kept talking.

"And these boys here won't want to get in a smackdown with a nasty old woman. But not me. I got no problem doin' that. So if you don't walk away, I've got enough bitch stored up, I'm aimin' it all at you, startin' with throwin' Nina's drink in your face."

At this, Nina slid her drink out of reach.

"Then," Kami went on, "if you, that snake of a brother of yours, or his sniveling wife get anywhere near Zara, phone her, or attempt to get in touch with her in any way, I'm unleashing all holy hell on all your asses until you beg for forgiveness or move to another state."

"Is there a problem here?" A mild-mannered-looking suited man I suspected was the manager entered the situation.

"No, I'm simply having a word with my niece," my aunt replied.

"Yes, this woman interrupted my wife's dinner in an extremely unpleasant way," Greg contradicted.

"She's not your wife," Ham grunted.

Uh-oh.

Shocking the crap out of me, Greg, with narrowed eyes and anger contorting his face, instantly fired back at Ham, "She'll *always* be my wife."

I went still. The table went still. I fancied the restaurant went still as I was pretty certain I watched ice form in a thick layer, crackling and groaning all around Ham.

"Well shit." His words were sarcastic but that didn't mean they weren't dripping icicles. "See I'm in a position to apologize since I fucked your wife against the wall before we left to come here."

This was when I plonked my head on the table again.

"Oh my," Nina breathed as she glanced at Max. "We haven't done that in a while, darling. We should do that again."

"Gross," Kami said.

"Foul," Aunt Dahlia snapped.

"I'm never comin' to The Rooster again," Max declared.

"Maybe we should take this outside," Greg suggested, and at the thought of Greg, five-nine and not having worked out since high school football, going up against Bruiser Ham, my head shot up.

"Stop it," I whispered and I felt all eyes come to me but I was looking at Greg. "This was gonna happen, either for you or for me. It was always gonna be unpleasant. I cannot fathom why you'd make it more so," I told him.

He knew what I meant. His face blanched, his eyes went contrite, but I looked at Aunt Dahlia.

"I'm never calling my father. I have nothing to say to him and he has nothing to say that I want to hear. You also don't have anything to say that I want to hear. I can't imagine after all that went down nearly a decade ago how you'd have the gall to walk up to my table, badmouth my man, and be all-around nasty but you did it. You did it well. Congratulations. Now, please, go away."

She sniffed, opened her mouth to say something, but I quickly looked to Ham.

"Please, darlin', sit down. They don't exist. This is our night. We're enjoyin' it with friends. Let's get back to doin' that."

Ham hesitated a beat before he slid in beside me.

I looked at Kami.

"Thanks for comin' to my rescue but it's all good now."

Kami didn't move, crossed her arms on her chest, and glared at Aunt Dahlia.

Aunt Dahlia shot her a look that only a shield of orneriness as world-class as Kami's could save her from bursting into flames and then Aunt Dahlia flounced off.

"Zara—" Greg started. Ham tensed beside me and I quickly looked to Greg.

"Please, don't. I'll call you later," I said quietly.

He looked to me, avoided all other eyes, and took off.

"Nina, Max, always a blast," Kami said to her brother and sister-in-law. "Guy I don't know, you treat her like shit, I slash your tires," she said to Ham. "Zara, later," she said to me, and then she sauntered away.

"All right now?" the suited manager asked.

"Yes, no thanks to you," Nina answered on a snap.

"I'll have complimentary drinks sent to your table," he muttered, backing away.

"That will be good ... to start," Nina returned.

He disappeared.

I took in a deep breath.

Ham curled an arm around me and pulled me into his side.

"You okay, cookie?" he asked.

I tipped my head back to look at him.

"How are you with grilling steak?" I asked.

"You know the answer to that," he answered.

I did. He was the master. Outside grill. Fried in butter in a skillet. Broiled. You name it, he did it, and well.

"Next time, we eat in," I told him.

He grinned.

"Cookie. I like that," Nina murmured.

I looked to her and she smiled.

I relaxed into Ham's side.

His arm around me got tighter.

The rest of the restaurant melted away.

Only then did I smile back at Nina.

*   *   *

We were in Ham's bed, Ham on his back, me pressed to his side, my cheek to his shoulder, my hand resting on his chest.

I was exhausted. A day of a lot of great sex, good food, good drink, and, in the end, good company made me that way.

Nothing else happened after the incident with my aunt, Greg, and Kami, thank God, although I noticed that Max seemed a little standoffish with Ham but hid it behind his friendly Max ways. This melted after the appetizers and by the end of the night, luckily, everyone was getting on great and we had a good time.

But right then, as exhausted as I was, I knew sleep wouldn't find me. There was too much on my mind. What Ham told me. How sad it was. How angry it made me feel that those women treated him that way, most especially his bitch of a wife. The fact that we'd been interrupted and I was worried there was more. Greg on the whole and what I was going to do about him.

But mostly, my aunt.

I would know that Ham also had things on his mind when he rumbled into the dark, "Somethin's gotta be done about that ex of yours, cookie."

I pressed closer and promised, "I'll talk to him."

"That is not gonna happen."

His words surprised me so much I lifted my head and looked down at him in the dark.

"What?"

"I'll have words with that fuckwit."

I felt my body get tight. "Babe, he's not a fuckwit."

"Called you his wife. Got in my face," Ham laid out the evidence.

"See it from his perspective," I urged.

"Got in your face while you were at work."

He did do that, though I wouldn't call it "getting in my face."

However, it must be said. The evidence was pretty damning.

"He didn't wanna let me go," I whispered.

"Well, he did. Papers signed. Months passed. It's done. He needs to get the fuck over it and I'm gonna communicate that to him. You are not."

"I think it's best if I—"

I shut my mouth when he declared, "I stepped aside for him."

Yes, actually, he did.

Ham kept talking.

And, in doing so, melting my heart.

"Didn't want to do it, hated fuckin' doin' it, hated losin' you for three years, but I did it. For you. For you to have him. So that means for him to have you. I wasn't in the place to give you what you needed then but if I was, you made it plain, I coulda made things not so fuckin' easy for him. I didn't. Now you're mine. He needs to back the fuck off."

I loved that. All of it.

I still felt the need to protect Greg from Bruiser Ham.

"But you don't know him, Ham. I do. And seein' me with you had to hurt him tonight."

"Zara, you bein' you, actin' like you, lookin' like you, he's fuckin' lucky he hasn't seen you with someone else long before this. And I'm not happy your life was fucked but that doesn't change the fact I'm lucky your life was fucked so you didn't even think about findin' another guy or I would be fucked."

I loved that, too. A whole lot.

That didn't mean I didn't keep trying.

"Let me try talkin' to him first," I suggested.

He weirdly cut me off with, "Babe, your clothes in my closet?"

"Yes, but—"

"They are. You're mine. Two strikes, he doesn't get a third. Now I'm dealin' with him."

"That makes me uncomfortable, Ham," I shared.

"I get that. I get why. I get you got guilt. I get you got feelings for him. I also don't give a fuck about him. You're my woman out to dinner with me and he stands there in front of me and calls you his wife? No fuckin' way. No one stakes their claim to what's mine, not behind my back, not across a room, and especially not to my face without a conversation."

That was when I knew I was right about Ham.

When it was no promises, no expectations, he was fair enough to give the same in return.

When there were, what was his was his and he marked his territory.

I was also right about something else.

Possessiveness was *hot*.

"Go easy," I said quietly, giving in.

"We'll start with that and see how it goes," he replied.

I decided to leave it at that and settle in.

We were silent for a long while but I couldn't fall asleep and I knew Ham couldn't either, so I laid something else on my mind on him.

"I'm worried about my aunt comin' to the table and what Dad might have to say."

I was worried even though I suspected I knew.

I'd been waiting. Waiting for years.

That didn't mean I *wanted* to know and wasn't worried about finding out.

"Put it out of your head," Ham ordered.

He, I knew, suspected, too.

"I'm not sure I can do that," I admitted.

He moved his hand to my face, fingers gliding along my cheek, through my hair, and he finished by wrapping his arm around me so I was snug in both.

"You made the decision to turn your back on that, cookie. We talked it out then and I still think you did the right thing. It was either they succeeded in destroyin' your sister or they got a shot at bringing the both of you down. They destroyed your sister. Even if it's not done, it's still done. We got you to the place of understandin' that. Don't give her the chance to drag you back in."

He was right. He was right back then when he guided me to that decision and he was right now.

I sighed.

Ham's arms gave me a squeeze.

"We need to finish our chat," I told him.

"We will, baby," he told me. "Though, not much left to say."

At least that was good.

I pressed even closer and whispered, "I'm sorry those women treated you that way."

"Me too," he agreed.

"Just sayin', serious, no joke, we have what wc have now or even what we had before, if we made a baby and I was carrying it inside me, no way I'd ever let it go."

I just got out the *O* sound in "go" when his arms got so tight, I was forced to slide up his chest and my lungs constricted, seeing as he was squeezing the breath out of me.

Therefore, I wheezed, "Ham."

He pulled me up his chest, his arms relaxed, and he slid one hand into my hair, bringing my mouth down to touch it to his.

When he let me lift away, he whispered, his voice jagged, "Thank you, Zara."

That meant a lot to him and it meaning a lot meant a lot to me, seeing as I clearly said the right thing and that was what I hoped I'd do.

"You're welcome, darlin'," I whispered back.

He shifted me back down his chest, his hand at my head settling my cheek back to his shoulder and ordering, "Go to sleep, baby."

"Okay. 'Night, Ham."

" 'Night, cookie."

I closed my eyes and tried to find sleep. After a while, I needed to move so I rolled, Ham rolled with me, bringing up his knees and mine and holding me close around my belly so we were spooning.

I felt his face in my hair and heard his voice murmur, "Softest hair I ever felt."

I felt my lips curl up, I snuggled my ass in his groin, and then I fell asleep.

CHAPTER TEN

Written in Blood

Reece

REECE DID NOT fall asleep when Zara did.

He didn't fall asleep at all.

And when his alarm clock showed seven thirty, he carefully slid away from her and moved out of bed.

Silently, he got dressed. Moving slowly so he wouldn't wake her, he grabbed his boots and went to put them on in the living room.

His girl slept deep and they'd gone to bed late, but he didn't take any chances with her getting up, finding him not there and wondering where he was. He left her a note in the kitchen saying he was getting something from town. He then went to her purse, found her cell, found her ex's number, and programmed it into his phone.

Then he went to his truck.

He drove into town and parked outside the police station. Slamming his door, he walked up the steps to the wooden boardwalk that served as a sidewalk along both sides the length of the main street of Gnaw Bone, making it look Wild West, which, in its day, it was.

He walked into the station seeing a woman at the desk, and standing at her side, a tall, fit man who nevertheless had a slight paunch over the big belt buckle he was wearing. If memory served, and for Reece it usually did, the man's name was Shaughnessy and he was a cop. He was wearing jeans and a flannel shirt, and it was likely he hadn't yet gotten around that morning to putting his badge on his belt.

Reece walked up to the front desk and the lady asked, "Can I help you?"

Before Reece could answer, Shaughnessy butted in. "Reece, right? New top dog at The Dog."

Reece looked to him to see the man's eyes sharp on Reece but there was a small smile on his face that was genuine.

"Yep," Reece replied. Shaughnessy leaned in with a hand raised and Reece took it. "Shaughnessy, right?" Reece asked to confirm.

"Mick," the man said after giving Reece's hand a deliberate, manly squeeze. Not too firm to make it a contest, nowhere near weak either, and Reece returned the gesture. "I got a title, which means I'm top dog around here, but no one uses it. Everyone just calls me Mick. You're welcome to do the same."

Friendly, approachable, the title didn't matter. The job did.

It was then Reece remembered he liked this guy.

"All right, Mick," Reece agreed.

To Reece's surprise, Mick invited, "'Spect, this early, you could use some coffee. Why don't you come around?"

He hadn't expected this to be that easy.

Then again, he'd chosen Gnaw Bone because people were that easy, his woman being one of them.

But even if Gnaw Bone wasn't so friendly, he still would have come for Zara.

He followed Mick to a coffeepot in a common area. Mick poured and slid the sugar Reece's way. Reece took care of his mug, Mick took care of his, and then Mick looked to him.

"Why don't we have a sit down in my office?" Mick asked.

Reece lifted his chin and followed Mick into an office that looked like the man who used it had not only been there a while, but also, he was busy.

"Jane, our girl up front, wants to tidy up. I just don't let her. If she did, I wouldn't know where anything was," Mick explained the mess as he rounded his desk and sat down, flicking his hand at the three chairs across from it. "Take a load off, son."

Reece did, took a sip of coffee, and trained his eyes on the cop.

Before he could say a word, Mick smiled and stated, "Glad you came down. Best we get things ironed out between us before we gotta iron them out during a situation. Been meanin' to come speak with you, things got in the way. Glad you reached out and beat me to it."

Reece felt his brows draw together as he replied, "Not followin'."

"The Dog," Mick returned. "Been around years, Reece, as you probably know from the last time you were in Gnaw Bone. Know things can get rowdy there. Know past management of The Dog preferred to deal with things on their own. It's good you know now that I don't turn the other cheek, son, not ever. But if the parties involved are good with walkin' away without callin' a cruiser, I'm good with that, long's there's no coercion for them to come to that decision, no weapons involved, and no lengthy hospital stays. You with me on this?"

He was talking about fights at The Dog and how he wanted them handled.

Reece had been handling bar fights for twenty-two years. He usually handled them by stopping them before they started. If that didn't work, he'd do it Shaughnessy's way.

So Reece told him, "I can agree on that. But that's not why I'm here."

It was then Mick's brows drew together. He took a sip of coffee as he cleared his features.

Then he asked, "So, son, why're you here?"

"Zara Cinders is livin' with me," Reece said as answer and Mick nodded but it wasn't lost on Reece that Mick's eyes grew even sharper.

Zara was liked. This was not a surprise. She was extremely likeable and she'd been around Gnaw Bone since birth so most everyone knew just how much there was to like.

Zara was also protected and this was also not a surprise. Kids who came from families like hers, if the town gave a shit, tended to be that way, too.

"Yeah. Hear you gave her a job, got her out of those apartments," Mick said. "Good owners. Just lazy. Keep tellin' 'em they should do somethin' about their locks and peepholes before somethin' not good happens and they keep tellin' me they'll get around to it. Zara, she's a good gal. Well-liked. Glad you got her out of there and in a job where she can get back on her feet."

"You don't understand me," Reece said. "She's livin' with me, as in she's mine."

Mick had no response but Reece again saw the man's already acute attention that he hid behind his good-ol'-boy ways get even more acute.

Reece didn't need a response.

He kept talking.

"Came in 'cause we were at The Rooster last night and Dahlia Cinders dropped by our table. She told Zara she had to speak to her father. This conversation did not go well, no information was shared, and it was, thankfully, brief. Zara's worried, though. 'Spect, you know what went down, you know why she is. I'm wonderin' if there's somethin' I need to know. That way I can cushion the blow when it's time that she does know. And I figure, the person who knows the most around this town is you."

There was a hint of surprise in his eyes when Mick asked, "Her father hasn't called her?"

"They don't speak," Reece explained.

"Yes, I know, but..." Mick trailed off, looked to his desk, took a sip of coffee, then looked back at Reece. "I'm sorry to be the one to tell you this, son, and I'm sorry that you're the one's gonna have to tell Zara. But, two days ago, Xenia passed away."

Just as he thought.

Reece's eyes slid to look out the window as his lips muttered, "Shit, fuck."

Nearly nine years ago, Xenia Cinders got high at the same time she got drunk. For reasons known only to her, and locked away now for near on a decade, she left her house, wandered into the street, and was hit by a car.

The car wasn't going that fast. Her body took some damage but not much. But luck that didn't shine often on the Cinders girls didn't shine on Xenia that night. The hit she took meant she landed with all her weight and a goodly amount of momentum on her head. The head trauma was extreme and irreparable.

She was brain dead.

Unfortunately, her body didn't know that.

Also, unfortunately, for a reason in the beginning but after that reason was no longer a reason it ended up being just plain stubborn cruelty, even though Zara had begged her parents to turn off the machines and let her go, they'd refused.

So now Xenia had lived an extra nine years without lifting a finger, blinking an eye, eating a bite of food, enjoying a drink, or actually living at all.

"You know anything about it, you know it's a blessing," Mick said quietly and Reece looked back at him.

"Not sure Zara's gonna look at it like that."

"I can see that." His eyes grew sharp again. "You care about her though, son, enough to make her yours, you'll guide her to that."

This, they didn't need. Reece had just got her back. They had shit to talk about, shit to do, and he wanted his girl to have it easy for a while. It'd been bad for her for too long. He'd guided her out. She was in a good place, close to happy.

They didn't need this, but more, Zara didn't.

Reece clenched his teeth, felt a muscle move in his cheek, and released his jaw to say, "Least they got that boy in a good home."

"Sorry, son?" Mick asked.

Reece locked eyes with the man. "'Spect you know, maybe you don't, but Xavier Cinders had no problem takin' his hand to his wife *or* his girls. Didn't do it often, used words most the time to make them feel shit, but he did it. Xenia got the worst of it but that didn't mean he didn't call Zara down to watch when her sister caught it. So it's good that when they finally got that baby out of Xenia, Cinders put him up for adoption."

Shaughnessy looked confused. "Zander Cinders is in a private school not too far from here, Reece. Xavier didn't put that child up for adoption. His sister, Wilona, just in the next county, has raised him since birth."

What the fuck?

"Are you fuckin' shittin' me?" Reece growled and he heard his voice. He suspected he knew what his face looked like and he suspected both were why Mick Shaughnessy straightened to alert in his chair.

"Son—"

"That motherfucker promised Zara he would put Xenia's boy up for adoption, make sure he got a good home."

"Reece—"

"I stood there when they came to the only agreement they came to durin' that mess. When he flat refused to let Zara raise him, he promised he wouldn't raise the boy. He promised he'd put that boy in a good home."

"It would appear he didn't lie, since he didn't raise him, but he did lie since he took custody of the child and placed him with his sister," Mick replied carefully.

"So you're tellin' me Zara's nephew has been growin' up in the next goddamned county for the last nine fuckin' years without him knowin' his aunt exists and without her knowin' her sister's boy is that close?" Reece ground out.

"I'm afraid that's what I'm tellin' you," Mick answered.

"All right, so now you wanna tell me why Zara doesn't know this?" Reece asked.

"I thought she did."

"Well, she doesn't," Reece pointed out the obvious. "This town is small and the people close. How does she not know this?"

"The Cinders aren't exactly social," Mick stated the God's honest truth. "The town rallied around Zara when all that happened, Reece. Not sure I know of anyone who gave their condolences to her folks, not that they wouldn't want to, just that they knew it wouldn't be welcomed so they didn't bother. What I'm sayin' is, not sure anyone knows where Zander is."

"Can I ask why you didn't tell her?" Reece pushed.

Emotion flashed in Mick's eyes before he answered, "Like I said, I thought she knew. Didn't bring it up because she essentially lost her sister and her parents through that and that's not somethin' you wanna bring up as a reminder for a sweet girl who kept her chin up and kept on keepin' on."

Fucking shit. That made sense.

"Shit, fuck," Reece clipped.

"Think you need to take a calming breath, son," Mick advised and Reece did exactly that before he looked out the window again.

However, the calming breath didn't work.

Therefore, he bit off, "I do not believe this shit."

Mick made no reply and the room lapsed into an uneasy silence before Mick broke it.

"Xavier took his hands to those girls?"

Reece sliced his eyes to the cop. "Repeatedly."

Mick closed his eyes, whispering, "Dear Lord."

"No marks, he wasn't stupid. But that didn't mean they didn't get their asses kicked," Reece shared and Mick opened his eyes. "I'm surprised you didn't know that," he finished.

"Didn't 'spect Xavier was a warm and loving father, way those girls cleared out when they hit majority and just knowin' the man, but didn't suspect that."

"Well, you were right. He was neither warm nor loving and he took that to extremes," Reece confirmed.

"Sins of the fathers," he muttered.

"Explain that," Reece demanded.

"Went to school with Xavier Cinders and his sisters, Dahlia and Wilona. Can't tell you how many times I saw one, the other, or all 'a them come to school with black eyes, fat lips, arms in slings. Back then, before school officials would report that to authorities and CPS would get called in, there was no help for them. Val Cinders was a hard man and the whole town knew it, just no one had the power to do anything about it. Reckon he taught his son to be just as hard. Sometimes the cycle breaks. Sometimes it doesn't."

"With Xavier, it didn't," Reece told him.

"I see that," Mick replied.

"And now that boy's livin' in that."

"We don't know that," Mick said quickly. "Maybe, by givin' him to Wilona, he was breakin' the cycle."

Reece felt his eyes narrow. "He lied to his daughter while his other daughter was near on nine months pregnant, brain dead, hooked up to machines, and lyin' in a hospital bed. He wasn't breaking any cycle."

"I remember that situation, Reece," Mick said quietly

and Reece knew he did. By the look on his face, he knew he remembered it like it was yesterday.

Then again, fucked-up shit like that wasn't easy to forget.

"This can't stand," Reece declared.

"Son," Mick started. "As Xenia's parents with no other legal arrangements in place, custody fell to them. I knew there was no love lost between Zara and her family and since not a lot of folks around here like anyone who lives in that den of vipers and give them a wide berth, I just suspected that he was an ass to her like he is to everyone. It's sorry news he took his hand to his girls and you gotta know I don't like hearin' it. But, I'll remind you, it's beyond the pale where Xenia took that. She got high *and* drunk when she was nearly full-term pregnant."

"She'd been clean for two years," Reece reminded him.

"She picked a sorry time to fall off the wagon," Mick returned.

"She'd been visited by her father that day," Reece told him and watched him suck in a hissing breath. "Yeah. I can see you can imagine that visit was cheery."

Mick's brows went up. "He take his hands to her?"

"That asshole who, according to him, has done no wrong in his life visiting his unmarried, ex-junkie pregnant daughter? Yeah, Mick, he took his hand to her. She was a vegetable lyin' in that bed but I still saw the bruise on her cheek. If you saw her, you couldn't have missed it."

"I thought she got that from getting hit by the car," Mick muttered.

"She got it when her father planted his fist in his nine-months pregnant daughter's face. After his visit, Xenia called Zara, lettin' her know that shit went down and Zara spent the day with her sister, talkin' her down from doin' somethin' stupid. But Zara had to go to work and Xenia did somethin' stupid."

Mick nodded.

Reece kept going.

"You don't hit kids, you don't hit women, and you only hit men when they give you call to do it. What would move a man to strike a pregnant woman is beyond me but he did it. Then again, he did the same to his baby girls and we could argue all day which one of those is more twisted with no answers since they're equally fucked up."

"This is true," Mick murmured.

Reece went on. "Xenia told Zara she got flashbacks, terrified of the state of her life, havin' a kid, not breakin' that cycle, not able to get away from that motherfucker. Zara left, shit kept twisting in Xenia's brain, and she made very wrong decisions that means she's been alive for a long time, same time she was good as dead. Think she paid a high price for her dick of a father bein' an asshole so, due respect, maybe you'll have a care, shiftin' blame to a dead woman."

Mick lifted his chin to acknowledge the rebuke but stated, "We're goin' over history."

"History doesn't live and breathe and that boy is doin' both one county over," Reece fired back.

Shaughnessy locked eyes with him.

Reece kept talking.

"Zara was in no place financially to fight them for custody. She was twenty-fuckin'-four years old and workin' nights, waitin' tables at a bar. She'd started with nothin' and worked her ass off since she was eighteen for everything she had. Not to mention, she had their promise that they'd find a good home for her sister's son."

"Not sure what either you or I can do about that. We can't rewrite history," Mick noted.

Reece stood and looked down at the man. "Yeah. You're absolutely right. But we can write the future and that chapter's gonna be written in blood."

Mick stood too and warned softly, "Son, you're talkin' to an officer of the law."

"Then you want this to go smooth, you start pokin' around, 'cause Zander Cinders is gonna be livin' with his aunt as soon's I can pull that shit off and it'd help if you did what you could do to see that kid out of that viper's den," Reece returned, putting his mug down on Shaughnessy's desk. "Obliged for the coffee," he muttered. Turning on his boot, he stalked out of his office.

When he left the station, he didn't go to his truck. He walked down the boardwalk, fury and adrenalin coursing energy through his frame that he had to burn off because it felt like his fucking head was going to explode.

His thoughts were assaulting him, an onslaught that caused a piercing pain to shoot through his right eye.

Zara was going to lose her mind when she found out her nephew was that close, being raised by a Cinders. He'd just guided her to getting it all together and now, fuck it, it was going to come flying apart.

He hated that for his girl but that wasn't what sent that pain stabbing through his eye.

He'd left her.

Back then, after that shit went down and he got her to the other side, he'd left.

Because of his own fucked-up history, his vow not to get tied to another woman, not to get tied to *anything*, he'd walked away from her.

He knew he'd go back. Even at that age, Zara was the kind of woman you went back to. Hell, even back then, Reece knew she was the kind of woman you *stuck* to. He just wasn't that kind of man back then and that was why he let her go, so she could have a man like that.

But he never knew he'd be where he was right then and *go back*.

It was no consolation that the baby had been taken by C-section by that time. The deal struck. Zara getting out of her end the knowledge her nephew would go to a couple who wanted a child desperately and couldn't have one so they'd treat the one they got right and a promise from her father and mother that she'd never see or speak to them again.

He'd had no idea that baby was handed off to an aunt.

He'd just taken Zara's pulse, saw she was moving on, healing, and he'd left.

He'd fucking *left*.

He could see it in his head, the image burning deep, that first good-bye, standing by his truck, her in his arms, smiling her sweet smile, her pretty brown eyes sad that he was going but understanding that was him. Giving him that. Giving him up. Letting him be who he was and taking him as he came.

He'd been her one. It took him years to realize she was his.

And she'd let him go so he could be who he had to be.

And he'd let her go so he could be a motherfucking asshole.

His girl, his cookie, abused by her father for as long as she could remember, having a mother who was so checked out, it was a wonder that bitch wasn't in a coma, too. Zara had broken away, forged a life for herself. Then when her sister essentially bites it, the baby Zara was looking forward to helping Xenia raise gone, she found it in her to move on and start to heal.

He told himself he could go. She was strong.

What really happened was he told himself what he had to hear so he could cover his own ass, deny the depth of feeling he had for a woman, and run away from history so he wouldn't have to learn one day she was a bitch like all the rest.

Even if she had given him no indication whatsoever she would be. There were no signs. No red flags.

Nothing.

He just left her.

The fury not subsiding, he wanted to punch something, and on that thought, mindlessly scanning as he beat back the pain in his head and tried to breathe through the weight in his chest, his eyes fell on a sign.

The instant they did, his feet took him there.

He walked through the door and saw that Nina Maxwell's law offices weren't swank but they were comfortable and understatedly plush. They were also professional. They were such that you walked in and instantly felt whoever worked there could sort your shit.

For it being such a shit day, it was still his lucky day because there was a receptionist behind the desk and Nina was standing at her side.

Both of their eyes came to him, Nina's immediately concerned, the receptionist's welcoming.

"Can I help you?" the receptionist asked.

"I know him, Nance," Nina murmured to her receptionist as she walked around the desk, a welcoming smile on her lips but it was wary. "Reece, this is a surprise."

Her eyes were scanning his face and he knew what she saw seeing as he wasn't hiding it.

"You got a second?" he asked when she stopped close.

Her head tipped to the side. "I'll make one."

"Neens, I'm sorry, but you have an eight-thirty appointment," the receptionist reminded her and Nina looked to her at the same time she wrapped her fingers around Reece's bicep and moved them to a side hall.

"Do me a favor. When they arrive, get them coffee and ask them to wait a spell. I'll try not to take long," Nina told the receptionist and led Reece into the hall.

She dropped his arm, guided them to a door, and moved them through to an office with a decent view of the mountains and the biggest desk he'd ever seen in his life.

He heard the door click and Nina ask, "Is Zara okay?"

Reece turned to watch her walk to the desk, not behind it, in front of it where she leaned her hips against the edge. She wasn't assuming a position of authority or dominance. Her position was open, friendly; this was a chat among friends.

Said a lot about her.

What said more was that she wore a tight skirt, stylish blouse, sexy spike-heeled pumps, and nice jewelry that added personality to a sexy but professional package. She wasn't a knockout but she was very pretty and with that hair, those eyes, those clothes, all of it screaming high-maintenance, she was a challenge many men would accept.

But getting to know her last night, she was a whole lot more. Nina was so goddamned smart it was borderline scary and she was able to speak her mind. A fact she'd demonstrated repeatedly.

In other words, not easy. Not even close. Attractive. Sexy. Stimulating. Cute as all fuck.

But not easy.

Reece knew it'd take a man like her husband to accept that challenge. And watching them together last night, Holden Maxwell lucked out he got hold of that spitfire and his wife lucked out she'd landed a man who got off on her not-unappealing brand of shit.

"She is now," he answered. "She's sleepin'. In a couple hours, she will not be."

"I'm assuming you care to explain that since you're here," she noted in her also not-unappealing voice with its English accent.

"And I'm assumin' with you two thick as thieves last night that you're tight with my woman," Reece returned.

She nodded. "We're close, yes."

"Then you know about her dad and her sister."

"Yes," she replied.

"All about it?"

"Yes, Reece."

"Do you *know* about her dad?" Reece pushed.

It sounded like the same question, but if she knew, she'd know it wasn't.

She studied him carefully. It took her a moment to trust him and he saw her body go tight with awareness before she spoke cautiously.

"If you mean about the physical and mental abuse, then . . . yes."

"I mean that," Reece confirmed.

Nina nodded.

"You know her sister was pregnant?"

Her face softened, sadness came into her eyes, and she replied, "Yes, Reece, I know that, too."

Zara had shared, which meant she was still torn up about her nephew.

Back then, he'd held her as she cried. They'd stayed up past dawn, drinking beer, shooting vodka, and processing what she was going to do about it and, when she came to the realization she had no money and no power, he'd helped her accept that. Helped her accept her sister might still be breathing with the aid of machines, but she was still gone. Then he'd helped her figure out how she would move on.

And she had moved on.

But looking at Nina, he knew she also hadn't.

"Xavier Cinders, Zara's father, did not put that boy up for adoption. He placed him with his sister one county over. And right now, I'm hiring you to start proceedings to get custody of her nephew."

He kept talking through her gasp as she straightened away from the desk and her eyes got big.

When he was done talking, she asked, "He didn't put him up for adoption?"

"No, he did not."

"Oh my God," she breathed.

"Yeah," Reece agreed. "Now you know that, you and me gotta get down to it. Life I led, didn't need money, made it and saved it so I had a lot of it. Coupla months ago, Zara's old house came up to auction from the bank. I bought it."

Her mouth dropped open.

Reece ignored that and kept talking.

"Needed cash to make that buy, used nearly all I had. So we'll need you to help us out and let us pay installments."

"I…you…of course, but"—her mouth quirked—"you bought her house?"

"Appreciate if you don't tell her that. It's taken some time for her to sort out her head, we just got where I want us to be. We still got things to get through, we need time to get used to each other again, and I'd like to ask her to marry me there, so it would suck, you fucked that surprise."

She shook her head quickly side to side. "I…no, I would—" She stopped abruptly to swallow a giggle, and then she went on. "I would never do that, Reece."

"Obliged," he muttered. "Now, this kid's name is Zander Cinders. I know he's in a private school one county over and he's with a woman named Wilona. Her maiden name will be Cinders but I don't know if she's married. I learned this shit from Mick, so you might wanna have a chat with him. But whatever legal shit you gotta do to start this ball rollin', do it. I'll be in with Zara after I break this news and some other fucked-up shit she's gotta know."

"What other fucked-up shit?" Nina asked and Reece drew in a deep breath.

His voice was quieter when he said, "Her sister finally passed."

Nina closed her eyes.

"Yeah," Reece murmured.

Nina opened her eyes.

"Poor Zara," she whispered.

"Give me the day, but, you got time, come around tonight. She won't be workin'. She just got the day off. But I'll have to go in, at least for a little while, and it'd be good she wasn't alone while I'm gone."

She immediately reached to a cell on her desk. "We'll exchange numbers so you can call me if she doesn't and I can call you to check to see if she's okay without disturbing her."

"Thanks," he muttered. They exchanged numbers as he continued. "You got any idea why your sister-in-law would run interference on Zara learnin' about her sister?"

"I don't right now but I will as soon as she picks up her phone," Nina replied.

He figured that was true. He suspected Nina Maxwell didn't let anyone in her life get away with shit.

And he was hoping that she did the same thing professionally.

"You're asking her to marry you?"

Fucking shit.

He didn't want to discuss this with a woman he barely knew and a good friend of his girl's.

"Yeah," he said shortly.

"Please take no offense, you know Zara and I are close. She means a lot to me, she's a good friend, she watches our kids." She pulled in a breath, then laid it on him. "Are you sure you're ready to settle down?"

Reece held her eyes.

He didn't answer to anyone. Spent years not doing that. Hated doing that shit. He didn't like her question and, eight months ago, he would walk right out the door without answering it.

But this was Zara's girl.

So he answered it.

"I knew when I drove away from her the first time, I

shouldn't be doin' it. I knew when I let her walk away from me three and a half years ago, it struck deep. I found out she lost her house, I sunk everything I had into buying it back. Never owned a piece of property in my life. Was once tied to a woman but never owned a house. Got myself loose from that woman and learned. What I learned after years was how to spot a good one. And what I learned seven months ago was that I was never gonna watch a good one walk away again. So yeah. I'm sure about settlin' down and I'll answer the question you didn't ask. I'm also sure about Zara."

Nina was silent and held his eyes through all that.

When he was done, she remained silent.

Then, slowly, her eyes lit, and she smiled.

And when she did, she smiled huge.

* * *

After finishing with Nina, Reece walked to his truck, angled in, and slammed the door.

Then he pulled out his phone, tamped down his still coursing anger, found the name, and hit go.

It rang three times before a man answered, his voice guarded. "Hello?"

"Greg, this is Reece, Zara's man, and before you get pissed and hang up, I just found out Xenia passed away two days ago."

To this he got silence.

So he spoke through the silence.

"It's fucked up I'm tellin' you before I tell Zara but once I tell her, I'm gonna need to be there for her so I won't have time to deal with you."

"Deal with me?" Greg asked, his voice unsteady and Reece didn't know why, anger or emotion for Zara about her sister.

Since Reece didn't give a fuck about this guy, it didn't matter.

"Deal with you," he confirmed. "I talk straight and I don't

got a lot of time so suck it up, man, 'cause here it is. Last night was fucked up. When you came to the bar was fucked up. Zara knows I'm gonna be doin' this, havin' this conversation with you, but she doesn't like it. That's because she cares about you. If you give a shit about her at all and want her in your life in the limited way you can have her, you end this shit. Now. You want to piss on my patch, we got problems. You followin' me?"

"Sorry, I'm still back at Xenia dying. I'm finding it hard to keep up through your threats," the fuckwit replied.

"Right, it's good you brought that up because I should make that clear. These aren't threats, Greg. When you pull that shit, it guts her. I'm not gonna let you do that and I'll find a way to make sure you stop. The way I'd prefer it to be is if you'd give the tiniest fuckin' shit about her and not make me do that because I got no problem fuckin' you up, but if I gotta go outta my way and lay the hurt on you that would fuck *her* up. *Now* are you followin' me?"

"It guts her?" he asked quietly.

"I don't know you so I don't know if you sound happy because you can do that to her or pissed at yourself you're doin' it to her," Reece told him.

"I'm not happy I'm hurting, Zara. God," he clipped.

"Then stop doin' it," Reece returned.

This was again met with silence.

"I gotta go lay a different kind of hurt on Zara now, man, so tell me this was a productive conversation so I can get that over with for her," Reece prompted when the silence stretched on too long.

"I never wanted things to get ugly between us," Greg shared.

"You don't want that, stop doin' what you're doin'," Reece advised.

"It was just a shock, seeing her with you last night."

"I get that. So does she. Doesn't change the fact that you didn't play that right."

"I didn't think. I guess I was mad."

Jesus. What kind of guy was this guy?

"I'm sensin' we're comin' to a positive end to this discussion so I don't wanna piss you off, but I'm not your counselor. I'm your ex-wife's man. You need to process shit, do it with one of your boys. I got shit to do."

"Right, that was . . . I'm being . . ." He trailed off and before Reece could end this and get on with his shit day, Greg kept going. "I . . . this is weird to have to ask but, I mean, I probably should but, later, I'd like to call her. About Xenia."

"Give it time. I'm lettin' her sleep until she wakes up. Then I'll lay that on her."

"All right."

It was time to end this.

"Thanks for givin' a shit, Greg, now I gotta go," Reece stated.

"Of course. Right. I'll, um . . . call her later."

"Fantastic," Reece muttered, trying to squeeze the sarcasm out of his voice and hearing he failed. "Later."

"Later," Reece heard before he disconnected, tossed his phone on his dash, started his truck, and headed home.

CHAPTER ELEVEN

Worthy of You

I watched as the coffee mug smashed against the wall, coffee splashing everywhere.

Then I ran straight to the door of the kitchen.

I didn't get there.

An arm caught me at my belly, my breath went out of me in a whoosh, and I found myself going backward.

Ham pinned me against the counter, his front tight to mine, his hands on the counter on either side of me, his head tipped deep to me, his face full of pain.

For me.

"Calm down, baby," he whispered.

"My sister's dead," I whispered back.

"Stick with me, cookie."

"My sister's dead," I repeated.

"Zara. Honey. Stick with me."

"My sister's dead!" I shrieked, watched him wince, and dissolved into body-wracking, throat-burning, uncontrollable tears.

Ham's arms closed around me.

My legs gave out. I slid down his front and fell to the floor.

Ham came with me, shifting to his ass. His legs spread and cocked at the knees, he pulled me between them, my chest against his. He wrapped one of his arms around me tight. His other hand was in my hair, forcing my face into his neck.

I wrapped both of my arms around him, held strong, and sobbed.

I'd known this day would come. In the beginning I waited, *hoping* it would come. Last night I understood deep down that it actually *had* come.

Even so, I was totally unprepared for it.

Ham held me close for a long time and when my tears went from wild and uncontrolled to the kind that settled in for a long time, quieter and punctuated by hiccoughs, he moved. Getting to his feet and taking me with him, he lifted me cradled in his arms and carried me to the living room.

He sat on the couch and then stretched out, arranging me on top of him, all the while holding me close.

We settled silently and I focused on something else and that something else didn't make the tears go away.

"My nephew really lives with my aunt Wilona?" I asked.

"It's true, darlin'."

"My aunt is a bitch," I told him.

Ham had no response.

"He's been there for nine years."

Again no response from Ham.

"My dad's such a dick," I shared.

That got a response.

"That he is, cookie."

I pulled in a deep breath through my nose and on the exhale relaxed into him.

"I don't believe this," I whispered.

"I don't either, baby," Ham whispered back.

I put a hand in the couch at the back, lifted up, and used my other hand to swipe at my face as I looked down at him.

There was pain in his face still. Pain for me. But it was now mingled with sorrow.

Sorrow for me.

If I didn't already love this man, looking at his handsome face showing plain all the feelings he was feeling for me, I would have fallen in love.

But I loved this man. It was just that, right then, I loved him more.

"His name is Zander?" I asked.

"That's what Mick says," he answered.

My eyes drifted to the armrest his head was lying on and I remarked, "Dad named him. That's for sure. He got that shit from Grandpa Val. Crazy-ass names."

"Zara's the most beautiful name I ever heard," Ham stated and my eyes flew to him as my chest expanded. "He's a dick but he named you sweet, baby. And, you find a way not to give him credit, Zander is pretty kick-ass, too."

Right then, I loved Ham even more.

So much I couldn't express it and I couldn't cope with it, so I dropped my head so my forehead was resting on his chest.

"Now that you got your shit tight, cookie, I'll tell you the rest," Ham said.

"Oh God," I moaned into his chest.

He slid his hand to curl around the back of my neck. "This is the good part, darlin'."

I lifted up to look at him. "There's a good part?"

"Yeah. When I was in town, after I learned this shit, got pissed, had to walk it off. I saw Nina's offices, paid her a visit, and she made time for me."

I was confused. What did Nina have to do with anything?

"I don't get it," I told him.

Ham gave it to me.

"Hired her to start custody proceedings to get Zander."

My heart lurched before it swelled, hope pushing out anguish.

Back then, I'd wanted my sister's baby. With my sister all but gone, I wanted a piece of her, especially a precious piece that she'd made. We'd had it tough, we'd stuck together through it, and after we escaped, but when we got older, she fell apart. Drugs. Booze. Meaningless hookups. She went off the rails and did it with flair.

That didn't mean I didn't always love her.

Xenia returned the favor.

She pulled herself together, though that didn't mean she still didn't fuck up. With my help, we got her into a program. She said sayonara to the drugs and booze but unfortunately kept up with the meaningless hookups and got herself knocked up.

When she'd learned she was pregnant and decided to keep the baby, we'd both been cautiously excited, considering our history—especially hers. I was looking forward to having a nephew. I was looking forward to helping Xenia right past wrongs.

Then it all went to shit.

If I'd had the money, the stability, the maturity, and the strength to fight my dad back then, I would have taken Xenia's baby on. I didn't fool myself it wouldn't be tough but I wanted that piece of my sister and I wanted her, wherever she was, to know I was taking care of her boy.

But I also knew that couples without the ability to have babies could give him a life maybe better than the one I could give him. I also knew my dad would see me a quivering mess and beaten so low I couldn't stand before he gave up. And last, I feared that even if I won him, Dad would find ways to fuck with me, and the baby. I also knew the ways my father could fuck with someone, and none of them were pleasant.

So I hated it but I let him be put up for adoption.

To get him safe, in a good, stable home with good people who would love him, I struck the deal.

Now I had my second chance.

Then my heart plummeted because I might have maturity but the money and stability were in even more of a shambles than they'd been back then.

This wouldn't work.

"Nina's my friend and I know she'd do a lot for me, Ham," I started. "But I really do not have the resources to go after custody and there's no way I could take that kind of freebie from Nina. She didn't even handle my divorce, since she insisted on giving me a huge discount. You know me, I couldn't accept that. So Greg and I used her partner, George. Since I wanted the divorce, I intended to pay, but in the end,

Greg insisted on paying for all that. He wouldn't stand down and I was seriously struggling so I let him. Nina didn't say anything but I unintentionally screwed her with losing a client, which isn't cool."

"Zara—"

"And you know Dad. He'd fight it. Tooth and nail. I have no idea how he paid for the care Xenia received for nine years, since she had no insurance. He isn't loaded even though they're comfortable, or they were, and that had to cost a whack. But obviously he did it and he'll throw everything at me to make sure I don't get Xenia's son."

"Honey—"

"And I'm not sure how a judge will feel, with my credit history, me workin' at a bar. Nothin's changed since back then except, if anything, it's worse. I'm a divorcée and I wasn't even married but a couple of years. I lost a business. I had a house foreclosed on. I'm doin' better but Dad will throw all that at me. It'll get ugly and go on forever. And if I make the decision to drag a child through something like that, well…I might be able to start it but I gotta be able to see it through."

Ham shifted his hand to the side of my neck, his fingers tensed, and he ordered gently, "Zara, quiet for a second and listen to me."

"Okay," I agreed.

"I got a little money—"

I was quiet only for the second he asked when I interrupted with, "Ham—"

His fingers tensing deeper into my neck interrupted me.

"Baby, *listen*."

I shut my mouth and nodded.

Ham waited a beat to make sure I kept my mouth shut before he continued.

"It isn't much, the money I got, but I got it. Nina knows

this. She's gonna let us pay in installments. That said, I make a good salary. Brutal hours, lots of shit to deal with, they learned with management turnover high for the last decade, they get a good one in, they keep him by payin' him. We got low overhead, livin' together. It may make things tight for a while but it isn't gonna break us and it'll be worth it."

When he stopped and I knew he was done, I ventured, "Yes, Ham, but you were a rolling stone. I just got out of making a mess of my life. A judge will—"

"A judge will hear that your father beat you, your sister, and your mom and take that into account. Hospital reports on your sister will bear to the truth that she appeared battered upon admission and I know she got hit by a car, babe, but they know the difference between kinds of bruises and when a body gets 'em. There were some that weren't fresh. Your testimony, baby, seein' as she called you that day, you went over there, and she shared your dad paid a visit, and you know from history and experience he's not above that, makes a former rolling stone who's got a steady job and a good income and a woman who got caught in the bite of a bad recession that lots of folks got caught in not so bad. My guess, if we can convince a judge of that, no fuckin' way he'd allow decisions about where Zander was or wasn't to be made by your father."

This made me feel better.

What did not make me feel better was the fact that we were talking about gaining custody of a boy neither of us knew, raising him, and Ham and I had been an official couple for approximately thirty hours.

He hadn't told me all his history. We hadn't worked through that. We hadn't worked through anything.

We began the day before.

We were nowhere near solid.

"I can't ask you to do this. We're just starting out and—"

"Babe," he cut me off, "you got a bad marriage under your belt. I got one, too. We're screwed if we didn't learn from that shit but I'll tell you somethin', I did. I lived decades not formin' ties with the women in my life because I didn't wanna get bit again by a bad one. I also know a good woman when I find one and I found a good one. I hope to Christ you feel the same way about me, cookie. And if you do, we got that. We intend to take this through the long haul, we commit to thick and thin. I'd have liked it to be thick for more than a fuckin' day before we got thin. But I don't step up for you now, then you should step through that door because that would make me a man who wasn't worthy of you."

Now I loved him even *more*.

So much more, I was going to cry again.

Therefore, as tears pooled in my eyes, I announced, "I'm gonna cry again."

"Sock it to me, darlin'. You cry happy tears 'cause I just told you I think you're the shit and I got your back, I'll take 'em."

Luckily, what he said made me smile, not cry.

It also made me slide up his chest and put my mouth to his.

This made Ham slide his hand into my hair and hold me to him as his mouth opened under mine, mine opened over his, and our kiss became a wet, sweet, amazing *kiss*.

Unfortunately, while it was moving from sweet to hot, the doorbell rang.

"Fuck," Ham muttered against my mouth.

"Yeah," I muttered against his.

Ham shifted his head, kissed my neck, then rolled me to the back of the couch so he could roll off of it.

I pushed up to sitting cross-legged in the couch, pulling my stretchy nightgown over my knees as I watched him move to the front door, look to the peephole. His jaw got tight, his eyes went over his shoulder to me then he turned and opened the door.

Mick Shaughnessy was standing there.

I didn't know if this was good or bad, considering, ten minutes after I got up, with teeth brushed, face washed, and pouring coffee, Ham told me he paid Mick a visit in town because he was also concerned about my aunt's performance last night and then I got the bad news.

"Mick, surprised," Ham said as greeting.

"Reece, my apologies but I got some information for Zara that I'm thinkin' she'll wanna know. I looked you up, found out where you lived, and came by so I could give it to her."

This indicated to me that Mick's visit was not good.

Ham looked at me, did a quick assessment of my emotional stability with his eyes, then stepped aside, murmuring, "As you can see from her face, I told her."

"Mm-hmm," Mick murmured back as he walked in and stopped across the room from me. With his eyes on me, I noted they were also sad.

For me.

Mick Shaughnessy was a good man, always was.

"Sorry for your loss, Zara," he said.

"Lost her a long time ago, Mick."

"I know, girl. Doesn't mean this doesn't bring it fresh," Mick replied.

My lip started quivering. I caught it between my teeth and nodded.

"You had somethin' to say?" Ham prompted. He'd closed the door and was standing a few feet to Mick's side, arms crossed on his chest.

"Asked some questions," Mick told Ham, and then his eyes moved to me. "Got some answers. Didn't muck about gettin' to you, seein' as time is of the essence but, there's a graveside ceremony for your sister today at Gnaw Bone

Memorial Cemetery, Zara. Three o'clock. No service at a mortuary and, since no one knows about this, figure the graveside services are closed. But I reckon—"

He got no further.

Even still in my nightgown, I planted a hand in the back of the couch, tossed my legs over it, and called, "Thanks Mick!" behind me as I raced down the hall to Ham's bedroom.

*　　*　　*

"It would probably be a good thing, if Dad's a dick, that you didn't punch him or something," I noted in the truck as I wrung my hands in my lap and Ham drove us to the cemetery.

Ham was wearing a dark-gray suit, deep-blue shirt, and even a nice black tie patterned in muted blues, greens, and grays.

I'd never seen Ham in a suit and he rocked it.

I was wearing the slim-fitting black dress I'd worn to my friend Kim's funeral years ago. Its lines were classic so luckily I didn't look like an out-of-style goofball. Also luckily, I didn't throw it away one of the million times I saw it in my closet, remembered Kim, her diagnosis of cancer, her very brief three-month fight with it, which mostly consisted of making her comfortable through it, and her funeral.

But I vowed to toss it in the trash after I took it off when we got home.

"Other way to look at that is, it would probably be a good thing for your dad not to be a dick so I won't punch him or something," Ham returned and I looked to him.

"Babe, we have to be cool. We can't get in graveside brawls right before suing for custody."

Ham glanced at me before looking back at the road. "Cookie, honestly, you think I'm gonna get in a bust-up with your dad at your sister's funeral?"

"You're unpredictable, lately," I shared.

That got me another glance, this one surprised, before he asked, "How's that?"

"Committed. Possessive. Forthcoming. You were always awesome but you're exponentially awesome... *er*," I explained.

I caught his grin before he asked, "I'm awesome... *er*?"

"*Exponentially* awesomer," I corrected.

That was when I got a chuckle and Ham's hand snaked out to grab mine and take firm hold.

"I'll be cool, Zara. Wouldn't do anything to fuck things up. Yeah?" he said quietly.

"Yeah," I replied, squeezing his hand.

He returned the squeeze and kept hold of my hand.

"You gonna be able to do this?" he asked.

I knew what he was asking and it wasn't about being graveside at my sister's funeral.

It was about seeing my mom and dad again.

"I'll likely require intravenous vodka after this is over but, yeah. For Xenia, I'll do this," I answered.

"Now that, baby, that's awesome," he replied, his deep approval unhidden.

I let the warmth of that move through me before I looked forward and began efforts to steel myself against seeing my father, my mother, and whoever else they deigned to invite. They didn't have a lot of friends but the ones they chose were nearly as awful as they were.

Therefore, I didn't figure we'd be in good company.

This sucked.

Not for me, for Xenia. My sister liked a good party. She was always social. Everyone liked her and she liked everyone *except* my dad, mom, aunts, and their friends. Therefore, during her last hurrah, those being the only attendees at this particular party was unfortunate.

Luckily, Mick got to us in the nick of time and she'd have at least one person she gave a crap about there.

I was closing in on having it all together when the wrought-iron arch of Gnaw Bone Memorial Cemetery came into view. My body went into hyperdrive trying not to fall apart.

As sick as this sounded, Gnaw Bone Memorial Cemetery was pretty cool. When we were in high school, my friends and I, including Xenia, used to go out there and hang out all the time. On the side of a mountain, its views sweeping, and nothing around it, so its feel was serene. It was also the resting spot for folks who lived in our town before it was our town.

Old gravestones and unusual, old-fashioned names gave credence to local lore that said that Wild West gunslingers were buried here—along with whores, gamblers, and prospectors. Suddenly, I saw myself going to Carnal Library and talking to Faye Goodknight. I bet there were local history books at the library. And I bet if I read those history books, I could tell my nephew all about the history of the town where his mother was born and where he was, hopefully, going to grow up.

That thought cinched my armor together, snug, no chinks, no way to get through no matter how much of a dick my dad could be.

Ready for this.

Not surprisingly, we were not met with faces wreathed with welcoming smiles as Ham and I parked.

I ignored this as I gathered up the flowers Ham called in while I was getting ready and we swung by the flower shop to pick up. We got out of the cab and made our way toward the graveside complete with elevated casket covered in an ostentatious spray of yellow roses that pissed me off because Xenia hated yellow.

As Ham and I made our way toward the casket, I noted, if the look on his face was anything to go by, Dad was very not cool with my appearance at the cemetery. And if he thought he could get away with it, I figured he'd launch himself at me, grab my arm, haul me back to Ham's truck, and forcibly shove me inside. Luckily, Ham was a bruiser and the pastor was there so Dad remained where he was and instead shot daggers at us from his eyes.

I avoided faces and concentrated on the not-so-easy trek through the grass in my spike-heeled pumps. I did this partly because I didn't like these people but mostly because I didn't want to lock eyes with my mom.

Dad, I hated.

Mom, any thought of her hurt me.

He was just a dick.

Mom, I didn't get.

It wasn't like, back in the day, I expected heroics, like her jumping in front of Xenia or me (mostly Xenia) and taking our beating. Dad was a big guy and Mom was an inch shorter than me and I wasn't exactly tall. I could see why she wouldn't do that because he'd just lose his mind, beat her down, and then haul off and wail on us anyway.

But I didn't understand why she didn't do something.

She had two sisters, too, and they were actually nice. Sure, they'd both moved out of state and stayed there but it wasn't like Mom didn't know how to drive a car or dial a phone.

Even if she felt their distance didn't make them an option, I couldn't fathom why she didn't go to Mick. As cops go, he was pretty approachable and even back then, when he wasn't head honcho, he *was* serious about his job and protecting the citizenry of Gnaw Bone. Everyone knew it.

Which took me to Gnaw Bone. I didn't have any experience of other places but back when Xenia did what she did and again very recently, they kicked in for me. They were just that way. If they had to do it on the hush-hush, they would. Or if they had to go all in, they'd do that, too. Hell, when Nina got kidnapped, she'd only been in town for over a week, most people didn't know who the hell she was, the ones who did didn't know her all that well, and everyone went out looking for her, even me.

I could understand that Dad cowed my mother. He wasn't just a big guy; he was a scary guy. And I didn't have any experience being a mother so who was I to say.

I just thought any mother would risk *something* for her daughters.

Not stand at the graveside of one dead one and watch your other one that you haven't seen or spoken to in nine years (and didn't try) walk up without even calling hello.

"Zara, lovely to see you here," Pastor Williams said meaningfully when we stopped next to the casket and my eyes went to him to give him a grateful smile. "Young man, welcome," he greeted Ham.

Ham lifted his chin.

"If you don't mind, pastor, we'd like to get this started. We're already unfathomably ten minutes late," my father cut in.

"Certainly, Xavier," Pastor Williams murmured, looking down to his Bible.

I did a scan that was far from thorough and saw, first, my mother's sisters weren't there, and second, only about six other people were, which meant the ones my father were expecting had likely been there awhile.

That was when I knew the source of Mick's information, considering Pastor Williams had delayed to wait for our arrival.

Therefore, if he wasn't a man of the cloth, older than my dad, and I didn't have my man at my side who I'd been waiting to be my man for years, once this crap was done, I'd kiss the pastor hard.

The service was short but sweet, seeing as Pastor Williams was a great guy, he knew Xenia, and he made it that way.

At the end, as he prayed, we all watched Xenia lowered into the ground, but even as my throat burned, I held it together.

"I'm sure Xenia would thank you all for coming," Pastor Williams started and I felt Ham's lips at my ear where he muttered, "I'm not."

I successfully stifled a half-nervous, half-amused giggle as Pastor Williams went on. "As do I, Xenia's parents, Xavier and Amy, and Xenia's sister, Zara. God be with Xenia and God be with all of you."

When he was done, I thought it safe to approach the opened earth and look down at those beautiful but inappropriate roses.

Then I tossed mine on.

Blood red. Her favorites.

Red. Means love, baby, she'd said to me once, a twinkle in her eye, still young enough to have hope for the future.

"I miss you," I whispered to the flowers. "I thank God you're finally at peace but I miss you, Xeens. Every freaking day."

I felt a hand slide up my back and curl around my neck, warm and reassuring as I stood still, stared at those flowers, and said one last good-bye to my sister.

Then I felt warmth at my back and lips at my ear where Ham murmured, "You ready, cookie?"

"Just a second, darlin'," I murmured back. The warmth at my back left but the hand stayed around my neck. I stared at the flowers and told my sister, "Got that, girl. Got that love, baby. Took a while. But I finally got in my life what the color of those flowers means. Wherever you are, be happy for me. I promise, we're gonna do right."

I said no more, waited for a wisp of wind that might be her reply, and got nothing.

It was disappointing but I had nine years of that, waiting for some sign that some part of Xenia's spirit was still with me and not getting it. I was used to it by then.

I moved away and the instant I did, Ham curled his arm around my shoulders and tucked me close to his side. I wrapped my arm around his waist and we didn't get a step before Pastor Williams stopped us.

"Zara, so pleased to see you here," he said.

"Thank you, Pastor. I'm pleased I got the chance to come," I replied. When his eyes went to Reece I introduced, "Pastor Williams, this is Graham Reece. Ham, this is Pastor Williams."

They shook hands as Ham said, "Pastor. Folks call me Reece."

"Fine, Reece. Nice to meet you."

"Same," Ham rumbled.

They broke contact and Pastor Williams looked to me. "I know this is not exactly a shock but it's no less distressing. I've said it before, I'll say it again. My door is always open if you ever need to talk."

"Thanks Pastor," I mumbled on a small smile.

He gave me a small smile back, nodded to me, nodded to Ham, and moved away.

I looked to my feet and muttered, "Hurry, let's make a quick getaway."

That was when I felt Ham go tight at my side and he muttered back, "Too late for that."

My head lifted and I saw Dad approaching.

Really, he was handsome. He'd given me his blond hair. Although his had since faded to gray in an attractive way. He'd also given me my brown eyes. He'd been built back in the day and he kept in shape, for an older guy. If you didn't know what a dick he was, and he didn't wear that fact on his face, he'd still turn heads.

Ham drew me closer.

"Zara," he greeted. These were the first words he'd spoken to me in nearly a decade and his voice was ice cold.

I refrained from replying, "Maker of the seed that spawned me," and just looked at him.

His eyes slid to Ham before coming back to me. "I see rumor is true."

I said nothing.

For some insane reason known only to him, Dad kept talking.

"Also heard you've traveled a rough road lately."

I kept my mouth shut.

His eyes again slid to Ham before they came back to me and I wasn't surprised it didn't take him long to show his true colors. "As always, you solve your problems in an interesting way."

"How's Zander?" I asked as a response to that vague slur on Ham *and* me and I was thrilled not only to get the supportive squeeze from Ham's arm but also to watch my dad's face blanch.

I scanned the attendees and saw Aunt Wilona standing with Aunt Dahlia and my mother, all of them with eyes on me. Aunt Dahlia's her usual nasty. Aunt Wilona looked a bit anxious but, weirdly, when I saw her eyes shift to Dad, they turned nasty. Mom's look I didn't allow myself to take in and quickly turned my attention back to Dad.

"I see Aunt Wilona didn't bring Xenia's son to his mother's funeral."

Dad's mouth got tight, his eyes went cagey, and his hands went into the pockets of his trousers under his suit jacket, likely to hide that they'd balled into fists.

"It's rather fortunate I was able to solve my problems

in an interesting way before I found out my nephew's living close by," I remarked and that was when Dad's torso swung in.

Toward me.

"Zara, you better—"

"Watch it," Ham growled and his menacing tone of voice even freaked me.

Dad's eyes cut to him and I looked at him, too.

But Ham only had eyes for Dad.

Angry ones.

"You're already closer to her than I want you to be. You get closer, say somethin' I don't like, the serious problems we already got escalate in a big way," Ham went on.

"Are you threatening me?" Dad asked.

"No, we'll let our attorney do that," Ham answered. Dad's eyes got big, and with Ham's arm firmly guiding me, he stepped us to the side and took us forward, past Dad, and straight to the truck.

Ham's gait was not swift, but it was determined as he got us the hell out of there. My heels dug in the turf but I managed to keep up.

He opened my door for me and helped me up before he swung it closed.

He was behind the wheel and we were on our way when I spoke.

"Do you think we should have exposed our hand early like that?" I asked.

"Don't know. Maybe not. Don't care. Seein' that asshole's face when you said Zander's name and when I mentioned our attorney was worth whatever play we might have just given up, though."

He wasn't wrong about that. I didn't get the chance to share that.

Ham asked, "You doin' okay?"

I looked out the windshield and clasped my hands in my lap. "Crazy, funerals suck, but you can't deny they give closure."

"True enough, cookie," he replied.

It was me who reached for his hand this time.

But when I caught it, it was Ham's fingers that closed around tight.

*   *   *

"Fuck, Zara. Ride that," Ham growled.

I was already riding his cock, bent over him, my face close to his, one hand in the bed providing leverage, the nails of my other hand scraping over his chest.

Ham had one hand to my hip, encouraging me with squeezes. The other hand was cupping my face.

When I went faster, he slid his thumb along my lower lip, then pressed it into my mouth.

The instant it cleared my teeth I sucked it deep.

"Jesus, baby," Ham groaned, his hips thrusting up.

Oh yes. I liked this. Now I was *really* riding him.

He slid his thumb out, then back in, and I took it again and again as I took his cock again and again and when I was whimpering against his thumb, he pulled it out and whispered, "Let's bring my girl home."

I knew what he meant and I wanted it.

Ham didn't delay. He slid his thumb away from my mouth, then glided his hand down my chest, between my breasts, over my belly, and that thumb I had in my mouth pressed in at my clit and twitched.

I slammed down on him, grinding, my head flying back, and with a breathy cry, I came. Hard. Beautiful. Loving it. Loving Ham.

"Ride me, baby, take me there," Ham encouraged, his voice thick and jagged and I started up again, faster, harder,

driving myself down on him through my orgasm, my finger-
nails digging deeper into his chest and one scored over his
nipple. His hips thrust up, he wrapped his arm around my
waist driving me down, and he groaned deep.

I bent closer as he came down and slid my lips from the
base of his throat up his neck and along his jaw.

Ham wrapped me in his arms and pressed me closer
before he turned his head and said gruffly in my ear, "Now
that's how I like my girl ridin' me."

I smiled against his skin, lifted my head up, and looked
down at him.

"Though, just sayin', you want it that other way, I'm
always available meat," he finished.

I felt the laughter bubble up and out before I rested my
weight on him and pressed my face in his neck.

He started sliding his hands soothingly along the skin of
my back, lifting one hand high, sifting it through my hair
and then down over my skin again. I was glad to have this
back. I loved this. I missed it. I hadn't had a ton of lovers
and Greg could be affectionate after sex for a while (in the
beginning) but then he was done and it was done.

I'd even tested it in the past and Ham could do it for hours.
I'd once fallen asleep just like this, my face in his neck, his
hands giving me love, because he did it so long, after ages of
that and an orgasm, I slid straight to dreamland, feeling his
affection as I fell.

"Thanks for doin' what you could to make a shit day less
shitty," I told his skin and his hands stopped so his arms
could wrap around me.

"Take care of my girl," was all he said.

He certainly did.

"It was cool of you to call Neens. She brought Becca and
Mindy, and Arlene heard about it so she came over too and it
was..." I paused. "It felt nice, Ham, to remember why life's

worth livin'. Good friends who care. A man who has your back." I kissed his neck and whispered, "Thank you."

"You're welcome, cookie," he murmured.

I lifted my head and looked down at him. "No more days off though. We need all the money we can get."

I saw the white flash of his smile through the dark and he asked, "Are you bossin' the boss?"

"Yes," I replied immediately.

His hands came to my face and there was firmness, not humor, in his tone when he assured me, "It's all gonna be good."

"It'll be better, I have more tips in my pocket," I returned.

His hands brought my face closer. "Zara. I swear, it's all gonna be good."

I held his eyes in the shadows and said, "Okay, darlin'."

"Now kiss your man and climb off. I got to see to things then we can get some shut-eye."

"Okay, baby," I replied, dipped my head, kissed him open-mouthed, and ended up not climbing off because Ham took over the kiss and rolled me so we ended it with me on my back.

Once he broke it, he dipped his head to touch his lips to my chest and slid out of bed.

I curled up facing the bathroom door counting it out.

We'd had forty-two hours of official togetherness and, notwithstanding outside factors, we were doing a little bit of all right.

Xenia had met Ham. She didn't come to the bar, too much temptation, but we'd met him on the boardwalk one day and I'd introduced her.

She'd liked him. I could tell because she told me he was hot and that was pretty much all my sister needed to like a guy.

She would have liked him more if she got to know him.

Ham's shadow entered the room and then he entered the bed and curled me into him.

Once I'd settled in, I told him softly, "Xenia told me she liked you when she met you but if she'd gotten to know you, she would have *really* liked you."

He lifted a hand to my hair and sifted his fingers through, asking, "You love her?"

"Oh yeah."

"Then I would have liked her, too."

I closed my eyes and whispered, "There it is."

"What?"

"You. Awesome...*er.*"

The last sound either of us made before drifting off to sleep was Ham's laughter.

I liked that.

So much I wanted it every night for the rest of my life.

CHAPTER TWELVE

Vaulted

Two days later...

"LET ME GET this straight," Maybelline, sitting with Wanda at a table in my section at The Dog, started. "Five days ago, you wandered down the hall and gave your boss-slash-roommate a booty call. A booty call that was so hot that he got pissed off and then for some reason, *you* went to apologize to *him* and he yanked you into his bed again. You did the nasty again,

freaked, and ran away. The next night he tells you, belatedly, mind, that he came back to town to commit to you. You
accepted that and all is hunky-dory for a few hours. You have
a scene at The Rooster, of all places, before settling down to
sleep with your boss, roommate, hot guy, brand-new but old
boyfriend. Then you find out your sister died, and girl, you
know I'm sorry about that…"

She waited for my nod, I gave it to her, and she launched
back in.

"And you find you got a long-lost nephew so you and your
boss, hot guy, new-old boyfriend decide to sue for custody.
You throw down with your dad at a gravesite and now you're
livin' the dream but with an impending nasty custody battle
hangin' over your head." She paused before she asked, "Do I
have all that right?"

Suffice it to say, I'd just filled them in on all that had gone
down with Ham and Dad.

I looked to Wanda. She was smiling down at her drink so
I looked back to Maybelle.

"Yes," I answered.

Her eyes went to the ceiling.

"Okay, just gonna say," Wanda began and I looked to her
to see her looking at Maybelle. "You need to give him a good
once-over 'cause it's clear you're not seein' what I'm seein'. If
that man right there"—she jerked her head to the bar, in other
words, Ham's way—"told me he came to town ready to commit
and then went gung ho with gettin' my long-lost nephew away
from some serious nasties, I'm not sure I would fight him."

Maybelle pinned Wanda with a stare and declared, "We
need to get you a man."

"No argument here," Wanda shot back.

Wanda was Maybelle except white, and without the
husband and three daughters. Wanda had two *ex*-husbands
and a son who was so wild, he did her head in.

She was currently giving her son tough love by grounding his ass every three days, which meant he was out getting in trouble even if grounded so he earned more groundings. Thus this was not working.

She was also looking for husband number three and Wanda pretty much had only two things she was looking for in her new man. One, that he had no problem taking a firm hand with a wayward teenage boy. And two, he just had firm hands that he knew how to use.

On that thought, a piercing whistle filled the air, and all heads, including mine, turned toward the bar and I saw Ham taking his fingers out of his mouth only to crook one at me.

"Seriously, I don't care if feminists hunt me down and burn me at the stake, that man crooked his finger and me, I'd follow him into a bank and rob it at his side," Wanda muttered.

I smiled at my boots before I gave them a glance and said, "I'll be back."

Then I walked to the bar.

Ham met me there and leaned into his forearms toward me.

God, I loved that.

"Did you just whistle for me?" I asked.

"Yeah," he answered.

"It was loud," I noted.

"Yeah," he agreed.

"You gotta teach me how to do that," I told him.

His eyes dropped to my mouth and he murmured, "Easy."

"Ham, no fair. Whenever you say that, my nipples get hard. I gotta work. I don't need chafing."

His gaze shot to my breasts, then to my eyes, and he smiled.

I smiled back before I asked, "You whistled, *mein herr*?"

His smiling lips twitched before he informed me, "I prefer Bruiser."

"Bruiser Ham drags me into his bed and shows me an

alternate universe I want to move to forever. *Mein herr* whistles at me to get my ass to the bar," I explained, then went on. "So, you whistled?"

"Right, cookie," he said through his still-present smile. "I'm your man but I'm also your boss and you been standin' at that table fifteen minutes. Don't mind that but you got empties on other tables, I get a bonus if I sell a shitload of booze, and the women you're talkin' to, one threatened me a few weeks back and is givin' me looks I don't much like. The other one is givin' me looks I don't much like that say she's thinkin' of drugging me, taking off my clothes, and tying me to a bed. She isn't ugly but she's not my type and, I think you know, I already got a woman."

I burst out laughing and found Ham still smiling at me when I was done.

"I'm afraid you're gonna have to win Maybelle over. She's feelin' we're goin' a bit too fast," I shared.

"She'll learn otherwise," Ham replied.

It was firm and I thought that was sweet.

I carried on.

"And Wanda's overdue for gettin' her some. Though, we'd just swung around to the topic of findin' her a man, and if we manage that, you're off the hook for the drugging and tying to a bed threat."

"Good news," he muttered.

"Do you really get a bonus if you sell a shitload of booze?" I asked.

"Last manager was lackadaisical. If the waitresses don't work the floor, remindin' them when their drinks are low, they don't sell a lot of booze. I up the bar's take, which I've done, keep it there six months, which I'm gonna do, they give me a bonus."

I felt a smile curve my lips, leaned into him, and stated, "We are *so* on that."

He gave me another smile in return and replied, "Then get that sweet ass on it, cookie. And, just sayin', the way to do that is not leanin' into me bein' all cute so I want you to take a break so I can take you to my office and make you moan. It's gettin' on the floor and not yammerin' with your girls."

I kind of wanted him to take me to his office and make me moan but I was getting the sense Ham wanted me to sell booze now and make me moan later. Further, talking about it would make me want it more so I ignored that and focused on something else.

"I have to yammer with them. A lot is happening and it's my sworn duty to the sisterhood, even if I'm workin'," I shared.

"Well, sell some booze in between," he shot back.

"That I can do," I told him.

"So do it," he returned.

I moved back, gave him a salute, and turned away. I lifted a one-minute finger to Maybelle and Wanda to share with them I'd be back and I got my sweet ass on selling booze.

My section included the left side of the bar, which included the recessed area that held the pool tables, the pool paraphernalia on the walls, and a few high tables and stools scattered around for people to rest their drinks and their asses during the taxing activity of playing pool.

I'd swung around to the dimly lit back corner when I stopped dead.

My mother, looking uncomfortable and even panicked, sat alone at the farthest table, her modestly expensive but classic handbag on the table in front of her, her hands resting on it like she was terrified someone was going to snatch it away.

My first thought was to hightail my ass back to the bar and ask Ham to make this go away.

My second thought was that would make me a sissy, and

if Ham knew my mother was there, there was a possibility he'd blow his stack. I tried to tell myself I felt nothing for my mother, but even so, I didn't think she could handle Ham blowing his stack. She could barely handle putting one foot in front of the other, so scared she'd do it wrong, Dad would lay into her.

So I kept my eyes on hers and she kept hers on mine as I walked to her table, taking her in.

She, too, was blonde but her blonde was lighter than Dad's and mine.

Xenia got her hair.

She was also petite and had blue eyes.

Xenia got those, too.

In fact, if Xenia had had another twenty years or so, I figured she'd look a lot like Mom.

I made it to her table and asked, "Get you a drink?"

"Zara—" she started, but I pinned her to the stool with my eyes and she abruptly stopped.

I knew my face was hard and my eyes unfriendly.

I also didn't care.

"Get you a drink?" I repeated.

She leaned into her hands on her purse and kept hold of my eyes. "Honey, please. I came here to talk to you and it's real important you hear what I have to say."

"Not to be a bitch," I began, intending to be just that, "but, lookin' back, I'm not sure you ever had anything to say that was real important."

She closed her eyes through her flinch and I felt something I didn't want to feel flow through me.

Guilt.

Guilt at hurting my mother and more guilt for doing it intentionally.

But she kept my nephew from me and I didn't have it in me to let that slide.

Still, I hated doing it, so I needed to get out of there.

"Now, Mom, can I get you a drink?" I asked yet again.

She opened her eyes and I saw the effort it took her to straighten her shoulders before she announced, "Your father isn't real happy you're back together with that man."

That man.

Dad had called Ham that back in the day, time and again, even though I'd corrected him dozens of times, telling him Ham's name.

I hated it then and I hated it no less now.

"Lucky for me, just like back then, I'm of the age of consent and can choose who I spend my time with," I told Mom. "Now, if you want to stay, you really need to order a drink. Ham's the manager. His job is to sell booze and he frowns on people hanging out, taking up tables, and not spending money."

"I . . . well, you know I don't imbibe," Mom told me and I did know that. I also never understood it. She wasn't militant antibooze but I'd never seen her even take a sip of wine. And that was even before Xenia went off the rails. Truthfully, even knowing it was wrong to think, what with my sister being a junkie alcoholic, with the life Mom led with Dad, I figured she could use a drink or two to get her through.

"We have soft drinks," I shared then I suggested, "Or the other option is you can leave."

She leaned farther into me, taking a hand from her purse and stretching it across the table toward me, palm flat. I looked down at it like it was a snake about to strike but held my ground.

"Your father's real worried about what you and that man have planned in regards to Zander," she informed me, and I looked back to her. "Zander's in a good place. He doesn't need any upheaval."

I felt my throat start burning with the effort to hold back the torrent of words that were getting caught in it.

"Are you kidding me?" I hissed and she leaned back, her hand sliding with her.

"Wilona never had kids," Mom stated. "Couldn't. She was over-the-moon happy she had her chance to raise a baby even if she did it later in life."

"Aunt Wilona is a nasty bitch only one step down on the nasty level from Aunt Dahlia and you know that because she's had not one nice thing to say about you in nearly forty years," I reminded her. "You were never good enough for Dad and she let you know it every chance she got."

And this was true. I'd heard it. Neither Aunt Wilona nor Aunt Dahlia had made even a vague attempt to hide these comments from Xenia, me, *or* Mom.

Even in the light of the bar I saw her face get pale, acknowledging this as truth before she said, "She may be a bit hard, Zara, but I promise, she's good with Zander."

At that, it was my turn to lean in. "If she was, then why has his aunt been livin' a county away and he has no clue I exist?" I locked eyes with her. "And he doesn't, does he, Mom? He has no idea his aunt has been as close as I am. Happy to spend time with him. Happy to tell him, when he was old enough to hear, which would be about now, how his mom had a beautiful laugh. How everyone liked her. How she had a way with tellin' a scary story and she knew a million jokes and she had a way of tellin' those, too. How she had soft hair and shining eyes and she was lookin' forward to bringin' him into this world. And how tragic that the one thing in her life she looked forward to was the most important thing she ever had a shot at and she didn't get it."

"Please don't," Mom whispered. "You know all this is hard on me."

Was she crazy?

"Hard on you?" I asked, my voice pitching higher *and* louder. "I lost my sister."

"I lost my daughter," she replied, her voice trembling, her eyes getting bright.

I leaned in farther.

"Well, I win because I lost my nephew, too," I spat.

"Zara—"

"And something else I lost, not that I had much of it in the first place, was any minute amount of respect I still had for *you*. *You* knew the deal that was struck. *You* knew Xenia and I were close. *You* know what Dad's like. *You* knew I wanted to be a part of my nephew's life. You also knew he was livin' not far away from me for the last nine years and you never *told* me."

"Your father—" she began.

"Yeah," I snapped. "My *father* would lose his mind if you went against his wishes and that might put you in a world of hurt." I leaned back and threw out an arm, my tone turning sarcastic. "And we wouldn't want that, would we? No way Amy Cinders would put anything on the line for her girls, or apparently her firstborn daughter's son."

Another flinch, this one I did not give one shit about, before she rallied with, "You knew how it was."

"Yeah, I did. I knew *exactly* how it was for eighteen years because no one shielded me from any of that shit except my sister," I shot back.

"Get out."

Mom's eyes flew over my shoulder and I turned to look, even though from that low, incensed rumble I knew what I would see and I was right. Ham was positioning himself close to my back but his infuriated eyes were locked on Mom.

"I got a right to refuse service," he stated. "And I'm exerting that right. Get out."

"Please, um...Mr. Reece?" Mom started and I looked back to her to see she'd slid off her stool and was looking beseechingly up at Ham. "I was trying to have a word with

Zara and it's good you're here because you should know, too, that Xavier isn't very happy about what you two might be—"

Ham interrupted her, repeating, "Get out."

"Really, I need you to listen to me," Mom begged.

"And, ma'am, I really need you to get the fuck out before I'm forced to eject you myself, and do not test me. I got enough years in bars, I won't hurt you while I do it but that doesn't mean you won't be set out," Ham returned.

Mom looked at Ham and then looked at me and saw she'd get no help from me so she reached for her purse.

Ham wasn't done, however.

"Also, a warning, and you take this to your husband. Things are about to get ugly and I mean that legally. You do yourself no favors, and I'd share it with him, if you harass Zara anywhere, but especially at work. You do, we'll be keepin' track of that shit startin' now and you might wanna think of what a judge will think of you keepin' a boy from his aunt and then hasslin' her when she decides she doesn't like that much and does somethin' about it."

"So you are. You are gonna fight for Zander," Mom breathed, eyes wide, face pale, terror written all over her features.

"Know the concept is foreign to you," Ham replied cuttingly. "But yeah, we're gonna fight for that boy. We're gonna do everything we can to get him in a safe place where he's got love that isn't fucked up and twisted."

"Wilona does right by him," Mom squeaked, terrified but weirdly holding her own.

"She did, she wouldn't keep him from his aunt," Ham said, much the same as me. "Now, you best be on your way, but one last nugget you get to share with that asshole you live with. Had a word with Dr. Kreiger."

Man, oh man. Ham *was* pissed if he was laying this particular nugget on Mom now.

And she knew what that nugget meant because her eyes went so huge, they had to hurt.

Ham didn't even take a breath before he kept going.

"He still works at County Hospital. He remembers Xenia. He remembers standin' right there with me, you, that asshole, and Zara when your husband agreed to put the baby up for adoption. He also remembers bein' surprised when he approached your man about seein' to that and your man reneged on that deal. He's pretty pissed to learn that your man lied to him at the time, sayin' Zara knew all about the change. And last, he's all fired up to tell a judge about this, seein' as he also thought that was a fuckwit move. So another piece of info you can suck up enough courage to tell him that might be useful is, what comes around goes around and I'm gonna make certain he gets his. Now, you got all that?"

This was all true.

Ham wasted no time the day after the funeral in finding Dr. Kreiger, who was the only witness to the deal I made with Dad. Ham didn't let me come, worried about my state of mind, seeing as my sister had just passed. However, he did fill me in when he got back from the hospital.

And during our meeting with Nina the day before that we had to officially get the ball rolling, Nina filled us in on the fact that Dr. Kreiger wasted no time e-mailing her a scanned letter to the effect that he had, indeed, witnessed the discussion, detailed all that came after, and he was willing to do whatever was necessary to help.

Mom nodded to Ham's words even as she whispered, "Please don't do this."

"It's gonna happen," Ham vowed on a growl, then finished, "Now, you best get on."

Mom looked to me. "Zara—"

But suddenly I couldn't see Mom any longer because Ham was not behind me. He was standing in front of me but I heard his voice rumble, "Mizz Cinders, I'm bein' very serious. This is the last time I'm gonna say it. You best get on . . ." He paused. *"Now."*

Not surprisingly, since Ham's scary tone degenerated to his *very* scary tone, I saw Mom scurrying to the door.

I also heard Ham murmur, "Be back," and watched him follow her.

No sooner had Ham hit the door when Maybelle and Wanda hit me, creating an instant huddle.

"What on earth was that?" Wanda asked, getting close as Maybelle did the same and studied my face.

I looked to Wanda. "That was my mom."

Wanda's eyes shot to Maybelle as Maybelle leaned back but her eyes were on the door where Ham had followed Mom.

"You need a drink, sweetie?" Wanda asked and I did. I totally did. I needed seven of them.

"I'm workin'. Ham has a policy, no boozin' it up while you're sellin' booze," I told her.

"He vaulted over the bar."

This weird comment came from Maybelle and I looked to her.

"What?" I asked.

Her gaze was still at the door, but it slowly slid to me.

"He watches you, you know," she stated, and I felt my insides begin to warm. "It's not boss keepin' an eye on his employee type of watchin' either. He likes what he sees. But it's more. Like he's makin' sure you're good, no drunk guys do anything stupid, stuff like that. You were outta sight for a while and I saw him do the scan he does a lot. He couldn't locate you. He didn't like that. Saw that plain as day. He moved to the front part of the bar, at the edge, looked around, and the minute he saw you with your momma, his face got scary, he put his hands to the bar, and vaulted right over it."

Ham vaulted over the bar.

For me.

How awesome was that?

That warmth spread through my chest.

"He did," Wanda affirmed. "He did do that. It was amazing. Seriously, after seeing that, I'd *so* totally rob a bank with that guy."

I didn't have a chance to smile at Wanda, Maybelline kept talking.

"I've never seen anything like it, man that big movin' like that," Maybelle declared. "He was lucky there was no one sittin' on the stools there because I don't think if there was that would have stopped him."

The warmth spread all around.

"I had an ex-boyfriend who was not such a great guy and didn't want us to be done," Maybelle went on. "Used to mess with me. I'd be at the same burger joint as him, he'd call out nasty stuff. So bad I'd have to run out, not even gettin' my burger. If he drove by while I was walking down the street, he'd do the same. I started seein' Latrell and that happened"— she lifted a finger—"*once*. Latrell took off after him and chased him fifteen blocks, caught him, bloodied his nose and then some. We were on our second date and I remembered, by the time he got back to me and word was already spreading what he did, I knew I wanted to spend the rest of my life with that man. I knew he'd never let anything harm me. And now, for near on twenty years, I was right. He hasn't."

I loved that story. Then again, I loved Latrell. Maybelline's husband was the bomb.

"Are you saying that you think Ham is like Latrell?" I asked, and her eyes, which were kind of dreamy with reminiscing, grew sharp on me.

"Heck no," she stated and I stared. Then she went on. "But he's one step closer to me not thinkin' he's all wrong for you and you're making the biggest mistake in your life."

Well, that was something.

"Can I have my girl?"

This was rumbled from behind us. We all jumped and I turned and looked up at Ham.

He didn't wait for a response. His big hand engulfed mine and he dragged me through the bar to the back hall, down it, and right into the office.

He closed the door and backed me into it, one of his hands going to the door by my head. He slid his other arm around me, pulling my hips into contact with his.

"You know I like it anytime and wouldn't mind christening the office, babe, but I just had a drama with my mom, story time with Maybelle, and we've got a bonus to earn so maybe we can give each other orgasms after we close," I quipped, knowing full well I wasn't there because Ham wanted to ravish me.

I was there because he wanted to make sure I was all right.

"Brave face, baby, I love that you got it in you to do that but you don't have to put that shit on for me," he replied.

I took in a breath, then dropped my head forward so it landed on his chest.

"She still has the power to hurt me," I said there.

"I get that," Ham replied, moving his hand from the door so he could wrap it around the back of my neck.

And he would get that, since I'd explained all about it back when Xenia got hurt and Ham, I was finding, didn't forget anything.

"I don't understand her," I shared.

"Means you're gonna make a great mom," he stated and I pulled back to look up at him.

"What?" I asked.

"My guess, you spent a lot of time thinkin' on it. My guess, if by now you still don't get it, there wasn't somethin' in your history with her that explained it. So my guess is, she was just shit at bein' a mom and if you don't get how she could do that, then you know how to be a good mom. Reckon that's the hardest job in the world just as it's the easiest."

I felt my brows draw together as I informed him, "That's a contradiction, Ham."

"Nope," he returned immediately. "You love a job, no matter how hard it is, it's still easy. Not sure, never studied up on the guy, could be wrong, but I reckon Michelangelo didn't wake up and think, 'Fuck, I gotta drag my ass outta bed. More painting at the Sistine Chapel. Wish that shit was done so I could get to a fuckin' beach.'"

His words made me laugh and move into him, pressing my hands against his chest and pressing everything else close.

When I quit laughing, I told him, "Okay, that makes sense. And it's very wise, Mr. Reece."

His brows shot up. "Now I'm Mr. Reece?"

"Bruiser drags me to bed. *Mein herr* bosses me around. And Mr. Reece is like a life professor, smart and generous with his wisdom."

His eyes got dark in a way I felt all through my body and he pressed me into the door.

"Right, we were in here for me to take your pulse. Now we're in here so I can fuck you against the door," he stated, his voice jagged, and I felt that all through my body, too, but I shook my head.

"I've got booze to sell," I reminded him.

"You can sell it in fifteen minutes," he muttered, his face disappearing in my neck as his hand slid over my ass.

"Fifteen minutes? Is that all I get?" I asked.

His teeth nipped my earlobe, his hand squeezed my ass, and his other hand, which I'd lost track of, was at the side of my breast and his thumb slid out, grazing the underside.

I shivered.

"All it'll take," he whispered into my skin as his lips slid up my jaw.

I wanted that, but I *needed* more.

"I'm thinkin' about giving Bruiser whatever he wants later, however he wants it, however long it takes him to get it. If he takes it now, that might not work out that great."

His head came up and his eyes burned into mine. "Whatever I want, however I want it, as long as it takes me to get it?" he asked.

"You got it."

His lips dropped to mine and I could feel them smiling as I saw his eyes doing the same. "You need to sell booze now."

"Right," I replied and I knew he saw my eyes smiling because my lips were doing the same.

He pulled me into him and kissed me, wet, hard, a promise of good things to come before he lifted his head an inch and looked in my eyes.

"You sure you're good?" he asked gently.

Every day in what seemed like a thousand ways, I fell deeper in love with this man.

I didn't share that.

I nodded. "Yeah, darlin'. I'm fine. Thanks for comin' to my rescue."

"Anytime, baby."

I grinned at him.

Ham grinned back.

Then we got to work and I kicked ass selling drinks to earn Ham his bonus, which was double good since it earned me more tips.

But I did it taking time while they were still there to gab with my girls and noticing that, when I wasn't at their table and I caught her studying him, Maybelle was looking at Ham a little bit differently.

Then again, he'd vaulted over a bar for me.

It wasn't chasing a guy fifteen blocks and beating the crap out of him.

But it was nothing to sneeze at either.

*   *   *

"No," I breathed my denial, pressing back against Ham.

I was on my knees, Ham on his behind me, his body pressed the length of mine. Ham had one of my breasts in his hand, his fingers doing amazing things with my nipple. I had my fingers linked behind my head and my knees were spread wide.

Ham had my toy.

He'd just taken me almost *there* with my toy, only to not let me go *there* by taking the toy away.

"I need it back, baby," I begged and his thumb dragged against my nipple, pulling at it hard. My hips jerked and I whimpered, "Ham."

"Not yet," he denied.

I tried another tactic.

"Okay, then I need your cock."

"Not yet," he repeated and I wriggled back into him but stopped when his finger met his thumb at my nipple and he pulled sharply.

Oh God, that felt good.

My head fell back and I moaned.

"Fuck me, so goddamned hot," he growled, pressing his groin into my back so I could feel just how hard he was.

"Okay, now I *really* need your cock," I pleaded.

"Hang tight, Zara," he returned.

"Honey," I implored as he kept torturing my nipple magnificently.

I could hear my vibrator going. I could feel his hard cock pressed against me and both were driving me mad.

I could take no more.

"Ham."

He positioned under me. I got the toy back just as his cock rammed up inside me. My head flew back, and my hands automatically went to where his were on me and I came, so primed by our play, the orgasm burned through me and I again cried out his name.

His hand at my breast went between my shoulder blades and he pushed gently as he ordered, "Down. I want that sweet ass."

I didn't hesitate. Even though it meant losing my toy, I went face to the bed and gave him my ass.

He turned off the toy, tossed it aside, and his fingertips glided over my ass as he pounded deep.

"Fuck, baby, love this ass."

"Take it," I gasped, rearing into his thrusts.

"Fuck," he grunted, slamming into me. He clamped one hand on my hip, yanking me back, the other hand flattened on my ass, the pad of his thumb pressing against the sensitive spot exposed for him.

"Yes," I breathed, jerking up to my hands, my thighs quivering. I slid my fingers between my legs and rubbed my clit.

Ham pressed the tip of his thumb inside me.

My head shot back and I cried out again as orgasm two seared through me.

"Fuck, my girl takes anything I got to give," he growled, still ramming hard and deep.

"Yes," I panted, still coming, still rearing back into him, wild, beautiful. "Ham, baby, I'm coming apart."

"I got you, Zara," he grunted.

I lost his thumb as his hand clamped on my other hip. He jerked me back, kept me there, and ground into me as he groaned.

I knew he was coming down, or close to it, when his fingers in my flesh relaxed and he started moving in and out slowly.

I dropped my torso back down, cheek to the mattress, and let him fuck me tender after fucking me hard.

Finally, he pulled out but I didn't lose him. His fingertips roamed my back and ass as the bed moved. Then I felt his lips at my ass, gliding, soft, one of his fingers slid along the cleft and down before it slid through the wetness between my legs and up inside me, filling me.

I made a contented mew and closed my eyes as he kept fucking me tender, this time with his finger, and I thrilled at it before he slid his finger out, gently glided it over my clit, sweet, light, but my hips still moved with the thrill of it and I made another low noise in my throat.

He kissed the curve of my ass before he muttered, "Relax, baby."

I fell to my side, curling my legs up to my chest.

Ham exited the bed.

I smiled into the covers.

He seemed gone for only a second before he was back, gathering me in his arms, my back to his front, his legs curling up with mine.

"I hope to fuck you liked that as much as you seemed to 'cause we're gonna do that again and we're gonna do it a lot," he said into the back of my hair.

"For a man who vaults over a bar for me, I'll do that again and I'll do it a lot but even if you didn't vault over a bar for me, I'd still do it again because it was fuckin' *awesome*," I replied.

"Vaults over the bar?" he asked and I twisted my neck to look at him.

"Maybelle and Wanda saw you when you vaulted over the bar to get to me," I informed him. "Wish I'd witnessed that display of athleticism, darlin'. But how did you vault over a bar?"

"Babe, there's a reason I do one-arm pushups and a shit-load of pull-ups," was his simple reply.

"I thought it was just so you can be hotter than hot and fuck people up when the occasion arises," I remarked and watched him grin.

"That, and bein' able to get over a bar when my cookie needs me," he returned.

Oh man. I really liked that.

"Well, hopefully your cookie won't need that kind of physical heroics again, but that said, if you get in the mood, you can give me a demonstration," I stated.

His mouth was still grinning even as my words reminded him that he'd needed to protect me, so his eyes went thoughtful before he cleared his expression and tightened his arms around me.

"You give me you, naked on your knees with your hands behind your head, I'll vault over the bar for you."

It was my turn to grin at him before I declared my stipulation. "I'm up for that, though no toy. That nearly undid me."

He pulled back a few inches in order to roll me to him, then he tangled us up, front to front.

Through this, he said, "Payback."

I felt my brows rise. "Payback for what?"

"Payback for takin' yourself there with your toy and makin' me listen."

That was when I felt my brows knit over narrowed eyes. "I didn't even know you were in the apartment, so I didn't *make* you listen."

"Still heard you. It did a number on me and you made me wait until I got in there again, so I get to play with you with your toy," he shot back.

"That doesn't seem fair," I retorted, and I felt his big body start to shake with laughter.

"Baby, you just came twice, hard, told me you were comin' apart the second time, and you're bitchin'?"

That *did* seem ridiculous.

"Whatever," I muttered.

At that, his body shook harder as his laughter filled the room.

My minor pique dissolved as I melted into him, smiling at him as he laughed.

When he was done, I noted, "All the awesomer you are got even more awesome, you vaulting over a bar for me."

Ham turned his focus and smile back to me. "You really liked that, didn't you?"

My smile faded and I pressed closer as I replied quietly, "Yes. I really liked it. I didn't see it but just knowin' you did it is beyond cool. But it's knowin' *why* that's what I *really* liked. Got a lot of good people in my life, people who were there always but who kicked in when it mattered. But when it really mattered, when the hurt could get extreme, only two people put themselves between me and it. One, two days ago, got laid in the ground. The other is lyin' in this bed with me right now."

When I was done talking, Ham was no longer smiling. His arms were also no longer holding me. One had clinched tight. He brought his other hand to cup my cheek as his eyes went dark and bored into mine.

"Fuck, shit," he whispered, his tone so jagged, if it wasn't so beautiful, it would have shredded me.

His face, his voice, his eyes, his fierce hold, it all did a number on me, making my throat itch and my eyes sting.

But the moment was too beautiful to mess up by dissolving into tears.

So I said, "I just want you to know I understand that, but I *need* you to know how much I appreciate it."

"Stop talking," he ordered gruffly.

"Okay," I whispered.

Ham's eyes moved over my face as his thumb glided over my cheek. I let him do this for a bit before I dipped my chin and shoved my face in his throat.

"What you said about your ex-wife, those women," I said softly there, "I get it. I get why you'd protect yourself from gettin' hurt. Still sucks you had all this to give and no one to give it to. But that doesn't mean I'm not grateful it got stored up over the years so you could give it all to me."

"Zara, I said, stop talking," he growled.

I shut up.

He slid his hand at my cheek, through my hair, and down my back where both hands started roaming.

I snuggled closer.

Eventually, Ham wrapped his arms around me to turn us so he could reach out and turn out the light. He kept hold of me as he located my toy and threw it on the nightstand and pulled the covers over us.

Then he settled on his back, me tucked close to his side, his fingers roaming the skin of my ass, my fingers sifting through the hair on his chest.

The air in the room was warm and heavy in a good way. I liked it. It didn't feel suffocating. I felt safe. But no way either of us could sleep in that air. I knew it by the tension I could feel in Ham's body and the same in mine.

So I moved to lighten the air.

"Any chance I'll get you naked on your knees with your hands clasped behind your head?" I asked.

"No fuckin' way," Ham answered and I smiled into his skin.

I knew it before I asked. Ham was sweet, kind, affectionate, and generous. But in bed, he was definitely in charge.

Still, I offered, "I'll vault over a bar for you."

"That's not gonna happen. You got the upper-body strength of a girl," he replied.

I lifted my head to look down at him through the shadows. "News just in, I *am* a girl, babe."

"Thank fuck," he muttered.

It was at that, I burst out laughing.

And that was the last sound either of us made before I settled back into my man and we both fell asleep.

CHAPTER THIRTEEN

He's Beautiful

Two days later...

"THINKIN' THIS IS too soon, babe," Ham said quietly.

"Shh," I shushed him, my eyes out the side window of his truck.

We were parked outside Zander's school. School had just let out, kids in private-school uniforms were streaming out the doors, and I was concentrating.

I had no idea what he looked like but I was certain I'd know him on sight.

"Cookie," Ham called.

"Shh," I shushed him again, this time adding waving my hand behind me.

Ham didn't want to come and he'd explained why. He figured I'd have the strength to fight the fight but I'd also have the patience if Zander was an entity out there I knew existed and wanted to connect with. But if he became real, in other words, I saw him, that patience would vanish and Nina had told us this wasn't exactly a quick process so we'd both need lots of it.

But it had been four days. Four days of knowing he wasn't too far away. Four days of knowing he was out there, living with Aunt Wilona, breathing, eating, studying, doing kid shit.

Four very long days.

I couldn't wait any longer.

So when I searched the Internet and found the name of the only private school in three counties, one close to where Aunt Wilona lived, I'd told Ham I was going. He told me it was too soon. I told him I was going even if he didn't go with me. Ham explained why it was too soon. I told him that made sense, but I couldn't wait any longer. Then I grabbed my purse and keys.

So Ham took me.

"Zara, baby, it's not too late. We can—" Ham started.

But I interrupted him by breathing, "Oh my God."

My heart slid up in my throat, choking me.

There he was.

Oh my God, there he was.

He looked like Dad.

Which meant he looked like me.

But he was already tall, not like me, like Dad. He was also lean and straight, his navy-blue blazer fitting well on him. He wore his charcoal-gray trousers casually, like they were jeans. And he had a graceful gait, like he already was in command of his little man's body.

And, last, he was laughing and walking with a bunch of boys as other kids called to them.

He had a posse. He had friends. He was clearly popular.

Like his mom.

"Oh my God," I repeated, my body stringing tight with the effort it took not to throw open the door and run to him.

As if he sensed it, Ham wrapped his fingers tight around my knee.

"Where is he?" Ham asked.

I barely controlled lifting my finger to point but said, "Right there. Blond hair, like mine. He's got four boys with him. He's almost to the end of the buses."

I knew Ham spotted him when he muttered, "Fuck, looks just like you."

"Yeah," I whispered, my eyes glued to the boy who was making the motions of saying good-bye to his friends.

After he looked both ways, I watched him jog across the street. I craned my neck and then watched as he climbed into an SUV with Aunt Wilona behind the wheel.

My heart, still in my throat, started burning, swelling, and I was finding it difficult to breathe.

I watched Zander smile at my aunt and then put on his seatbelt.

Aunt Wilona smiled back and eased the car into the street.

I stared as they passed us. Neither of them turned to look, not that Zander would know who he was seeing. But they were gabbing to each other, sharing their days, like they probably did every day after school since kindergarten.

"Get us out of here, Ham," I ordered, my voice husky and unsteady. "Get us out of here now."

Ham wasted no time turning the ignition and moving into traffic.

"Okay, that was a bad idea," I admitted softly when we were on our way.

"Fuck," Ham replied.

"A really bad idea," I stated.

"Knew that'd wreck you. Fuck," Ham murmured.

"I think I'm gonna cry," I told him.

"Do it," Ham invited.

"I hurt all over," I shared and I did. The pain was radiating out of my throat, blocking every pore.

"Baby."

My eyes filled with tears. "He's beautiful, Ham."

Ham said nothing but his hand came back to my knee.

"She'd be so proud," I whispered then I lost it.

Leaning forward, I buried my face in my hands and my shoulders started shaking with silent sobs.

About a second later, the truck was at the side of the road, my seatbelt was gone, and I was pulled across the cab and in Ham's arms.

He held me until my emotion was spent and he kept holding me when, lips at my ear, he stated gently, "From now on, cookie, you gotta listen to me, okay?"

I nodded.

"This is gonna be hard enough, don't make it harder," he went on.

I nodded again.

"You listen to me, swear to Christ, honey, I'll break my back to make that hard as easy on you as it can be."

Every day in every way I loved this man more and more.

"Okay, darlin'," I whispered.

"Now kiss me, napkins in the glove compartment, clean up, and let's get you a mile-high mud pie at The Mark," he finished.

I smiled a shaky smile into his neck.

Graham Reece *so* knew me.

I pulled back and gave him my shaky smile before I gave him a light kiss. Then I pulled away, cleaned up my face, and Ham took me to The Mark, where I could mute my sorrow in chocolate cake, fudge frosting, whipped chocolate mousse, and ice cream.

And although The Mark's mud pie was amazing, what muted my sorrow was the hope that, one day, I'd be sitting there with Ham and Zander, watching my nephew eat one, too.

*   *   *

Reece

Reece stood in the doorway to the kitchen, shoulder resting against the jamb, eyes aimed through the living room to the doors of the balcony where he saw his girl sitting outside, feet up on the railing, beer in her hand, gaze on the mountains.

He had his phone in his hand. He looked down at it, hit the button, glued his eyes back to his woman, and put the phone to his ear.

"Reece, how's everything?" Nina asked in his ear.

"We had a situation today," Reece replied. "Zara couldn't wait anymore. We went to Zander's school to see if we could spot him. We did. She lost it."

"Oh dear," Nina murmured.

"We need to discuss a new strategy," Reece informed her.

"And that would be?" she asked cautiously.

"She's holdin' it together but I 'spect that's gonna dissolve. If we gotta make concessions without harmin' the end goal, we're gonna have to do that. But we need to get them to agree to arrange for a meeting with Zara and Zander and then regular visits."

There was a long, weighty pause Reece did not like before Nina shared, "I received word from Xavier Cinders' attorney today, Reece, and I'm sure it won't surprise you that they're already taking a hard line."

She was right, it didn't surprise him. But it did piss him off.

"Explain that," he ordered.

"More things that won't surprise you but mention of Zara's divorce, the brevity of that union, the loss of her home and shop. And you and I may need to have a sit down so you can share anything I might need to know, because they didn't say it up front, but my guess is, they're investigating you and if you've got skeletons in your closet, I have to know about them."

"I don't," Ham stated.

"That's good but maybe I need to be the judge of that," Nina replied.

Fuck.

"It was also noted that you were caught up in that mess with that serial killer," she went on.

Fuck.

"Not my fault that guy had me in his sights," Ham returned.

"Agreed. But that doesn't mean they won't twist it in some way to make it work for them."

"Goddamn it," Reece muttered.

"Do you want good news?" she asked.

"If you got it," he answered.

"I've had long conversations with both Zara's maternal aunts. I know she primed them before they called me but I'm pleased to report they told me what they told her. They're willing to assist us any way we need it. As you know, they, too, were under the impression Zander had been adopted and they're about as happy as Zara is that he wasn't. They're also a bit put out they weren't invited to Xenia's final services."

"Know that already, Nina," Reece told her and he knew this because Zara had reported it to him after the lengthy phone calls she'd had with her aunts two days ago.

"Yes, well, it's still good they've confirmed with me. One minor problem with this is they never witnessed any physical abuse of Amy, Xenia, or Zara. That said, they often saw Xavier lose his temper, he did it quickly, they found it alarming, and they watched how their sister cowed and how the girls were not saved from this by father or mother. They've also heard Wilona and Dahlia pile verbal abuse on Amy. I don't know how far that will go but they've both agreed to be deposed locally. We'll add their depositions to our evidence but neither can afford back-and-forth trips and we're on a budget, too. So we'll save their visits to Colorado if we need them, or hopefully when they come out to meet their great-nephew."

"Fine," Reece replied.

"And another bit of news I'm not entirely certain what to do with," she said, and Ham's focus on Zara dimmed so he could focus on her words mostly because of how she said them.

"That is?" he prompted.

"Max and I were out with the kids last night and we got a visit at our table from Pastor Williams."

This was so surprising, and considering how the man handled Zara, the service, and Zara's guess that he was the one who shared about the service with Mick, Ham straightened away from the door. "And?"

"My sense is, he's in a pickle. He's a man of the cloth and thus there are many things he can't share. However, I also got the sense he knew what was going on in that house while the girls were growing up and he wanted to help. I don't know if Xenia went to him, or if it was Zara or Amy. But my guess is, one of them did. If it was Xenia, he may be free to share as she's no longer with us and yet he wasn't very forthcoming during our strange chat last night. If it was Zara, she would have told us. So, unfortunately, I'm thinking it's Amy."

"Shit," Ham muttered.

"There are many angles to any fight, Reece," Nina told him. "I don't know his but what he said and how he said it was curious. It was also intriguing. I'm going to look into it as he seemed frustrated and very concerned. So, guessing again, he can't do anything to help us unless Amy allows it. But he *can* talk to Amy."

"Not sure that'll do any good. That woman was broken a long time back. She doesn't have it in her to do shit. Right or wrong," Reece explained, something he suspected Nina knew.

"Miracles happen," she replied.

"I wouldn't hold your breath," Reece advised.

"I won't," she said, a smile in her voice. "But I'll hope. I'll also think about how to approach regarding a meeting that will take us into a regular visitation schedule while we fight the big fight. But, Reece, my advice is to keep Zara away from Zander. I know it will be hard on her but we can't risk her approaching him, what that would say about her that she wouldn't have a mind to how he'd react to the shocking news of her living a county over. We have to go cautious in every step we take. If we can't come to a private agreement and this sees court, the judge will want to see us taking the high road."

"Tried to talk her out of it, she wouldn't listen. It didn't go well. She's promised to listen," Reece told her.

"Good," Nina murmured. Then she stated, "A lot has been going on but you should know I found out Kami didn't want Zara to know about Xenia because she wanted to save Zara from either being shoved out of any services they had for her sister or having to go and be around her father. So Kami, Lynda, Kami's mom, Arlene, and now me, Mindy and Becca are hoping to plan a memorial for Xenia. It wasn't meant to be a surprise but it is meant to be a celebration of Xenia that Kami suspected Xavier wouldn't give. They wanted to have it sorted before they went to her. Now, with all that's going on, I need you to check with Zara to see if she'll be okay with something like that. If she is, we'll proceed. If she isn't, we'll let it go."

"We'll have a chat," Reece said.

"Thanks," Nina replied. "Now, I'll have a think about

how to move forward after what happened today, and when I come up with a plan, I'll call you."

"Right. Thanks, Nina."

"No problem, Reece."

They wrapped it up and Reece went into the kitchen, got a beer, got another one for Zara, and headed out to the balcony.

She looked up at him and smiled but the smile didn't cut through the sadness he knew she was trying to hide.

Silently, he handed her the beer. She took it, chugged what was left in her bottle, and leaned forward to set the empty on the railing.

He dragged a chair close, sat in it, and lifted his cocked legs to rest his feet on the railing.

The chairs were cheap white plastic and every time he sat in one, he was sure it would give out.

At her house, a house that stood empty waiting for the time he gave her the diamond sitting in his nightstand, another expenditure that cut into his nest egg, she had a great deck. Or, *they* had one.

Big enough for nice furniture, a table, chairs, umbrella, loungers, and a kick-ass grill.

He'd intended to use the money he had left to set them up, create a space for her that she deserved. Build a home. Start to build a life. While doing that, build a family.

Now he was thinking he needed to talk another landlord into voiding another lease because rent on the apartment when they had a house all paid for was something they could no longer afford.

Which meant giving his girl her diamond a lot sooner than he intended, not giving her time to settle into the us he was building them to be.

"Well, at least I timed my magnificently stupid visit to first lay my eyes on my nephew during a day off so I can sulk and drink beer and not lose tips because of it," she joked to the horizon before she took a draw off her beer.

But Reece smiled.

Even back in the day, with her sister laid up, brain-dead in a hospital bed, she'd found it in her to joke. To smile. To bury the shit of her life and find ways to enjoy it in spite of all that.

It was why he took her to his bed. She was fucking pretty, great hair, fantastic tits, an even better ass, and he'd been thinking of doing it but held back because he thought she was too young. He didn't need to get hung up on a woman but it was far worse when a woman got hung up on you, and the younger ones were prone to that shit. Extricating yourself from that kind of situation was not fun, so he avoided it.

But when that shit storm hit and the way Zara handled it, he knew she might be young in years but she was not young in any other way, so he took her back and took her to his bed.

When he did, he found out why she'd grown up fast and he hated learning it. But it brought him to the understanding that this pretty woman with her great body, great hair, fast smile, quick wit, and easy disposition was a whole lot more even if that already was a fuckuva lot.

And he wanted it.

So he got it.

And now he *had* it.

And he had no problem putting a ring on it, even if that meant doing it faster than he'd planned.

But the bottom line was, it was too late, way too late. He'd let her down and done it in the worst way.

He sure as fuck was going to make up for that now.

"Just got off the phone with Nina," he told her.

"Heard you talkin' to someone," she murmured and took another drag, her focus on the mountains, not on their conversation.

He bumped her leg with his. "Cookie, you gotta listen."

He watched her sigh and look at him. "I had one breakdown today, Ham. You know me well, darlin', but not well enough to know that I'm only allowed one breakdown a week. Sister dead and seein' Zander, I'm already over my quota. I don't know what'll happen if I have another one but I suspect either spontaneous combustion or projectile vomiting. Neither are pretty, so be forewarned about that when you share what you gotta share."

He grinned before he requested, "Would you stop bein' funny when I got important shit to tell you? You can go back to bein' funny after we're done."

"Sock it to me, *mein herr,*" she invited and his grin turned into a smile.

Then he socked it to her, everything, except his asking Nina to arrange a meeting and visitation with Zander. He didn't want to get her hopes up.

When he was done, she immediately replied, "Right. First part, Dad's a dick. We knew that already. No surprise. Onward from that, I hope he goes bankrupt paying for an investigator to investigate you, which, incidentally, invading your privacy like that elevates him from a dick to a dick-ish douchebag, which, I'll grant, is a vague distinction but I think you get me."

Reece began to laugh softly, not missing the fact that, unlike Nina, Zara didn't even question the idea that he might have something in his past that could hurt them. He didn't. He'd been a traveling man but that didn't mean he had anything to hide. But Zara didn't waste even a single breath to question it.

She wasn't done.

"And the second part, I'm shocked as shit Kami would be so thoughtful. That's sweet. And I'd like to celebrate Xenia's life, but right now, I don't have it in me. A week, two, maybe we can arrange a big blowout. I'll get out pictures and invite all her old friends. Now"—she shook her head—"no."

"You got it, cookie."

"And just so you know, even though my sister was an alcoholic, that doesn't mean after seeing my beautiful, obviously popular, smiling nephew today, I don't intend to use beer as a crutch and drink until I pass out. So advice, keep an eye on that so you can get in there and get yourself drunk sex before it turns unpretty and drunk sex ends with me puking and/or passing out during the act."

"I'll keep an eye on that. I'll also order a pizza so we can draw that out, seein' as you goin' down on me rocks my world but when you're smashed, you ratchet that shit up so it's so fuckin' good, I don't know whether to come in your mouth or fuck you then hold you until you pass out, before I slip out while you're asleep and buy you a trophy."

He was damned gratified when she threw back her head and laughed with no sadness hidden behind the sound. It was all genuine.

And Reece took a drag off his beer as he watched her laugh.

Her laughter waned and her eyes focused on his. "You know, of course, that now I really need a Blowjob Trophy."

"Then I'll get you one, you earn it."

She grinned. "Challenge accepted, Bruiser."

Reece moved his gaze to the mountains, muttering, "Good to hear, cookie."

She butted her leg against his, not to get his attention, just a show of affection, and he heard her soft giggle before she squelched it to drink more beer.

His girl.

Drama.

Then easy.

Jesus, but he'd fucked up. He could have had that for a decade and, more, given it to her.

Oh yeah. Fuck yeah.

He'd fucked up.

They sat in silence awhile before Reece got up and ordered pizza.

Then they drank, ate, and drank some more.

And, later, Zara earned her trophy.

Then she passed out.

But she did it cuddled close in his arms.

CHAPTER FOURTEEN

Two Different Things

Six days later...

"You know, Cotton," I called to the old man's back as we trudged through the mountains, "they have digital cameras these days. Most of them are small and none of them require film and all this other stuff I'm lugging through the perilous off-trail Rocky Mountains."

I wasn't joking. We weren't on a trail. I had to admit, the views were stunning but still, the terrain was treacherous. So treacherous, the old guy's easy pace moving through it flipped me out. Then again, he wasn't carrying a heavy camera bag on his shoulder like I was.

"Did you come to bellyache or did you come to see a master at work?" Cotton asked, not turning back to me.

"I came to see a master at work but, prior to that, you failed to divulge you were a slave driver."

He stopped abruptly, murmured reverently, "There she is," then reached an arm back toward me, again without looking at me but snapping his fingers and demanding, "Give me my bag, girl."

I gratefully pulled the strap off my shoulder and positioned the handles in his hand.

His fingers curled around the handles and he went right to work, unzipping the bag, yanking out his camera, then dropping to a knee with the camera up to his face.

I got close and looked at the view he was shooting.

Then I lost my breath.

All my life, I'd lived in the Rockies and never, not once, did I get used to their splendor.

They might be hard to climb, difficult to traverse, and the weather in them unpredictable, but none of that meant that God didn't know exactly what He was doing when He created them.

Once I'd drunk in the view, my eyes moved to Cotton.

I was more than pleased that I'd found time to go out with him on a shoot. Or more to the point, I was more than pleased he'd phoned me way early that morning, waking me after a few hours of sleep since I'd had a shift the night before, and telling me to haul my behind to his place to get him because we were going out.

I left a disgruntled but soon-back-to-fast-asleep Ham in his bed in order to have this opportunity.

But navigating dangerous mountain passes was worth the view. More, watching Cotton, who looked like Rocky Mountain Santa with his shock of white hair, white beard, jolly belly, and red nose, focused on creating what I knew once the photos were done would be sheer beauty made it even more worth it.

I drank this in, too, and did it until Cotton dropped the camera then sat on his ass on the boulder we were perched on and looked up at me.

"Thermos 'a joe in that bag, Zara, coupla mugs. Pour us some lead," he ordered.

I dropped to my ass on the boulder and did as told. I handed him his travel mug and wrapped my gloved hands around mine.

"How'd you know this was here?" I asked after I took a sip, motioning to the view with my head.

"Lotta years on me, girl," Cotton answered. "Spent 'em high and low, traipsin' through these hills. Saw this spot years ago. But this spot, the light's gotta be right. Woke up and just got the feelin', the light would be right. Luckily, I was not wrong. So here we are and, finally, I caught that old girl's glory."

I looked to the "old girl," a sweeping range of Rockies that punctuated a cloudless blue sky, the sun stark on its planes, shaded through its angles.

It was phenomenal. Cotton's feeling was spot on. Then again, that was why he was world famous and became that way exposing the beautiful mysteries of America's mountains' majesty.

"You gotta know, whole town's talkin' about your boy," he muttered and my eyes went from the majesty to Cotton.

I didn't know which "boy" he was talking about. Ham could be a boy to him, considering Cotton's age. Or he could mean Zander. I did know that whatever this was he was bringing up was why I was there, he'd asked me to come before the Zander news broke, so I suspected it was Ham.

"You wanna explain that, Cotton?" I asked.

He took a sip from his mug and his eyes came to me.

"Xenia's son," he answered, surprising me but I nodded.

I'd told Mindy and Becca about Zander the night of Xenia's funeral. I'd also told Arlene. Mins and Becs could keep their mouths shut. Arlene, no way in hell.

" 'Spect you know this already, Zara, but your daddy's a sumabitch," Cotton shared.

I drank from my coffee and looked to the mountain. "Yeah, Cotton, learned that when I was around three."

"He hurt you girls?" Cotton asked, and my gaze shot back to him.

"Cotton—"

"Did Xavier take his hand to you girls?" Cotton asked firmly.

"Yes," I whispered, telling him something only Ham, Mins, Neens, Becs, Maybelle, Wanda, and my dead friend Kim knew, outside of Xenia, of course, but she was there.

"Dang nab it," he muttered.

His head dropping, he looked at his lap.

"Cotton, it was a while ago," I told him gently.

His gaze came back to mine before he said bizarrely, "Takes a village."

"What?" I asked.

"It takes a village, Zara. You won't know this, won't have remembered her that way. If I recall, by the time you and your sister could cipher, she'd lost it so you didn't get her that way, but Amy Cinders before she became a Cinders was the prettiest girl in town before she gave our town you and your sister. And that's sayin' somethin', seein' as we got a lot of talent about. Thing about her was, she wasn't just pretty, she was sweet. Couldn't tell a joke and wouldn't, seein' as she was a might shy, but you'd work hard to make her laugh, hear that sound that was pretty as her, watch her face light up."

His eyes grew sharp on me before he finished.

"And she laughed a lot back then, girl."

I didn't like this, knowing Mom was pretty...once. Happy...once. Laughed...once.

Cotton was right. I never saw her smile, definitely not laugh, and by the time I could "cipher," although it wasn't lost on me she was vaguely attractive, that was defined as "vaguely" due to the fact that timidity shrouded her and fear poured off her in waves.

I didn't like knowing she'd lost that. More, I didn't like knowing she gave it up, apparently without much of a fight.

"I'm not sure I want to hear this," I told him carefully, also not wanting to offend him.

"What I'm sayin' is, he broke her. So we knew. The town did. Xenia and you hightailin' it outta there the minute you could. Xenia abusin' her body in an effort to dull the pain. We knew. And we shoulda done somethin' about it."

I felt bad for him because he clearly felt bad about all this but it was way past the point anything could be done now.

"You seem to be takin' this hard, Cotton, and I won't say it wasn't tough but it was a long time ago and there were people closer to the situation who should have done something about it."

"Your mother," he said.

"Yes," I agreed.

"You're right," he stated.

"I know I am," I told him.

"Your man now, what's that about?" he changed the subject suddenly.

And there we were, just as I suspected.

That didn't mean I wasn't confused at his question.

"I'm not following," I replied.

"He's got years on you, girl," he shared something I knew.

"And you had years on Alana," I returned the favor, referring to his wife, a beauty, Native American, statuesque, graceful, soft-spoken, kind, and now, upsettingly, gone.

It was before the time I could "cipher," but I knew she'd been in her twenties when they married, Cotton in his forties. That didn't stop them from building a family, which they did, all adopted because Alana got ovarian cancer when she was way too young, had her entire womb removed, enjoyed a good spell with her man then it came back and devoured her.

But unlike my friend Kim, who died within months of diagnosis, for Alana, it took its time the second time around, drew it out, so when Alana finally faded away, it was a relief, even to Cotton, who was ravaged by her illness, his powerlessness against it but not her loss. His relief was so great, you could see it, feel it. It wasn't a celebration. It was a stillness of expression and manner. And it lasted a long time.

Then he got crotchety and now he was a new Cotton, one who didn't smile as much as I remembered him doing when I was a kid. And he didn't laugh as much either.

He found his way to live on without the woman he adored.

But it wasn't the same.

"We're not talkin' 'bout Alana, Zara. We're talkin' 'bout you," Cotton shot back.

"Cotton, you're grumpy but I love you. You know it. Still, I don't know where you're aimin' so I don't know where to put my shield."

He didn't pull any punches when he finally spit it out.

"Girls come from homes like yours sometimes find their daddies."

I blinked.

Then I stared.

After I did that for a while, I burst out laughing.

"I'm not bein' funny, girl," Cotton groused through my laughter.

Also through my laughter, I forced out, "You so totally are."

"Zara, straighten up and listen to me. I'm bein' very serious."

I choked down my laughter and looked at him.

"Darlin', he even looks mean," Cotton stated quietly when he got my attention.

"Yeah, he does," I agreed. "But he's the gentlest, most affectionate man I've ever met."

"Zara—"

I cut him off.

"When I broke my wrist, he drove hundreds of miles to cook and clean for me for a week. When Kim died, he couldn't get here until two days after the funeral because of work but he busted his ass to get here. He had only three days off and he didn't sleep a wink in those days due to driving and spending time looking after me. And when I found out about Xenia, I couldn't hold myself up and Ham was right down on the kitchen floor with me, holding me in his arms while I cried."

I leaned forward and batted his knee with my hand before I leaned back, but through all this, I held his eyes.

"He's not my dad, Cotton. He's a big man who's worked in bars his whole life so he's got a look about him that you just don't mess with him. But he got that through his profession. He doesn't practice it in life."

"Max likes him," Cotton told me, sounding peeved, like he didn't want to admit that.

But that was when I knew that Max also had reservations about Ham, maybe because of the way he looked, maybe Nina had shared some of our history, and that was why Max was cautious at first at The Rooster.

But Ham had won Max over and Max had shared this with Cotton.

"Give him a chance. There's a lot to like," I assured Cotton.

"He gonna give me that chance or is he gonna blow town and leave you again but leavin' you this time maybe with a boy to raise?" Cotton asked.

"You know, I love you all the more because you care enough to bring me out here and have this talk, even if your honesty is off-base. But Ham's stayin'," I replied and Cotton's eyes grew shrewd.

"You sure about that?"

"Yes."

"And how are you sure?"

"Because he told me."

"Girl—"

I scooted across the boulder to get closer to him and once there, I leaned in farther.

"He loves me, Cotton."

"He tell you that?"

I felt my chin jerk back.

He hadn't.

Ham had never said that.

He showed it, all the time.

But he'd never said it.

Not when he talked about committing to Gnaw Bone, committing to me. Not while we were cozied up, watching TV. Not during sex. Not cuddling after sex prior to falling asleep.

Not ever.

"You got a whale of a fight on your hands, darlin'," Cotton said and I focused on him again. "Choose who you got in the corner of your ring wisely. You take on a child, your life becomes about that child and it's harder to take life's knocks when they hit *you*. You definitely shouldn't be courtin' them."

"Ham's a good guy," I whispered.

"I believe you," Cotton replied. "But a good guy and good for you are two different things, Zara."

It was getting on my nerves when people made sense when they were talking about Ham even when I knew deep down they had no clue what they were talking about.

"I'm suddenly rethinking being your camera-bag-lugging girl," I shared in order to express this and he grinned. It didn't quite catch his eyes but he did it.

"Truth hurts. Then again, it also sets you free," he stated. "Talk to your man and make sure his head is where you need it to be. You get that boy away from your daddy's family, you gotta teach him to look after himself and the best way to do that is by example."

"Ham'll win you over," I promised.

"Not me he's gotta win," Cotton returned. "But I'll take it, though only after I know he's pulled out all the stops to win you."

That was sweet but I felt my eyes narrow. "How can you be scary, nosy, irritating, and lovable all at the same time?"

Cotton grinned even as he shrugged. "It's just me."

It was and had been since Alana died.

"You gonna take pictures or is there more of my world you wanna rock?" I asked, being flippant in the face of sudden uncertainty.

"I'm gonna take pictures but only after I say one more thing."

I looked to the blue skies and muttered, "Great."

"Zara," Cotton called.

I looked at him.

"Alana was like you," he said quietly and I pulled in a breath because, from Cotton, this was the highest of compliments. "She was young but old at heart. She knew what she wanted and God smiled His Heavenly light on me when she found that in me. Never happier in my life than when I had her, not before, absolutely not after. The age we had between us never touched us, not with the love we had. Her parents didn't like it but she didn't care. The day I won them over, I reckon, was the day she died. They'd watched me stick by her side through the better but mostly through the worse. This man of yours is who you think he is, I see you think you got that, too. And, if this man is who you think he is, I couldn't be happier for you."

"Now you're tippin' the scales, Cotton." I kept up with my flippancy, this time in order not to cry. "You're supposed to balance lovable and grumpy. Now you're bein' way more lovable than grumpy."

He sucked back more coffee, then handed me his cup, stating, "Then you best get off your keister, girl. There's mountains to climb and pictures to take."

I looked again to the skies and repeated, "Great."

"Up," he grunted, shoving up to his feet.

I sucked back my coffee and followed him.

Then I followed him through the scrub and rocks and boulders and I did this successfully not falling down the side of the mountain or, less dramatically, twisting my ankle.

And Cotton showed me beauty.

It was what I knew it would be, a marvel watching a master at work even if it was simply watching a man snap pictures.

That didn't mean I didn't do it with my mind weighed heavily with thoughts about what he said.

This sucked, shadowing a great morning.

But Ham and I had never finished talking about his history, his problems with women. So much had happened since then—we'd been involved with Zander, Xenia dying, work, and settling into life together—we never got back to it.

And he'd never told me he loved me. I'd told him he was the love of my life, but he never shared anything close to that sentiment. Not with words.

And I'd learned the hard way with how I grew up, with the way Xenia went off the rails, that Cotton was right.

I had to look after myself.

Which meant I had to talk to Ham.

* * *

I sat on the couch in Ham's office at The Dog, my legs crossed under me.

After my early morning in the mountains with very little sleep and an evening on my feet carrying drinks, I was dog-tired. There was nothing I wanted more than to fall into bed and sleep until tomorrow where I could go back to work and make more tips in hopes of using them to win my sister's son into my life.

But my eyes were on Ham at his desk. He was standing, bent over the desk scribbling stuff in books and shoving money in moneybags he'd put in the safe when he was done cashing out completely. And it occurred to me that, unless we were in bed or Ham was stretched out watching TV, he rarely sat. Years of life working on his feet, he was used to it and kept them, probably out of habit.

"Tell me about February."

Those words were said in my voice because they came from my mouth.

Ham, still bent over the desk, tipped only his head back to look at me.

"What?" he asked.

I'd started it. I didn't mean to. I had other things to say. Other things to ask.

But I'd done it because I wanted to know. I'd wanted to know for a while. So I had to go with it.

"We never got done talkin' the other night at The Rooster. You didn't get to the part about February Owens."

Ham didn't move, body nor eyes, when he asked, "What about her?"

This wasn't new, awesomer, forthcoming Ham. This was don't-ask, don't-tell Ham and him going back to that, especially on this particular topic, sent a chill spreading over my skin.

Even so, I carried on.

"I don't think it'll come as a surprise, darlin', that after that went down, I didn't avoid it. They had a special report on what happened with Dennis Lowe, an hour long, on one of the channels and I watched it. They said all the men who got killed were her"—I paused before I said—"lovers. Even her ex-husband got it."

"And?"

And?

That was it? *And?*

I couldn't say I knew what I wanted to get. His confirmation they were lovers coupled with a firm declaration it was over, he was over it, and he'd moved on would be good. What would be better would be his firm declaration he'd moved on because he'd realized he'd always been in love with me.

What wasn't good was *and?*

"Were you her lover?" I pushed.

"Yes," he answered.

I waited.

He said no more and went back to scribbling something.

I had no idea how to take this except badly.

"Ham?" I called.

"Yeah," he said to the desk, not looking at me.

That chill on my skin grew colder.

Then I looked to the side. This was not the right time. I was tired. It was after three in the morning. And Ham obviously wasn't in the mood.

I should never have said anything.

"Zara, you got somethin' to say?" Ham asked and I looked at him to see him again looking at me.

I shook my head. "No."

Ham nodded and went back to doing the shit he had to do to finish the night at the bar.

It wasn't until we were in the truck that either of us spoke again and it was Ham who did it.

"Care about her," he declared.

I looked to him, seeing his face illuminated only by the lights of the dash so I couldn't read it, and I asked, "What?"

"Feb," he answered. "Care about her. Always will."

It was then I knew I *really* should never have said anything.

It was not a surprise he cared about her or always would. He was that kind of guy. He was also the kind of guy who was honest. I'd asked. He gave me the truth.

I still found this unsettling and I figured this was mostly because his declaration was present tense, which wasn't bad, as such. It was just that nothing came after it.

I looked out the side window.

"She's got a man, babe. She's havin' a baby. She might already have had it."

In other words, beautiful February Owens was very taken.

So what did that mean? Was I the consolation prize? Ham rethought his life after getting literally axed by an ax murderer, his first choice was shacked up so he turned to Gnaw Bone?

I thought this.

I said nothing.

"Care about you, too, cookie," he said softly.

He cared about me.

That I knew. I'd always known.

But that didn't mean shit when you were planning on building a life with a man. Suing for fucking custody of your nephew with him.

Getting Zander was Ham's idea in the first place and, by the way, what was *that* all about? Hell, Ham seemed even more determined to win Zander than I was. That wasn't true but that didn't mean he wasn't driving hell-bent for leather on that.

He wanted kids. He'd wanted them since his bitch ex-wife, Rachel, aborted the two he could have given to her. Decades, he'd wanted kids.

So was Zander his shot for getting one and quick?

"Zara, you're quiet," Ham observed.

"I'm tired," I semi-lied.

"Next time that old man wants to drag you up a mountain, I'm keepin' you in bed with me," he replied.

I again said nothing.

We went the rest of the way home in silence and, once there, I wasted no time going to the bathroom and getting ready for bed. I didn't look up at Ham as I passed him when I left the bathroom and he was on his way to it. I just climbed into bed, turned my back to Ham's side, and curled up under the covers.

Minutes later, Ham joined me. Seconds later, his hands were on me, attempting to roll me into a cuddle.

I resisted, pulling away and muttering, "I'm not in the mood tonight, darlin'."

I felt Ham still before I felt him retreat.

The light went out and the bed moved with Ham settling then there was nothing.

Not until he said into the dark room, "Before, you were flippin' me out. Now, you're pissin' me off."

"Why?" I asked.

"This shit you're pullin'," he answered.

This shit I was pulling?

I decided not to rise to the bait. "I'm just tired, Ham. I'm not pullin' any shit."

"You are, and you're full of shit, too."

That, I couldn't let slide so I lifted up on a forearm and twisted my head to look in his direction. "How am I full of shit? I went to bed last night at three thirty in the morning and got out of it at seven thirty. I've had four hours of sleep."

Ham, being all I knew that was Ham, didn't hesitate to lay it out honestly.

"You asked that shit about Feb, didn't like my answers, now you're pouting."

Unfortunately, although this was somewhat close to the truth, now I was pissed off.

"I'm not pouting," I snapped.

"Tell me when we have ever shared the same bed and, even if we didn't fuck, you didn't sleep the whole goddamned night somehow cuddled into me."

I had no reply mostly because there was never a time, not once, when we shared the same bed where I didn't sleep snuggled close to Ham.

"Yeah," he stated, knowing from my nonresponse that he'd made his point.

With no other retort open to me, and angrier because of it, I repeated, "I'm not pouting, Ham."

"You weren't my first, babe, but you're gonna be my last," he declared.

Unthinking, too ticked to think, I shot back, "Lucky me Feb was taken, or I wouldn't get that."

After I finished speaking, I noted the air in the room instantly got heavy, and not the good, warm, safe kind. The bad, dangerous, suffocating kind.

And I didn't care.

He cared about her.

He cared about me.

What the hell was I supposed to do with that?

"What the fuck was that remark about?" he growled, and it wasn't his good, warm, sexy growl but his bad, dangerous, angry growl.

"Forget it," I mumbled and collapsed back in bed.

"Do you honestly think I'm gonna let you get away with that shit you just spewed?" he asked.

"Apparently not, since I should be sleeping and you're still talking," I replied.

The bed moved and the light went on.

I sighed, loud and heavily.

"Look at me, Zara."

"Can we do this in the morning?"

"Fuckin' look...at...me."

That was said in his downright terrifying, bad, dangerous, angry growl.

Since I had no choice, I sat up and turned to him, crossing my arms on my chest and my legs under me. Ham was up, too, back to the headboard, legs cocked at the knees under the covers, arms also crossed on his chest. I didn't know how he could be frightening, essentially lying in bed, but he pulled it off in a big way.

Luckily, I knew he'd never hurt me so I ignored that, too.

"Now, explain that shit," he ordered.

"I'm not exactly going to do cartwheels, knowing you care about another woman," I stated the obvious.

"Then why the fuck did you ask about her?" he asked.

"We still have more of your shit to talk through and I figured she was part of that."

"Well, she's not part of any shit I gotta talk through. But, advice, babe, you wanna have a deep conversation, don't start it when you're tired and in a bitchy mood."

I felt my temper spiking as I informed him, "I wasn't in a bitchy mood until you switched back to ask-no-questions, tell-no-lies Ham."

Ham lost patience and I knew this when he clipped, "Fuckin' hell, Zara, I don't know this shit you got goin' on in your head but there's only one me."

"That's bad news," I fired back, "seein' as the Ham I know cuts ties and takes off when the spirit moves him."

His brows drew together over narrowed eyes and he asked low, "Is that what this shit is about?"

"Actually, this shit is about me wanting to go to sleep, you not letting me do it, picking a fight, and me being so fucking tired I could fall asleep right now, sitting up, and you not letting this shit go."

"Zara, you started it by bringin' up Feb," he reminded me.

"Then point taken, big guy," I retorted, shoving the covers aside and jumping off the bed. Standing beside it, glaring at him, I went on. "I'll know next time not to bring up February. In fact, never to bring her up, seein' as you care about her so much, thinkin' about her puts you in a shit mood."

Ham angled out of bed and faced off with me across it, contradicting me. "I'm in a shit mood because you're pullin' this shit."

"Right then, your mood will get a whole lot better when I leave," I announced, then stomped to the door.

I was halted with a hand curled firm around my elbow when I was three feet away.

I looked up at Ham.

"Where the fuck you goin'?" he asked.

"My bed," I answered.

"Zara, you just rolled out of your bed," he told me.

"Ham, I just rolled out of *your* bed."

His brows shot up and that was a scary look, too.

"Jesus, seriously?" he asked.

"Let go," I demanded.

"Babe, get in bed."

"Let go."

"Fuckin' get in bed," he bit out.

"Fuckin' *let go*," I snapped. Not giving him the chance to comply, I twisted my arm from his hold and bolted out the door.

Once in my old bedroom, I slammed the door.

Then I stood staring at it, breathing heavily and waiting.

It didn't open.

I didn't hear Ham come down the hall. I didn't hear him knock.

I got nothing.

So be it.

I crawled into my own bed and curled under the covers.

He cared about me.

He also cared about February.

That's all he gave me.

Just that he cared about me.

But he also cared about February.

I lay in the dark knowing that was far from enough.

And, incidentally, I didn't sleep that night either.

CHAPTER FIFTEEN

He's What He Does

THE NEXT MORNING, I was in the kitchen rinsing out my cereal bowl, dressed, and ready to roll, when Ham walked in wearing loose track pants, running shoes, and a tight Under Armour crewneck that made his already massive chest seem colossal.

He gave me a scowl, which meant he, like me, wasn't over it, and he headed to the coffee.

I headed to my purse sitting on the countertop.

I almost had a hand on it when I heard Ham state, "I'm runnin'. When I get back and showered, we'll sort out our shit."

I nabbed my purse, pulled the strap over my shoulder, and, not looking at him, returned, "Sorry, we won't be doin' that, seein' as I'm takin' off right about now and I'm not comin' back. I'll see you at work. We'll talk tomorrow."

"Not comin' back?" he asked my back.

"Not until after work," I answered, pulling my hair out from under the strap. "Then, I'm sleepin'."

"Where the fuck you goin'?"

"Away from you," I replied, moving toward the door.

"Zara, you are not leavin'. I'm runnin' then we're workin' this shit out."

I turned at the door and glared at him. "Another thing to learn about me is no one tells me what I can and cannot do. I got away from that shit when I was eighteen and I'm never goin' back. So we'll talk tomorrow when I've had time alone to think things through. I haven't had much of that, us workin' together and livin' together, and I need it."

He had an empty mug in his hand and his eyes on me were narrowed as he asked, "Think what through?"

"This." I threw a hand in the air. "You and me."

His scowl got darker. In fact, it was midnight dark and scary to boot.

But he rested a hand on the countertop before he said, "Babe, tell me. What…*exactly*…is there to think through?"

As scary as his scowl was, the prospect of making the wrong decisions now that could possibly eventually affect three lives was far scarier.

So I explained. "The fact that it seems you want a commitment. To commit to me but, also, me to commit to you. And you want me to do that knowin' you care about another woman."

"February is not standin' in my kitchen with me," he pointed out and it was the *wrong* thing to say.

"Yeah, and when I asked you about an ex-lover, Ham, you gave it to me straight," I shot back, my heart starting to race, my head beginning to hurt, not wanting to do this now but caught up in it anyway, which was *not* making me happy. "I have no qualms with that. It's you. The problem is, after that, you gave me nothing. No woman in her right mind, especially with our history, knowin' you had others besides me, is gonna hook her star to a guy who's maybe hooked to someone else."

At my words, his scowl instantly went dark as pitch and I fancied the lights in the kitchen dimmed from the force of his glower.

"Are you fuckin' *shittin'* me?" His voice was also lower, rumbling, and pissed way the hell off, matching his expression precisely.

But I threw up my hands in exasperation because, again,

he did not contradict me. He did not assure me. He didn't do anything but get *more* pissed at me.

"Do I look like I'm shitting you?" I asked, then locked eyes with him. "You can't possibly think this isn't hard on me, Ham."

"No, you're absolutely right. I can't think that. What I don't get is, why you're *makin'* this so fuckin' hard, Zara. And just sayin', you're doin' all this shit to yourself," he retorted.

Man, oh man, now I wasn't just exasperated. I was getting angry.

Therefore, I snapped, "How's that?"

"Feb is not an issue," he fired back but again gave me no more.

"Right, well, I'm still in love with Greg. Is that an issue for you?" I returned nastily and dishonestly.

"Jesus, fuck, now you're makin' shit up and, worse, actin' in a way that I feel like I've been hurtled back to fuckin' high school," he bit out. "You need to grow up, Zara. We got issues, we talk 'em out. You don't get nasty just for the sake of scorin' a blow."

I couldn't believe he just said that. But he did, and because he did, I was no longer getting angry, I was there.

Therefore, I slammed my hands on my hips, leaned into him, and shouted, "My God, Ham! I'm not throwing an adolescent hissy fit. You say you want to start a life with me at the same time you care about another woman."

"I care about a lot of people, babe, but I'm not fuckin' any of them," he clipped.

"Yes, well, call me stupid, seein' as my life has been how it's been, havin' hope that one day, one fuckin' day somewhere in decades of them, I'll get what I want, but I'd kinda hoped, starting my life out with the love of my life, it wouldn't happen with my man carin' about another woman *and* carin' about me."

"Jesus, there's a difference," he replied.

"And that would be?" I pushed.

"Clue in, Zara, I'm standin' right in front of you. I'm here. And, like I said, I'm fuckin' *you*." And on the "you" he lifted a finger and jabbed it my way.

Heart racing, skin prickling, I retorted, "So, tell me, Ham, February Owens wasn't pregnant somewhere in Indiana, livin' with her high school boyfriend reunited, would you be standin' here with me?"

From the change that instantly came about him, something about that struck him. It appeared it was deep and that absolutely did not bode well.

Not at all.

"You can't be serious," he whispered.

"Explain why you think that," I returned. " 'Cause, see, where I'm standin', I see how I'm bein' *very* serious. I'm also *hearin'* that you haven't answered my fucking question."

"Fuck me, you're still so far up your own goddamned ass, you aren't payin' a lick of attention," he ground out.

"Explain that too, Ham, seein' as I feel I'm payin' so much goddamned attention, my head's about to explode."

"I suggest you pay more," he advised caustically.

"Actually, I was thinking of suggesting the same thing to you," I shot back.

"Zara, I have been so in your space, in your business, in your life, takin' your back and sortin' your shit, consumed by all that, I feel like it's been months I haven't breathed just for me."

"Then today's your lucky day, Ham. Breathe easy 'cause you're off the fuckin' job," I hurled at him, my tone ice cold but the blood in my veins was boiling even as my throat constricted.

I gave him no chance to say more. When we fought, we didn't do it fair and we went for the kill and I didn't have the energy to take more.

And I definitely didn't have the energy to come to the realization, again, the way Ham danced around the subject, that he was not in love with me. He might not be in love with February Owens, either. But he was honest enough to say it right out, share how he felt about me, and he didn't.

So he wasn't.

And I could not cope with that.

Not then.

I was too freaking tired.

I'd cope with it later and I'd figure it out, like everything I'd figured out in my life. I'd find my way past it, like I did with every blow I took. And I'd move the fuck on.

So I turned and marched to the front door, yanked it open, and stopped dead when I saw a woman standing at it, hand raised to the doorbell. She jerked in surprise, went solid, and stared at me.

I stared at her right back.

She was pretty, very pretty but in a way that it looked like she'd once been beautiful. In fact, a raving beauty. But she was older than me, if not by much, and the years had not been kind. There was a sadness to her face that even seeing her just then for the first time was easy to read. And it was so immense, that sadness had worn the beauty she once held clean away leaving her a dimmer vision of what was once glorious.

She was also blonde, her hair long and thick and cared for. She had hazel eyes. Her makeup was carefully applied to try to hide the wear of sadness, but it failed. She was dressed well, taller than me, and even more so in the high-heeled boots she was wearing. And she was very slim. Too slim, seeing as her breasts were large enough that they were either fake or her frame had endured more dieting than it needed, which made her seem top heavy and her shape unnatural.

"I, uh...gosh, um...I'm sorry. I thought Graham Reece lived here," she stated.

"Rachel?"

It was at hearing Ham's incredulous, displeased growl that I went solid.

This was Rachel? Sneaky aborter of babies, ex-wife *Rachel*?

As I stared in shock (and maybe a bit of abhorrence), her eyes went beyond me.

Her face changed in a way that another chill slid over my skin and she said, "Reece?"

"What the fuck?" he asked from closer and I felt his heat hit my back.

"I...well." Her eyes darted from Ham to me to Ham again. "I know this is a surprise—"

Ham cut her off. "Fuck yeah, seein' as I haven't seen your face or heard from your ass for twenty years, you show up out of the blue at my front door, it's a big fuckin' surprise."

He was most assuredly not being welcoming and she didn't miss it, not that she could. In fact, she barely hid her wince but she still managed to power through it.

"I saw you on the news," she told him.

"So did a million other Americans," he returned.

"And I...a few days ago, a man came to me, asking about you," she went on and I felt Ham tense at my back even as my body strung tight.

Dad's investigator.

"I thought you should know. I was worried and"—she shook her head—"I thought you should know."

"How'd you find me?" Ham asked what I thought was a very pertinent question, one of many, seeing as Ham grew up in Nebraska and he hadn't said it, but since they married young, my guess was that she was there, too.

"I have, well"—she hesitated—"my husband has a friend. He's a police officer. He...I'm sorry if you find this intrusive but he looked you up for me."

"And he couldn't look up my phone number?" Ham clipped and he was being kind of funny but it was far from amusing.

Her eyes went to me, then Ham again, and she said quietly, "You were injured by a serial killer, Reece. I've obviously upset you but after that... after that man visited, I wanted to see if you were all right. Not hear it. *See* it." Her eyes finally came to me and she whispered, "I'm sorry. It was—"

Ham interrupted her again, "What'd you tell this guy?"

Her gaze shot back to him. "Sorry?"

"What'd you tell the PI who came callin'?" Ham clarified.

"Well... the truth," she told him.

"There's your truth and my truth, Rachel, and back in the day, those two didn't sync," Ham returned.

She held Ham's eyes and requested softly, "Can I not do this out in the breezeway?"

Ham hesitated a second before he moved. Curling an arm tight around my shoulders, he tucked me deep into his side and backed us up three steps.

It wasn't much and wasn't intended to be much. She had just enough space to move into the apartment and close the door. That was all he was giving her.

I didn't want to be there, now for a variety of reasons. But Ham had clamped me so tight to his side, I couldn't move and I didn't want to because of what that might say to her.

But also, someone kill me, because Ham obviously wanted me right where I was, and because I loved him, I couldn't move.

"Now you aren't in the breezeway, woman. So what'd you tell the PI?" he prompted.

She straightened her shoulders, ignored me, and stated, "Like I said, I told him the truth."

"Rach—" Ham began but she kept talking.

"I said you were a good man, a good husband. We were young but you still gave me a decent home and that was because you worked hard. I told him that you wanted a family. You were ready for it. You were prepared for it, and you would have made an excellent father. But I was too young, I didn't...I didn't..." She faltered, probably because the extreme hostility rolling off Ham was hard to miss and all of it was aimed at her, then she rallied. "I didn't know what I wanted. I screwed up, our marriage went bad, you worked to save it, but I was too young and I...I...screwed it up." She pulled in a deep breath and finished. "That's what I told him, Reece."

I felt Ham's body relax and some of my tension flowed away when it did.

When Ham made no reply, she continued.

"Obviously, I didn't want to tell him anything but he was determined. So I asked him what this was about. He wasn't forthcoming but he did say the custody of a young boy was at stake."

Finally, her eyes slid to me, then around the apartment for the first time, maybe looking for clues a child lived with us, maybe just curious.

She did this quickly before looking back to Ham.

"He claimed it wasn't your boy," she told him.

"He isn't," Ham confirmed.

She nodded, looked swiftly to me again, failing at hiding her curiosity, then back to Ham before she said quietly, "Still, whoever it is, I told him what kind of man you were and made sure he knew you'd do right by the boy and he wouldn't find any help from me if he was trying to keep you away."

"So am I supposed to say thanks?" Ham asked sarcastically and that was when I decided to jump in.

"Rachel, I'm Zara," I stated belatedly, feeling awkward, but then again, I hadn't yet been given the opportunity to mind my manners and Ham certainly had no intention of minding his.

At my butting in, Ham's arm got tighter around me. A warning, but I ignored it.

"It's my nephew this is all about," I shared. "I'm uncertain he's being raised in a healthy environment and I've decided to do something about it."

Rachel nodded.

I continued. "It means a lot to me to get him safe, so I appreciate you being honest about Ham."

"Ham?" she asked.

"Reece," I clarified.

She nodded again, her eyes drifting up to Ham and it was then we both discovered that Ham was done with this unexpected visit and he was going to do something about it.

"So now that you came well out of your way to share your benevolence, we got shit to do," he declared. "I'd offer you a cup of coffee but I think you get why I'm not gonna do that."

"I live in Fort Collins now, Reece," she shared.

"Congratulations," Ham replied.

"Ham," I whispered, curling into him and looking up at him. His stubbled jaw was hard and a muscle was ticking there. I stared at that muscle jumping in his jaw.

Twenty years and she had the power to move him to this kind of emotion.

Twenty years.

This meant he wasn't over her, either. Twenty years was a long time. Yes, she did him wrong in a very, *very* bad way. But he had not moved on. He might have reflected years after she'd broken him, after he'd had an ax in his shoulder, and made the decision to try to move on.

But he hadn't moved on.

More not good in a situation between us that was already really not good.

"Seein' as you're standin' in front of the door and you know how to use it, I suggest you do that," Ham invited.

I looked to her to see she looked even sadder, she was pale and this was already hard on her but Ham was making it infinitely harder.

She didn't delay in nodding again and stepping to the door.

With effort, I pulled free of Ham and followed her. I put my hand on the door once she was through it and called her name.

She hesitated before cautiously turning back.

"I know your history," I told her quietly. "And I hope you understand Ham's reaction to your visit. But I thank you for being honest with the investigator. In the end, it will help Zander, and that's what's important."

"Of course," she murmured.

"Thank you for coming all this way."

She nodded, glanced beyond me, then turned and walked away.

I closed the door and found the living room empty so I moved to the kitchen.

Ham was pouring coffee in a travel mug.

He must have felt my presence in the doorway because he announced, "Don't wanna talk about that shit." He screwed the lid on the mug and turned to me. "Now I'm goin' for a run. You're here when I get back, you're here. You aren't, you aren't. Suit yourself."

Then he prowled to me and I had to jump out of the way or be bowled over.

But I followed him, asking stupidly, "You're running with a travel mug of coffee?"

Ham's answer was to walk through then slam the front door.

When I had aloneness and silence, both for the first time in a long time, suddenly, exhaustion overwhelmed me.

I couldn't think of shopping. I couldn't think of finding a friend who might be free to have lunch with me, but more, I didn't want to talk this shit through with anyone. I didn't want anyone to know. And I couldn't face saying it out loud.

I couldn't think of driving to Carnal and going to the library, studying up on Gnaw Bone history so I could teach Zander all about the town where he was born.

I couldn't think of doing anything but what I did.

I walked to my old room, closed the door, dropped my purse to the floor, took off my clothes, put on my nightgown, and crawled into bed.

I stared at the pillow, mind blank, skin cold, heart hurting, for a long time.

But Ham hadn't even come home from his run before my eyes drifted closed and I fell asleep.

*   *   *

I felt my hair slide off my neck and heard Ham's soft voice saying, "Baby, wake up."

My eyes fluttered, then stayed open. I turned my head on the pillow and looked up to see Ham sitting on the edge of the bed. I was curled with my back to him. He was leaned over me, his hand in the mattress by my belly.

"You been asleep for six hours," he told me. "Now, you got a choice. You can get showered and we'll go to work or I'll see if Christie can take your shift and you can keep restin'."

"I'll work," I mumbled, shifting out from under the covers and avoiding his body as I moved around him and out of bed.

Then I avoided him as I shuffled out of the room and down the hall.

Even half-asleep, I made the decision to get ready in his room. I didn't have the energy to move my stuff and I really didn't have the energy to deal with Ham if he had a negative reaction to that.

So I gathered my clothes and went into his bathroom.

I might not take long showers but I was a primper and more so before a shift at work. I'd learned that tips were adversely affected if you looked like shit.

But fortunately, I was able to primp at the same time blanking my mind. If it wandered to Ham, February Owens, or Rachel, I thought of a mental stop sign and shut it down.

I didn't have the energy for that either.

By the time I was gussied up, we barely had time to make it to the bar to start my shift on time but Ham didn't say a word.

We drove to The Dog in silence, my part of that weighty, Ham's seemed reflective.

He did speak when we got there. I'd dumped my purse and jacket in the office, and he did this to say, "You got the front of the house tonight, babe."

I'd simply nodded and got to work.

I didn't avoid him during the shift. I expended the effort to turn it on for customers in order to sell drinks and earn tips but I shut it off when I approached the bar.

Ham, on the other hand, was back to laidback Ham. Leaning into me, being funny (though not earning even a grin, I was like a robot, on switch with customers, off switch with Ham), but this didn't seem to affect him, although he did his thing watchful, even cautious.

The thing was, he could be charming and flirty. He was very good at it and now was no exception, but, for the first time in my life, I was too heartsore to respond.

I wasn't sure what he wanted.

What I was sure of was that he could tell me until he was blue in the face that he'd reflected, come to some decisions, but I didn't think he even knew what he wanted. He was entirely fucked up about women and I had to make a decision about where I fit in that.

Did I take Ham as he was, all of it good, but knowing he didn't love me, maybe couldn't love anyone after what Rachel had put him through, and hope that was enough not only for me but also for him? Enough that he wouldn't revert to his old ways, find he couldn't stick, cut ties and roll on?

In the meantime, possibly winning Zander and maybe even beginning a family of our own?

Or did I decide that I deserved better? That maybe there was something out there for me where I had it all, all the good stuff Ham gave with the bedrock of love to keep it solid. Making this decision even knowing there was a possibility I'd never find it.

I'd come to no decisions and was no less tired at the end of shift.

In fact, I was so exhausted, I fell asleep with my head on the back of the sofa in his office, sitting up, legs crossed under me, as Ham did all the shit he had to do after he closed down The Dog.

This meant I woke up when he was lifting me in his arms.

"I can walk," I muttered.

"You're out. Stay out," he told me.

"Ham, please, put me down," I demanded but my voice was quiet.

He hesitated before he set me on my feet but kept a hand on me to keep me steady. I steadied, reached down, grabbed my purse, and followed Ham out. I waited for him to lock the office and I waited for him to lock the back door of the bar.

We rode home again in silence.

When we got up to the apartment, I repeated what I did the night before, going directly to the bathroom, washing my face, brushing my teeth, pulling on my nightgown. But in the end, I gathered up all my clothes, and when I passed Ham leaving the bathroom, I didn't go to his bed.

I went to mine.

I closed the door, dumped my clothes on the floor, and without even turning on the light, I slipped between the covers.

I was there ten minutes and so tired I was nearly asleep before I felt the covers slide down and I was up again in Ham's arms.

"Ham, I'm really tired," I protested, putting my hands to his chest and giving him a feeble push to underline my point.

"I know, cookie, and that's good, seein' as I got shit to say, you're gonna listen to it, but you don't got the energy to open your mouth through it," he replied.

I stopped pushing and gave in.

I'd get this done, then I could sleep, and tomorrow, hopefully on a full night's sleep, I'd be able to make some decisions.

The jury was out on whether I'd have the strength to carry them through.

Ham's room was dark when we made it there and he didn't turn on the light when he put us to bed, front to front, gathering me close and tangling his long, heavy legs in mine.

I closed my eyes and dipped my chin, my forehead colliding lightly with his collarbone.

This, feeling just this, how good it was, could make me believe I could take Ham as he came even if he didn't love me.

"February," he stated and my body tensed.

Suddenly, I had all the energy in the world and started to pull away.

But Ham's arms got tight, his legs tightened around mine, and he said quietly, "Settle, cookie, and please, God, listen."

Something in his tone, the intensity of it, made me still.

Ham felt it. His arms loosened but one hand started stroking my back and that, too, could make me believe I could take Ham as he came.

"I didn't talk about it, not back then with you, 'cause no need to get into that kind of shit with the way we were. But I was with Feb like I used to be with you," he shared.

I closed my eyes again and rested my forehead back on his collarbone.

Ham kept stroking my back.

"Feb's different though, baby. She's not like you. Even in the beginning, you gave you to me and I had all of you, even when I was gone. I knew that. I knew it wasn't fair. But I wanted it, it mattered to me, so I kept it. Feb never gave herself to me. I didn't have it in me to be the man you needed me to be back then. Feb didn't have it in her to be that woman to me."

"But you wanted that," I stated, my heart breaking, my mind thinking I should have fought harder when he carried me to his bed.

His hand slid up my spine and curled around the back of my neck. "No," he declared firmly. "I wanted from her what I told myself I wanted from you. And I got that from her."

I said nothing.

"That shit went down with Lowe choppin' people up and the feds had to contact me 'cause I was a target. I called her, her man answered. Not gonna lie to you. That stung."

I pressed my lips together but stayed still and quiet.

"She's a good woman," he whispered, his fingers at my neck tensing, his arm around me giving me a squeeze. "Can't lie to you, baby, 'cause it's true. Wish I could. Wish I could make this easier. But I've fucked up so much of my goddamned life, I gotta do it right when I straighten it out."

That didn't exactly make sense.

Before I could ask, Ham kept going.

"We had good times, her and me, and the way she was, I suspected that would never end. Never figured she'd settle down. I was the only one she had, though, and she's a good-lookin' woman so I suspected there'd be a time when she might hook up with someone else but not settle down. I thought I had that, that safety with Feb, and would never lose it. When I did, it did a number on me, and that was before Lowe caught up with me."

He paused but I said nothing so he carried on.

"When that conversation went down, I'll never forget it, the last thing she said was, 'You find another, don't watch her walk away.' All I could think was how many times I'd forced you to watch me walk away. "

Thinking he still was carrying a torch for February, that was not what I expected to hear.

So much not, my eyes opened.

"And then it got worse. I thought about the one time I'd watched you, when you'd done the same as Feb, somethin' I knew you were eventually gonna do, walkin' to somethin' you deserved to find, a man who would make you happy. And how I stood there watchin' you walk away and thinkin' how easy it was to walk away from you 'cause I did it always knowin' I'd be back and how much it fuckin' killed watchin' you do it, 'cause at the time, I didn't think I'd ever have you back."

Oh my God.

"Ham—"

"February Owens is a good woman. She was good to me. I was good to her. And I care about her. But she was never gonna be mine, and it sucked, losin' her, but thinkin' on it, I knew that deep down from the moment I met her. And that's precisely why I started it up with her. But, cookie, you were mine from the moment I met you. That mattered to me. I took care of it as best as I could, until I came to a place in my life where I could give you what you should have and lucked the fuck out you were available for me to give it. And that's the big difference you gotta get."

I tried again to cut in. "Darlin'—"

It didn't work.

"And I don't like thinkin' about her because, like I said, it sucks losin' her. Her man is not the kind of guy who wants me checkin' in. But I gotta tell you, it's more. And it's more in a fucked-up way only because a man lost his mind and went on a killin' spree in her name. She lost people she cared about and not in a quiet, slippin'-away kind of way. She watched someone get shot. She saw a friend of hers die. She's gotta live with all that and do it with reporters and writers breathin' down her neck, knowin' movies are gonna be made of that mess and documentaries are gonna air on TV. You care about someone, you wanna be there for them and this is a time when I'd wanna be there for her. I can't and, baby, that stings, too."

"Babe—" I tried again.

But Ham kept going.

"So I don't wanna talk about her because I lost her and she means somethin' to me. But it upsets you so there it is. The thing you gotta take from all this is, Feb is not you. She was never an option. She would never be where you are right now. She wouldn't give me that. And I always knew that. I also always knew, from the first time I said good-bye to you, that I was a special kind of fuckwit for doin' it because I was drivin' away from the best woman I'd ever known. And years have passed, Zara, and you're still that woman. It's just that now, I'm never gonna drive away. I'm never gonna leave you and I'm not gonna let you leave me."

He stopped talking finally, but I couldn't start.

I didn't know what to say.

What I did know was, being the best woman he'd ever known was a lot better than his just caring about me. And his vowing he was never going to leave me wasn't shabby either.

But he still had not told me he loved me.

Then again, I was Zara Cinders and until I was old enough to go out and make friends, only one person in my life loved me truly, completely, and unconditionally. And, even though she stepped up repeatedly to take beatings meant for me, eventually made me watch her go through a junkie stage, through empty hookup after hookup that didn't mean a thing, and finally made me watch her essentially die, she never stopped loving me.

So I should probably learn to take what I could get.

"You with me on all this?" he asked when I said nothing.

"Yes," I answered and I felt him let out a long, silent sigh.

I said no more. Ham didn't either.

Then he did.

"You fight nasty, cookie," he stated gently.

"Yeah, I do. When what I'm fighting about matters," I replied.

"I get that," he said. "What I don't get is that you were in no state to start a conversation about Feb. You had to read I was not in a place where I wanted to talk about that, and you still threw it in my face, which was not cool."

He was right.

However, he was also wrong.

"That mattered," I declared and his hand came to my chin, moving it up so he could catch my eyes in the dark.

"All I'm sayin' is, in future, wait for your right time and give me the same. Yeah?"

Seriously, I hated it when he was gentle and reasonable when I didn't feel like being the same.

So I laid it out why I wasn't.

"Ham, you're the one for me and it doesn't feel good knowin' you don't feel the same."

"What?" he asked.

"You heard me," I answered.

"Jesus," he muttered, rolling into me so I took on a lot of his weight.

"Ham—"

"Cookie, quiet," he ordered, his voice jagged and at that tone, I didn't know what to expect so, even tired, I pulled all I had left close and braced. "Please, baby, I know a lot of shit is swirlin', but pay some fuckin' attention."

"I am," I snapped because I damned well was.

"Get this," he stated, his voice not jagged any longer, but suddenly harsh. "That bitch walked into our home."

The shadow of his face dipped close to mine, a move so swift I held my breath.

"*Our* home," he repeated, saying that like the space we rented was sacrosanct. "And I don't give a shit if that woman finally did right. My girl and I were fightin', it was intense, it didn't feel good for either of us, she takes off to blow off some steam and opens the door to my ex?" He shook his head. "No. *Fuck* no. I don't give a shit she drives for hours to show me she's changed, she wants redemption. Zara, babe, you do not open the door to *our* goddamned house and be confronted with that shit. Not ever. Not if I can help it."

I'd been wrong. Rachel didn't have the power to push Ham to extreme emotion.

It was me having to deal with her that had royally pissed him off.

But Ham wasn't done.

"She showed me how it felt to be stripped of power when she aborted two of my children. Then she pops by out of the fuckin' blue to *do right*." He said the last two words with extreme sarcasm. "And in doin' that strips my power fucking *again* by makin' it impossible, unless I acted a bigger dick than I was or got physical, to shield you from that. The only thing I could do to protect you was hold you close and that is not cool. Not in any way."

I was right.

His not being able to protect me was what pissed him off. And he didn't put his arm around me because he needed me. He did it because he thought I needed him.

Okay, maybe I'd been a bit of a moron.

Ham still wasn't done.

"The point I'm makin' is, I do not feel that way about *anyone,* Zara. I'm a good man and I'll take a friend's back but *no one* gets that shit from me. Not ever. Not since Rachel. Not Feb. Not anyone. But *you*. Now, are you finally gettin' *how* you need to start payin' attention?"

"Yes," I whispered because, finally, I was.

Ham *still* wasn't done.

"Then pay close attention to this. A man is not what he says, babe. He's what he *does*."

Was he saying what he actually wasn't saying...but was?

"You care about me," I stated quietly, testing my theory.

"Fuck yeah, Zara. I care about you enough to lay roots with you. I care about you enough to fight for your nephew with you. I care about you enough to make babies with you."

His hand grabbed mine, yanked it up, and pressed it flat against his shoulder where the smooth, puckered skin of the ugly scar left by an ax marred his flesh.

"I care about you enough to take another one of these if a man was comin' after you. Both my parents are dead. I got no siblings. I got no roots. The only thing I got, the only thing I realized months ago I've had for a long fuckin' time, is what I've kept as close as I could until I was ready to take it all the way, and that's fuckin' *you*."

That was me.

"I think maybe I've been kind of a bitch," I blurted.

"I think you want what you gotta learn I'll give when I'm ready to give it, honey," Ham replied. "And until I'm ready to give it, you gotta *pay attention* so you'll know you have it already."

I had it already.

Like I thought when I was talking to Cotton.

Ham had never told me he'd loved me.

But he'd shown me.

That meant he loved me.

Man, oh man.

"Okay, now I think I need to kiss you and, maybe, go down on you to make amends for having my head up my ass," I shared.

His body relaxed, the mood in the room shifted, and he dropped his forehead to mine.

"Sweet offer," he murmured and the firm was out of his tone. It was filled with tender. "But I'm in the mood to go down on you. You get how you get when I do, we may switch it up and while I'm givin', so are you. But you get distracted when I got my mouth on you at the same time you're suckin' my cock so I think it's best one of us stays focused."

And I had him back.

All that, fighting, heartbreak, Ham laid it out the way Ham always laid it out, I find I'd been a moron and he doesn't rub it in my face or make me pay in any way.

He's back to joking.

And offering to go down on me.

"You know I love you."

I said it and then I couldn't breathe because suddenly the entirety of Ham's bodyweight was pressing into me. But only for a moment before he rolled us, taking him to his back, me on top of him, and he shoved my face in his neck with his hand cupping the back of my head even as his other arm continued to squeeze the breath out of me.

And finally, I paid attention.

So I said not a word. I just let everything he was saying to me without saying it flow through me.

It felt beautiful.

His hand and arm relaxed and his voice was soft but jagged when he replied, "Yeah, baby. I know."

I tipped my head back and kissed the underside of his jaw.

Ham bunched my nightgown in his fist at my ass, murmuring, "Get this off, cookie. You might be tired but not too tired to sit on my face, which is what you're gonna do right now."

Usually, when Ham gave an order while we were on mattresses, I did what I was told mostly because I got a lot out of it.

This time, I deviated from Ham's plan by shifting up and laying a hot, heavy, wet one on him.

Ham let me and he did this by participating fully.

It was sweet.

It was hot.

And I paid attention to that, too.

Then he let me go so I could take off my nightgown and sit on his face.

Which was exactly what I did.

CHAPTER SIXTEEN

Bury Him

Reece

Four days later…

REECE WAS RUNNING along the road by the boardwalk in town when a burgundy Jeep Cherokee passed. He saw the brake lights illuminate and, as he moved alongside it, he heard a woman shout, "Reece!"

He looked left and saw through the open passenger window that Nina was in the driver's seat.

He jogged to the opened window and stopped.

"Yo," he greeted.

"Hey, I don't want to interrupt your run but I actually just called you, twice. I left messages but you obviously don't take your phone with you while you run, and we *really* need to talk."

The "really" was emphasized in a way Reece couldn't ignore, not that he would, mostly because she looked excited, her eyes lit with a fire he hadn't seen in them before, and she was normally fiery.

"You don't mind me sweatin' in your office, I'll meet you there," he told her.

"See you in a few," she replied on a bright smile.

He backed away from the SUV. She took off, her hand waving as she did, and he followed her, his pace steady but faster.

She gave the impression she had good news.

Christ, please make this good news.

He entered her offices, sweating, breathing heavy, and when he did her receptionist was putting the phone in the cradle, her head coming right up.

"Neens says to go right on in, Reece," she invited. "She just called. She's comin' in the back way. You should get to her office at about the same time she gets there."

Reece nodded and moved to the hall toward Nina's office.

Nina was still dumping her stuff on her desk and shrugging off her stylish coat when he struck his knuckles on her open door.

"Come in," she said, waving at him excitedly and tossing her coat on the back of her chair. "And if you could shut the door?"

He moved in and closed the door as she rounded the desk and slid her round ass up on the front of it.

"Okay," she launched in. "I'd offer you coffee, water, a towel but seriously, this is too good not to share and do it fast. I'll get you that stuff after."

"Spill it," Reece demanded, his breath still heavy and his heart thumping deep, the latter not having anything to do with his run.

They'd had no recent news except Nina being frustrated with Xavier Cinders' attorney's stonewalling. She'd explained that this would happen. Nina was gung ho, but they wouldn't be. She also repeatedly told them this was a process that didn't happen overnight.

Even so, it was wearing on Zara. She was keeping a brave face, but if something didn't give soon, Reece worried that mask was going to crack.

"Right, well, it's about what Pastor Williams said. Do you remember I told you I thought what he said was curious but intriguing?" she asked.

"I remember," Reece agreed.

"I didn't want to say anything to you because I really didn't understand what *he* was saying and I wanted to understand it before I mentioned it. So, I know we're on a budget but I still thought it worth the risk to talk to our investigator. She's good. Really good. We don't use her often, not enough business for that, but she's excellent. So I hired her for this job, limiting her hours, and she found it. I just had an early lunch with her and she told me all about it."

Nina stopped speaking and Reece's patience started slipping.

"And?" he prompted.

Nina smiled huge, an expression that belied her next words.

"Xenia's care for nine years cost a fortune."

Reece shook his head. "Not followin', Nina."

She leaned toward him animatedly. "Xavier kept her on life support in a private facility for nine years. That requires more than tubes and machines but staff time and lots of other stuff. Did you ever think to wonder how he could afford that?"

"Try not to think about him at all," he answered.

Although that was true, the man worked at an aeronautical factory a county over. He was union, blue collar but skilled labor, and had worked there decades so he made a whack. But not that big of a whack. So even though Reece didn't think of him, that didn't mean he didn't wonder.

Leaning back, she nodded. "Well, couple that with Zander

Cinders going to a school that cost fourteen thousand dollars a year. Then add the fact that Wilona Cinders works a part-time job. And she does that and still can seemingly financially handle the upbringing of a young boy and the mortgage on a four-bedroom house even though her husband cut ties as in *cut ties*. They bought that house to fill it with children and when she couldn't give him any, he divorced her, moved to Alaska, and left her with a house they had some equity in but still had fifteen years of a mortgage on."

Not much had been happening with the case but Nina knowing all this meant the woman had been seriously busy.

"Maybe you need to do the verbal arithmetic for me," he suggested when she stopped talking again.

Instead of doing that, enjoying herself too much, Nina asked, "Has Zara ever talked about her grandfather Val Cinders?"

"He passed when she and her sister were teenagers. She liked him well enough, but bein' a Cinders, only as much as he'd let her," he replied.

She nodded, her eyes lighting further.

She was coming to the good stuff, thank fuck.

"Okay," she continued. "Now, the Cinders being an old Gnaw Bone family, and I mean *old,* did you know that, before Val Cinders death, he sold huge tracks of land to Curtis Dodd? Land Dodd developed on. And that deal included Val Cinders getting a percentage of the profits off those developments."

Reece felt his head jerk. "What?"

Curtis Dodd, who had been murdered a few years ago, was the town's land magnate. He developed all over the county. Hell, you couldn't drive through town without seeing his huge-ass, ostentatious house up the mountain, lording over it all. A house he built to do just that. A house that no one lived in now that his wife was in prison for conspiring to murder him.

Nina leaned in. "We're talking *millions*."

"And this makes you happy because..." he prompted.

"It makes me happy because Xenia and Zara Cinders were minors when Val Cinders died. That meant that the money he left to them, and when I say he left them money, he left them *all of it,* Reece"—Reece's frame froze but his gut clenched as she went on—"was supposed to be held in trust for them. They were supposed to receive it when they reached thirty years of age. Xenia never reached that age and, therefore, her money should have gone to Zara or, alternately, Zander. But I'm guessing with all that's happened to her in the past year, Zara never saw a dime. Which means Xavier stole it from her, used it to keep her sister alive against her wishes, and is using it to help his sister raise the son he also stole from Zara."

Reece stood completely still and stared.

She wasn't done.

"I have no idea why Val Cinders didn't divvy it up between his kids, but he didn't. Then again, word on the street is that they didn't like him much and he returned the favor. And my investigator reports that will was ironclad. He wanted none of that money to go to Xavier, Dahlia, and Wilona, and he made certain that it wouldn't. Apparently not a nice guy, he set his wife up with only a stipend to come off the interest of that money but that stopped when she passed. Bad blood runs in that family, it would seem."

Reece remained silent.

Nina kept going.

"My investigator dredged this up and she also looked into Xavier's finances. He isn't even hiding it. He's got all those funds, *not* in trust, held local, and he's been accessing them almost since the girls inherited them. We haven't figured out quite yet why that money never was put in a trust, though. That said, there is still a very large sum of money in those accounts. In fact, as my investigator sees it, there's three million nine hundred and seventy-five thousand, two hundred and two dollars and sixty-seven cents."

Reece said nothing and moved not an inch.

Nina continued, declaring enthusiastically as she clapped her hands in front of her, "We've got them!"

"She lost her home," he replied, his voice low, dangerous. *Angry.*

Nina's smile faded.

"She lost her business," Reece went on.

"Reece—"

"She lived in a shit, unsafe, studio apartment, sat on used furniture, had a crap TV, and worked for near-on-minimum wage to keep her shit together."

"I—"

"He knew it. Everyone in town did."

"He probably did, but—"

"That money was hers. That money was her sister's. She could have approached the courts to release it and used it to raise her nephew."

"That's likely true. However—"

Reece leaned in and interrupted her, rumbling, *"Bury that fucker."*

Definitely reading his words and tone, Nina jumped off the desk and, lifting a placating hand, tried again. "Reece—"

But he cut her off.

"I want the money. I want the boy. Zara's thirty-two, almost thirty-three. She had access to that money, she could have taken care of Zander. She had that money when she needed it, she could have ridden it through that rough patch and he fuckin' knew it. He let his daughter swing." He leaned back and ordered, "Bury him. You can land his ass in jail, do it. I want him fucked up, Nina. I want fuckin'"—he leaned in again, barely controlling the fury boiling through his frame—*"blood."*

"Okay, Reece," she agreed quietly, dropping her hand.

"You throw everything you got at him, Nina," he ordered. "I don't give a fuck what the cost. You…make…him…*bleed*."

She nodded, studying him carefully. She did this for long moments.

Then Nina Maxwell smiled.

*   *   *

So pissed, he could barely see, after leaving Nina, Reece ran an extra two miles to try and work that shit off.

It didn't touch it.

Now he had to get back to Zara. Share more news about her fucked-up family. Rock her world yet a-fucking-gain.

She already knew her father was an extreme asshole. He had no idea how she'd respond to those extremities expanding.

But he had to get home. He'd been gone longer than normal and she'd worry.

He wished he could keep running.

He couldn't get it out of his head, the state of her house when he first walked into it months ago, that couch, that shit-ass coffee table, that fuckin' TV. And her studio without a peephole and a chain he popped with no fucking effort.

His cookie, living like that. His woman, unsafe. His girl, nearly broken.

All because her dad was an asshole.

If Reece hadn't come back, she'd still be there and she'd stay there. Even if she found out about Zander, she'd never approach Nina to fight for him. She'd never know she was a millionaire.

But he came back and it was fucking whacked but he had Dennis Lowe to thank for it. An ax murderer woke his shit, made him sort himself out.

It was insane but it was true.

Dennis Lowe had taken lives but saved his.

And Reece did not at all like thinking that shit.

Trying to control his fury, when he hit the parking lot to their apartment building, he slowed to a jog and forced his mind to the fact that, when they got her money, she'd be set. She wouldn't have to worry about that shit ever again.

They also finally had the means to fuck her father and get her nephew.

And last, not the best of this news but not shabby either, the conversation he'd had with their landlord a while back had borne fruit. She'd not wanted to let them out of their contract unless they had someone to rent the space. But she'd called that morning to say she'd found someone to rent the unit. They were free to leave at the end of the month.

A new start. A nice house in a good neighborhood, shit-loads of money in the bank, three bedrooms, one Zara's sister's boy would sleep in.

And finally, after a shit life and taking way too fucking many hard knocks, his girl would have it good.

On that thought, Reece felt his anger subside.

"Mr. Reece!"

His head turned and he stopped dead at what he saw.

Wilona Cinders, Zara's aunt, was walking swiftly his way.

His fury instantly came back.

But instead of letting it loose, he forced himself to shake his head.

"We got attorneys. Your brother does, too. We talk through them," he told her, turning away and moving toward the stairs that led up to their breezeway.

"Mr. Reece, please, you'll want to hear what I have to say," she called.

He could hear her heels on the tarmac and he didn't pause.

But he replied, "That's extremely doubtful."

"Mr. Reece!" This was a cry. "Xavier is threatening to take Zander away from me!"

"Your problem," Reece returned, taking the first four stairs in two strides.

"He's taking him away because I told him about his mother and aunt," she said, slightly breathless and her words made Reece stop.

He turned and looked down at her.

"Thank you," she mumbled the instant he did.

"You got two minutes," he declared.

"I need to talk to Zara," she stated and he shook his head again.

"You talk to me first. Then I decide if you get to my woman."

She straightened her shoulders. "I want her to meet Zander."

At this unexpected announcement, Reece sucked in a breath before he crossed his arms on his chest.

"I'm listening."

"I...I don't want him taken from me. I don't want to lose him. I don't want his life disrupted. He's only nine. He wouldn't understand all this. He shouldn't have to. I've been trying to protect him from what's going on but it's getting harder. He gets good grades. He likes his school—"

"Zara will make the decision about whether Zander stays in that school. If we can swing it, I'm sure he'll stay," Reece informed her, not letting on that he knew about the money, and that as soon as they broke Zara's father, Zander's school tuition would be no problem.

She took a step toward him, shaking her head. "You don't understand. Xavier and I...we've, well...not agreed on a variety of things through Zander's upbringing. I never got any legal documents to make me his guardian, so Xavier has all the power and—"

He interrupted her. "That'll be changing."

She lifted both hands, and her face, not unattractive and he'd only seen her a few times but her usual closed, hard expression made it less so, now looked pained.

"Please, Mr. Reece, I beg you, listen to me."

Jesus.

If he could believe it, by the look on her face, the tone of her voice, she cared about this kid and not just a little bit.

Reece went silent.

"I don't know what's happening with the attorneys," she stated. "I do know that any child will eventually want to know about their parents. And any child should have all the family they can get. From the beginning, Xavier and I didn't agree about who would be in Zander's life and he made it clear that if I didn't toe his line, he'd take Zander away from me. But I always knew there'd come a time when Zander would ask questions about his mother and father. And when Zander started doing that, Xavier and I disagreed on how it should be handled. Now all this is happening but even before that…" She paused and then she admitted, "I wanted him to go to his mother's funeral."

"Clearly you didn't get your wish," he noted.

She shook her head. "No, but I got mad that he didn't… It was the perfect time to tell him, if there ever was a time to tell him such things. Zander wouldn't really understand it now but he might one day be angry that he'd been kept from his mother's funeral. But Xavier wouldn't let me bring him. Wouldn't let me share about his mother, his aunt, so he wouldn't be curious or upset if he saw Zara at the funeral. And then I saw Zara at the funeral and got angrier about all the pain Xavier has caused, keeping this family apart. So, after the funeral, I took him to get a sundae and I told Zander about his mom." She held his gaze, took in a deep breath, and finished. "And I told him about Zara."

Zander knew about Zara.

Reece tamped down the urge to howl with elation and guessed, "And Cinders knows this and he's pissed."

"Very much so," she confirmed.

Reece said nothing.

Wilona Cinders did.

"Zander wants to meet his aunt."

"You name the day and time, she'll be there and you know it," he said instantly.

She nodded.

Then she shocked the shit out of him when she added, "And I want to help you with your custody case."

Reece blinked. "What?"

"I have stipulations."

He uncrossed his arms from his chest and planted his hands on his hips, saying sarcastically, "Why does that not surprise me?"

She didn't respond to that.

Instead, she announced, "I want to raise him."

Reece's anger started edging back.

He dropped his arms and made to move away. "Not gonna happen."

"No!" she cried, lifting a hand toward him. "He'll meet Zara. She can come over any time. I promise. Any time, Mr. Reece. And Zander can come to your place. He can spend the night. Have his friends over if he wants. We'll do Christmases together. Thanksgiving. All of it. I'll do anything, and I know Zara and I haven't been close, but I promise. I'll do anything. Between us, we'll make it good for Zander. I swear."

She lifted her other hand, turning both palms up, beseeching and, fuck him, with her posture and the look on her face, the bright in her eyes, even he wasn't immune.

"But he's my boy," she whispered, her voice breaking on the word *boy*. "I've had him since he was so little. He couldn't even hold his head up. And he's happy. I've worked hard to make him happy because I *want* him to be happy. I don't want Xavier to hurt him. I want him to have people around him who love him. And I don't want him to be caught up in any of Xavier's nastiness. I don't want scars on him like that."

The tears glistened in her eyes as her voice dropped lower.

"I don't want him to have scars like his mother had. I don't want him to *survive* childhood like she did..." She pulled in a breath and shared, "Like I did. I want him to be *happy*."

A tear slid down her cheek and Reece closed his eyes.

Probably unintentionally, Xavier had broken the cycle, giving his grandson to a woman who'd learned. A woman who couldn't conceive. A woman who knew the precious entity she had in her hands and handled it with care.

He opened his eyes. "I'll talk to Zara. We'll want a meeting with Zander the minute you can arrange it. We'll speak to our attorney about the rest of it and either Zara or our attorney, Nina Maxwell, will contact you to discuss things further with you."

"Zander can't wait to meet her," she said immediately.

"She feels the same."

"Tell her..." She lifted her hands to her face for a second before she dropped them. "Please, Mr. Reece, tell her that it wasn't my decision to keep him away from her. I would have gone to her but I didn't think..." She trailed off.

She was right not to think Zara would be receptive to a visit. Zara was not a fan of either of her aunts. But times apparently were changing.

And Reece was fucking glad she didn't. This was news he wanted to share.

"I think she's got a pretty clear understanding of how her father works, Mizz Cinders. But I'll tell her."

She nodded.

He turned to leave her.

"Mr. Reece?" she called.

He heaved a heavy sigh and turned back.

"Thank you."

Fuck him. She meant that.

And she meant it deeply.

Reece nodded.

She looked up the stairs as if seeing them she could see Zara, tell the future, understand how she'd react.

Then she moved away.

Reece watched her go.

Then he jogged up the steps.

*   *   *

"Oh my God. Oh my God. Oh my God, God, *God*," Zara chanted as Reece stood in his sweaty workout clothes and watched her dancing around their living room, her soft hair bouncing, her face lit with a massive smile.

Needless to say, she took all that day's news better than he did.

She stopped, whirled, dashed to him, and halted abruptly so she could slap her hands so hard on his chest he had to swallow a grunt.

"Zander wants to meet me!" she shrieked in his face, then threw her arms around him, also throwing her body at him. She did this so he had to go back on a foot so they didn't topple down.

He wrapped his arms around her, noting with little surprise her priority in dancing around in joy was her nephew, not the fact that she was a millionaire.

Before he could say a word, she jumped away, breaking from his arms, and cried, "Oh God! I need a new outfit!"

Reece felt his lips curve into a smile.

Jesus.

Women.

"Not sure a nine-year-old boy'll care what you wear, cookie," he told her.

She shook her head and started pacing, declaring, "I have to go to the mall." She whirled on him again. "Immediately!"

"Maybe you should let me call this new shit in to Nina before you head to the mall."

He wished he could eat those words when her face instantly fell.

"Do you think Aunt Wilona will renege?" she asked.

"No. The woman I spoke to would lay her life down for that boy. But your father is unpredictable."

"Then we need to do this on the hush-hush," she stated and he grinned.

"That'd be good. So you be good. Don't go spreadin' word around town with all your girls. Don't fly off to the mall and buy a meet-with-Zander outfit. Your dad's investigatin' me. We already know that. We don't know what else he's up to. He could have someone watchin'. He might even already know about that meet I just had with your aunt outside. We just got a couple of huge breaks. You need to play it cool."

She nodded, her head bobbing vigorously. "I can be cool."

She was totally not going to be cool.

"Arlene's out," he told her and she scrunched up her nose.

"This is true. Arlene has a big mouth," she agreed.

"Inner circle, babe. Nina only until she sorts shit out and you get a sit-down with that boy. We do not want to tip our hand that we know about that money or it might disappear. We do not want to set your father into doin' somethin' stupid that'll hurt Zander if he knows Wilona made an approach. The more people who know, the more chance word will spread even if folks don't mean any harm. We keep this under our hats. And that means more than keepin' it from Arlene."

She again nodded.

"Now I'm gonna call this in to Nina. Then I'm gonna take a shower. Then we'll celebrate this shit private-like in a way no one will know."

She nodded again but this time with a huge smile on her face, but asked, "Can I make an alternate suggestion?"

"Give it to me," he invited.

"We could speed up the celebration. I take a shower with you."

That was when Reece smiled.

Then he muttered, "You're on."

Then he braced because she again flew at him, and landed in his arms. He had to take another step back to keep them from falling. Her hand slid up into the back of his hair, pressing down, and her mouth found his.

Which meant their plans were derailed.

They celebrated on the living room floor.

Then he called Nina.

After that, they celebrated again in the shower.

CHAPTER SEVENTEEN

Out of Harm's Way

Two days later...

"CALM, COOKIE," REECE muttered.

We were sitting in a booth at The Mark, both on one side. I was fidgeting, a ginger ale in front of me, my eyes glued to the door.

Aunt Wilona had not reneged.

Ham called Nina, Nina called Aunt Wilona, and the meeting was set up.

And it was set up for that day after school, or as soon as Aunt Wilona could drive Zander there after school. We were meeting at The Mark for mile-high mud pies.

After a life that was so far from a dream it wasn't funny, this was yet another dream come true.

I'd had time to buy a new outfit, and since Nina was the only one Ham allowed me to talk to about all this, she'd gone to the mall with me. So I was wearing a new berry-red sweater, Lucky jeans, a killer belt, and a pair of high-heeled boots that were so expensive, even back in the day when things were good in the shop, I would never have even looked at them.

But now I was going to be a millionaire.

Since her impromptu meeting with Ham, Nina had actually looked at Grandpa Val's will and she said it would take an act of God to break it. This was her professional opinion, of course, but she had added evidence, seeing as she'd also discovered from court papers that all three of Grandpa's offspring had tried to do that at the time Grandpa died and they'd all lost.

Unfortunately, after this battle was fought, the executor of the will, one of Grandpa's cronies, had taken a trip to the Pearly Gates. For some reason now lost with him, he'd not set the money up in trust and he'd not made provisions for his demise, so there was no one official to keep track of the money and Dad had jumped on that, taking control of it.

To keep Aunt Wilona's mouth shut, he eventually gave her Zander and the money to keep him.

But to keep Aunt Dahlia's mouth shut, he'd just given her money.

Money Nina was making moves to get back, either from Dad, whose money it wasn't to give, and if that didn't work, she was going after Aunt Dahlia, seeing as she knew this was ill-gotten gains and she accepted it anyway.

So, although Nina shared that it might be tied up while all the legal stuff was handled, I'd eventually get it.

She'd done what she had to do and, tomorrow, those accounts would be frozen until the legal issues were settled.

Therefore, since I was eventually going to be a millionaire, I could afford Zander's school *and* an expensive pair of boots.

I knew Ham thought I was insane, me being hell-bent to buy a new outfit to meet my nephew in. I knew this because he was wearing a wine-colored shirt I'd seen him wear more than once since he'd been back and his standard faded jeans that were so broken in, they looked like they'd been bought around the dawn of time.

Still, he looked great, like always, even if his outfit wasn't new.

But to me, that day I'd be meeting my nephew.

And my nephew would be meeting the only good part that was left of his mother.

So I had to do it right. For Zander.

And for Xenia.

"I know you're excited, baby," Ham started and I tore my eyes away from the door to look at him. "But you gotta pay attention, all right?"

I nodded.

He kept going.

"Decisions to be made, big ones for Zander. Your aunt's right. He grew up with her. Tearin' him from his home. The woman who raised him. You gotta have a good reason to do that. But she's a Cinders and she might give you one. So you got any bad feelin' about him, you clock it, we talk about it, we share it with Nina, and we make our plans. Yeah?"

We'd already discussed the plan, at length, and I was down with the plan so I nodded again.

"She's fuckin' him up, though, don't 'spect she'd walk

him right to you. Also don't 'spect this first meeting will expose if shit's not good. This has gotta go good so we can get another meet without her there. So you play it cool."

"I'll play it cool, Ham," I assured him, still fidgeting, moving my ass in the seat nervously, unsure what to do with my hands, all this saying my words were a lie.

Seeing as Ham didn't miss much, that would be, he didn't miss *anything,* he didn't miss this. So he turned fully to me, grabbed both my hands in both of his, and pulled them to his chest.

Then he declared, "No one, man, woman, or child would not love you, Zara."

At his words, I went completely still.

After I let them sweep through me, I whispered, "Again, awesome...*er.*"

He grinned.

I heard the door open and my eyes shot to it.

Ham let me go and turned away but I sat there, hands still raised where he'd released them, staring at Aunt Wilona and the blond-haired boy in front of her wearing a private-school uniform and craning his neck to look around.

My heart started hammering so fast, so hard, if I could pull my eyes away from my nephew and look down, I would have sworn I'd see it beating in my chest.

But I couldn't tear my eyes away so I saw Aunt Wilona put a hand to Zander's shoulder and point our way.

His eyes came to our table.

I held my breath.

He smiled, then bopped toward us with nine-year-old-kid exuberance.

Ham slid out and I slid out after him so I was on my feet when Zander came to a halt two feet in front of me.

"Jeez, you look like me," he declared.

I felt my eyes sting.

"Yep," I replied.

His eyes went to Ham and his head tipped way back.

"Whoa, you're, like, *really* tall," he remarked.

"That I am, boy," Ham stated.

"Zander, honey, this is your Aunt Zara and your, um…I guess, your uncle, uh…" Aunt Wilona stammered.

"Reece," Ham grunted.

"What kind of name is Reece?" Zander asked.

"It's my last name," Ham answered.

"What's your first name?" Zander went on.

"Graham," Ham replied.

"Don't you call yourself Graham?" Zander queried.

"Would you call yourself Graham?" Ham returned.

Zander grinned.

My heart flipped.

"Nope," Zander said.

"So you get me," Ham noted.

"Yep," Zander agreed.

"Why don't we sit down?" I butted in. "Get you a drink and something good to eat."

"Cool," Zander muttered and scrambled into the other side of the booth.

I watched and then my eyes went to Aunt Wilona. She was looking at Zander then she looked at me. I nodded and gave her a small smile. She returned the gesture.

After that, we all piled in.

Once we were settled, Zander launched in.

And he did it looking at me.

"Okay, so, I forgot to bring my clothes to school to change but I wanted to get here so I told Nona to just come here and that's why I'm wearin' this," he stated, flipping his hand in front of him. "I go to a school where they make you wear uniforms."

He was excited to meet us.

My heart squeezed.

"I know," I replied.

"The girls hate it 'cause they can't wear fingernail polish or different shoes but I don't mind much," he shared.

"Well, that's good," I told him.

He kept chattering. "Nona says girls that age shouldn't wear fingernail polish anyway and 'spose she's right, but really, it's the older girls who're always whinin' about it. The school goes from first grade to twelfth," he stated proudly, then added, "Though, first to fifth is in one building. Sixth through eighth in another and the high school is all the way across the way so we don't see them much except at assemblies. Still, I hear the high school girls complaining about nail polish, even at assemblies." He paused, then finished with, "The older kids talk a lot during assemblies."

"They probably shouldn't do that," I remarked.

"Nah, they shouldn't," he agreed. "But they're better at it. They've learned to talk quiet so they don't get into trouble."

"Well, uh . . ." I trailed off, not knowing what to say to that.

Zander didn't need a response. He kept right on yammering.

"What I don't get is, who cares about fingernail polish? I mean, is it that important?"

"I'm thinking that at nine you probably shouldn't tax yourself to try to understand the female mind," I advised and he grinned at me.

My heart turned over again.

"Just sayin'," Ham put in, "I'm way past nine but I quit tryin' to do that a long time ago."

Zander laughed.

It sounded beautiful.

So beautiful my hand shot under the table and I curled my fingers tight around Ham's thigh.

When I did, his hand covered mine, pried my fingers away so he could wrap his fingers around mine and hold them close.

Trudy came to the table with menus. Drinks were ordered and I got my chance to suggest Zander try the mile-high mud pie.

Without even looking to see if it was okay with Aunt Wilona (Dad never let us have dessert unless it was a special occasion), he went for it.

Aunt Wilona went for one, too. In fact, Ham was the only one who took another road and got a slice of turtle cheesecake.

After Trudy left, Zander turned back to me.

"So, do you look like my mom?"

My fingers still held in Ham's squeezed hard and I felt the tension coming from Aunt Wilona but I powered through all that and held Zander's gaze.

"No, darlin'. She was blonde but lighter. And she had blue eyes but they were very pretty," I told him.

He nodded.

"You're gonna be real tall, I can tell, and she wasn't all that tall either," I went on.

He scrunched his lips to the side and I didn't know if that was disappointment or him simply not knowing what to do with this information.

"I"—my eyes went to Aunt Wilona and back to Zander—"brought a picture if you'd like to see?"

Zander looked at Aunt Wilona. She gave him a shaky smile and then he turned back to me and nodded.

I let Ham's hand go and went to my purse that was shoved into the seat at my side. My fingers fumbling with nerves, I found the picture of Xenia I'd chosen to bring. I'd done it carefully. And I hoped I'd done it right.

In the picture, Xenia and I were outside at a party. A barbecue some friends were giving in a park. I was sitting cross-legged on the top of a picnic table. She was beside me, standing, leaning into me. We were both smiling, big and bright at the camera, but my goofy sister had her hand behind my head, giving me rabbit's ears.

She looked beautiful, young, and happy.

I pulled in a breath, put the picture to the table, and slid it across to Zander.

"That's her," I whispered. "That's your mom. My sister. Xenia."

Eyes riveted to the picture, hands in his lap under the table, he just stared.

"She joked a lot," I told him, my voice husky so I cleared my throat and felt Ham's arm slide across the back of the booth and around my shoulders. "She was always joking around," I continued. "And she told really good scary stories."

Zander's eyes lifted from the picture. "Scary stories?"

I nodded. "She'd have you trembling so bad, you'd shake your bed. And when she went in for the kill, you'd jump out of your skin."

He turned his head to look up to Aunt Wilona and then he looked back down at the picture.

Moments passed and no one said anything.

Zander broke the silence. "Do you remember those stories?" he asked, eyes still on the picture.

My throat started tingling and through it I forced my lie, "Every last one."

It was a lie but if I got my shot to tell him the ones I remembered, I'd then make up new ones and lie again and say they were Xenia's.

I just hoped I made up ones that were as good as hers.

He looked again at me and tipped his head to the side, his eyes weirdly astute.

"Why didn't you come see me before?" he asked and Ham's arm curled tighter around my shoulders as more tension came from Aunt Wilona.

"I—" I started.

"I don't live real far away," Zander pointed out.

Surprisingly, Aunt Wilona spoke.

"Your granddad and Zara aren't close," she said and Zander looked up at her. "Grownups do funny things and your granddad does a lot of them."

Unfortunately, the look on his face stated that he knew that and that didn't make me feel all that great.

Aunt Wilona wasn't done but what she said next shocked the crap out of me.

"I should have explained this when I first told you about your Aunt Zara, but your grandfather didn't want your aunt seein' you so he made that happen. We'll talk about that more when you're a little older, honey, but right now all you need to know is he didn't do right and your aunt didn't even know you were as close as you were. She thought you were far away and she couldn't get to you. But when she found out you were close, Zara made a point to find a way to do what we're doing right now and she did it. Fast. So here we are."

Zander looked my aunt straight in the eyes when he stated, "But you knew Aunt Zara was close, too. You told me when you told me about her and my mom."

I winced when I saw the pain slide through Aunt Wilona's face.

It was then I came to Aunt Wilona's rescue by announcing, "Your granddad wouldn't let her tell you, and I suspect we'll explain that more when you're a bit older, too, but she didn't have a choice but to do what he said."

He glanced at me when I spoke, nodded when I was done, then looked back at Aunt Wilona and asked, "Why would Granddad do that?"

"Your granddad is a mysterious man," Aunt Wilona replied vaguely.

"I'll say," Zander muttered, looking back down at the

picture and his words and all they exposed meant my body tightened and Ham's arm around my shoulders pulled me into his side.

"You're here now," I declared in an effort to lighten the mood and Zander looked up at me. "And I'm here. Aunt Wilona's here. Reece is here. We're getting chocolate cake. No, we're getting the best chocolate cake *ever*. So it's all good. And if you want to keep that picture," I nodded to the picture, "it's yours."

"Yeah?" Zander asked.

"Yeah," I answered, smiling at him. "And now, before your mouth is busy shoving cake in it, I want to know everything. What subjects you like in school. Your best friends' names. Do you play sports—"

"Linebacker. Football. Like Tate Jackson!" he stated immediately. "And after I finish my pro career, I'm gonna be a bounty hunter like him, too."

Tate Jackson lived one town over. He'd also had a short-lived NFL career that led to a longer career as a bounty hunter.

And thus his life path was any nine-year-old boy's dream.

"You could be a bounty hunter," Zander advised Ham. "You'd scare them into givin' up with just a look."

"Might be too late for a profession change for me, kid. But also, thinkin' you might reconsider, as it looks like you're givin' both your aunts heart palpitations with your future career plans," Ham replied.

"Don't worry. In ten, fifteen years, I'll be a bada...uh... I mean, I'll be tough. They'll be good," Zander reassured Ham. Then he asked, "Do you work out?"

"Most every day," Ham answered and it occurred to me that Zander was bonding with Ham and this might not be because he was uncomfortable around me, being his newly-learned-was-dead mother's sister, but because he had no man in his life.

"Looks like you do it, like, five times a day," Zander noted, his eyes moving to Ham's wide chest.

"Only need to do it once, boy, just do it right," Ham replied.

"You know," Aunt Wilona broke in, "if... erm... Uncle, uh... Reece would be okay with it, maybe you could, I don't know... go running with him or something."

My eyes went to my aunt and for the first time in my whole entire life, I wanted to hug her.

Then I looked to Zander as he bounced in his seat, completely oblivious that Trudy had arrived with a tray full of drinks and plates of cake.

"That would be *so cool*!" he cried.

"I run five miles every day, Zander. Can you keep up with that?" Ham asked.

"Totally," Zander answered, then looked at me. "Are you going to run with us?"

I really wanted to say yes. I really, really did. But I also didn't want to drop dead of a heart attack trying to run with Ham and Zander when I'd never run for exercise in my life. In fact, I couldn't even remember the last time I ran *at all*.

"I'll get the protein shakes ready for your arrival home," I offered.

"Awesome," Zander whispered and finally looked at the cake that was sliding in front of him.

It was then he burned a whole straight through my heart.

Because Trudy got too close to the picture of Xenia with the plate of cake.

So Zander's hand darted out, snatching it up, taking it to safety, and doing this by pressing it face-first to his chest.

I dropped my head, stared at my lap, and deep breathed as my eyes filled with tears.

Ham wrapped his hand around the back of my neck.

I kept doing this until I heard Zander say, sounding like his mouth was full, "This is really good!"

I looked up and saw his mouth was full and getting fuller as he was shoving more cake into it.

The picture of Xenia was propped up on the table by the wall, face out and out of harm's way.

I swallowed, pulled gently away from Ham, and grabbed my fork.

I took a bite and looked to my aunt.

She was concentrating on her cake so it took a minute before she felt my eyes, lifted her head, and caught them.

I swallowed cake and mouthed, *Thank you*.

Tears brightened her eyes as relief washed through her face. Then she nodded and looked down at her cake.

Ham gave my thigh a squeeze and then picked up his fork.

Zander looked at me and, still with mouth full, announced, "I get all A's in science but don't get excited, I get C's in English. It used to drive Nona nuts but finally she said as long as I can speak it, it isn't necessary for me to live and breathe it and scientists are way cool so I'm good."

I smiled as he went on talking and I experienced something very weird as he did.

The weird part wasn't falling in love with my nephew. I knew I'd do that.

The weird part was falling in love with my aunt.

That was something I never thought I'd do.

*   *   *

We were on the sidewalk outside The Mark, Aunt Wilona and I a bit away from Zander and Ham, who'd walked down to take a look at his truck.

But not too far away that we didn't hear Zander yell, "That truck is *huge*!"

I watched Ham smile down at him and my belly felt weird. Like I had butterflies. And it hit me that this was because, at that moment, I understood in a visceral way that

Ham would be a good father. And that would mean a good father to *our* kids.

And a good uncle to his nephew.

Holding that feeling close with the warmth of sharing a mud pie with my nephew, I turned to Aunt Wilona and did what I had to do.

I reached out, touched her forearm, and stopped.

She looked down to her arm where my hand had touched, looked at me, and stopped, too.

"Does he ask about his dad?" I asked, bracing for her answer because Xenia had narrowed it down to two guys. Only one was still in town but Zander didn't look like either of them.

She gave a brief nod. "Started asking about his parents a year or so ago. Being careful with it. Xavier didn't want me to say anything so I danced around it until, of course, after the, uh…"

She trailed off and I nodded to let her know I understood.

"I don't know who his father is, Aunt Wilona," I admitted. "And neither did Xenia. Not for certain."

She looked toward Zander and murmured, "My niece had demons."

I was grateful she understood that. In the coming years, sharing with Zander about his mother, it would be important.

"I'll need to understand how Dad is with him," I said quietly.

"You know your father," she replied and my eyes sharpened on her.

"Yes, Aunt Wilona, I do and I'll need to understand how Dad is with him," I repeated firmly.

She held my eyes and whispered, "He doesn't hurt him."

"Zander seems very high-spirited," I noted. "Except when he's talking about Dad. Then he seems confused."

"Your father is a hard man," Aunt Wilona said. "Zander is a nine-year-old boy. He doesn't understand hard."

"Abuse comes in many forms," I returned. "And all of them are hard."

"I wouldn't allow that to happen," she retorted quickly and sharply. "We'd disappear before that happened. Zander hasn't been alone in your father's presence since he was six months old."

I let out a relieved breath for a variety of reasons.

It was coming clear that Aunt Wilona was not like my mother. She was a lioness with my nephew. She raised him. She obviously loved him. And most important, when it came to my dad, she protected him.

"It's very difficult living under this cloud, especially since I have to keep it from Zander," she went on and I focused on her. "Do you and Reece know what you intend to do?"

"About Zander, not yet," I answered, then gave her a hint of the relief she gave me. "We're concerned about him gettin' caught in this storm. We'd like to avoid doing that and we want to find ways to work with you to accomplish that. But you should know, the clouds are gathering and, tomorrow, Dad is not going to be very happy."

Her eyes narrowed on me but she simply nodded and didn't ask questions.

"You seem to have done well with him," I noted carefully.

"He's my life," she replied.

"Aunt Wilona—"

Her face twisted with emotion and she turned fully to me.

"I know I didn't get him the right way but that doesn't mean a thing. I told your man and I'll tell you, Zander wants you in his life. I want him to have his aunt. You were close with Xenia. You can give her to him in a way I can't, and you did that tonight, seeing as I don't even have any pictures of her. And a boy should have his mother however he can get her."

She stopped and I nodded so she continued.

"And I want to mend fences with you. Having him, he's

taught me a few things, and I've learned you're never too old to learn. So, I'm saying this because I want to keep him, I want him safe, I don't want his life disrupted, but nine years under Xavier's thumb, nine years with Zander in my life, I've learned what's important. And doing everything I can to give that boy the life he needs to build a good one when he gets older is the only thing that's important. And that includes family." She leaned into me. "The *right* kind."

That meant so much to me, of course, I went flippant.

"If you're not careful, I might start liking you."

"Same goes for you," she replied instantly and Aunt Wilona even being minutely funny shocked the shit out of me so I burst out laughing.

When I started to get control of it, I was shocked further to see Aunt Wilona smiling at me.

"What are you guys laughing about?" Zander asked and I looked down to see him come to a jumping halt close to my aunt.

He'd obviously run there because Ham was still down the way, sauntering toward us, eyes on me, assessing.

"Your Nona was being funny," I told Zander when I looked away from Ham to him.

"She's like that all the time," Zander surprised me by replying.

"Good," I whispered and looked at my aunt.

"Get this!" Zander started, grabbing Aunt Wilona's hand for a quick tug before letting it go. "Uncle Reece has a *Harley*."

"Oh God," Aunt Wilona moaned, looking up to the heavens.

"I know!" Zander replied, interpreting her reaction as only a nine-year-old boy would. "Isn't that cool?"

Aunt Wilona looked to Reece and shocked the hell out of me yet again.

"He gets on the back of that with you, he wears a helmet."

"Of course," Ham murmured.

"No way!" Zander shouted. "Tough guys don't wear helmets!"

"Tough kids mind their aunts or they don't get a ride," Ham commented and Zander looked up at him, scrunched his nose, and then looked at his feet.

"Whatever," he muttered, then he looked up at me. "Do you ride with him?"

"Yes," I answered.

"Do you wear a helmet?" he pressed on.

Stupidly, I hadn't seen that coming.

"Well . . ." I started, trailed off, and Ham saved me.

"My bike, my rules. And my rules are, you follow your aunt's rules. Yeah?"

Zander looked to Ham then my aunt and I followed his eyes.

Aunt Wilona was staring at Ham with what might have been respect before she looked down at Zander and said, "We should go, honey."

Zander nodded and looked up at me. "Nona says you can come over for dinner. You wanna do that soon?"

I wanted to do that that night.

"Whenever you want us, we'll be there," I said.

"Awesome," he mumbled.

"Say good-bye, sweetheart, we should get going," Aunt Wilona urged.

"Right," Zander said, looked at Ham, and waved. "Bye." He did the same to me and repeated his "bye."

"Bye, kid," Ham rumbled.

"Bye, darlin'," I replied, grinning at him, and then I grinned at Aunt Wilona. "Bye . . . Nona."

She rolled her eyes before she gave her farewells and they moved away.

Ham moved to my side and curved an arm around my shoulders as we watched them go.

Then, suddenly, Zander turned around, raced back, and wrapped his arms quickly around my hips, giving me a barely there hug before he jumped back and looked up at me.

"Thanks for the picture," he whispered.

I wasn't breathing, too moved by his touch, his words, but I still opened my mouth in an effort to speak but before I could, he turned and dashed back toward Aunt Wilona, stopped again, looked to Ham, and called, "I'll wear a helmet!"

Then he ran back to Aunt Wilona. She gave us another wave and I stood in the curve of Ham's arm as we watched them get in their SUV then I returned Zander's wave as we watched them drive away.

"How's my cookie?" he muttered as I continued to watch the street where they'd disappeared.

"He's a great kid."

"Yeah, he is."

"Did you see that with the picture?"

His arm curled me closer to his side. "Yeah, baby."

"Aunt Wilona doesn't let him alone with Dad," I told him.

"That's good," Ham replied.

"I'm in love," I declared and Ham curled me even closer, fitting my front to his side, and I tipped my head back to catch his eyes.

"I figured that'd happen," he noted.

"Aunt Wilona's done a good job," I whispered.

"Seems so," Ham agreed.

"I miss her more right now than I have in nine years," I shared.

He knew I was talking about Xenia and I knew he did when his eyes warmed, his face got soft, and his lips murmured, "Baby."

I shoved my face into his chest.

Ham wrapped his other arm around me and I wrapped both around him.

We stood there on the boardwalk for a long time, holding on, saying nothing.

Eventually, I broke the silence.

"I want nine kids," I declared, my voice muffled by his chest.

"Seems I'm done with condoms," was his reply.

I tipped my head back, caught his beautiful, intelligent, smiling eyes, and burst out laughing.

CHAPTER EIGHTEEN

Show and Tell

THE NEXT MORNING, I was woken up when Ham dragged his thumb over my nipple.

My eyes opened slowly as that scored straight from nipple to between my legs and I whispered, "Ham."

The second I said his name, his heat left my back, he rolled me, rolled over me, and his mouth took mine in a deep, soft, sweet kiss.

I slid my arms around him.

Thus Ham commenced making love to me before I was barely awake. Something he did on occasion. Something I liked very, *very* much.

And when he did it, he made it all about me. Taking his time through kisses and touches to remove my nightgown and panties. Then it was all about his hands, lips, and tongue trailing over my neck, chest, my breasts, ribs, and belly. His mouth closing over my nipples and gently suckling. His fingertips gliding through the wetness between my legs, tender, reverent, loving. His lips coming back to my mouth to kiss me deep, wet, sweet, beautiful, and *long*.

It was a slow burn he built, taking his time, like we had years for Ham to taste me, touch me, give me everything.

With experience, I'd learned to ride the burn, not push it, not demand more. Moving my hands over him, tasting him when I had the chance but, when we did this, it was about Ham giving to me.

And that was what I got that morning.

Until Ham changed it and, doing so, he altered my world.

Because, when he finally slid inside, no condom, just him and me, he moved, slow, deep, beautiful but he did it holding my eyes, his weight braced onto a forearm in the bed under me but his hand connected with me, fingers wrapped around the back of my neck while he drifted the fingers of his other hand through my hair.

"Softest hair I ever felt," he murmured.

My arms, already wrapped around him, tightened and I lifted my legs to curve them around his hips as I whispered, "Ham."

He brushed his lips against mine, pulled back, kept sliding in and out, the rhythm sure, leisured, amazing, as he held my eyes.

"Drove away from you nine years ago, knew it was wrong then, didn't know that it was the biggest mistake I'd make in my life," he whispered back.

My arms and legs convulsed around him, I lifted my hips, deepening his invasion, and his rhythm escalated.

"Darlin'," I breathed, not knowing where this was going but liking how it made me feel.

"You're an unbelievable woman, Zara," he told me softly.

I liked how that made me feel even more and tears filled my eyes.

But I ordered, "Shut up and make love to me," and when I did, my voice was trembling.

Ham ignored me.

"Best woman I ever met," he went on.

My hands slid up his back, rounding him, shoving between us and up through the crisp hair on his chest. I cupped his jaw and slid my thumbs over the stubble on his cheeks.

"Be quiet, baby," I begged.

His thrusts got faster and he dropped his head, his lips a whisper away from mine.

"Took hit after hit, started life takin' 'em, literally, you never even went down to a knee," he murmured against my mouth.

"Be quiet."

"So fuckin' strong."

"Quiet, honey."

"So goddamned pretty."

"Ham," I whispered.

"Mine," he growled, that noise sounding against my lips sweeping through me, his hips moving much faster, driving harder, going even deeper. "All mine," he finished and, before I could say a word, he slanted his head and took my mouth.

Then he took us both there.

Timing it perfectly, I gasped into his mouth before I moaned, my limbs clenching around him, the climax rolling through me, gentle but beautiful and lasting. Seconds later, Ham planted himself to the root and groaned down my throat.

When he came down, he started gliding in and out as his lips trailed down to my neck and moved there. He did this awhile before he slid in, filling me, connecting us, and stayed put.

Then he said against my neck, "Want you off The Pill, honey. We start now."

"Okay," I agreed quietly, liking that.

Ham and me, we'd already started. But a family, we were going to start now.

Yes, I liked that.

And he'd obviously liked Zander, and meeting him reminded Ham, like me, of the bounty we had before us. No reason to delay. We started now.

He lifted up and looked down at me. One of his hands was still curled around the back of my neck, the other one he used to drift his fingers lightly across the skin on my face as his eyes watched.

Then they caught mine.

"Loved Rachel," he stated and his words were so unexpected, considering the mood he'd created, I blinked.

Where did that come from? And why was he talking about Rachel *now*?

"Ham, I think—"

"Bear with me, darlin'," he whispered.

I shut my mouth.

Ham continued. "We met after high school. She was beautiful, think I fell in love with her the minute I laid eyes on her. Stopped at nothin' to get in there then bind her to me."

He paused and I said nothing, doing my best to bear with him.

When I didn't say a word, he kept going.

"Had a good life with my folks. Mom bein' so sick, she took a risk havin' me. She couldn't take more risks after that, though. But, the love they had to give, love they gave me, I knew the only thing that would have made growin' up better was havin' brothers and sisters. Never, when I was a kid, when I was growin' into a man, did I dream of doin' big things. Goin' to the moon. Makin' lots of money. Bein' some kind of hotshot. I just wanted to build on what my parents gave to me and showed me. A man in love with his wife. Dad takin' care of her, me, our home. A woman in love with her husband. Them makin' a child outta that love and workin' together to teach him to be a good man. Havin' that I knew that was the only thing I needed."

"Okay," I said softly, liking this part of what he was saying even as my heart broke, knowing Rachel took away that simple dream.

"So young, in love, I shared all that with Rachel. Laid it out for her. Stupid," he stated and I tensed my limbs around him.

"She was the one who was stupid, Ham."

He gave me a small smile, dipped his head, and touched his mouth to mine before he lifted it and kept talking.

"She told me she wanted the same things. She agreed with me on everything, our life path, how we'd get there, how many kids we were gonna have."

I nodded.

Ham went on. "I believed her. So gone for her, I sucked that shit up. Woke up in the morning, told her I loved her. Left for work, told her I loved her. Rolled into bed at night, worked bars then, too, babe," he shared something I knew. "Woke her when I got home and told her I loved her. Every time, she said the same thing back. She'd even call me durin' the day for no reason, she said, except to say she loved me."

This wasn't fun to hear but I held him close, held his eyes, slid one of my hands up his back so I could sift my fingers through his messy hair, and stayed silent.

But I did it thinking the woman I'd met a few days ago still loved my man. Back then, she was young, stupid, selfish, and I didn't understand her kind of love, why she did the things she did. I just understood in that moment with the sadness I read in her face, the gesture she'd made for Ham driving all the way out to Gnaw Bone, that she'd spent twenty years paying a big price for doing them.

And the price she paid was losing Ham and, after doing that, knowing exactly how much she'd lost. But it was worse. She had to live with the fact that it was what she did that meant she had lost him. She'd actually thrown all that was Graham Reece away.

Ham broke into my thoughts to ask, "After what she did to me, I didn't get it. How could you love someone and do that to them?"

"I don't know," I answered on a whisper.

"No," he replied. "You wouldn't."

The way he said that, like he really believed it, meant the world to me.

Ham continued. "The two after her, cookie, same thing. I wasn't stupid, though I was still young. But I'd learned. With them, I didn't lay it bare, open myself, but we eventually got to the discussion and they told me they wanted the same things as I did out of life. They also told me they loved me. Swore it. Said it over and over. Then they *showed* how they felt, who they were, and it was not that."

"No," I agreed.

"And after the third, I really learned. After the third, I knew those words were empty. You can say anything but it's what you do that says it all."

My hand in his hair clenched as where he was going with all this finally dawned on me.

"Never said those words again, cookie," he told me. "Women said them to me, didn't believe it. Those words had lost their meaning."

Yes, I now knew where this was going.

"Darlin'," I murmured.

"Then you said it."

I closed my eyes as beauty scored through me.

Because when he said those four words, his voice was jagged.

"Baby, come back to me," Ham urged.

I opened my eyes and his fingers still drifting over my face stopped as he cupped my cheek.

"Suddenly, those words again had meaning," he said.

"They totally do," I replied, my voice throaty.

"Only 'cause you show they do," he returned. "With all her bullshit, the way she burned me, time and again gutting me, Rachel taught me, and fuck but I learned, love is a show, it's not a tell."

I nodded, swallowing, fighting the emotion that was building inside me.

"All the time, people say one thing, but they do another. You feel somethin' for them, you wanna believe what they say but you gotta learn to read what they do. I think, the other night, you got what I meant when I asked you to pay attention. But now, I'm sayin' all this because I want you to know why that man is me. Why I couldn't give you what you needed, say the words you needed to hear."

"I understand, baby," I told him.

"I love you, Zara."

My breath caught loudly in my throat even as my body bucked under his with the force of emotion that had built so high, it exploded inside me.

Unthinking, overwhelmed, holding on to him tightly, I lifted my head, shoved it in his neck, and mumbled brokenly, "Ham."

His lips against my ear, his hand at the back of my neck squeezing, he whispered, "You get those words because you give them. You say them and you mean them. No bullshit. No lies. Not tellin' me what I wanna hear to get my dick, my money, my protection, whatever the fuck it was that they wanted outta me. Nine years ago, you let me go so I could be the man I was. You took me only as I could give because you knew that was the way it needed to be for me. You gave me that because you love me. And I took it, fuckin' up huge. But now, baby, you get it all back. Now's your time where *you* get everything *you* need."

I loved all that, *adored* it.

But part of it made me uneasy.

So I dropped my head to the pillow, Ham lifted his, and when I caught his eyes, I asked, "You fucked up huge?"

"Left you," he answered.

"Ham—"

He shook his head and his hand came back to my face so he could press his thumb to my lips.

"No. No, cookie. None of this shit woulda happened to you if I didn't have my head so far up my ass back then."

"Ham—" I tried again but his thumb smushing my lips made it come out "Humm," and he talked right over me.

"I fucked up. We lost near on a decade. You endured some serious shit. You lost nine years of Zander—"

I moved my hand to his wrist, pulling it slightly away, and told him, "You probably wouldn't have known about Zander either. Dad went to great lengths to keep that from me."

His brows rose. "You think I stood by your side where I should have been, I wouldn't have kept my eye on that asshole?"

No, I didn't think that. New, awesomer Ham, if he'd been able to be that Ham back then, would have definitely kept his eye on Dad if only to make certain Dad didn't screw with me.

"It's done now," I decided to say to let him know all was cool.

"Babe, you lost your home. You lost your shop. You lost nine years of your nephew. You been sittin' on millions of dollars you didn't know you had for nearly three years. You got married to a guy you cared about but you picked him for safety, figured out you fucked up, cut those ties, and moved on but did it torturing yourself because you picked wrong even though he did too. None of that shit would have happened if I'd been where I knew when I fuckin' drove away nine years ago I should have stuck. At your side."

My belly warmed at his words and my hand still wrapped around his wrist gave him a squeeze as I replied, "Okay, Ham, maybe all that's true and I love it that you think that but don't you think that even if you were here, other shit might have happened? You can't protect me from everything. You can't stop life from happening."

"You got love, you got someone at your back, when life happens, it's a fuckuva lot easier to deal and move on and you know that, cookie."

He was not wrong. I did know that, having Ham these past months, and before that, having him look after me in the times when we were together (but weren't), riding into town to come to my rescue when I most needed him.

And that was when it hit me. All of it.

So my body melted under his and both my hands moved back to his jaws and I shared, "You gave me that."

"Yeah, *now.* For the last coupla months. Not the last nine years," he returned.

"Kim died and you were there," I whispered and Ham's head jerked. "Kim got diagnosed and you were the first person I called. We talked for three hours, Ham. You listened to me cry, and in two days, you showed up at my house just to spend the night holding me then you had to go and drive back so you could work. I broke my wrist, you took a week off to be with me. Except for when I let you go, you were *always* there for me. And you *let* me let you go because you thought I needed that. And Ham"—I dug my fingers gently into his face—"when I lost everything, you were there and you gave it back."

By the time I was done speaking, his eyes were burning into mine and when I finished, he dropped his forehead to mine and groaned low, "Fuck, Zara."

"Rachel burned you, she gutted you, she killed your

dream," I whispered. "And that would mark anyone. It changed you, made you protect yourself, made you into the man you had to be. But if a woman loves you, truly loves you, baby, she *lets* you be the man you have to be. She doesn't change you into the man she wants you to be."

And by the time I was done saying that, Ham had angled his head and crushed his mouth to mine.

This was not a slow, tender, sweet, deep, long kiss.

This was a hard, devouring, intense, wet, deep, long kiss.

It was a show, not a tell.

And it said everything.

And when we were done, Ham had rolled us so he was on his back, I was on top, one of his arms was clamped tight around me, his other hand in my hair, holding my mouth to his, but when he let me lift my head, we were both breathing deeply.

"I love you, Zara," he growled.

And I loved that.

So freaking much.

"I know, darlin'. I love you, too," I replied.

His eyes still burned but then that burn muted to a warmth I felt flowing through me in a way I knew, down deep, without a doubt, that warmth would never leave me.

"I know, cookie," he whispered.

"Good," I whispered back, then I watched Ham grin.

It was the most beautiful thing I'd ever seen.

But even so, I grinned back, dropped my mouth to his, and kissed my man's grin right off his face.

* * *

Late that night (or more accurately, early the next morning), we were in the truck after work, Ham driving, me with my phone to my ear listening to the voice mail Aunt Wilona left while I was lugging drinks around the bar.

It was late. I was tired. I had a shitload of tips in my

pocket because Ham had hired a band and the place had been packed.

But, even as tired as I was, I was happier than I'd ever been in . . . my . . . *life*.

"Aunt Wilona called," I told him after I listened to her voice mail and shoved my phone into my purse. "Says the next night we both have off, she'd like us to come over for dinner and she wants to know what you don't like to eat."

"Eat anything, babe," he replied.

That wasn't strictly true. The not strictly true part about that was that he didn't quibble about food. It was just, if he didn't like it, he left it on his plate.

I made a mental note to share with Aunt Wilona the stuff I'd noticed Ham left on his plate and turned my eyes to the windshield.

When I saw where we were, I felt my brows draw together.

"Where are we going?" I asked.

"Got a stop to make," he answered.

I looked to him. "At three thirty in the morning?"

He was silent a moment before, gently, he ordered, "Bear with me, cookie."

Man, oh man, he'd asked me to bear with him once already that day, to spectacular results that lit my world with a rosy glow, so I had a feeling I needed not only to bear with him but bear up because as awesome as our morning was, I was not a girl used to awesome so I knew I had to prepare. Therefore, I shut my mouth and looked back to the road.

Five minutes later, I opened my mouth because we'd turned into my old development.

What on earth were we doing here?

My eyes went back to his profile and I started, "Ham—"

"Five seconds, baby."

I'd heard that before too, another time he'd colored my

world with a rosy glow when he told me he'd come back to Gnaw Bone for me.

I pulled in a breath, confused, uncertain, but since this was Ham, I let it out.

Ham drove right to my old house, right up into the drive where he parked, and my heart started beating hard.

I hadn't been back since I packed up and left, a very unhappy day, and I was surprised by the way the house looked. Many foreclosures looked unkempt, what with no one to take care of the yard.

Mine looked like it had when I lived there except the house had that empty feel any empty house had.

Ham opened his door, I followed suit, and he was at my side when I'd jumped down. He slammed my door, grabbed my hand, and led me to the front walk.

"Ham, this is weird and kind of—" I began.

"Five more seconds, cookie."

I again shut up.

Ham walked us to the front door. Not letting my hand go, he flipped his keys around and inserted a key in the lock.

My breath caught.

I forced it to flowing again so I could ask, "Darlin', how'd you get a key?"

He didn't answer.

He unlocked the door, shoved it open, and pulled me through with him.

The blinds I'd left behind were pulled, the space almost dark so I could barely see a thing. Ham kicked the door closed with his boot so even the minimal light coming in from the streetlamps outside was extinguished.

I knew where we were going by memory when he walked us into the house and stopped by where I knew there was a light switch.

He flipped it on.

When the lights came on, I stopped breathing.

Mindy's furniture was there.

Also, in the built-in cabinets was Ham's TV, under it the DVD player, cable box, and a new stereo and receiver. On either side of the cabinets sat two attractive standing speakers. Arranged in the built-in were my knickknacks, books, and what appeared to be Ham's as well as my CDs, not filling the spaces but making it appear homey.

My eyes drifted and I saw in the dining room a new oval, distressed dark-wood, gorgeous dining room table with six dark wicker, woven chairs all around. New attractive, green-and-blue woven placemats were on the table and even new matching napkins folded in rectangles on top of them. In the center of the table there was an enormous spray of blood-red roses, no baby's breath, no greenery, just those stunning stems.

Against the wall next to the table, there was a matching hutch and above it was mounted a large, black-and-white, beautifully framed print.

A Cotton.

And not just any Cotton (not that there was such a thing).

It was a picture of "the old girl." A picture Cotton took when he was with me.

Breathing again but having trouble doing it, my eyes stinging, throat burning, I gently pulled my hand from Ham's and wandered in two steps. Turning woodenly, I saw all my stuff in the kitchen, dishtowels folded over the oven handle, canisters on the counter, crock holding wooden spoons and spatulas sitting by the range, another huge spray of blood-red roses resting on the bar.

Lips parted, vision swimming, I turned to see Ham standing in the entryway, arms crossed, watching me.

"How?" I breathed.

"Came up for auction, I bought it," he replied.

My breath hitched. I swallowed, opened my mouth, closed it, opened it, and asked disbelievingly, "You bought it?"

"Months ago, cookie. Bought it with cash. It's paid for. No mortgage. Then I waited until the time was right to bring you home."

Bring me home.

I didn't know what to do. I didn't know what to say. I couldn't even cope with all I was feeling.

So I just stood there.

"Talked to our landlord," Ham carried on. "She got another tenant for our unit, so we were free to move. Your shit is sorted. Time was right. Made a couple of calls, folks I made a couple of calls to made a couple of calls. Your girls Maybelline and Wanda as well as Nina set all this up."

He jerked his head toward the dining room table.

"Deluxe Home Store," he said. "They got it at a discount. Maybelline, her husband, and Wanda's gift to you."

I started deep breathing.

Ham wasn't done.

"Obviously, Cotton gave you that print. The stereo and surround sound, I bought that, but Arlene arranged delivery and Mindy's man, Jeff, set it up. Flowers are from me, too, but Arlene picked them up for me. Nina got Max to sort out some guys. They were waiting in the parking lot at our pad, saw us leave tonight, they got to work and did the heavy lifting. Nina, your girls Mindy, Becca, and Jenna, as well as Maybelline and Wanda, sorted the other stuff." He jerked his head toward the built-in, obviously referring to the arrangement of CDs and knickknacks before he concluded, "Our clothes are in the closet. Your bed is in the guest room. Our bed is in our room. We're home."

We were home.

Ham had bought my house.

We were home.

I stood immobile, unable to move, but more, unwilling just in case movement would pierce the fragile bubble that had formed over this crazy-beautiful dream.

Ham didn't have a problem moving and he did so to come to me.

But he stopped a foot in front of me, bent, grabbed my left hand, and lifted it. He held it between us, dug in his jeans pocket, and pulled his hand out. Arranging my ring finger straight with his thumb, he moved his other hand to it and my head dropped, this all feeling like it happened in slow motion.

And it was then I watched his long, strong, calloused fingers slide a princess-cut diamond on my finger. It was simple, no adornment, set in white gold or maybe platinum. But the diamond needed no ornamentation. It was not small, not by a long shot. It wasn't massive and ostentatious, either. But it made a statement.

A huge one.

Again I quit breathing.

"Like I said," Ham began and my head drifted back up so I could catch his eyes. "Now's your time where you get everything you need."

"I love you," I forced out in a whisper.

"I know." He did not whisper.

"No. I love you," I repeated.

"I know, cookie."

"No," I stated, his fingers still holding mine. I didn't move but kept my eyes locked to his. "I *love* you, Graham Reece."

Ham said nothing but I knew he understood me when his eyes started burning and his hand, which had been gently holding mine, engulfed it, squeezing tight.

"You're an unbelievable man, Ham," I told him softly.

His burning eyes flared and his hand pulled me closer.

But his lips ordered, "Shut it, honey."

His voice was jagged.

"Best man I ever met," I went on.

With me closer, his free hand came up, curling around the side of my neck, sliding up and back into my hair.

"Be quiet, baby," he whispered, those jagged words tearing through me beautifully.

"So fuckin' strong," I kept going.

"Quiet, honey."

"So goddamned handsome."

"Cookie—"

"Always there for me."

His hand cupping the back of my head pulled me up as his head came down and he crushed his mouth to mine.

He let my other hand go so his arm could knife around my back. My arms circled his shoulders and we made out, hot and heavy, in our new house.

It was the best kiss I'd ever had, even better than the ones he gave me that morning before and after he told me he loved me.

Then again, this time, he was doing it after he put his ring on my finger and gave me back my house, so that was hardly surprising.

When we were done, Ham kept me in his arms but shoved my face in his neck as he pressed his jaw to the side of my head.

"You bought back my house," I said there.

"Yeah," he confirmed what was proved all around.

"You're pretty good with show," I shared in a massive understatement.

"Glad you appreciate it," he replied.

"Though, that said, you're also pretty good with tell," I stated.

"Pleased I got both bases covered," he returned.

"Just in case there's a doubt, the answer is yes, I'll marry you," I told him.

"Good to have that verified." His voice was now holding a smile.

"And, my guess, you corralled Maybelle into helping with all this, she probably likes you now," I stated.

"She said much the same thing when I stole her number from your cell and we had our chat," he informed me.

That was good to know.

"The ring is beautiful," I kept blathering.

His arm gave me a squeeze. "Glad you like it, cookie."

"No, I mean it's *really* beautiful."

"Love that you think so, darlin'."

Finally, I shut up and held on to my man.

He held me back.

We did this for a while, that was to say, we did it until Ham was done doing it.

"We gonna stand here huggin' in the hall all night or are you gonna pick where we start? Break in the livin' room or fuck in bed?" he asked.

A shiver slid through me and I pulled my head back to catch his eyes.

"Dining room table," I gave him my decision on an alternate location and I watched his eyes flash in a way I liked a whole lot.

"Yeah?" he asked.

"I wanna smell my roses while you're inside me," I whispered and I got another flash before he dipped his head and his mouth was on mine.

"You got it, cookie," he said there.

And he was right.

I did.

I had it.

I had everything I needed.

For the first time in my life, even though with the life I lived I never thought it would happen. And for the first time in my life, it happened without me having to work my ass off to get even close to it.

In other words, for the first time in my life, I just plain had *everything*.

*   *   *

"Cookie?" Ham called

We were in our bed in our new bedroom, my new-old one. We were spooning and I was nearly asleep.

Still, I had the scent of roses lingering in my nostrils and the feel of Ham still lingering between my legs.

"Yeah, darlin'?" I answered, my voice sleepy.

"Just sayin', want that day to come soon that you got my name so you best get on that."

I smiled into the dark.

"You got it, *mein herr,*" I teased.

His arm around me grew tighter.

"Babe?" he called again.

"Right here, honey."

"You take my name, you do it knowin' you'll never lose it."

My hand found his at my belly. I linked my fingers through, feeling the band of his ring biting lightly into my flesh, and I sighed a contented sigh.

Then I replied, "I know."

"And you know what it means."

I knew what it meant to Ham.

Ham giving me his protection. His money. His love.
Him.

"I know what it means," I confirmed and I did.

I knew it meant everything.

So I didn't yet have everything.

But I was going to.

I felt Ham's face burrow into the back of my hair.

"Zara Reece," I whispered.

"Yeah," he whispered back.

"Sounds good."

"Fuck yeah, it does."

"Ham?" I called.

"Right here, cookie."

"I'm uncertain I can take you gettin' any awesomer," I admitted.

His body stilled for a brief moment before it started shaking then the rumble began and, shortly after that, his laughter filled the room.

I smiled again against my pillow.

Still chuckling, he pulled me even closer and muttered, "You got a lifetime to get used to it."

I did.

I finally did.

Thank God.

CHAPTER NINETEEN

Survivors

One week and one day later…

"THIS IS GROSS."

These words were spoken by Zander, who was standing in Ham's and my kitchen and squirting devilled egg yolks through a pastry bag into the waiting halves of hardboiled egg whites.

The house was filled with people, every available surface

groaning with food. The bar separating the kitchen from the dining room/living room also had food, a big devil's food cake on a tall cake stand (Xenia's favorite), a massive spray of red roses, and all this was intermingled with framed photographs of Xenia.

It was Xenia's memorial party.

Zander might have missed his mom's funeral but when I told Aunt Wilona about Kami's idea, we agreed that it should happen and I gave the green light for plans for liftoff so I could have this and Xenia could have this, but more, so Zander could.

"It's not gross. It's delicious," I contradicted Zander.

He squirted some devilled yolks into an egg, didn't do a very good job of it, and I didn't care. Then he looked up at me.

"I don't like eggs," he informed me.

"No?" I asked, loving every smidgeon of information I learned about my nephew, even the knowledge he didn't like eggs, and I didn't care one bit if that made me a freak.

He kept sharing the wealth. "My breakfasts of choice are pancakes or waffles or Nona's hash brown casserole."

Although I found the concept of Aunt Wilona's hash brown casserole intriguing, I returned, "Eggs make you strong. Rocky Balboa drank raw ones before going out for a run."

Zander scrunched up his nose.

"Raw ones?" he asked.

I nodded.

"That's gross . . . *er*," he decreed, then asked, "Rocky who?"

"Rocky Balboa," I answered.

"Who's that?" he queried and I blinked.

"You don't know Rocky Balboa?"

Zander shook his head.

Therefore, as any conversation about Rocky Balboa was wont to make you do, I tipped my head back and cried in a deep guttural tone, *"Adrian!"*

When I was done shouting, I knew eyes had come to me

but I only had eyes for my nephew, who was laughing and staring at me.

"You're crazy," he declared, still laughing.

"That's what Rocky shouts after his big fight against Apollo Creed. Adrian is his woman," I told him.

"Is he a cage fighter?"

I shook my head in mock disgust, leaned down to him, and allowed myself to do what I'd wanted to do during both of the dinners Ham and I had shared with him and Aunt Wilona at her house.

I ran my hand over his hair and cupped the back of his head, dipping my face close. "*Rocky* is a movie. A *great* movie. One of the best movies of all time. And, if you want, you can come over, I'll pour a bunch of stuff in bowls, all of it not good for us, and we'll eat and watch Rocky Balboa be awesome."

"That'd be cool," he said quietly, his eyes having changed. He looked somewhat uncertain but at the same time not uncomfortable and also pleased.

It was not lost on me in the time we'd shared with him and Aunt Wilona that she was affectionate with Zander. She wasn't fawning and he was a growing boy so she didn't get into his space being too motherly. That didn't mean he didn't get many indications in a variety of ways that he was loved.

But he'd never had one like this from me.

And, if I was reading him right, he liked it.

So I pushed it, lifted up, kissed the top of his head, and then moved quickly away so as not to freak him out.

My eyes swept through the house as I did but they stopped on Ham, who was across the room, beer in hand, talking to Latrell and Jeff, but his eyes were locked on me.

And his mouth was smiling.

I smiled back and then turned my attention to dumping stuff that was not good for anyone into bowls in order to replenish the generous but swiftly disappearing food supply.

"Are all these people really my mom's friends?"

These words were asked by Zander but his voice was quiet and strange.

I looked down to him to see the eggs done, the pastry bag still in his hand, but he was looking over the bar into the house that was a crush of people, rock music on low drowned out by happy chatter with spurts of laughter.

"Yep," I answered.

"She knew a lot of people," Zander noted and I again got close to him but not too close.

Conversationally, I said, "Yeah, she did. She knew a lot of people but these aren't just people she knew. These are her friends."

He set the pastry bag aside, tipped his head to look up at me, and remarked, "She had a lot of friends."

I went down in a mini-crouch so we could be eye-to-eye and told him, "Your mom was funny. She liked people and showed it. She was generous and she'd do just about anything for anybody. And people liked her because of all that. If you're like that, you get a lot of friends and that's what she did."

Suddenly, his face changed again, definitely uncertainty and something I didn't get until he spoke.

"I'm scared to go out there," he whispered.

Surprised at this admission, I asked, "Why?"

"Because they liked her so much. What if they don't like me?"

My heart squeezed and it dawned on me why, since Aunt Wilona and Zander arrived half an hour ago, he'd stuck to her or me like glue.

He was nervous and he wanted his mom's friends to like him.

Carefully, I asked, "Why wouldn't you think they would like you?"

"'Cause you said I'm not like her. They'll be expectin' me to be like her."

I shook my head even as I smiled.

"You don't *look* like her," I clarified. "But you told me you have a ton of friends. You're funny. You're open." I got closer and dipped my voice low. "As far as I can see, you're *just* like her."

When his eyes lit with hope, my heart squeezed again and I lifted a hand to curl my fingers around the side of his neck. Feeling the warmth of his skin, his pulse beating against my palm, for some reason I fell in love with him more just because he was so . . . very . . . *real*.

"You go out there, they'll love you," I promised. "But I'll stick close anyway."

He tipped his head to the side but did it careful not to break contact with my hand.

Yes, he didn't mind affection from me and, knowing that, I sent my thanks to the heavens.

"You sure?" he asked.

I nodded.

"Okay," he murmured.

I gave him a grin and a squeeze and left it at that, even though I wanted to kiss his hair again. I'd had enough for now and I didn't want to push it.

I straightened and I did it just in time to hear the loud thud of a motorcycle helmet hitting the countertop.

Both Zander and I turned our eyes to Ham, who was now standing with us in the kitchen but his eyes were on Zander. Ham had gone to Carnal to buy Zander the helmet just the day before.

"Try that on for size, kid," he invited.

Zander's head whipped to the helmet, then back to Ham.

"No way!" he yelled.

"Way," Ham replied.

"This is *so cool*!" Zander shouted.

His hands darted out to the helmet and my heart didn't squeeze at Ham's actions.

It warmed.

So I gave him a huge smile.

Ham's eyes took in my mouth and his lips twitched.

Zander pulled the helmet on then tipped his head back to Ham. Lifting his hand to the kick-ass visor, he pushed it up.

"Does it fit?" he asked.

Ham crouched in front of Zander, put his hands to the helmet, moved Zander's head around, checked for snugness, then gave the top of the helmet a mild smack before he answered, "Yep."

"Cool," Zander breathed.

"We got good weather, kid. You want a ride?"

"Really?" Zander asked, rocking up to his toes in excitement.

"Sure," Ham replied.

"Totally!" he shouted but then dashed around Ham, still yelling, "Nona! Nona! Look what Uncle Reece got me!" He gestured to the helmet. "He's takin' me for a ride!"

Aunt Wilona's head whipped around at Zander's shouting. She spied the helmet, her face went straight to alarmed before she smoothed it out and forced a smile at Zander.

"I'll have a word," Ham murmured to me. "Put her at ease. We'll go easy."

"Okay, darlin'," I murmured back.

Ham moved in, touched his mouth to mine, and, when he lifted up, I smiled at him again.

This time Ham gifted me with a smile back.

Then he moved out of the kitchen and toward Zander and Aunt Wilona.

I put the devilled eggs and bowls of snacks out and me and a variety of other people followed Ham, Zander, and

Aunt Wilona out the front door. We stood in a group and watched Ham throw a leg over his vintage Harley that hc'd obviously moved out of the garage for this purpose earlier and unbeknownst to me. Then we watched him instruct Zander how to get on behind him.

I got close, as did Aunt Wilona, and when we did, we heard Ham order, "You hold on to me tight and don't let go for any reason. You with me?"

"Yeah, Uncle Reece," Zander agreed instantly, wrapping his arms around Ham's middle.

My belly fluttered and I got a little tingle between my legs.

Ham's eyes came to me, and my physical reactions must have shown on my face because his eyes got dark and then he grinned a sexy grin.

That got me another tingle between my legs.

Two seconds later, the bike roared, they took off, and, even over the roar, we could hear Zander's shout of glee.

"Dear God, save me," Aunt Wilona muttered.

I burst out laughing and for the first time in my life, touched my aunt in affection of my own accord.

I reached out and slid my arm around my aunt's shoulders, pulling her close.

"It'll be good," I assured her.

"I hope so," she said to me, eyes pinned to where we last saw Ham and Zander.

My voice was firm when I stated, "Zander means everything to me. I mean everything to Ham. And anyway, Ham thinks Zander is the bomb. He'd *never* let anything harm him."

Aunt Wilona turned her head to look at me, the fear downshifted to worry in her face, then she smiled and slid an arm around my waist.

And it was then I had the weird sensation that, even when you thought you had everything, life found ways to give you more.

I pulled her closer and we walked into the house, following the partygoers who had already gone back inside.

I let her go after a squeeze and went to find my beer.

I'd located it, pulled back a drag, and dropped my beer to find Arlene standing right in front of me.

"Mindy's pregnant," she announced and I stared.

Then I whispered, "What?"

"You didn't hear it from me," she declared, then walked away.

After she did what Arlene was prone to do, dropped a gossip bomb, my eyes flew around my living room until they caught on Mindy. She was standing with Becca and Bonnie. She was smiling. And she was drinking lemonade.

I felt my face split in a huge smile.

The doorbell rang.

I set my beer aside, moved through the crowd to the door, opened it, and there stood Pastor Williams.

Knowing from Ham what he'd done, I buried my desire to fling my arms around him and give him a big kiss. Instead, I just smiled.

"Hey, Pastor Williams," I greeted.

"Zara." He smiled back.

I stepped aside. "Please come in."

He moved in, and I shut the door and threw out an arm.

We walked toward the crush, stopped at its edge, and I asked, "Can I get you a drink?"

"Unfortunately, I still have work to do on tomorrow's sermon, so no. I just have time to stop by and pay my respects."

"Bummer," I replied.

He looked down at me and grinned.

Then he looked through the crowd, his face softening.

"I suspect your sister would enjoy today's gathering," he remarked.

She totally would.

"Yeah," I agreed.

He kept looking through the crowd before, cautiously, he turned to me. "It seems there are some who haven't yet arrived."

I felt my back straighten when I asked, "Mom and Dad?"

He shook his head slowly. "No."

I studied him then got it. "Zander's out for a ride with Ham on his Harley."

His face cleared, and he nodded once and mumbled, "Ah."

"It's all good, Pastor Williams," I told him.

"Good," he replied.

"Okay, no. That isn't right. It's all *very* good," I shared and he again smiled.

"Good," he whispered with feeling.

"Thank you," I whispered back and watched his face change again before he socked it to me.

"I have been waiting years, Zara, turning it over in my head, talking to God, trying to find answers, my way to intervene," he stated and I took in a deep breath at understanding his plight, knowing that Mom probably spoke to him or maybe he saw what other people didn't see and knowing that he must have grappled with his powerlessness against it. "I still struggle, what I . . . when I spoke with Nina . . ." He paused. "I'm uncertain it was right."

"It was right," I assured him.

He shook his head. "When you make a decision to help one, or two, or five, but doing so might harm just one, it isn't right. But it's just and you simply hope that God can assist you in living with that balance."

He was talking in circles, trying not to expose anything, but from what he said, I surmised, "You're worried about Mom."

"That I am, Zara," he surprisingly confirmed. "Your father is a man who likes to get his own way. It's crucial to him to control any situation with an iron fist," he told me something I very well knew. "He's lost access to a variety of targets. Therefore, his focus on the one he has left will be more acute."

I didn't like this for my mom but I'd long since learned the only person who could save her from being a target was herself. And for reasons I'd never understand, she was unwilling to do that. And for reasons I *really* didn't understand, she *was* willing to put others in her path so when Dad's attention turned to doing his worst, he'd focus on those targets rather than her.

So there was nothing I could do. But more, with my life the way it was, my sister gone, and all that had gone on that Mom might have had no control over, but still, doing nothing made her a party to it, there was nothing I wished to do.

I leaned slightly in to him. "I hope He does that for you, Pastor Williams, assists you with living with the balance. Because, in truth, I don't know if there's any hope for her. But I *do* know there's no hope for Dad."

"I have no doubt He will," he replied. "That doesn't mean it will all be well. Just that He will see us through."

I lifted a hand and squeezed his arm, uncertain if God would see everyone through, this meaning my mom, but He was doing His bit for the rest of us.

"He might see you through even better, if He saw you sitting in one of my pews more than just for the Christmas choir performance," he went on, and at his pointed quip, I laughed, dropping my hand.

"Point taken," I said.

"Good, then I'll see you tomorrow morning at church. I have a very good sermon planned so I'm certain you won't want to miss it."

I gave him another smile then leaned closer, got up on my toes, and kissed his cheek but stayed there to say in his ear, "God chooses well."

He gave my arm a squeeze as he murmured, "That's a mighty compliment, Zara. Thank you."

I rocked back, caught his eyes, and nodded.

He gave my arm another squeeze before he nodded back. His eyes went through the crowd, he did a few chin lifts when they fell on people he knew, and then he turned to the door.

I watched him move through it, and as he did, I saw Greg moving up my walk.

I'd called Greg and invited him. He'd never met Xenia but he'd gone to visit her with me once. I didn't go to see her very often. It was too difficult. But since he was my husband, and she was my sister, and I loved them both, I thought he should meet her even if that meeting was macabre and bizarre.

Incidentally, when I went with Greg that was the last time I visited my sister.

I'd also invited Greg because we'd promised we wouldn't lose each other and I knew Ham talked to him, so I hoped Ham had gotten through to him. Greg had called and spoken with me briefly after Xenia died. But other than that, I had no idea, with Ham in my life, his ring on my finger, if we could keep our promise.

I just hoped we could.

"Hey," I greeted, walking to him as he shut the door.

He turned to me, his eyes catching mine for a brief moment before they scanned the house and then came back to mine.

"Hey," he replied.

"You okay?" I asked. "Being here, I mean. And—"

Greg interrupted me. "Zara, this is your sister's memorial and you're asking me if I'm okay?"

"I, well . . . yeah."

"Okay, then . . . no. I'm not okay since I've been worried about you since I heard your sister died."

"Greg," I said softly. "I understand that, appreciate it. That's really sweet and I mean it when I say I'm glad you came. But I know this has to be weird. You and me. Me and Ham." I swung my arm out behind me. "This house. I just want to be sure you're okay with all this."

He shook his head and his face went gentle as his hands came to my shoulders and then slid up to curl around the sides of my neck.

He leaned his face down to mine. "Zara, honey, after your, uh…Reece phoned me, it forced me to think. Weigh my options. What's done is done and I know there's no way I could win you back. I screwed that up. After he called, I came to terms with that. So I had to choose whether I wanted to have you in my life how I could have you or if I wanted to be a jerk and not have you at all." He grinned and admitted, "I'm not much good at being a jerk."

His words made me relax and I grinned back. "You never were."

"It's going to be weird. It'll probably be hard, but we'll get there."

I closed my eyes as relief swept through me and when I opened them, I whispered, "Thank you."

"Just that, um…until I sort things out, get used to, uh… *him,* or your being with him, if we have a cup of coffee or something, maybe for a while it can be just you and me. Will he be okay with that?"

I wasn't sure he would. Ham was pretty possessive.

Then again, Ham knew I loved him, he loved me, he knew I didn't feel that way about Greg, so I suspected he'd also trust me.

"I'll talk to him," I promised.

"Okay," Greg replied, then his eyes went over my head. He dropped his hands and muttered, "I'm going to go say hi to Latrell."

"You want a drink first?" I asked and Greg looked back at me.

"If you're cool with it, I know my way."

"I'm cool with it, darlin'."

He grinned, lifted his hand to curl his fingers around the side of my neck again to give me a quick squeeze, then he wandered toward the kitchen.

I wandered to the end of the entryway and was immediately set upon by Maybelle and Wanda.

My eyes went from one to the other to see both of them examining my face but it was Maybelle who spoke.

"You all right?" she asked.

"Yes," I answered.

"Girl, seriously," Wanda began. "You're a drama magnet."

I looked to her and assured, "It's all good."

"Mm-hmm," Maybelle mumbled. "It's all good right about now, when your man is off on his bike with your nephew. He walks into this house and your ex is here, I do not see good things."

"Ham knows I invited Greg," I told her.

She nodded but went on. "Then you best be thankin' your lucky stars he wasn't here when your ex put his hands on you. I could see it was all platonic-like but I think your man doesn't have that filter when it comes to you and any man puttin' his hands to you."

This was true and I thanked my lucky stars Ham wasn't there for that either, not to mention thanking them for the fact that Greg was not the type of man who would push that kind of thing if Ham was there, or at all.

"We had a moment. The moment's over. It won't happen again," I told Maybelle.

"Well, you bein' a millionaire, a new auntie, back in your house with a hot guy who's actually a good guy who'd move mountains for you and, with that body of his, I'm thinkin' he actually could, I'm also thinkin' your lucky stars finally started to shine their light, thank the heavenly Father above," Maybelle remarked and I turned fully to her.

"Is this your official stamp of approval on Ham?" I asked.

She leaned back and her brows went up.

"Girl, he had us all rushin' around like an army of ants settin' you up in your new-old house so you could come home from work and take a load off. That is, you could take a load off after he planted a huge-ass diamond on your finger," she returned, gesturing to my hand. "How could I not give that my official stamp of approval?"

I knew it.

And I loved it.

So I smiled huge and crowed, "Told you."

"Whatever," she replied, looking away.

Not done, I turned to Wanda. "You're my witness. I told her."

"You so did," Wanda replied, grinning big.

"I need another drink," Maybelle noted as the doorbell rang.

"I'll get that, hon. You find yourself a fresh bottle and suck back more beer," Wanda offered and moved away.

Maybelle looked back at me and her eyes were lit with joy when she did.

"Happy, baby?" she asked softly.

"I'm at my sister's memorial, celebrating her life, and my man is taking her son for a ride on his Harley, a ride Zander couldn't wait to get. I'm back in the house I love that my man bought for me. And his ring is on my finger. So yeah. I'm happy," I answered. "I've never been happier in my life. I thought yesterday, I'd never been happier. And the day before. And the day before that. But I'm wrong every day. It keeps gettin' better."

Her eyes went soft and bright when she whispered, "Then that means I couldn't be happier for you."

"Zara!"

My name said in that voice sent all my happy flying out the window.

"Oh no you do not!" I heard shouted from the other direction and I knew that was Kami Maxwell.

But I ignored Kami and, stiltedly, I turned and saw my mother, her face a mask of alarm, staring at me.

What the hell was she doing there?

Greg was invited. Sixty other people were invited.

My mother was absolutely not.

"What are you—?" I started, feeling Maybelle edge close as Wanda did the same on my other side.

But I didn't finish because Mom's hand shot out, clamping on mine and tugging hard.

"We must talk," she demanded.

I tried to pull my hand free as I said, "We have nothing to say and, Mom, I don't wanna be ugly but you aren't welcome here. Not to mention, with what's happening legally, you shouldn't *be* here."

"Zara, you don't under—" she began but didn't finish when I felt a wave of hostility blast through the front door.

Maybelle and Wanda felt it, too, and edged even closer as my eyes flew to the door to see my father storming in.

Without hesitation, he walked right up to Mom and me, grabbed Mom by the back of her neck, and yanked her away so hard she went flying.

Wanda gasped.

Maybelle whispered, "Heavenly Father."

My body strung tight.

My father's eyes sliced through the crowd and locked on me. "Look at you. Look at this. Your sister's dead and you're yukkin' it up with beer and booze. What's the matter with you?"

"Get out," I whispered.

"I will. Happily. You give me the boy," he shot back. "He doesn't need to be around this, and mark my words, girl, the judge will hear about this."

"Get out," I repeated, louder this time.

Dad again ignored me. "Waste of time. Waste of space. You always were. Just prove it over and over since you first started breathin'. Just like that sister of yours. Now, give me the boy and I'll go."

"Xavier." Aunt Wilona was there, standing close to Maybelle. "Let's speak outside."

Dad turned blazing eyes on his sister and announced, "You're done. You'll see that boy again over my dead body."

Aunt Wilona paled.

"Sir, you really should leave."

This was said by Nina, who was also now in my huddle, which had been joined by Arlene, Kami, Becca, Mindy, Jenna, and Cotton, with Max and Jeff patrolling the outside, bodies loose and in motion, eyes locked on Dad. I felt a presence at my back and I didn't have to look to know it was Greg.

Dad spared Nina barely a glance before he looked back to Aunt Wilona.

"I gave orders," he reminded her.

"He missed his mother's funeral," she returned, her back slamming straight. "He was not going to miss this."

"That isn't your decision," Dad fired back.

"You're wrong. I gave him bottles. I changed his diapers. I cooked his dinners. I made his lunches. I baked his birthday cakes," she retorted. "You simply showed every once in a while, acted an ass, confused him, didn't let his grandmother love on him, like she was tainted by his mother when his mother was tainted by *you*, and you were a general all-around pain in the behind, so I think I *definitely* get to make those decisions."

"You'd be wrong," he clipped.

"Since I got my boy, I've never been wrong, Xavier, and you've never been right," she leaned in and hissed.

And it was then, Dad lost it. Given his target, not one to miss that kind of opportunity, his hand went down and across his front, then he swiftly and powerfully backhanded Aunt Wilona across the cheek.

She went flying and the crowd around us flew into motion but Dad had a lot of practice with this and no sooner had he clocked Aunt Wilona, he took two steps my way and suddenly had his hand wrapped tight around my throat. His other hand was up and fisted in my hair, pulling hard, making pain shaft over my scalp and down the back of my neck as his hand at my throat squeezed, this making it hard to breathe.

"Take your hands off her," I heard Max growl from close even as I felt Greg move in behind me, his hand at my dad's hand in my hair, but Dad had such a firm hold, there was nothing Greg could do without hurting me more.

Dad's face was in mine, oblivious to all this, his eyes blazing with his brand of righteous fury that I'd seen time and again, remembered like he'd burned that look into me just yesterday, and I stood immobile with terror.

"You think to take *my* money?" Dad snarled in my face.

"Get...your hands...*off* her," Max bit out and he was even closer but I didn't tear my eyes away from my father's.

No, that wasn't right. I *couldn't*.

"My lawyers say we're gonna have to sell our house, pay back what *they* say *we* owe *you*," he spat.

I tried to suck in air as his hand squeezed.

"Got one more chance," Max warned.

"Sell our cars, sell fuckin' *everything*," Dad clipped, yanking on my hair and I whimpered.

"Greg, move away. Jeff, get behind Zara," Max ordered.

I stared into Dad's eyes.

"You're a piece of shit," he whispered, his voice filled with venom. "Your sister was a piece of shit. The minute your mother pushed the both of you out, I should have done what you do with a piece of shit. I should have flushed you away."

That was when I'd had enough.

My knee moving without me telling it to do so, I brought it up, brutal and sharp, and connected violently with my father's privates.

He grunted in pain, released me instantly to curl into himself, but he didn't get there.

That was because he was yanked back by his hair, turned, and Ham had his hand in a death grip at his throat. Ham was advancing, shoving Dad toward the front door even as he rumbled in an absolute, downright terrifying tone, "Get Zander clear."

My hands went to my throat. Maybelle and Wanda came to me. I sucked in breath and watched Max, Latrell, Cotton, Jeff, Greg, and Pete follow Ham as he shoved Dad out the front door.

"You okay, hon?" Wanda asked.

I didn't answer.

My head turned to see Mindy, Becca, and Aunt Wilona guiding a pale-faced, terrified-looking Zander down the hall. Ascertaining he was in good hands, I ran out the front door.

I also had to run through the front yard because Ham had Dad pinned to the side of an SUV parked at the front of the house. Dad's face was so red, it was purpling, his mouth opening and closing and Ham was in his face, his hand still wrapped around Dad's throat. He was obviously squeezing. Hard.

The men were huddling close and I tried to push through but they stood firm so I could find no opening.

"Reece, stand down," I heard Max order.

With a mighty heave, I shoved between Latrell and Pete.

"Reece, Zara," Max warned, telling him I was there.

Dad made a choking noise.

Ham didn't move.

"Reece." Jeff got close and Jeff, incidentally and at that moment frighteningly, was an officer of the law. "This is not the way you want this to end."

At these words, Ham shoved Dad off so hard Dad's head cracked against the SUV.

He stepped away, scowling his scary, scarier, *scariest by far* scowl at my dad.

I got close and plastered myself against his side. The instant I did, Ham's arm slid around my shoulders and he tucked me even closer but his eyes didn't leave Dad. Still glowering at Dad, Ham then lifted his other hand and rested it curled light, warm, and I could tell he wanted it to be healing, at the front of my throat.

Finally, he whispered to Dad in his still scary voice, "You put your hands on her."

Dad had both hands to his throat and was sucking in air, slightly bent, but he was still able to glare at Ham.

"First time you put your hands on her that she remembers, she was five," Ham announced.

A squeak came from the crowd surrounding this tableau as well as some movement, gasps, and whispers but I knew that squeak was Mom's.

"You beat her, you beat her sister, you made her watch that *and* you made her watch when you took your hand to her mother. Then you stole her nephew, stole her money, watched her swing and you got the balls to walk into *our house* and put your hands on her?" Ham asked.

Dad coughed, then bent over and spit in the yard.

Ham pulled in a mighty breath, turned to Jeff, and let it go, stating, "We're pressing charges."

Dad's head shot up and I heard Mom squeak again.

"You just accosted me!" Dad yelled.

Ham cut his eyes to him. "You were in my home, abusing my woman in front of witnesses. I got a right to defend my home and I definitely got the right to defend my woman."

"He's not wrong," Jeff declared and he looked at Pete, asking, "You got cuffs?"

Pete, also an officer of the law, nodded while moving and replied, "In my vehicle." Then he took off on a run toward his car.

"Sir, face the vehicle, hands behind your head," Jeff ordered.

"Are you insane?" Dad asked, eyes round, face red now for a different reason.

"Sir, I said, face the vehicle," Jeff repeated.

"I will not do that," Dad snapped.

"Then you'll face resisting arrest on top of the other charges you got, and I see you aren't thinkin' all this through, but the ones you already got aren't real good. My advice, you need to start actin' smart and you need to do that right about now," Jeff advised.

"She's my daughter," Dad spat, like that entitled him to do what he did and more gasps and whispers slid through the crowd.

"She's an adult whose home you entered without permission and against her wishes and then proceeded, in front of witnesses, to assault her and another woman. But, just sayin', even if she wasn't an adult but she was a kid, that shit would actually be"—he leaned in to Dad, his usually mellow expression dissolving into fury before he finished—"*worse.* Now, face the vehicle and put your goddamned hands behind your head."

Dad glared at Jeff a moment, his eyes shifted through the

people watching, and then he did as Jeff told him to do but with his head turned to Mom.

As Jeff kicked Dad's feet farther apart with his boot and Pete approached with cuffs, phone to his ear, Dad ordered Mom, "Call our attorneys."

"But Xavier," Mom started in a small voice, "in our last meeting with them, they told us, with our bank accounts frozen and us not able to pay them, that we—"

"Call them!" Dad barked.

She nodded swiftly, glanced at me, and as usual gave me absolutely not one bit more. Even after witnessing that whole debacle, she looked after herself and her safety and scurried away, digging in her purse.

It was just then, at that moment, held by my man, this suddenly lost its power to hurt me.

I took my eyes from Mom and, held close to Ham, his hand still at my throat, I watched my father get patted down, handcuffed, and read his rights.

It.

Was.

Awesome.

"I so totally wish Xenia was here," I whispered to Ham. "She would freaking *love* this."

"Cookie," Ham started. I looked up at him and even when I did his hand didn't fall away from my throat. "How in *the* fuck can you make me want to laugh when I'm this goddamned motherfucking pissed?"

I shrugged and replied, "It's just me."

His eyes studied my face then his hand slid down to my chest and his gaze moved over my throat before his hand slid back up and his eyes again caught mine.

"Yeah. It's just you," he murmured and the warmth and approval in his eyes made me melt into him.

"Thanks for nearly choking my dad to death after he

assaulted me," I said and Ham blinked before he stared and finally his lips twitched. When I saw the lip twitch, I went on. "And also, thanks for making that *nearly* choking him, seein' as it might be difficult for us to get married and me to get knocked up if you were serving time for involuntary manslaughter."

At that, Ham's lips stopped twitching and curled up.

I shifted to his front, got up on my toes, and wrapped my arms around him before I assured him quietly, "I'm all right."

"You always are, baby," he replied just as quietly.

"And you're always there when I need you," I returned.

Ham's eyes flared. His hand at my throat shifted around and up into the back of my hair and he bent his head to touch his lips to mine.

"Champagne!" I heard Nina shout as Ham lifted his mouth from mine and we both turned to see her close. "Two counts of assault and trespassing!" she declared and clapped with excitement. "Isn't that great?" she asked but didn't wait for an answer.

She turned to Arlene.

Before she could say a word, Arlene started toddling toward her car, announcing, "I'm on it."

"I'll go with," Kami called, following her.

I didn't get the chance to look to see what was happening to Dad as, with Maybelle as sentry at my free side, Latrell playing sentry to her, some of the crowd following close at our backs, others staying to watch the finale to my Dad's arrest, Ham firmly led me back into the house.

But I was able to break away in the excited shuffle once we got inside.

When I did, keeping an eye on a mindful Ham, who clearly wanted to keep an eye on me, I managed to perform a miracle. I snuck to the front door and looked out the window at the side so I could watch as the cruiser pulled up and Jeff and Pete shuffled my dad to one of the back doors, Jeff putting his hand to Dad's head after Pete opened the door, and folding Dad in.

So engrossed in this, when my hand was taken in a firm grip, my body gave a slight jump and I turned to see Aunt Wilona, her eyes aimed out the window.

"It's all but over," she said to the window.

"I figure it is," I agreed.

She looked at me.

I smiled at her.

Her eyes dropped to my lips then came back to mine and she smiled back.

"Cookie, get away from the fuckin' window!" Ham ordered loudly even though he was only five feet away.

I rolled my eyes at my aunt, gave her hand a squeeze, then moved from the window.

Lifting my hand to my forehead in a salute directed Ham's way, I yelled, "As you wish, *mein herr*!"

Ham shook his head.

I turned to my aunt, looked at her cheek, and whispered, "Let's go to the kitchen and get you some ice."

She nodded. We did that. I left her with Wanda in the kitchen, found Zander with Mindy and Becca in the guest bedroom, and I relieved my girlfriends.

Once they left, I gave him a good onceover. I didn't know him all that well but I could still tell he was freaked mostly because you couldn't miss it.

I sat next to him on the bed and took his hand. "It's all cool, darlin'."

"Uncle Reece was real mad," he replied.

He was not wrong about that.

"Yep, he likes me a whole bunch and doesn't like it when someone hurts me, but he's okay now," I assured him.

"Is Nona okay?" he asked.

I nodded. "I've got a good friend takin' care of her."

Zander's eyes moved over my face, possibly in an attempt to make sure I was telling the truth.

I figured he believed me but still, he asked, "Can I go to her?"

He was a good kid and he loved his Nona. Which meant she'd earned that love.

Without delay, I got off the bed, pulling him up with me. "Let's go."

I took Zander to Aunt Wilona. They huddled. I hung with them, taking their pulse, and when it seemed Aunt Wilona had it covered, I wandered out of the kitchen and found Ham.

I moved right to him and fitted myself to his side.

When I did, one of his arms went around my shoulders and he lifted his other hand, shifting my hair away. His fingertips gliding over the shell of my ear, and they slid down my neck and across my throat.

"All good?" he murmured.

"Better than ever," I replied and when he looked like he didn't believe me, I leaned into him and whispered, "I think you may have noticed this already, but some of us Cinders, we're survivors."

He held my eyes and lifted his hand to cup my jaw as he bent his head to mine.

"Don't know about the others, but I know that's true about you."

My arms already around him tightened.

"Love my cookie," he said softly and I felt a smile curve my lips.

"And I love my bruiser," I replied and watched a smile curve his.

Then he dipped his head farther to touch his lips to mine, and when he was still doing that, we heard Arlene shout, "Got the champagne!"

Ham broke our contact and we turned our heads to see Arlene and Kami at the door and each held a bottle of champagne in both their hands. Arlene's eyes were on Ham.

"Big bear of a hot guy, there's a case in my car. I reckon you won't have problems liftin' it. So get your hind end out there and do that," she ordered.

I laughed as I heard Ham's chuckle. Then I got two squeezes and my man let me go in order to move to the front door.

I watched him go.

Then I looked through my house at my friends, Xenia's friends, knowing my nephew was in the kitchen with my aunt, and listening to muted music, unmuted chatter, then finally hearing a champagne cork pop.

My eyes slid to one of the framed photos of my sister on my bar.

"Wish you were here, darlin'," I whispered across the room to the photo.

As ever, I got no reply.

Then I moved that way in order to find cups.

EPILOGUE

Everything

Three months later...

"BUT I'M NOT CRAZY!"

I shouted this and Zander, lying beside me in the dark on a blanket over the snow on Xenia's grave, jumped a mile and gave out a strangled scream.

I'd just told him one of Xenia's doozies, a scary story that was the best of all her scary stories, with the kill line being the one I'd just delivered.

I knew it was weird, me and my nephew out at night in the cold dark lying on my sister's grave.

I also didn't care.

I wanted her with us and this was as good as we were both going to get.

Anyway, Zander thought it was awesome. I'd heard him with his friends when he didn't think I could hear and he told them I was the coolest aunt ever, primarily because I was crazy and part of this craziness was me taking him to his mom's grave at night, this being something all his friends thought was totally weird and therefore *awesome*.

Since Xenia's memorial, Ham and I saw Zander and Aunt Wilona frequently. We went to their place for dinner, they came to ours, and Zander came often, Aunt Wilona dropping him or Ham and I picking him up so he could hang, watch movies, go out to movies with us, or whatever.

And we'd had Zander and his friends over for two sleepovers and, as I mentioned, his friends thought I was awesome because I was crazy. But they thought Ham was awesome because he was big and scary, had a bike, worked at a bar, and exuded such badass awesomeness that any nine-year-old boy would appreciate it.

Zander and I were both on our backs and when he screamed, I turned to my side and got up on my forearm.

"I got ya," I stated the obvious, smiling at him through the dark.

"Yeah," he replied, pushing up to both his forearms in the blanket behind him and I could see his smile lit by moonlight. "That was a good one."

"I always get ya," I reminded him.

"One of these times, you won't get me," he returned.

I knew he was right. I'd run out of stories or he'd grow up and not be so easy to scare.

But we had this now. What Xenia gave to me, telling me these stories, I gave to her son because she couldn't. And I thanked God every Sunday at church, dragging myself and Ham there even if we worked the shift the night before, in order to do it.

"Tomorrow's gonna be killer," Zander stated and I focused back on him.

He was right. Tomorrow was going to be killer.

Because tomorrow, in a small ceremony officiated in the church by Pastor Williams, followed by a party in a function room at The Rooster, I was marrying Ham.

"Totally," I agreed.

"It's cool Uncle Reece asked me to be a groomsman. He barely knows me."

I agreed, absolutely. It was cool.

When Ham told me he was going to ask Zander, I'd had to fight back tears. Then I jumped his bones.

I figured Ham asked Zander because he liked Zander a whole lot. I also figured he did this so I could have part of my sister standing up with us.

Yes, still, every day in every way I was falling deeper in love with my man.

"He's gettin' to know you and what he knows, he likes," I shared. "And you mean a lot to me so I think it's way cool, and we're both glad you said yes."

"That's awesome," Zander whispered in a way I knew he definitely thought it was awesome.

Suffice it to say, I was right on our first meeting. With Dad the only man in Zander's life, not around a lot, and when he was, not in good ways, Zander was sucking up all he could of Ham. And Ham did not mind at all. Each time they saw each other, they got tighter and tighter.

I loved it and what I loved even more was that Aunt Wilona loved it as well. Any hesitancy she might have had with Ham, she lost the day of Xenia's memorial. But we'd all been growing close, and it wasn't hard to read she was relieved and grateful that her boy had a good man in his life. Finally.

"Seein' as I have to be all gussied up and to the church on time tomorrow, we probably should be gettin' back," I told him, even though, to save the drive for them tomorrow, which wasn't long but we had the space so why not, Aunt Wilona and Zander were spending the night with Ham and me.

Still, I was cold, it was growing late, and I wanted to get my nephew warm and myself back to my man.

"Okay," Zander mumbled, shifting up to his feet.

He helped me pick up the blanket and shake the snow from it. Then I folded it and tucked it under my arm.

We started to move to my car but Zander glanced back

and I stopped when he muttered, "Just a sec," and moved to Xenia's tombstone.

The bouquet of blood-red roses that we brought, the newest one since we always brought one to Xenia when we came, had tipped to the side. Zander went down to his knees, righted it, shoving it into the snow and mounding more around it to keep it steady.

I swallowed against a tingle in my throat as he jumped to his feet and came back to me.

"We can go now," he told me, his head tipped back to catch my eyes.

"All right, darlin'," I replied softly, lifting a hand to squeeze the back of his neck before I let it drop away.

We walked side-by-side to the car and it had been so long, I had searched for it so often and never got it, I gave up on trying to feel it.

So I missed the light, cool, gentle breeze that followed us to the car.

*   *   *

Two hours later...

"Ham," I breathed and I did it quietly, since they were probably asleep, but my aunt and nephew were in the house, Ham was driving inside me, and I didn't want them to hear me coming.

"Love that, baby," Ham growled, his hips moving faster, harder, driving deep. "Love *you,* Zara."

At that, I lifted my head and shoved my face in his neck, my limbs tightening around him, my orgasm searing through me, and with his words came a warmth after the burn that had nothing to do with my climax.

And everything to do with love.

*   *   *

Reece

The next evening...

Reece stood alone at the bar in the function room at The Rooster, his eyes aimed at his wife.

Zara Reece.

Fuck, Zara was his wife. Something he never thought he'd have again. Something he thought he never wanted to have again. Something, in having, it being her, that day Zara taking his name, something he thought was the most precious gift he'd ever received.

Zara was laughing with Nina and a now-showing Mindy. Always damned pretty, today, no doubt about it, his new wife was beautiful.

The ceremony was small, this party the same, but she'd pulled out all the stops when it came to her appearance.

She'd bought a strapless ivory dress that was covered in lace and had shimmering flakes that caught the light. It skimmed her curves and fanned out in a kick with a short train at the back. Her soft hair was curled and pulled up away from her face and neck. Her makeup highlighted every pretty feature on her face. She wore pearls at her ears, neck, and wrist, borrowed from Maybelline, who'd worn the same on her wedding day.

Since his bride was fancy, Reece had bought a new suit and worn a tie.

The tie was long since gone, his ivory shirt opened at the collar, a beer in his hand.

Zara had divested him of his tie in the back of the limousine that took them up to The Rooster and she'd done this about ten minutes before she'd yanked that lacy, shimmering skirt up her hips and climbed on his lap, slid down on his cock, and rode him slow and easy, then hard and rough until they both found it.

The Rooster was damned good food and worth the long, one-hour drive to get there.

Still, that night in their limousine, his wife riding his cock, wearing her wedding gown, smelling good, looking better, feeling fucking great, and bearing his name, Reece wouldn't have minded that drive being a fuckuva lot longer.

Zara might be ticked off, but although there were arrangements of red and ivory roses on the tables, a three-tiered wedding cake they'd eventually get to cutting, and a DJ, this was not a formal reception.

This was a party.

None of that traditional stuff, speeches, special dances, and bouquet and garter throwing.

Just booze, food, good friends, good music, and good times.

Easy.

Reece watched and felt his lips curve up as he did so when Nina said something that made Zara laugh. His lips curved deeper when Wilona approached and, without hesitation, still laughing, his wife slid her arm around her aunt's waist and pulled her close, Wilona returning the favor and smiling at her niece.

Tearing his eyes from her, they drifted across the room to see Zara's maternal aunts chatting and smiling with Zander. Zara's mother wasn't there, wasn't invited, but when Zara had called her mother's sisters, told them Amy Cinders would not be invited but asked them to come, they said they wouldn't miss it for the world.

He looked back at his wife.

His girl lost her sister, never had a mother or father to speak of, and it might have taken her a while, but she finally got herself a family.

"Took a gol' darned long time but does a body good to see that."

Reece's head turned at these words and he looked down at Jimmy Cotton who had his eyes aimed Zara's way.

"Agreed," Reece murmured and Cotton looked at him.

"'Spose congratulations are in order," Cotton grumbled in a way that said he'd give them but he didn't like it. Then again, the man grumbled out of habit so Reece took no offense.

"Seein' as I'm wearin' this fuckin' suit and my woman's in a dress that cost a shitload more than our TV, yeah," Reece agreed.

Cotton's lips twitched and, his fingers wrapped around a bottle of beer, he settled in beside Reece.

Reece stayed silent and waited. Maybelline and Wanda had given their approval of his being in Zara's life. His girl had told him so. Arlene did the same, showing it grumpily but still hilariously.

In the past few months, not around often but around, Cotton had not. And now the man, who never looked in a good mood and rarely acted like he was in one, seemed the same.

"Hear things are still a bit tied up," Cotton noted, and if Reece knew where Cotton was going with this comment, he also knew Cotton wasn't wrong.

Nina had been able to get a judge to schedule a hearing so they could unfreeze the accounts in order to access some of the money to continue to give Wilona the funds to keep Zander and to pay his tuition. But they hadn't yet had a judge hear their full suit.

Seeing as Xavier's case was weak, he had no money and was currently out on bond, awaiting trial for assault and trespass, and he was a jackass to boot, he'd been unable to find legal representation. That and the fact he had no leg to stand on meant he'd eventually lose. They just needed to wait it out. But the trial was now scheduled and although it was several months away, Xavier's criminal trial coming fast on its heels, their wait had an end.

And even if he was stubbornly declaring his innocence for whatever twisted reason the man would do that, considering the number of witnesses he had to the acts he perpetrated in the home Reece gave Zara, Xavier was going down. This meant, in the coming months, he'd see jail time. Even if it wasn't much, it was something.

And he'd lose everything.

Nina was not backing down and she was going after everything they owned as well as Dahlia Cinders, who'd put her house on the market but left town, whereabouts unknown until Nina's investigator found her living in an apartment in Denver.

As a recipient of stolen funds she fully knew were stolen, Dahlia had been named in the lawsuit.

And she might try to escape but Nina didn't let any shit slide. She wasn't getting away.

And she'd be going down, too.

In other words, Nina Maxwell did as asked. It hadn't happened yet but when all was said and done, Xavier Cinders would be broken, homeless, cleaned out, an ex-con, and lucky if he landed in an unsafe studio apartment. And she'd one-upped this by making moves to bury Dahlia Cinders, too.

Absolutely worth every cent of their monthly payments to Nina's firm, the balance of which would be easily paid off when Zara got what she was entitled to. And Wilona and Zander wouldn't have to worry as Nina was acting on their behalf as well and half of the money to be won would be put in trust for Zander but accessible by Zara in order to help Wilona keep him and educate him.

By all reports, even if he hadn't seen the woman, Amy Cinders was a mess.

That wasn't his problem nor was it his wife's. Reece knew Zara struggled with it but he also knew she always found her way and she would with this.

Amy had not reached out. Amy had made her choice.

And Amy had to live with that choice. If she someday reached out, that would yet again be something his woman would have to struggle with. But if that happened, she'd find her way with that, too.

"It'll get sorted," Reece responded to Cotton's remark and Cotton grunted his agreement, then verbalized it.

"Nina pulls no punches."

"Nope," Reece agreed.

"Spitfire," Cotton noted about Nina.

"Yep," Reece agreed.

"Keeps Max on his toes," Cotton noted.

Reece's eyes went to Max, who had a toddler attached to his hip and was smiling at something Mick Shaughnessy said. But not unusually, even listening to Mick, Reece watched as Max's eyes slid to his wife and his smile stayed firmly in place.

"And he loves every fuckin' second," Reece murmured.

"That's the truth," Cotton replied.

They both watched Zara break away from Nina, Wilona, and Mindy and move toward the DJ.

"'Spect she's up to somethin'," Cotton remarked as Zara smiled at the DJ and the DJ nodded his head.

"Probably," Reece said.

"Then I best say this fast, seein' as I don't got a lot of time."

Reece tipped his eyes down to the man and said nothing.

"Didn't know about you," Cotton stated. "Warned your girl to be careful. See I shouldn't have bothered. Her daddy may be a snake, but all the poison he injected in her didn't make her blind and in pain like it did her sister. Always knew that, good kid who grew up to a good woman, loving, hard-workin', kind. So I shouldn't have worried."

It didn't make Reece happy the man had warned his girl about him but seeing as she'd slid a band on his finger that day and he'd done the same with her, he let that slide and simply replied, "No, you shouldn't have."

Cotton nodded, then declared, "So now, I'm just gonna say, I'm still gonna watch, keep my eye on you. See, this life, the way it goes, usually you get the better then you get the worse. But for you two, you got the worse and now you get the better. And, I gotta admit, I'm sure gonna enjoy watchin' that."

Before Reece could respond, over the microphone the DJ asked, "Could I ask Graham Reece to join his wife on the dance floor?"

"Fuck," Reece muttered and Cotton grinned.

"A groom's lot, havin' his bride make a spectacle of him durin' their big day. You've had it easy. You just got the spectacle at the church and this one to get through."

"Thought I'd get away without this shit," Reece replied.

"None of us do, boy. But she gets somethin' outta it. No clue what, but she does so it's worth it."

Unfortunately, it was.

"Yo! Bruiser!" Zara, standing alone on the dance floor, hands on her hips and smiling, shouted his way.

"Go," Cotton whispered. "Walk to your wife, leavin' behind the worse, and meetin' the better on that dance floor."

Reece held his eyes.

Then he jerked up his chin and moved to his wife, leaving the worse behind and joining the better on the dance floor.

*   *   *

Zara

Thirty seconds later...

The piano intro to The Zac Brown Band's "Colder Weather" began as Ham pulled me into his arms.

"I just had to," I whispered in his ear as my arms slid around his shoulders. "It says it all. But, just to say, I sure am glad you got out of colder weather."

Ham made no reply. He just held me close and started swaying. Maybe he was listening to the words (at least I hoped so). Maybe he was just putting up with me.

As our friends and family looked on, I stood in my wedding gown, swayed in my husband's arms, and I knew Ham was listening to the words and not just putting up with me when his arms got super-tight and his cheek slid down and pressed to mine.

My eyes unseeing on the ceiling, everything that was me focused on my man's big bearness engulfing me. Dominating me. Making me feel safe as the song flowed around us, his warmth beating into me, his cheek pressed to the softness of mine. I reveled in the feeling of being where Ham promised me I'd be and knowing my man was no longer stuck in colder weather.

Cookie, pay attention. I'm gonna give you everything.

That was what Ham had promised.

And, since that day, and even before, that was what Ham delivered.

When the song began to die away, my lips close to his ear, as I'd planned for that very moment since I found out two days before, I gave that feeling to Ham.

"Just thought you'd wanna know, baby," I whispered. "I'm pregnant."

The song died away but Ham didn't move. Not an inch. Not even to twitch. He just held me close, tight, his cheek pressed to mine as the song ended and silence surrounded us.

And that felt so good, it would take a moment before I felt it.

When I did, I knew I was wrong, as I'd been wrong day in and day out from the day Ham told me he loved me.

I didn't have everything.

Because, if you worked hard for it, if you didn't give up, even when you found your way and you thought you had everything, life found a way to give you more.

And I knew this when I felt the wet coming from Ham's eyes gliding along my cheek.

And I again had more.

*   *   *

Thirty-two hours later...

Outside the bungalow with its big windows open, the breeze wafting through the filmy curtains, if you walked through the heat of the sun beating on the soft sand and out into the cool, blue water, all the way up to your neck, and you looked down, you could see your feet as plain as if you were standing on shore.

The couple in the bed in the bungalow hadn't experienced this yet.

They were sleeping. The big bear of a dark-haired man on his side, his small, blonde woman tucked close in the curve of his body.

But even in slumber, his big, calloused hand with the wide, platinum wedding band on his ring finger rested lightly, splayed wide on her belly.

And he appreciated the soft silk of her hair.

Seeing as he had his face buried in it.

*   *   *

One year, five months later...

Outside the apartment with its arched windows wide open, over the tile-floored balcony, down a story, the gondoliers glided their gondolas gracefully through the canals.

But the family in the bed in the bedroom of the apartment hadn't experienced this yet.

They were sleeping. The big bear of a dark-haired man on his side, his small, blonde woman tucked close in the curve of his body, their baby boy tucked close to her belly.

But even in slumber, his big, calloused hand with the wide, platinum wedding band on his ring finger rested lightly, splayed wide on his son's diapered behind.

And he appreciated the beauty of what lay in that bed.

Seeing as he slept the peaceful, dreamless sleep of a man who had everything.

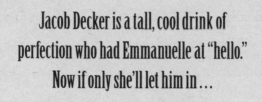

Jacob Decker is a tall, cool drink of perfection who had Emmanuelle at "hello." Now if only she'll let him in …

Please see the next page for an excerpt from

KALEIDOSCOPE

CHAPTER ONE

Dimple

"JACOB DECKER!"

Deck turned at hearing his name called in a voice he knew but hadn't heard in years. A voice he liked.

A voice he missed.

A voice that made his blood run hot.

He scanned the relatively busy lunchtime wooden sidewalks of Gnaw Bone and couldn't spot her.

What he could see was an amazingly beautiful woman walking his way. She was in tight dark wash jeans tucked in stylish high-heeled brown leather boots that went nearly up to her knees, a distressed, feminine, brown leather modified motorcycle jacket with an expensive-looking scarf wrapped loosely around her throat. Her long, gleaming dark brown hair shone in the cold winter Colorado sun, subtle red highlights making an attractive feature stunning. From under a knit cap pulled down to her ears, her hair came out in sleek sheets flowing over her shoulders. Covering her eyes were huge, chic brown-framed sunglasses.

Her full rosy lips were tipped up in a grin.

She stopped two feet in front of him and he stared down at her with surprise as, even in her sunglasses, her face showed fond recognition, warmth and a fuck of a lot more.

But he'd never seen this woman in his life.

And Deck never forgot a face.

Never.

But if he did, he would never forget that face.

Or any other part of her.

Then her grin turned into a smile, a dimple he remembered vividly depressed into her right cheek, his surprise switched to out-and-out shock and she leaned into him. Lifting a hand and placing it lightly on his shoulder, her other hand she rested on his chest, she rolled way up on her toes and pressed her cheek to his.

"Jacob," she murmured, and he could feel her fingertips dig into his shoulder even through his coat.

Jacob.

That name, a name he allowed very few people to use, said in that voice, a voice he missed, sliced through him.

Deck tipped his chin and felt her soft hair slide against the skin on his cheek. His blood still running hot but his chest now felt tight.

"Emme," he whispered, lifting a hand and wrapping his fingers around the side of her trim waist.

She pulled her head back; he lifted his and their shades locked.

She was still smiling that smile, that cute dimple shooting a flood of piercing memories through his skull. Memories he'd buried.

Memories about Emme.

"It's been a long time," she said quietly.

"Yeah," he agreed.

And it had. Years. Nine of them.

Too long to see Emme again.

"How are you?" she asked, still not moving away.

"Alive," he answered, that dimple pressed deeper and he knew, if she wasn't wearing shades, he'd see her unusual light brown eyes dance. He'd made her eyes dance frequently back then. And he hadn't had to work for it. She just gave it to him. And often.

"Em!" a man's voice snapped.

Deck's head came up and Emme moved slightly away, dropping her hands from him as she turned. They both looked at a tall, good-looking, well-built blond man wearing a mountain man uniform of flannel shirt, faded jeans, construction boots and jeans jacket standing three feet away, scowling.

Emme shifted to the man, her dimple gone but her lips still tipped up. She wrapped a hand around his bicep and leaned into him in a familiar way that said it all about who he was to her.

Deck felt that slice through him, too, but this time in a way that did not feel good.

"Dane," she began, "this is an old friend. Jacob Decker." She threw a hand out Deck's way as she lifted her sunglasses to his face. "Jacob, this is Dane McFarland. My, um... well, boyfriend."

Again, shocked as shit that Emmanuelle Holmes had a boyfriend, but not shocked this slim, stylish, stunning Emme had one, Deck opened his mouth to offer a greeting but McFarland got there before him.

"An old friend?"

Deck felt his body tighten at the man's terse tone as he watched Emme's head turn swiftly and her shades lock on her boyfriend's face. He also noted her grin had faded.

"An old friend," she stated firmly.

McFarland, not wearing sunglasses—his were shoved up in his hair—took Deck in top to toe through a glower.

He had the wrong idea.

McFarland's eyes sliced to Emme and what he said next proved Deck right.

"What kind of old friend?"

It was the wrong thing to ask. Deck knew this because, even if a man had suspicions his woman just introduced him to an ex-lover, he should wait until they were alone to call her on it. He also knew this because Emme's smile was not only gone, her face had grown slightly cold.

"The kind I'd introduce to my boyfriend?" she replied on a question that didn't quite hide its sarcasm, her smooth alto voice—something among many things he'd always liked about her—having grown nearly as cold as her face.

Emme didn't take shit from her man.

Another surprise.

Dane's glower subsided, he started to look contrite, but none of the cold left Emme's face and Deck decided to wade in.

"Let's start this again," he stated, offering his hand. "Dane, like Emme said, I'm Jacob Decker. An old friend of Emme's, just a friend from back in the day. Everyone calls me Deck."

McFarland's eyes came to him, dropped to his hand then back to his face when he took Deck's hand. He squeezed and he did it hard, a challenge, a competition. His ludicrously strong grip saying either he didn't like his girl having men friends no matter how they came or that he'd noted Deck had three inches on him and likely forty pounds, but he felt he could still take him.

Or it said both.

This guy was a dick.

He was also a moron. Just with the difference in their sizes, any man would be smart enough not to issue that kind of challenge or think he could best Deck. But the fact that those forty pounds Deck had on him were all muscle and McFarland couldn't miss it made him more of a moron.

And Deck did not like that for Emme.

Unable to do anything but, he squeezed back, saw McFarland's flinch, felt his hand go slack in reflexive self-preservation in order to save his bones getting crushed, and his point made, Deck let the man's hand go.

McFarland flexed it twice before shoving it into his pocket.

Emme missed this. She was looking up at Deck.

"What are you doing in Gnaw Bone?" she asked.

"Could ask you the same thing," he returned.

"I live here now."

Another shock. Her family was in Denver and they were tight. She didn't have a shit ton of friends but they were in Denver, too. And she was the kind of woman he thought would settle early in a life she found comfortable and stay forever.

Then again, he thought a lot of things about the Emme he knew including the fact she was sweet, funny, interesting, and no one but his best friend Chace Keaton gave better conversation. But even if it made him a dick for thinking it, she was always sexless. She made it that way. Worked at it. Her looking like she looked, dressing like she was dressed, having a man, meant her making the move to Gnaw Bone shouldn't be that big a surprise since she'd made a lot of changes.

But he didn't like that she lived in Gnaw Bone.

It wasn't her living there. It was that he had no idea how long she'd been there, but he couldn't deny the fact that knowing she lived close for however long it was, he found upsetting.

"Your turn," she prompted when he said nothing as to why he was in that town.

"Business," he answered, and the dimple reappeared.

"That's great," she replied. "Please tell me you're going to be around for a while. I've got to get back to work but I'd love to meet you for dinner."

He'd be around for a while. He didn't lie. He was in Gnaw Bone for business. But he lived in Chantelle, a twenty-minute drive away.

And he didn't have plans. So he definitely could make dinner.

He grinned down at her. "You're on."

"Uh, Em, I got shit on tonight," McFarland broke in, and both Deck and Emme looked at him.

"That's okay, babe," she told him, and Deck fought back his grin turning into a smile when McFarland's eyes flashed with annoyance. "Jacob and I can have dinner without you. And anyway, we have a lot of catching up to do and you probably would be bored seeing as you won't know who or what we're talking about."

McFarland did not like his woman making dinner plans with another man, or having history with him even if it was platonic. It showed clear on his face but he'd learned from moments earlier and kept his mouth shut.

Emme looked back at Deck.

"Do you know The Mark? It's just down the street." She pointed behind him but he nodded as she did.

"Know The Mark, Emme," Deck told her.

"Great." She gave him another dimple. "How's seven o'clock sound?"

"Works for me," he agreed.

The dimple pressed deeper even as unhappy vibes rolled off her boyfriend.

"Looking forward to it, honey," she said softly, words meant just for him, an endearment that made her boyfriend even less happy and that was reflected in the vibes rolling off him getting barbed.

But those words shifted through Deck like a razor blade through silk.

She'd always called him honey. Elsbeth had hated it. Then again, Elsbeth had eventually not been a big fan of Deck's friendship with her BFF.

In his surprise at seeing Emme here in Gnaw Bone, hours

away from where he knew her to live. Seeing her as he saw her, completely changed, hair much longer, those highlights, becoming clothes, at least twenty, probably more like thirty pounds off her frame. Seeing her with a man. Fuck, seeing her at all after what went down, how things ended and the last thing she did the last time he saw her.

With all that, belatedly, he realized he should have taken more care. He should have kept his shit together. He should maybe not have agreed to go to dinner with her. He'd shut the door on her, literally, after things ended with Elsbeth. It had hurt her. And he'd been so hung up on Elsbeth, he'd never gone back to open it.

But he did make dinner plans.

And he did because she didn't look a thing like her, Deck wondered why, and Deck didn't like puzzles. He found a puzzle, he solved it. This colossal change in Emme was a puzzle he intended to solve.

He also did it because of the last thing she did the last time he saw her.

And last, he did it just because she was Emme.

He may have hurt her but if he was reading her current behavior correctly, she held no grudges.

"Me too," Deck murmured.

McFarland slid an arm around her shoulders, pulling her into his side and stating, "We gotta get back to work, babe."

She looked up at him and nodded. "Right." Her shades came back to Deck and she gave him another grin, no dimple. "Tonight. The Mark. Seven o'clock."

Because her boyfriend was a dick, and because it made sense, Deck suggested, "Give me your number. I'll give you mine. Just in case shit gets screwed, one of us is late, or whatever."

As expected, McFarland didn't like this and he gave Deck a hard look.

Deck ignored it and pulled his phone out of his back pocket as Emme moved out of the curve of her boyfriend's arm to dig in her purse.

"You first, or me?" she asked, head bent, hair shining in the sun. He had her profile and the elegant curve of her jaw was on display. Something he never noticed before. Something else that surprised him not only because he noticed it but also because it was elegant, alluring, inviting touch, even taste and it also surprised him because he always noticed everything.

But he'd never noticed that.

And he didn't need to be thinking about how Emmanuelle Holmes's jaw might taste when she was standing next to her boyfriend.

"Me," he said. She nodded and he gave her his number.

She did the same when he was done and shoved her phone in her purse.

"Now we're good," she told him.

"We are," he agreed.

"See you at seven," she said.

"Yeah," Deck replied then looked up at McFarland. "Later."

McFarland jerked up his chin, said nothing, slid his arm around Emme's shoulders again and pulled his woman around Deck.

She wrapped an arm around McFarland's waist but still twisted to wave at Deck and give him another smile with dimple as she walked away.

Deck stood on the relatively busy sidewalk and watched McFarland load Emme up in a big, red, flash, totally pimped out, my-dick-is-small GMC Sierra.

Another reason to go to dinner with Emme. That was, find out what the fuck she was doing with that asshole.

He turned away, burying how seeing Emme again made

him feel as he moved down the wooden planks toward the police station. All that shit went down a long time ago. It was over. He was over it. Finally. After nine years.

And the bottom line truth of it was, in the end he'd eventually learned that the biggest thing he lost in all that was Emme.

So, thinking on it, it didn't suck that maybe he could get her back.

He pushed into the police station, shoved his sunglasses back on his head and moved to the reception desk seeing the receptionist eyeing him.

The instant he stopped in front of her, before he could introduce himself, she stated, "You're Jacob Decker."

He wasn't surprised. There were men that were hard to describe. Deck, a few words, people would know him from two blocks away.

"I am," he confirmed.

"Mick and the others are waiting on you," she informed him, eyes going up, down, up and stopping every once in a while to get a better look at something, his hips, his shoulders, his hair.

This also didn't surprise him. Women did this often. At six foot four, there was a lot of him to take in. It wasn't lost on him that most of it, women liked looking at. And, if he liked who was looking, he didn't hesitate to use this to his advantage.

"Just go on around the counter, back down the hall, second door to the left. You want coffee, keep goin', get yourself some and backtrack," she finished.

He nodded, muttered, "Thanks," and moved.

He didn't bother with coffee. He had the means to have the finer things in life and therefore accepted nothing less. And from experience he knew police station coffee was far from the best. Deck ground his coffee fresh first thing in the morning. He bought it on the Internet. It cost a fucking whack. And it was worth it.

He went to the second door to the left. It was closed. He gave a sharp rap on it with his knuckles and entered when he heard the call,

The gang was all there, as Chace had told him it would be.

Mick Shaughnessy, captain of the Gnaw Bone Police Department, standing by his desk.

Jeff Jessup, one of Gnaw Bones' detectives, standing by the window.

Henry Gibbons, captain of the Carnal Police Department, leaning on a table across the messy office.

Carole Weatherspoon, captain of the Chantelle Police Department, standing close to Gibbons, arms crossed on her chest.

Kenton Douglas, County Sheriff, standing shoulders against the wall.

And last, Chace Keaton, Deck's best friend since school and a Carnal detective.

It was Chace Deck was watching as he closed the door behind him, and he was watching Chace because he knew the man well and he didn't like the look on his face.

But it was Shaughnessy who spoke first, taking Deck's attention.

"May be rude but I'll start by welcoming you to this meetin' but statin' plain, I don't like it."

"Mick," Chace murmured.

Deck ignored his friend and informed Mick honestly, "I'm a big fan of statin' shit plain."

"Good, then I'll state it plainer," Mick went on. "We talk this through with you, you take this contract, Kent deputizes you, you are not a maverick. Chace suggested your services and I looked into you, found nothin'. No man's got nothin' but a fully paid truck, a fully paid house, a credit card with no balance, taxes fair and square and a load of cash in the bank. Makes me nervous."

"I see that," Deck allowed, not annoyed by the check—he'd expect nothing less—but he said no more.

"So, before we talk this through with you, you know that if you take this on, you do this by the book. You're deputized, you report, you take orders and I'll repeat, you don't go maverick," Mick continued, and Deck drew in breath.

Then he stated it plain.

"My understanding of this meet is, if I wanna take this on, and seein' if I do, my usual charges will need to be significantly discounted considering you can't afford to pay them as I charge them, it'll need to be somethin' I really wanna do. And you got a reputation I admire, Shaughnessy, so I hope you take no offense but I don't take orders. I work a case how I feel it needs to be worked. I report what I feel is necessary. And last, I only do maverick."

Mick looked to the room and announced, "This isn't startin' good."

"Why don't we lay it out, see what Deck thinks and get the other shit sorted if it's somethin' he wants to do?" Chace suggested, moving to a wide whiteboard set at an angle in the corner.

No one said anything. Deck settled in but Chace's eyes came to him.

"You're gonna see somethin' you might not like on this board that probably will make Mick's warnings moot seein' as I figure you are not gonna want this case. I would have told you about it sooner, but if I did, you might not have come in, and, respect Mick," Chace glanced at Shaughnessy before he looked back to Deck, "with what happened a few days ago, we need you."

With that, he flipped the whiteboard and Deck's eyes scanned it.

Half a second later, his body froze solid.

This was because there was a picture of the man he just met on the street, top center of the whiteboard, his name in red marker written under the picture, "Boss" under his name. Coming off his picture were a variety of red, black and blue lines that led to smaller pictures with names and other information. And last, the reason he knew Chace knew Deck would not like what he saw was the blue line that led from McFarland's picture down to the bottom right corner where there were two pictures.

One, a color shot of McFarland and Emme making out at the side of his pimped-out truck. The one next to it, a black-and-white shot of Emme walking down the boardwalk, head turned to the side looking at something. She was wearing different but no less fashionable shades over her eyes, her long hair was unhindered by a hat showing she had a deep, thick, sexy-as-all-fuck bang that hung into her eyes, her body was encased in different jeans, coat and shoes but her outfit was no less stylish. Her lips were smiling, the dimple out.

Under the picture it said "Emmanuelle Holmes." Under that "Girlfriend/Lover." Under that it said "Partner?"

With practice and deduction, Deck knew that the black lines were definite alliances the team had confirmed. Red lines were hot, lieutenants or those with records, possible weak links. And blue were unconfirmed members of the crew.

"Doesn't look like it, but it's Emme, man," Chace said quietly, and Deck tore his eyes from the picture of Emme and looked at Chace. "Saw the name. Couldn't believe it until they showed me her trail. It all fits. That's her. Totally changed."

"Saw her outside, just now, with him," Deck told the room, watched Chace blink and jerked his head toward the top of the whiteboard. He then declared, "He's no boss. She's no partner."

"So you do have a history with Emmanuelle Holmes," Carole stated, but it was a question and Deck looked to her.

Shaughnessy ran his men his way and word was, Shaughnessy took his job seriously but he was as laidback as they come otherwise. Even his officers didn't wear uniforms. They wore jeans and tan shirts with their badges but that was as far as they got.

Gibbons was mostly the same, his two detectives dressed as they wanted. Officers wore uniforms, however.

Weatherspoon, who oversaw Chantelle, a town with more money, coming in top of the heap of the trinity it held with Gnaw Bone (second runner-up, a town that depended a great deal on tourist trade and took that seriously) and Carnal (not even close, it was a biker haven, mostly blue collar, definitely rougher). She was in full uniform. Her officers wore full uniforms. Her detectives wore suits or sports jackets and trousers. Her elite citizenry would expect nothing less.

Deck's eyes shifted to Kenton Douglas.

That man was a wildcard. Recently voted sheriff, he came out of the blue, young, attractive, African-American, in the Sheriff's Department only ten years, and he'd wiped the floor with his opponent who held that spot for twenty-five years. The old sheriff also held it while a serial killer hunted his patch and a police chief in his county got so dirty he was foul. The county was ready for change. Douglas was smart enough to know the time was ripe and slid in on a landslide.

Then he made sweeping changes.

And one of those changes was taking his sheriff's police out of uniform and giving them the Mick treatment. Tan shirts. Badges on belts. Jeans. Boots.

It was a smart move. His county was a rural, mountain county. His residents liked easy and familiar, but they were scared after all that had gone on and many of them had learned not to trust the police. Easier to trust a badge wearing jeans and boots than one kitted out in full gear.

It wasn't only smart, it was subtle. And so far, successful.

Change wasn't easy and it wasn't easily accepted.

Douglas breezed his through, didn't take a breath, and kept on keepin' on.

Deck didn't know what to make of him. He was handsome. He was slick. He was personable. He was sharp. And he had balls. So Deck was leaning toward admiration.

"She's an old friend," Deck answered Carole's question about Emme.

"What kind of old friend?" she asked, and Deck tamped down his annoyance at going through this again.

"My ex's best friend," he answered. "That kind of old friend."

"How do you know she's not involved?" Jeff asked and Deck looked to him.

"I know Emme. She wouldn't do this shit," Deck stated.

And she wouldn't. He knew what was happening. The whole county knew. It was bad shit that, four days ago, got a hell of a lot worse. With all the shit going down in that county over the last few years, they wanted this nipped in the bud and they wanted that three months ago.

Problem was, they had a multi-department task force set up to do it and they still were finding fuck all.

This was why Chace suggested Deck. Deck would find everything they needed to end this and he wouldn't dick around finding it.

"How well do you know Emme, son?" Henry asked, and Deck's eyes went to Chace's boss.

"Well," he answered.

"They spend a lot of time together," Jeff noted. "Holmes and McFarland."

"She's his girlfriend. They would," Deck told him. "But this shit?" He shook his head. "No way."

"Sometimes," Chace started, and his tone was cautious, "girls like her, girls like she used to be who turn into girls like she is now, get a guy's attention, a good-lookin' guy like that, and they can go—"

Deck cut him off. "Chace, you know Emme. You know that's bullshit. She's always known her own mind. And she's always been cool. Even when she wasn't a knockout, she wasn't that kind of person."

"It's been years, Deck," Chace reminded him. "A lot of them. People change, and it isn't lost on either of us she has in a big way."

"Yeah, and I just met her on the street. I'm havin' dinner with her tonight and she looks good, man, but she acts the same. And her man is a dick but he's also a moron. So he's no boss," Deck declared and looked at Shaughnessy. "And you just got yourself a maverick."

The mood in the room shifted. It had been alert. Now it was relieved.

Shaughnessy was the only one who didn't want Deck stepping in.

The rest of them, after all they'd seen for the past few years, wanted this done, and they were willing to take risks to get that.

"Terrific," Shaughnessy muttered, his eyes moving through the room.

"Decker, this needs to be discussed," Douglas stated, and Deck looked to him.

"You want me on the team, we talk money. I'll give a discount, see this shit sorted. I'll want a full brief. I'll want the entire file. I won't take orders. I'll keep you in the know of what I do and what I find. But, just sayin', that woman means something to me." He threw out a hand toward the whiteboard. "So even if you don't put me on the team and pay me, I'll still be seein' her clear of this shit."

"You can't let her know we're investigating her boyfriend," Carole said swiftly.

"This isn't my first rodeo," Deck returned. "What's goin' down, I wouldn't fuck your investigation. But she's still clear and she's clear in no more than a week. Not months. Not as long as it'll take you to track this crew, the way you're goin', and stop their shit."

"As contract to this task force, you cannot engage in illegal activities. We can't prosecute with fruit from the poisonous tree," Douglas told him.

"Again, not my first rodeo," Deck replied.

"You have a crew or do you work alone?" Henry asked.

"This, I'll be bringin' in my crew," Deck answered.

"They'll all need to see me," Douglas stated. "Contract is signed, you all work for my department until the case is done."

Deck nodded and his eyes went to Chace. "Want a picture of that board, want the file."

"Deck, not sure this is a good idea. You got a conflict of interest with this—"

Deck again cut Chace off. "This is Emme."

"I know it's Emme," Chace shot back, concerned for Deck and losing patience because of it. "Until just now, I had no idea you'd react the way you have when you saw it was Emme. So *Emme's* the goddamned conflict of interest."

"You know her," Deck whispered, also losing patience, and he watched his friend's face. Definite concern but also indecision.

He knew Emme.

Chace went from the academy into Carnal's Police Department and stayed there but that didn't mean Deck didn't spend time with Chace throughout all Deck's travels. Chace had met Elsbeth. Chace had spent time with her. And with Elsbeth came Emme. So Chace had spent time with Emme too.

"Her change is remarkable, Deck," Chace noted again. "That's something to take into account."

At his words, Deck felt the ghost of her fingers digging into his shoulder through his coat. Saw the dimple. Heard her call him honey.

And he knew her history. Elsbeth told him. He knew what she'd survived. He knew what made her what she was.

He didn't know what made her what she was now, but he was going to find out at dinner.

Last, he knew Emme would not be a part of a crew who burgled homes across an entire county and recruited high school students to do it. Not for the attention of the likes of Dane McFarland. Not for money. Not for power. Not for anything.

"She's up first. I investigate her. Clear her. Then clear her of this shit," Deck stated.

"You work that with me," Chace returned.

"Suit yourself. But dinner with Emme tonight is just her and me."

Chace studied him.

Deck took it then looked to Douglas. "You got a file for me?"

"It'll be delivered to your house by three thirty," Douglas replied.

"Contracts will be emailed to you by then. My crew will be in tomorrow at eight to be deputized," Deck replied.

"You gonna be with them?" Douglas asked.

"Wouldn't miss that shit for the world," Deck answered, cut his eyes through the people in the room, noting Henry Gibbons looked amused, Mick Shaughnessy looked annoyed, Carole Weatherspoon looked reflective and Chace still looked worried.

Then he walked out of the office, out of the station and to his truck.

Fall in Love with Forever Romance

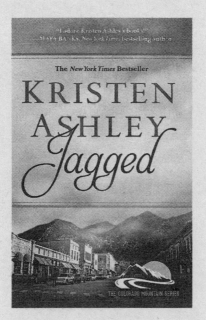

JAGGED

Zara is struggling to make ends meet when her old friend Ham comes back into her life. He wants to help, but a job and a place to live aren't the only things he's offering this time around...Fans of Julie Ann Walker, Lauren Dane, and Julie James will love the fifth book in Kristen Ashley's *New York Times* bestselling Colorado Mountain series, now in print for the first time!

Fall in Love with Forever Romance

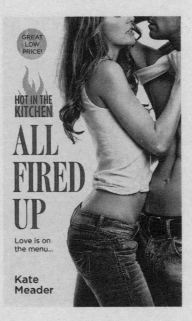

ALL FIRED UP

It's a recipe for temptation: Mix a cool-as-a-cucumber event planner with a devastatingly handsome Irish pastry chef. Add sexual chemistry hot enough to start a fire. Let the sparks fly. Fans of Jill Shalvis will flip for the second book in Kate Meader's Hot in the Kitchen series.

Fall in Love with Forever Romance

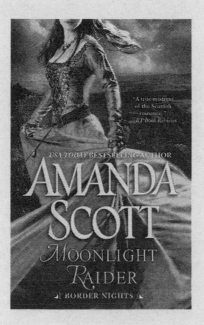

MOONLIGHT RAIDER

USA Today bestselling author Amanda Scott brings to life the history, turmoil, and passion of the Scottish Border as only she can in the first book in her new Border Nights series. Fans of Diana Gabaldon's *Outlander* will be swept away by Scott's tale!

Fall in Love with Forever Romance

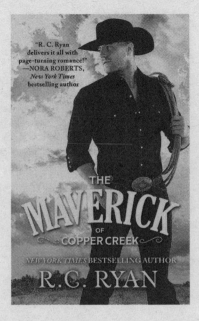

THE MAVERICK OF COPPER CREEK

Fans of Linda Lael Miller, Diana Palmer, and Joan Johnston will love *New York Times* bestselling author R. C. Ryan's THE MAVERICK OF COPPER CREEK, the charming, poignant, and unforgettable first book in her Copper Creek Cowboys series.

Fall in Love with Forever Romance

IT HAPPENED AT CHRISTMAS

Ethan and Skye may want a lot of things this holiday season, but what they get is something they didn't expect. Fans of feel-good romances by *New York Times* bestselling authors Brenda Novak, Robyn Carr, and Jill Shalvis will love the third book in Debbie Mason's series set in Christmas, Colorado—where love is the greatest gift of all.

Fall in Love with Forever Romance

MISTLETOE ON MAIN STREET

Fans of Jill Shalvis, Robyn Carr, and Susan Mallery will love this charming debut from best-selling author Olivia Miles about love, healing, and family at Christmastime.

Fall in Love with Forever Romance

RING IN THE HOLIDAYS

For Matthew McPherson, what happens in Vegas definitely doesn't stay there, and that may be a very good thing! Fans of Lori Wilde and Rachel Gibson will fall in love with this sexy series from bestselling author Katie Lane.

Fall in Love with Forever Romance

A CHRISTMAS TO REMEMBER

Jill Shalvis headlines this touching anthology of Christmas stories as readers celebrate the holidays with their favorite series. Includes stories from Kristen Ashley, Hope Ramsay, Molly Cannon, and Marilyn Pappano. Now in print for the first time!